RED CITY

Christopher Mitchell is the author of the epic fantasy series The Magelands. He studied in Edinburgh before living for several years in the Middle East and Greece, where he taught English. He returned to study classics and Greek tragedy and lives in Fife, Scotland with his wife and their four children.

Brigdomin Books Ltd
First Edition, September 2021
ISBN 978-1-912879-62-5

For Alayne

ACKNOWLEDGEMENTS

I would like to thank the following for all their support during the writing of the Magelands Eternal Siege - my wife, Lisa Mitchell, who read every chapter as soon as it was drafted and kept me going in the right direction; my parents for their unstinting support; Vicky Williams for reading the books in their early stages; James Aitken for his encouragement; and Grant and Gordon of the Film Club for their support.

Thanks also to my Advance Reader team, for all your help during the last few weeks before publication.

DRAMATIS PERSONAE

The Aurelians
    Emily Aurelian, Queen of the City
    Daniel Aurelian, King of the City
    Elspeth Aurelian, Princess of the City
    Lady Aurelian, Daniel's Mother
    Lord Aurelian, Daniel's Father
    Lady Omertia, Emily's Mother

The Mortals of the City
    Quill, Adjutant of the Bulwark
    Rosie Jackdaw, Artificer Blade
    Inmara, Royal Guard
    Darvi, Royal Guard

The Former Royal Family
    Amalia, Former God-Queen (Lady Sofia)
    Montieth, Prince of Dalrig; Prisoner
    Mona, Chancellor of Royal Academy, Ooste
    Salvor, Royal Advisor, Pella
    Naxor, Demigod; Former Emissary
    Vana, Demigod; Cousin of Naxor
    Yvona, Governor of Icehaven
    Amber, Elder Daughter of Prince Montieth
    Jade, Commander of the Bulwark
    Ikara, Former Governor of the Circuit
    Lydia, Governor of Port Sanders
    Doria, Courtier in the Royal Palace
    Collo; Former Courtier

The Lostwell Exiles

Kelsey Holdfast, Blocker of Powers

Van Logos, Commander of the Banner

Lucius Cardova, Officer in the Banner

Flavus, Scout in the Banner

Silva, God; Descendant of Belinda

Felice, God; Former Governor of Lostwell

Kagan, Former Gang Member

Maxwell, Son of Amalia and Kagan

Gellie, Fordian Housekeeper

Saul, Torduan Chef

Vadhi, Brigade Worker

Nagel, Brigade Worker

The Exiled Dragons

Deathfang, Dragon Chief

Burntskull, Deathfang's Advisor

Darksky, Deathfang's Mate

Frostback, Deathfang's Daughter

Halfclaw, Green & Blue Dragon

Dawnflame, Blue & Purple Dragon

Bittersea, Dawnflame's Mother

Firestone, Dawnflame's Son

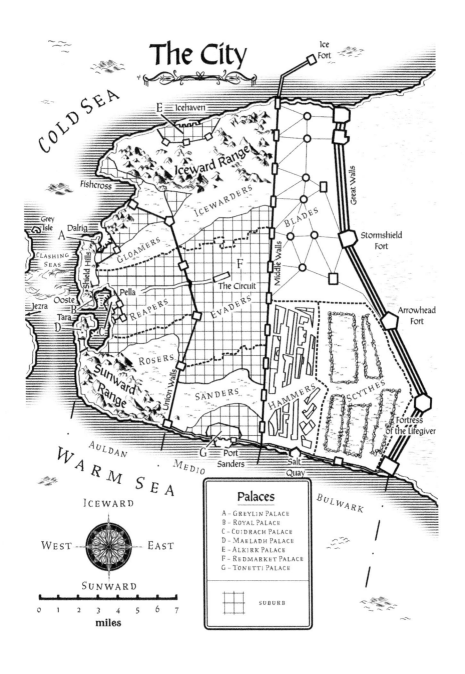

CHAPTER 1

BACK TO THE FRAY

O uter Pella, Auldan, The City – 20th Marcalis 3422

'Your grandmother would be very proud of you, dear,' said Lady Omertia, as Emily rocked the baby girl back and forth in her arms. 'If she were still alive,' her mother went on, 'she would be your strongest supporter. I'm proud of you, too, my daughter; you've accomplished more than anyone could have dreamed.'

Emily tried to smile, but the motion of the carriage over the cobblestones was threatening to awaken the baby at any moment. The journey from the Aurelian villa in the Sunward Range had been smooth, but the rougher paving of Outer Pella was causing the inside of the carriage to judder. She glanced out of the window, in an attempt to judge the remaining distance to Cuidrach Palace. Outside, the sky was a resplendent pink, with darker patches to iceward, ahead of them.

Her mother caught her eye. 'Would you like me to take Elspeth for a minute, dear?'

Emily looked down into the baby's sleeping face, then reached over, passing the blanket-wrapped bundle to her mother.

'Thanks,' said Emily, as Lady Omertia settled into her seat with the child. 'Do I look as bedraggled as I feel?'

'You spent over an hour getting ready this morning, dear,' her mother said, 'and you don't look any different from then. Our time on the Aurelian estate seems to have reinvigorated you; you looked worn out when we left Pella at the beginning of the month. When you get back to the palace, I do hope that you take it easy, at least for the first while.'

Emily pulled her shoulder bag onto the seat next to her and began rummaging in it. 'You know I have to get back to work, mother. I've been idle for nearly a year.'

Her mother laughed. 'Idle? Dear me. You call pregnancy, giving birth and looking after a baby "idle?" You need to eat more. You've been half-starving yourself recently; don't think I haven't noticed. And that ridiculous training regime; one would assume that you were preparing for battle. Is it really so important to you that you appear slim again?'

Emily pulled a hairbrush from the bag and gave her mother a look.

'Maybe I have forgotten what it is to be young,' her mother went on, 'but I worry about you, dear. You are a mother now, and you need to keep your health.'

'It's about being fit again,' Emily said, drawing the brush through her blonde hair, 'and about feeling good about myself.'

'So, it has nothing to do with turning the head of every man in the Royal Court? I know how you've always enjoyed the attention of boys. Your father used to say...' She paused, and her face flushed. 'Sorry, dear.'

Emily tugged at a few tangles. 'What did he used to say?'

'Never mind.'

'No, mother; tell me.'

'I don't think so, dear. It was nothing complimentary, as I'm sure you've already suspected. Your father had very little to say that was kind.'

'Would you have divorced him, if the Roser laws had allowed it?'

Lady Omertia glanced away.

'You wouldn't have, would you?' said Emily. 'You would have stayed with him, despite everything he did to you, and to me. You preferred propriety over your own happiness.'

Her mother continued to say nothing, her eyes fixed on the view through the window. Emily frowned. She knew she should probably leave it there, but her mother's refusal to completely disown Lord Omertia had always rankled.

'He used to tell me that he wished I'd been a boy,' she went on. 'Of course, that was before he or I knew the truth about where I was really born. "Why couldn't you have been a son? Girls are nothing but trouble." I heard that a lot, and now I wonder – why didn't you obtain a baby boy, if that's what he so clearly desired?'

'You were meant to be a boy,' her mother said. 'A boy was what I had requested, and your grandmother was supposed to ensure that I received a boy. I didn't know that you were a girl until she handed you over to me, and, by that time, it was too late. Your father was furious. He called you the death knell of the Omertia line, and demanded that I produce more children for him; but one such deception was all my heart could bear.'

Emily's anger rose within her. 'If Daniel spoke like that to me, I'd leave him. In fact, if I even suspected that he thought that way, then I'd be out the door, taking Elspeth with me. I would never allow her to be raised by a man who despised her.'

Lady Omertia gazed down at the baby nestled in her arms. She blinked away a tear and shook her head. 'You shame me, daughter.'

Emily lowered the brush and took a breath. Lord Omertia had been dead for over two and a half years; how was it possible that he still had the power to hurt her?

'We shouldn't quarrel, mother,' she said, 'especially not over Lord Omertia; I can't bring myself to call him "father." All of that is in the past, and there's nothing anyone can do to change it.'

'I know you think I was a bad mother; I...'

'Please,' said Emily; 'don't. Your fault was being loyal to someone who didn't deserve it. In the grand scheme of things, that's hardly a hanging offence.'

'But you spent much of your childhood in fear, Emily, and I am partly to blame. I wish I could...'

'Stop, mother; I mean it. I shouldn't have brought it up. We have Elspeth to think about now, and the future. Dwelling on the past will get us nowhere.' She glanced out of the window. 'We're entering Pella; not long to go.'

Her mother said nothing, so Emily kept her glance on the view. The rougher suburbs of Outer Pella had been left behind, and their carriage was being drawn through the neater streets of the old town. To their left was the edge of the inner bay, its calm waters reflecting the reds and pinks of the sky, and she could see Tara upon the opposite shore. The bulk of Maeladh Palace was visible against the dark cliffside, and she shuddered at the memories of her incarceration at the hands of Prince Montieth, one and a half years before.

The carriage bore to the right as the road joined the main esplanade. The harbour of Pella was bustling with vessels of all sizes, from small fishing boats to large masted galleys filled with supplies for the Jezra colony. Ships that had returned from Jezra were also berthed by the long piers, unloading their cargos of building stone, and saplings destined to help reforest the Iceward Range. The waterfront was packed with people, and many stared as the long line of soldiers and carriages passed on their way to Cuidrach Palace.

'Sit back from the window, dear,' her mother said. 'The Queen should have some mystery about her.'

Emily glanced down at her hands, to make sure they weren't trembling. She needn't have worried; they were as steady as a rock, despite the growing anxiety she felt bubbling away. It wasn't the people that she was nervous of, she realised; it was the politics. For eighteen days, she had been secluded within the Aurelian estate with her mother and her baby daughter, and had ignored any news coming from the rest of the City.

'When I walk back through those doors,' she said, 'I'll be back at work; and not just the part-time bits and bobs I was doing over Sweetmist – I'll be full-time. I'll have to pay attention to every little detail again.' She glanced at her mother. 'To be honest, part of me wishes I could just continue like I've been doing the last few months. Elspeth is getting easier to look after; well, a little, and I didn't want our holiday on the estate to end.'

'You are the Queen, dear; surely you can delegate?'

'I might if I trusted anyone.'

Her mother shifted the baby onto her other arm. 'You were never paranoid as a child.'

'And I'm not paranoid now. The demigods of the City despise me; their contempt is written on their faces. I have come to believe that only their shock over the death of Yendra prevented them from acting in the months after her death, and then when the riots started last summer, they decided to sit back, and wait to see how long it took before the mortal monarchy unravelled.'

'It hasn't unravelled yet.'

Emily slipped her crown over her head. 'Which is why I have to go back to work. Daniel's been practically ruling alone for months; he needs my help.'

The carriages pulled into a courtyard on the sunward side of the palace, and the soldiers closed the gates. Various courtiers and servants stepped down from the other carriages ahead, and an officer from the Royal Guard opened the door of the Queen's carriage.

'Your Majesty,' he said, bowing; 'we have returned to Cuidrach.'

He extended his hand and Emily took it. A crowd had formed by the courtyard gates, and they cheered as Emily emerged into the crisp morning sunshine. She smiled and waved to them, then the officer helped her to the ground. Emily waited as her mother came out from the carriage, holding the infant princess in her arms. The crowd cheered again at the sight, and Emily lingered for a few moments, before they turned for the palace. Courtiers lined the driveway, and all bowed to her as she passed. At the grand doors, one of several entrances into the palace, Lord Salvor was waiting.

He bowed low, hiding the smile on his features. 'Welcome back, your Majesty. And to you, Queen-Mother; I trust your stay upon the Aurelian estate was a pleasant one?'

Lady Omertia smiled. 'It was wonderful, thank you.'

5

They walked into the palace, and Emily felt a strange sensation of apprehension, and of being glad to be home at the same time.

'Are you rested, your Majesty?' said Salvor, as they passed more lines of bowing courtiers.

'Do you mean, am I ready for work?'

Salvor said nothing, but a smile persisted at the edge of his mouth.

'I'm ready,' she said.

Salvor glanced at the child in the Queen-Mother's arms. 'The princess has grown since I last saw her, your Majesty,' said Salvor, 'but she remains the very image of you. Now, shall we walk to my office? His Majesty is there; he is most eager to see you.'

'Yes,' said Emily. They turned and began walking along the marble-lined hallway. They passed a squad of soldiers and entered the wing of the palace that held the main administrative areas.

'Anything changed in the last while?' she said, as they walked.

'Several things have changed, your Majesty.'

'Anything important? Is Montieth still locked up safe and sound?'

'Of course, your Majesty; the prince has made no attempt to escape. Lady Jade is keeping a close eye on her father.'

'Good.'

Salvor pursed his lips. 'There have been some concerns about other aspects of Lady Jade's leadership of the Blades. I included them in a report I sent to the Aurelian estate, your Majesty.'

'I have a confession, Salvor; I read nothing political while I was in Roser territory. I needed to clear my mind before entering this world again. I needed to remember what it was like just to live for a while.'

'Then we are fortunate, your Majesty,' he said, 'that you are a quick learner.'

The infant began to awaken, and wriggled in the arms of the Queen-Mother.

Emily leaned in towards her. 'We're going to see daddy, Elspeth.'

Guards opened two tall doors for them and they strode into Salvor's grand office, leaving the courtiers behind at the entrance.

The King rose from his seat at the head of a table.

'Emily,' he said, a smile spreading across his face.

He pushed his chair to the side and hurried towards her. They embraced in the middle of the room, and Emily pulled him close.

'It is great to see you,' he said. He turned to his mother-in-law, and she passed him the baby.

'Woah,' he laughed; 'you're getting heavy, little Elspeth.'

The child stared up at Daniel's face, then started to cry.

'That'll teach you for making a comment like that,' Emily said.

'She's eight months old,' Daniel said, rocking the infant; 'she doesn't know what I'm saying.'

'Perhaps, but she can tell it wasn't a compliment.'

A woman arose from the table, and clasped her hands in front of her waist, her head bowed.

'Lady Mona,' said Emily. 'I didn't see you there. How are you?'

'Welcome back to the palace, your Majesty,' said the demigod.

'Lady Mona is on her way to Jezra, your Majesty,' said Salvor, 'to take a look at the scrolls that were found there after the invasion.'

'Yes,' said Mona. 'It's taken me this long to sort out the mess caused by the Gloamer militia using the Royal Academy as a barracks during their occupation. I heard you were returning this morning, your Majesty, and so I thought I'd come and pay my respects.'

Salvor eyed the Queen. 'Lord Naxor is also in the palace, your Majesty.'

'Really? What is he doing here?'

'Visiting his sister, your Majesty.'

Emily frowned. 'I didn't think Naxor and Ikara got on very well.'

Salvor gave a slight shrug.

Emily turned to Lady Omertia. 'Mother, will you please take Elspeth to the apartment?'

Her mother curtsied. 'Yes, your Majesty.'

Emily kissed her baby daughter on the forehead, then watched as her mother strode away. A squad of guards joined her at the entrance to the office, along with several servants hurrying to keep up. When the doors closed again, Emily turned back to Salvor.

'I thought Naxor was restricting himself to Port Sanders? Has he reneged on our agreement?'

'He assured me, your Majesty, that he wished only to speak with Lady Ikara for a couple of hours, and then he will return to his mansion in Sander territory. He is here in a personal capacity, and does not wish to jeopardise the agreement he made with the Crown.'

'I hope not,' said Emily, 'because I was being generous. He hasn't lifted a finger to help us since he returned from Lostwell.' She paused for a second. 'You're older than him, aren't you?'

'Yes, your Majesty; by precisely two hundred years.'

'I see. Could you read his mind without him knowing?'

Salvor glanced away. 'No, your Majesty. I'm afraid it doesn't work like that. Naxor is one of the most powerful of the generation of demigods, and his vision skills outweigh mine. I can enter his mind, but only if he allows it.'

Emily turned to Mona. 'You have vision as well, don't you?'

Salvor and Mona's eyes met for a moment.

'Don't do that,' Emily snapped.

'What's this about?' said Daniel.

Emily sat down by the table, and the others followed her example.

'When he first got back here,' she said, 'Naxor was over-friendly, trying to wheedle his way in, and reading our minds whenever he felt like it. Then, we rebuked him and sent him to liaise with the Evaders. After that, he seems to have skulked off in a huff to his mansion in Port Sanders, where he's been doing Malik knows what. Meanwhile, the Evader delegates get assassinated, and no one seems to know anything about who did it.'

Daniel frowned. 'You're not suggesting that Naxor was to blame, are you? The Circuit is riddled with warring factions; the delegates had plenty of enemies without Naxor needing to intervene.'

'I examined the minds of several dozen Evaders, and others of interest,' said Salvor, 'and found no trace that my brother was involved.'

Emily gave a wry smile. 'All the same... Lady Mona, could you gain access to Lord Naxor's mind without him knowing?'

'No, your Majesty. It is as Salvor said; Naxor's vision skills are powerful; in fact, since the tragic death of Princess Yendra, his vision skills are the best in the City.'

'You mean there's no way to get into his mind that he won't be able to prevent?'

Salvor and Mona eyed each other again. Emily frowned as she watched them silently communicate, her fingers drumming on the tabletop.

Salvor broke off the glance and turned to the King and Queen. 'There might be a way, your Majesties. If I were to link minds with Lord Naxor, and occupy him in conversation, then Lady Mona could slip in unnoticed.'

'This is highly unethical,' said Mona.

'But possible?' said Emily.

Mona hesitated, then sighed. 'Yes, your Majesty. As long as Naxor doesn't delve too deeply into Salvor's mind while they talk, then he shouldn't suspect anything.'

'Just a quick in-out is required,' said Emily. 'Let's keep this as focussed as possible. I'm not asking anyone to strip away Naxor's secrets – he can keep them – no, all I want to know is if he was involved in the assassination of the delegates. That way, we shan't be rousing any moral qualms. Are we agreed?'

'I am a little uncomfortable about this, your Majesty,' said Mona; 'but I bow to your sovereign will.'

Salvor said nothing for a moment, his eyes on the table, then he nodded. 'I also agree, your Majesty.'

'Should we not also... how should I put this?' said Daniel. 'Should we not be checking his loyalty? I mean, if we're going to take a look inside his mind anyway?'

'No,' said Emily. 'That seems to be crossing a line. Knowing if Naxor was responsible for those deaths is enough; I don't want to know any more.'

'Should I summon my brother, your Majesty?' said Salvor. 'Lady Mona will need to be in eye contact to increase her chances of success.'

'No,' said Emily. 'If he comes in here, then he'll probably be in my mind within seconds, and then he'll know what we're up to.'

Salvor nodded, then dipped into his pocket. He extracted a small box, and laid it onto the surface of the table.

'What's in there?' said Daniel.

'Two pairs of eye protectors,' said Salvor. 'As far as I know, they are the only sets left in the City.'

Emily raised an eyebrow. 'And you just happened to have them in your pocket?'

'I don't always carry them around, your Majesty, but when I discovered that my brother was visiting, I decided to bring them along. I know how much you both dislike Naxor reading your minds.'

Daniel reached forward and opened the box. Emily glanced inside, and saw four small, clear discs lying upon a bed of soft velvet.

'They are uncomfortable to wear,' Salvor went on, as Emily and Daniel peered into the box, 'but they work against all vision powers. I found them in the Royal Palace in Ooste a couple of years ago.'

'Why didn't you tell us you had them?'

'With the passing of Princess Yendra,' he said, 'there are only four gods or demigods left in the City who possess vision powers – myself and Lady Mona, Naxor, and the prisoner from Lostwell, a Lady Felice. I know that you do not need to be protected from me or Mona, your Majesties, and so I didn't think that they would be required. If you put them on, you will be safe from my brother.'

Emily and Daniel glanced at each other, then she lifted one of the discs from the box. She held it up between her fingers and squinted at it in the light coming through the windows.

'Who made them?' she said.

'No one in the City, your Majesty,' Salvor said. 'They must have been brought here from outside; they may even have been with Malik and Amalia when they first arrived. They are beyond anything that even the most skilled artisans in the City could manufacture. The material is of a quality and delicacy that cannot be replicated here.'

'And, I just slip one over each eye?'

'Yes, your Majesty.'

Daniel laughed. 'I can't wait to see Naxor's face when he realises we're wearing them.'

'Before we do this, your Majesties,' Salvor said, as he watched Emily trying to place the first one onto her left eye; 'I feel obliged to ask if you are entirely sure that this is a sensible course. If my brother discovers our subterfuge, he may not react well.'

Emily blinked as the clear disc settled over her eye. 'Then, tell me honestly – are you sure Naxor is completely innocent of the deaths of the Evader delegates?'

'No, your Majesty. However, have you thought about what we should do if we discover he is guilty?'

Emily paused as she edged the other disc onto her right eye. It smarted, and she could feel the slight weight of them press against her eyes.

'You were right; they are uncomfortable,' she said, her eyes watering. She glanced at the blurry figure of Daniel next to her. 'Your turn.'

The King reached into the box, and dropped the discs onto his eyes.

Emily frowned. 'You made that look easy. Salvor, please summon Lord Naxor.'

Salvor's eyes glazed over for a second. 'It is done, your Majesty.'

'I'm still not altogether happy about this,' said Mona.

'Enter his mind as soon as my brother and I are linked,' Salvor said to her. 'Ten seconds should suffice to find what their Majesties are looking for.'

The demigod nodded, though her face showed plainly what she thought of the idea. Salvor stood, and clasped his hands behind his back, his eyes on the main doors.

'I hope you know what you're doing with all this,' Daniel whispered to Emily. 'Naxor would make a powerful enemy.'

'But that's just it, Danny – we need to know if he really is an enemy.'

A courtier opened the door. 'Your Majesties, Lord Naxor is here to attend the court.'

'Show him in,' said Salvor.

Naxor strode through the door, a half-smirk playing on his lips. He walked over to where Emily and Daniel were sitting, and bowed low.

'Your Majesties,' he said; 'to what do I owe this enormous honour?'

'I felt it was time for a catch-up,' said Emily. 'It's been a while. According to the terms of the agreement we made last year, you were to remain in Port Sanders, while we were to turn a blind eye to your activities. Why have you come to Pella?'

'To see my sister, of course; and my cousins. I am merely on a social call, your Majesty.' He noticed Mona sitting by the table, and raised an eyebrow.

'Why didn't you use your vision?' said Emily. 'You don't need to be here in person to talk to them.'

'Yes,' said Naxor, 'but that seems a little cold, don't you think? For example, you could have simply asked my brother to talk to me using *his* vision, but instead, I find myself summoned into your royal presence. Were you looking for some political advice, perhaps? If so, then here it is – you should...'

'We weren't looking for your advice, Naxor, thank you,' said Daniel. 'We have everything under control.'

Naxor started to laugh. 'Apologies,' he said, his lips settling back into a smirk; 'I see that wasn't meant as a joke. A pity. If you had any sense, you'd cancel the upcoming elections immediately, and withdraw your constitutional changes before the City tears itself apart. Only the Reapers and the Hammers are behind you, you do know that, yes? The Rosers, Gloamers, Sanders, Evaders, and the Blades, let's not forget them – they are preparing to resist you with everything at their disposal, while you have alienated nearly every demigod in the City. Without Princess Yendra to support your reign, I fear the worst, your Majesties.'

'The elections shall go ahead as planned,' said Daniel, his eyes narrow. 'The people will not have their voice taken away from them.'

'The people?' said Naxor. 'Which people? The five tribes I mentioned are planning on boycotting the elections, and ignoring the new laws. Are you hoping to use the Banner Exiles and the dragons to enforce your will? Will you send troops into the Circuit? Into Tara? The riots that plagued the City last summer shall return; will you not compromise?'

'We have tried to compromise,' said Daniel. 'Now is the time for a firm will to steer the City.'

'That might have worked if Yendra were alive,' said Naxor; 'but you've lost the Blades. They don't respect Jade; they might fear her, but they don't respect her. If she ordered them to occupy Medio, I believe they would mutiny. Face facts – at the moment, your rule extends to Pella, Ooste, Jezra and the Hammer territory; nowhere else is listening any more.'

'That's enough,' said Emily. 'Thank you for your opinions, Lord Naxor.'

He smiled, and gazed into her eyes. His smile dropped, and he turned to Salvor. Emily's heart raced as she watched the two brothers communicate. She kept her glance away from Mona, trusting that the demigod was following her instructions. Mona let out a shriek. She jumped to her feet, and staggered backwards.

Naxor glared at her. 'Were you in my head, dear cousin?'

Salvor glanced at the main doors. They opened, and a squad of soldiers from the Royal Guard entered, their crossbows trained on Naxor.

'Don't move, brother,' said Salvor.

'You cowardly dog,' sneered Naxor.

'What is it?' said Emily. 'What is he hiding? Did he kill the Evader delegates?'

'No,' said Mona, her eyes wide. 'He is innocent of that.'

'Then, what's the matter?'

Mona stared at her. 'The God-Queen is back.'

'Impossible!' cried Daniel. 'Vana and Silva have scanned every inch of the City – the former God-Queen has not returned. They would have seen her.'

'Secure Lord Naxor,' said Salvor to the soldiers. 'Bind his wrists and hood him.'

'Can it be true?' said Emily, her voice rising. 'Naxor – is it true? Is Amalia hiding in the City?'

'Why don't you ask Salvor?' Naxor said, winking. 'He's been working with her for months.'

Salvor gasped. 'Lies. Don't listen to him, your Majesty.'

'Where is she?' said Emily, standing.

'I have nothing more to say,' said Naxor, as soldiers bound his wrists behind his back. 'You can try to read my thoughts again, but you won't succeed, not now that I know your little tricks. Mona and Salvor will never get into my mind again, I swear it.'

A soldier reached forward, and pulled a hood over Naxor's head.

'Take him away,' said Salvor. 'Place him in solitary confinement. No one is to see him without our express authority.'

The soldiers saluted, and led Naxor away.

Emily turned to Mona as soon as the doors closed. 'What did you see? Tell me everything.'

Mona sat back down at the table and put her head in her hands. 'Only that Amalia is here, your Majesty. Hiding, somewhere in the City. I was too alarmed to dig any further.'

'But Naxor and Amalia were enemies,' said Daniel. 'Why would he be hiding her presence here? Salvor, what did he mean? Did you know that Amalia was here?'

'No, your Majesty. I had no idea until Mona saw it in his mind. You must not believe his lies.'

Emily glanced from Salvor to Mona, wondering who she could trust.

'Summon the three demigods living in Cuidrach,' she said; 'one at a time, and question them. You can read their minds, can't you?'

'Yes, your Majesty. Vana, Collo and Ikara's powers are less than my own.'

'And fetch Lady Silva; we shall need to look over the City again.'

'But it can't be true,' said Daniel. 'How could the God-Queen be hiding, without us...' His eyes fell and he groaned. 'Anti-salve.'

'Dear gods,' said Emily. 'That's how Prince Montieth hid from us.'

Mona's face shone with fear. 'But that would mean that Amalia was in contact with Montieth the whole time. If she's really back, then... then...'

'Calm yourself, cousin,' said Salvor. 'We need facts, not speculation.'

Emily turned to Mona. 'When you get to Jezra, tell Major-General Logos to attend the palace, with Kelsey Holdfast. I think it might be time to have another chat with Lady Amber.'

CHAPTER 2

SHIPS IN THE NIGHT

J ezra, The Western Bank – 20th Marcalis 3422

Greenhides scuttled through the narrow ravine, the smouldering trees sending sparks and smoke whirling around them as they fled the dragon. Frostback hovered, her silver wings extended, and she unleashed another barrage of fire down at them. Trees crackled, split and erupted into flames. A dozen greenhides fell, the rest scattering along the slopes of the forested hillside.

From atop the harness, Kelsey watched, her eyes scanning the trees for more greenhides. Frostback banked, then turned, and Kelsey had a view of the entire ridge. Where a lush forest had once stood, were half-built walls, mud, and hundreds of Brigade workers. Halfclaw was fifty yards away, lowering a long stretch of pre-built stockade wall into position. Frostback rose above him, circling, her gaze on the churned up and broken landscape. The scene looked chaotic, but Kelsey knew how much preparation and planning went into each day's work. Mud-covered Brigade workers secured the new stretch of stockade wall, joining the two ends to the sections that had been laid down earlier that day. As soon as the thick wooden posts were in place, the workers began to withdraw, Banner soldiers escorting them back towards the main walls ringing Upper Jezra. Frostback and Halfclaw soared overhead, ensuring no greenhides returned to attack the humans as they retreated.

'Another good day,' said Kelsey; 'over a hundred yards of new walls put in place.'

'I think I preferred the Fog of Balian,' said Frostback. 'Flying over mist-covered lands was wonderful. This feels like work.'

'That's because it is work,' said Kelsey. 'It's our jobs.'

'It strikes me that humans are contented with very little. They drudge all day long; building, digging, repairing, and yet they seem to find this acceptable. Life is for living, not for working.'

'We'd all be living in caves if we thought like that.'

'And what is wrong with living in a cave? You humans scurry about like restless ants, but does it make you any happier?'

Halfclaw joined them as they flew over the outer walls of Upper Jezra. Below them, the last of the workers and soldiers were hurrying through an open gate.

'I need some warmth on my scales,' said Halfclaw. 'Do you want to fly down to the desert for a few hours? We could rest by an oasis.'

'Yes; I would like that,' said Frostback. 'Rider, do you wish to come?'

Kelsey could tell which response the silver dragon wanted by the tone of her voice.

'No,' she said; 'I need to talk to the Brigade officers about tomorrow.'

'Then I shall set you down in the lower town. Try not to get too drunk; I don't like it when you're hungover in the mornings. It makes you tetchy.'

'Me; drunk? I don't know what you're talking about.'

'If you say so, rider. Where will I send the humans to look for you in the morning? At your own home, or will you be staying in Van's quarters again tonight?'

'I don't know. It depends how drunk I get.'

The final soldiers crossed through the gates in the walls, and the stout iron-rimmed doors were closed and barred. Frostback and Halfclaw banked, and flew over the sprawling area at the top of the cliffs that had been reclaimed from the greenhides. Lines of old defences from the previous summer were being dismantled, and wide baskets of fresh supplies were being hoisted up from the lower town by cranes, their spindly arms stretching out over the side of the cliff. Workers looked up from the muddy roads, and several waved at the dragons as they passed. Frostback reached the edge of the cliff and plunged downwards, leaving Halfclaw circling above. Kelsey held on as the buildings of Lower Jezra rushed towards them, then the dragon pulled up at the last second, and gently landed onto the open space covering the foundations of the ruined palace. The rear of the foundations backed onto the cliffside, and a new quarry had been opened up, both to provide stone for building, and to create a space where the two dragons could shelter.

Kelsey unfastened the straps and clambered down to the ground. Frostback's crew approached – four Brigade workers, whose jobs revolved around making sure the young silver dragon was fed and looked after.

Frostback gazed at them. 'I shall not be requiring your services this evening,' she said; 'I am going to fly sunward. I will rest there, and return at dawn.'

'Very well, ma'am,' said Nagel, the Fordian sergeant in charge of the dragon detail.

Kelsey winked at him. 'She has a date with Halfclaw.'

'It is not a "date,"' said Frostback. 'Dragon mating customs are far removed from the capricious and flighty notions of love that humanity seems to hold dear.'

'Have fun,' said Kelsey, as the dragon beat her wings and lifted into the sky.

'Poor Halfclaw,' she muttered; 'she's been keeping him waiting for a year and a half.'

Nagel passed her a canister of water.

'Thanks,' she said. 'It looks like you guys have the night off.' She noticed a young woman in the dragon crew that she didn't recognise. 'Who's this?'

'Her name's Vadhi, ma'am,' said Nagel. 'She's been transferred from the Thirteenth Brigade to replace Yannic. The Colonel said that if you don't like her, then he'll find you someone else.'

The young woman saluted.

'Welcome to the dragon crew,' said Kelsey. 'If you're half as good as Yannic, then you'll be fine.'

'I'll do my best, ma'am.'

'Are you Torduan?'

'Yes, ma'am.'

'I must be getting better at the accents,' said Kelsey; 'though I guess we're all Exiles now, eh? Do you fancy a drink later? I always want to get to know the new members of the crew.'

Vadhi smiled. 'Definitely, ma'am.'

Kelsey glanced at Nagel. 'You're coming too, sergeant. Where will we go? I fancy a change from the Brigade Common Rooms.'

Nagel raised an eyebrow. 'Are you hoping to bump into a certain Commander of the Exiles, ma'am?'

'I'm not bothered about meeting Van,' said Kelsey.

Nagel suppressed a smile.

'Right,' said Kelsey, ignoring him. 'We'll meet in the Common Rooms after dinner, and then hit the taverns. I'd better go and brief the Brigade command on today's progress up on the ridge. See you later.'

Kelsey strode down the steps leading away from the high platform, and joined a busy street that ran from the old palace to the harbour. New brick buildings lined both sides of the paved road, and wagons were competing with workers as they squeezed along the crowded thoroughfare. A few Exiles nodded or called out to her as she passed, and she acknowledged them. Everyone in Jezra knew who she was – the famous dragon rider who had saved the King and Queen from the mad prince. Her actions from a year and a half before had ensured that Kelsey had never had to pay for a drink in any of the taverns in the town; a privilege of which she had taken full advantage.

She stopped in at a formidable, five-storey structure, where the Brigade had their operational headquarters, and spent an hour discussing that day's work up on the ridge. Their orders were to slowly expand the territory under human control, pushing back the green-hides yard by yard, and enclosing all conquered areas with new lines of defensive walls. Trial and error had, over the space of a year, evolved into the process that they all followed – laying down prefabricated lengths of stockade under the cover of the two dragons' fire. At the end of the meeting, the next day's targets were handed out, and Kelsey left the building as it was starting to get dark.

She walked along the streets until she reached her cottage, a small red-brick building next to a long line of high tenements. It had only three rooms, but as a dragon rider, she was one of the few people in Jezra entitled to her own place. She unlocked the door and went inside. She had a tiny living room, a bedroom, and her own bathroom, complete with a pipe that carried hot water from the Brigade Common Rooms. She pulled off her scruffy work clothes, washed herself, then dressed in her bedroom. Occasionally, she wished she lived in the shared accommodation where the rest of the young, unmarried Brigade workers slept, but at other times she treasured her privacy. Van had offered her a larger house, but she had declined, not wanting it to seem as though she felt herself to be better than everyone else.

When she was ready, she pulled on her boots and winter coat, and stepped back outside into the street. She made her way towards the harbour, where a huge storage depot was located. Two floors of the building were taken up with the Brigade Common Rooms, where many of the workers spent their free time. She queued up at the refectory, and ate some dinner alone at a table, then walked into the busy bar room. The tiled floor was covered in small wooden tables, at which dozens of Brigade workers were sitting. At one end of the room, six enormous barrels were positioned on their sides, and staff were filling large mugs with the ale that they contained. The Exiles brewed their own beer, and each worker was entitled to a quantity of tokens every ten days, which they could swap for alcohol. Kelsey nodded at a few of the people whom she recognised, then she spotted Vadhi and Nagel sitting together at a table. Nagel was one of a growing number of Fordians who had moved from the City to Jezra over the previous year. Some of them had started their own businesses, but Nagel had volunteered for service in the Brigades.

He waved at Kelsey as she approached.

'I already got you an ale,' he said, gesturing to a spare mug as she sat.

'Cheers,' she said, taking a long drink. 'Just the one here, mind. I want to go out tonight.'

The Fordian nodded. 'I heard you laid over a hundred yards of new wall today.'

'Aye; that's right. We should have the sunward extension sealed off by the end of the month, and another three hundred acres will be added to Upper Jezra. I mean, it's all a muddy wasteland at the moment, but give it a couple of years, and there will be farms, and a new woodland is getting planted.'

'I've never even been up there, ma'am,' said Vadhi, her voice quiet against the noisy background of the bar room.

'Don't call me ma'am when we're not working,' said Kelsey; 'we're not in the army. And, what do you mean you've never been up on the ridge? You must have been to Westrig at least?'

'Nope, never,' said Vadhi. 'I was too young to be out on the front lines when we first landed, so I got a job at the harbour office. I started off carting supplies about, and then they taught me to read and write, and I've been working as a clerk ever since. I've never been within a hundred yards of a greenhide.'

'How old are you?'

'Eighteen.'

'Pyre's arse, you make me feel ancient,' said Kelsey. 'You must have been sixteen when we got here from Lostwell. Were you in a gang?'

'Yeah. Well, my big brother was, and I ran up the ramp to Old Alea with him.'

Kelsey took another drink. 'Do you have any experience with dragons?'

'No. I just wanted a change.'

'There were over a hundred applicants for the role,' said Nagel.

'That many?' said Kelsey. 'I didn't know I was that popular.' She frowned. 'I'm joking, Nagel. Obviously, it's the dragons that must be attracting them. Wait until I tell Frostback that a hundred humans were trying to get Yannic's job; that'll put a smile on her scaly face.'

'What's she like?' said Vadhi.

Kelsey thought for a moment. 'Whatever you do, don't bullshit her; she'll see through it and hate you for it. And, if she ever does anything for you, for Pyre's sake remember to say thank you. Right, drink up; we're going.'

They stood, and pushed their way through the press of workers in the bar room, then left the towering building behind. The air was cold and crisp outside, and Kelsey saw her breath mist in front of her. They made their way along the brick-lined streets towards the harbour. The quayside was busy, with a large supply ship from Pella being unloaded onto the docks. Heading away from the harbour was a narrow lane squeezed between buildings. The upper floors were built of brick, but the ground levels had been adapted from the original stone ruins of the town. All six of Jezra's privately-owned taverns were located down the narrow lane, with three on either side.

'Here we are,' said Kelsey.

'I've never been inside any of these taverns,' said Vadhi. 'I can only afford to drink in the Common Rooms.'

'We'll let you into a wee secret,' said Kelsey; 'the Brigade pays my bar bills, so tonight won't cost you a single coin.'

Vadhi's mouth opened. 'I just thought that you were rich.'

'Nah,' said Kelsey; 'I get paid the same pocket money as the rest of the Brigades, but after that thing with the King and Queen, I never have to pay for drinks.'

'The perks of being a dragon rider,' said Nagel.

They entered the narrow lane. On their left was the corner of one of the main harbour depots, and on the right was the first tavern.

'That's the *Queen of Khatanax*,' said Kelsey; 'named after an old friend of mine. It's where the crews of the Pellan ships drink. We'll head to the next one down – *Exile's Rest*.'

The front of the *Exile's Rest* was built into the stone foundations of an ancient structure, and they went down a small flight of steps to get to the main entrance. A tall doorman nodded at Kelsey as they walked through the front door. They went into a narrow lobby, then entered a low-ceilinged hall, filled with tables, and with small alcoves dotted along each wall. The stonework had been reinforced and repaired with hundreds of red bricks, but the place had an ancient feel to it.

An older man approached. 'Miss Holdfast,' he said; 'good evening. Are these your companions for the night?'

'Aye, that's right,' said Kelsey.

'Excellent. I will set up a tab for you. Would you like your usual booth?'

Kelsey nodded, and the man led them through the hall to a quieter area at the back, where there were several dimly-lit alcoves. They sat at a table, and the man lit a few candles for them.

'Ale, please,' said Kelsey.

'No problem,' said the man, 'and would you like me to inform you if the Commander of the Exiles comes in?'

Vadhi and Nagel shared a short glance.

'Aye,' said Kelsey. 'Thanks.'

'Are the rumours true?' whispered Vadhi, as the man left them.

'What rumours?' said Kelsey.

'Um, that you and the major-general are, em, very friendly?'

'I told you not to bring that up,' said Nagel, his eyes narrowing.

'Sorry,' muttered Vadhi.

Kelsey pretended she hadn't heard. She knew that everyone in Jezra was aware that there was something going on between the dragon rider and the Commander of the Exiles, but as Kelsey didn't understand their relationship, she was in no mood to discuss it. She also knew that it wasn't by chance that she had chosen to go into that particular tavern on that particular evening, and her nerves jangled at the prospect of seeing Van.

She glanced at Vadhi as a waitress brought over a tray of ale. 'A hundred applicants, eh?'

'I think so,' said the young Torduan.

'How did you get the job? I mean, you seem alright, but how did you beat ninety-nine others?'

Vadhi's face went red.

'Her brother is an officer in the Fourth Brigade,' said Nagel; 'he's close to the colonel.'

'Ahh,' said Kelsey.

'I got the job on my own merits,' said Vadhi. 'My brother recommended me, but I still had to put in the work.'

Kelsey laughed. 'Don't worry; we'll give you a fair chance. Though, all newcomers have to start off by cleaning out the dragon's lairs. Let's see if you're still keen after a few months of shovelling shit.'

Vadhi's eyes hardened. 'I'll do whatever you ask me to, ma'am.'

'Quit the "ma'am" nonsense. Call me Kelsey when we're out.'

The tavern began to fill up as they drank their first ales. The patrons appeared to be mostly off duty Banner officers, sprinkled with a handful of private citizens – all Exiles from Lostwell who had moved to Jezra from the City over the previous year. A Fordian merchant in rich robes nodded to Nagel as he walked past, and several officers also acknowledged Kelsey's presence.

They were on their third ale when the owner of the tavern strolled by to let Kelsey know that Van had arrived, and a few minutes later the Commander of the Exiles appeared at their table. Vadhi jumped to her feet, saluting. Nagel also saluted, but remained in his seat.

'Sit down,' said Kelsey. 'Van, this is Vadhi; a new girl in Frostback's crew. Vadhi, this is, well, you know who he is, and that giant next to him is Captain Cardova.'

The captain nodded to Vadhi. 'Call me Lucius when we're in the *Exile's Rest*. Nice to meet you.'

Vadhi's face went red.

They moved up to make space for Van and Cardova, and the two officers sat. Within moments, a small team of waiters and waitresses were attending their table, taking down the commander's order for brandy and more ale.

Cardova poured brandy for everyone, while Van and Kelsey glanced awkwardly at each other.

'They managed over a hundred yards up on the ridge today,' said Nagel.

'I heard,' said Van. 'The new techniques are working well. Best of all, there were no casualties. Frostback busy tonight?'

'Aye,' said Kelsey. 'She's flown off sunward with Halfclaw to get some warmth in the desert. She's not a big lover of winter.'

'I know how she feels,' said Van. 'At least Sweetmist is over. It's hard to believe that we've been here for two years.'

'This is the longest I've been in the one place since I was a lad,' said Cardova. 'It's almost starting to feel like home.'

'This is home,' said Vadhi. Her face went red again as the others looked at her. 'I mean, if Lostwell really has been destroyed, then we're stuck here forever, aren't we? Maybe "stuck" is the wrong word.'

Van shrugged. 'It's accurate. I guess we just have to make the best of it. To be honest, I wouldn't choose to live anywhere else. Everything I want is right here.'

Kelsey glanced away, wanting to avoid the way Van was looking at her.

'It's better than Dragon Eyre,' said Cardova, 'but I miss Implacatus. Not the place, but the people, well, some of them. I'd like to walk into my old Banner headquarters, to see how they're all doing.'

'Which Banner were you in?' said Vadhi.

Cardova pulled up the sleeve on his left arm, showing her a tattoo. 'Black Crown.' He nodded in Kelsey's direction. 'Her brother killed a whole regiment of them in Fordamere.'

'That's Corthie for you,' said Kelsey.

'Did you actually see Corthie Holdfast?' said Vadhi.

'I caught a glimpse of him,' said Cardova, 'and I saw the big black dragon that he was friends with.'

'Wow,' said Vadhi; 'you saw Corthie.'

'Hold on,' said Kelsey; 'I've seen Corthie too, you know. He was an annoying child.'

'I'd like to meet the rest of the Holdfasts,' said Cardova. 'Van's told me about Sable and Karalyn; they sound intriguing.'

'My sister is mental,' said Kelsey; 'she'd eat you alive. Mind you, so would Sable.'

'I think one Holdfast is enough for the City,' said Van.

'Aye, though I'll bet the Queen would prefer it was Corthie, rather than little old me.'

'That's not true,' said Van; 'and I should know. I meet with the Queen every month.'

'I shouldn't be here,' said Vadhi. 'Yesterday, I was a clerk in the harbour office, and now I'm out drinking with... with...'

'Get used to it,' said Kelsey. 'You've moved up the food chain, Vadhi.'

'People will try to get to Kelsey and the major-general through you,' said Nagel. 'Watch out for them; and don't ever gossip about what you see or hear.'

'I won't,' said Vadhi.

Cardova laughed, as he refilled their glasses with brandy. 'You can gossip about me all you like.'

'Tell us about yourself,' said Van.

They listened as Vadhi talked about her impoverished childhood in the slums of Alea Tanton, and about how her brother had saved her by dragging her up the ramp on Lostwell's last day. Kelsey eyed Van while the young Torduan spoke, trying to sort out her feelings towards him. She knew that he still liked her, but he had been so busy with his work that they rarely saw each other. She had learned his schedule, and knew which of his evenings were free, but wanted to make it seem as though each time they met in the *Exile's Rest* was nothing more than a coincidence.

The staff kept the drinks coming to their table, and it was past midnight when Sergeant Nagel announced that he was going back to his room in the barracks. He helped a slightly unsteady Vadhi to her feet, and they made their farewells.

'I think I'll call it a night too,' said Cardova, a faint smile on his lips as he glanced at Van and Kelsey. 'I'll see you at work tomorrow, boss.'

Van nodded.

'Your new girl seems alright,' Cardova said to Kelsey, as he stood. 'Don't drive her away.'

'I'll try not to,' she said.

The captain smiled, then made his way out of the tavern.

Van glanced at Kelsey. 'So, here we are once more.'

'Aye.'

He nodded. 'Do you want to...?'

'Aye. Sure.'

Van gestured to a waitress, who came over to the table.

'We're leaving,' he said; 'make sure the bill is sent to my office.'

'Yes, sir,' said the waitress.

Kelsey and Van got to their feet, and walked through the busy bar towards the door. Several Banner officers saluted their commander, and Kelsey noticed plenty of glances in her direction.

'They all know, don't they?' she said, as they emerged out onto the cold street.

'About what?' said Van.

'About us.'

'Does that bother you?'

'I don't know. What are we?'

'Is tonight going to be one of those nights?'

'What do you mean?'

'I mean, are we going to stay up half the night debating the exact terms of our relationship?'

She frowned. 'I might just go home.'

Van paused as they reached the dockside. 'What? But...'

'Are you only interested in getting me into bed?'

'Hang on, Kelsey. If I remember right, that's what you told me you wanted. You said you didn't want the emotional burden of a "proper" relationship, but that you still wanted to get together. And, did I say that I didn't enjoy sitting up talking to you? I do enjoy it. Maybe not as much as being in bed with you, but I'll take what I can get.'

He started walking again, heading in the direction of his apartment in the new Command Post. Kelsey watched him stride away, then sighed and followed him.

'This isn't doing me any good,' she muttered, as she reached his side.

'Then, go home,' he said. 'I'm not forcing you to come back with me.'

'Do you want me to come back, even if I sleep on the couch tonight?'

He stopped, and looked into her eyes. 'Of course I do.'

Kelsey felt a shiver ripple through her body. It was probably a mistake, but she couldn't help herself. After everything she and Van had been through, there was no one in the City she felt closer to. She was convinced that she didn't love him, but there was something about him that kept drawing her in. He took her hand and they carried on, passing the ships tied up for the night in the harbour until they reached the Command Post. Sentries on duty saluted Van as they entered the tall building, and then they made their way upstairs to Van's private quarters. He unlocked the door and lit a couple of lamps, as Kelsey sat on his long couch and poured herself another brandy from a half-empty bottle on a table.

'Are you happy with our arrangement?' she said, as he sat next to her.

He gave her a wry smile. 'You know what I want.'

'Tell me.'

'I want us to be together; I want you to move in here with me. You are the only woman I have ever really loved, Kelsey.'

'So, you're not happy with this arrangement?'

'I'm happy that I get to see you.'

'Then, why do you never come round to visit me at work? And, you've never once been in my house.'

'That's because I don't want to pester you. You know my feelings – I'm not going to grovel or beg. Are *you* happy with this arrangement?'

'I don't know.'

'Do you know what I think? If it hadn't been for that damned vision,

I believe that we'd be together. It ruined everything. No, not everything, but it ruined our chances of having a normal relationship.'

Kelsey said nothing, knowing that he was probably right.

'What do you want from me?' he said.

'Sometimes nothing,' she said; 'and, at other times, everything.'

'Are you sure that it's not just because you're lonely?'

'No. For the first time in my life, I could probably snag just about any single boy in the Brigades, just because I'm a dragon rider; but I haven't even kissed another guy since coming to the City. You know me better than anyone else here; you... understand me.'

He stared at her for a moment, then swallowed and got to his feet.

'I'll get you some blankets,' he said.

'Wait,' she said, reaching up and taking his hand. 'Sit back down.'

He sat next to her. She placed her glass onto the table and kissed him. He pulled her close, the fingers of his right hand pushing through her long brown hair. Her senses came alive, and she closed her eyes, drowning in his embrace. His left hand went to her waist, while her own hands began to fumble with his clothes. Her fingers reached the bare skin of his chest, and they fell back onto the couch, entwined in each other's arms.

There was a loud thumping on the front door.

Van glanced up. 'Damn it.'

'Ignore them,' said Kelsey.

The thumping sound came again.

Van swore, and sat up. He took a breath, then stood and walked towards the door. Kelsey glared at his back, then sat and poured herself another brandy. She heard the door open, and the sound of voices.

'We have a visitor,' Van said, as he walked back into the living room.

Kelsey looked up. Following Van into the room was Chancellor Mona. The demigod's eyes flickered over Kelsey sitting on the couch.

'I'm glad you're here, Miss Holdfast,' she said. 'It'll save me time. I've already wasted several hours this evening trying to locate Van Logos.'

'Please, sit,' Van said.

'I've been in the Command Post since sunset,' Mona went on, as she sat opposite Kelsey. 'None of the officers seemed to know where their own commander might be found.'

'It's my night off,' said Van, sitting next to Kelsey. 'I only have one day a month when I'm free, and my officers know when to be discreet.'

'But this is an emergency,' said Mona.

Kelsey frowned. 'We knew you were coming over to Jezra at some point, but I'd hardly call the research into the scrolls here an emergency. Could this not have waited until the morning?'

Mona glanced from Kelsey to Van, as if realising what she had walked into. 'Was I interrupting something?'

'You're here now,' said Van. 'What's wrong? I assume that something is wrong?'

'Something is very wrong, Commander,' she said. 'Naxor has been arrested and thrown into prison.'

Kelsey shrugged. 'Oh well.'

'Why would Naxor be arrested?' said Van.

'He was hiding something,' said Mona; 'and I'm here to tell you that the King and Queen require your presence in Pella as soon as possible; you too, Miss Holdfast.'

'Why?' said Kelsey.

Mona's expression fell. 'God-Queen Amalia has returned to the City.'

CHAPTER 3
MORAL PERSPECTIVE

The Circuit, Medio, The City – 21st Marcalis 3422

Kagan glanced around the small, walled garden. 'What is this place?'

Lady Sofia said nothing, her attention on the three tombstones that sat against the rear wall of the garden. Kagan shivered in the cold morning air, and rubbed his hands together.

'Is this a graveyard?' he said.

Sofia glanced at him. 'It's the Shrine of the Three Sisters. It's a little ironic, me being here, because when I was the God-Queen of the City, I didn't know where it was. Had I known, I would have ordered its destruction.'

They sat on one of the benches that ran next to the flower beds.

'Why would you have destroyed it?' said Kagan.

'The three sisters were enemies of mine; as was their mother.' She bowed her head. 'They were Yendra's daughters.'

Kagan said nothing. Sofia's feelings regarding the death of her daughter seemed to change as abruptly as the weather in the City. Some days, she seemed almost jubilant that Yendra was dead, but on others, a dark melancholy would fall upon her if the subject was broached.

'Such a beautiful garden,' she said. 'The Evaders built this place because they loved Yendra and her daughters. If I had died, they would have spat on my corpse.'

'Do you remember the three daughters?'

She narrowed her eyes at him. 'Of course I do. My eldest son killed two of them, before he, in turn, was slain by Yendra. And now, another of my sons is responsible for Yendra's death. What a mess. If Malik and I had known how much pain and suffering would be inflicted by our children, I wonder if we would have had any. We had six, and now only one remains.'

'You have Maxwell now,' said Kagan. 'You have another son.'

'Yes, but Maxwell is a demigod, not a full god,' she said; 'due to the fact that you are a mere mortal. Don't look at me like that, Kagan; you know what I mean. I love little Maxwell, and you are a good father to the child. That is, after all, why I selected you as a companion. However, Malik was an immensely powerful god, and you cannot compete with that.'

She stood again, and began plucking a few weeds from one of the flower beds. Kagan watched her, his feelings torn. He adored Sofia, or Amalia as she truly was, but knew that, to her, he was only a temporary fixture in her life. He would age and die, while she and their son would live on forever. It hurt, but he was coming to terms with it. She could have chosen anyone, but she had picked him to father her child, and that had to count for something. His thoughts went to the baby boy. He had been left in Port Sanders in the care of Gellie and the two new servants who had been employed to care for him, and Kagan missed him. He had been surprised when Sofia had suggested a trip out of the mansion, as she hadn't left the house in over a year, and had assumed that they would be bringing Maxwell with them.

Sofia stood in front of him. 'Let's go.'

'Are we travelling back to Port Sanders?'

She raised an eyebrow. 'No. I didn't come out here to visit this shrine; it just happened to be on the way.'

'The way to where?'

'You'll see. When we get there, you are not to mention anything about the existence of our son; understood?'

He nodded, and got to his feet. They left the walled garden through a narrow door and came out onto the twisting streets of the Circuit. It reminded Kagan of the slums of Alea Tanton, and had the same air of quiet desperation about it. Children played barefoot in the gutters along the narrow roads, while the heavy grey of the concrete surrounding them felt suffocating. Sofia didn't seem to care; she kept her chin high as they navigated the narrow lanes, ignoring the looks from some of the Evaders they passed. They reached a wider road, where their carriage was waiting, and Saul opened the side door for them. They climbed on board, and Saul returned to the driver's bench, where he urged the ponies forward.

Sofia closed the shutters on the windows of the carriage and settled into her seat, her eyes half-shut.

'I don't think I shall ever return here,' she said. 'The memories do nothing for my mood.'

'And maybe, if you're trying to stay hidden, you should remain in Port Sanders.'

She frowned at him. 'No one will recognise me. When I was God-Queen, I barely left Maeladh Palace in three hundred years. Furthermore, I've taken so much salve, that I look ten years younger than I did the last time I was here.'

'It's still hard for me to believe that you're not twenty-one.'

She laughed. 'I am over five thousand years old, Kagan. Somewhere in this City will live my great, great, great, great grandchildren. I missed out a few "greats" there to save time, but you get the idea. That's one reason I chose you. Being from Lostwell, there is absolutely no possibility that we are related to each other.'

'I thought it was because of my suave good looks.'

'That too. It does help that you are an attractive boy; it gives Maxwell a better chance that he'll be handsome when he's older.'

'Will he have powers?'

'I will be extremely disappointed if he doesn't. I can sense his self-healing, so he's definitely immortal, but we won't know what range of skills he possesses until he reaches his teenage years.' She caught Kagan's glance. 'By that time, I hope we will have had a few more; I intend to get my money's worth out of you.'

'I'm up for that.'

'Good, because I want to start trying for another one soon.'

He raised an eyebrow. 'Soon?'

'Not while we're in a carriage, Kagan; I do have some standards.'

'Oh, I just thought...'

'I know what you were thinking. Maybe tonight, once we have dealt with today's business.'

He shrugged. 'It was worth a try.'

***

Kagan dozed as the carriage was drawn through the City. With the shutters closed, he had no idea where they were, and he awoke with a jolt as the carriage came to a halt.

'We're here,' said Sofia, watching him from her seat.

He rubbed his eyes and sat up. The side door opened, and Kagan saw the back of a large, dark building. Militia soldiers were standing around, wearing uniforms that he didn't recognise.

'Help me down,' said Sofia. 'Remember, you are my servant while we are on this visit.'

Kagan stepped from the carriage, then extended his hand to assist Sofia down onto the cobbled ground. He glanced around. He could smell the sea air, but the scent of it was different from that which pervaded Port Sanders – colder and fresher.

Saul remained by the carriage, while Sofia and Kagan walked towards a tall set of doors built into the side of the dark building. As they crossed a bridge over a dry moat, the militia on guard at the gates moved to block their way.

'I am here to see Lady Amber,' said Sofia.

She reached into her purse and withdrew a ring, which she showed to the guards.

'Wait here,' said one, taking the ring. He opened the tall doors and went into the building.

'Is this Dalrig?' Kagan whispered.

Sofia nodded. 'We are standing in front of Greylin Palace.'

Several minutes passed before the guard returned. He handed the ring back to Sofia and nodded, allowing her and Kagan to enter the building. There were no windows inside, and thick shadows draped every wall. They were shown to a room with worn carpets and faded tapestries, and escorted to seats by a cold hearth.

'Lady Amber will come down to see you shortly, ma'am,' said a guard.

Kagan leaned over to Sofia as soon as the guard left them. 'Lady Amber is your granddaughter, is that right?' he whispered.

'Yes. However, as of this moment, she has no idea that I am in the City. That ring bears the crest of the Port Sanders Merchants' Guild; that's what got us through the door. We'd best be prepared.'

'For what?'

'Anything. I cannot predict how she will react when she sees me.' She glanced around. 'My, what a dreary place this is. No wonder Amber is so miserable.'

The door opened and a young woman walked in, a frown on her lips.

'I have very little time,' she said, as she approached. 'Tell me what you want, and be brief.'

Sofia laughed. 'Is that any way to greet your grandmother, Amber?'

The woman halted. Her eyes went to Sofia, and she stared for a moment in incomprehension, then her mouth fell open.

'No,' she muttered. She raised a hand. 'Don't come near me! Stay back, I... I...'

'Really, Amber; is this necessary? If I wanted to kill you, you would be dead. I'm only here for a little chat. Come; sit.'

Amber remained where she was. 'This can't be happening. You're not supposed to be here – you were supposed to have died with Lostwell.'

'Yes, well, I didn't. Do you have any wine?'

'Wine?'

'Yes, for you. I think you need something to calm your nerves.'

'What do you want with me? I had nothing to do with my father abducting the King and Queen; nothing. Do they know you're here? You have to leave; now.'

'I'm not leaving, Amber. Sit down, and stop being such a cry-baby.'

Amber took a step forward, then fell into an armchair, her eyes never leaving Sofia's face. 'You look different; younger.'

'Thank you,' said Sofia. 'This is Kagan, my companion and servant. He is from Lostwell, so some of the subtleties of our relationships here in the City are rather lost on him.'

'Does he know who you are?'

'Of course he does. It doesn't mean much to him; in fact, your reaction to my arrival is the first time he's seen anyone who truly knows me.'

Amber stared at Kagan for a moment, and she seemed to calm a little. 'Why did you come back, grandmother?'

'Back to the City, you mean? It's not as if I had much choice – the Ascendants on Lostwell were hunting me, and I'd have been executed if they'd found me. Where else was I supposed to go? But, Amber, you're worrying over nothing. I fully intend to hide here, unnoticed, for a long time to come. Only necessity has brought me to your door this day.'

'What necessity?'

Sofia smiled. 'It's quite simple. I have run out of the anti-salve that your father gave me.'

'Wait; my father knows that you're in the City?'

'Yes. He's not always been a model son, but he was prepared to help me when I came begging at his door two years ago. I needed to hide, and so he provided me with a supply of anti-salve, to mask my powers.'

'And what have you been doing since then?'

'Keeping my head down, dear,' Sofia said. 'It was difficult at first, but when Belinda sent the Exiles here, I assumed the identity of a rich noblewoman from Lostwell, and blended in.'

Amber nodded, her eyes narrowing. 'Are you going to try to take over the throne?'

'Perhaps in a century or so,' she said. 'Right now, I am enjoying living as a private citizen. I have a nice mansion, and plenty of money, and no horrible pressures of having to rule. I might wait until the mortal monarchy falls apart on its own, and then make my move, or perhaps I'll remain hidden. However, if you try to deny me the anti-salve, then I'll have no choice but to come out into the open. I assume that Lady Vana is in the City? She would be able to track me once the anti-salve in my bloodstream wears off.'

Amber stood, and raised her hand again. 'You mean you have no powers at the moment?'

'That's more like the Amber I know,' said Sofia; 'ruthless and calculating. Unfortunately for you, my powers have returned. So, you can lower that hand and sit back down; you won't be killing me today.'

'But, if your powers are back, then Vana will be able to see you here.'

'Only if she happens to be looking, my dear.'

'The Queen has another demigod who can also track us – a Lady Silva.'

Sofia smiled. 'Silva survived? Excellent. I like her, though she'd probably betray me in a heartbeat. It was only really Belinda that Silva doted on, not me. Did any other gods make it here from Lostwell?'

'Naxor did.'

Sofia shrugged. 'Well, we can't have everything, I suppose. Anyone else?'

'Someone called Felice, a god from Lostwell; and Kelsey Holdfast.'

Sofia groaned. 'Not her again. Though, I confess that I already knew that she had made it here. I heard she was involved in your father's arrest.'

'Do you know her?'

'Let's just say that we have had occasion to bump into each other.'

'She can block powers, can't she? The Crown refuses to confirm it, but it's the only explanation I can think of. Whenever she's around, my powers stop working.'

'That is her particular skill.'

'From what you said, it sounds like you arrived back in the City before the Exiles appeared.'

'That is correct.'

'Then, does that mean that you have a Quadrant?'

'Well done, Amber. That is the case.'

'Do you have it with you?'

Sofia reached back into her bag and pulled out a copper-coloured metal device. Kagan frowned, having no idea what he was looking at.

'I thought it best to bring it today,' said Sofia, 'in case you tried anything stupid.'

'Is it the same device that you used to leave the City in the first place?'

'My dear, it is the same device that brought me to the City two and a half thousand years ago. It sat unused in the Royal Palace for centuries, and then in Maeladh Palace, when I left Malik and moved to Tara. Call it my insurance policy. So, tell me, Amber, how is your relationship with the Crown these days?'

Amber frowned. 'Not good. I have been left in charge of Dalrig, but no one trusts me. I think everyone believes that I was helping my father, though, if they had any evidence, I'd be locked up in the Fortress of the Lifegiver along with him. But, that doesn't mean that I'm willing to rebel against them, so don't get any ideas. Like you, I want to keep my head down for a while.'

'We can help each other, Amber.'

'I don't want your help, grandmother. Do you remember the last time we met?'

Sofia frowned. 'Not particularly.'

'Let me remind you. It was in the Royal Palace in Ooste, after you had elevated Duke Marcus to become a prince. You melted the skin from my body.'

'Did I? You must have done something to deserve it, dear.'

'I refused to acknowledge Marcus as my sovereign ruler.'

'Well, there you go. Treachery should not go unpunished.'

'You made a terrible mistake with Marcus; when will you realise that?'

'A mistake? Please enlighten me.'

Amber shook her head. 'Marcus was a fool. Your love for him blinded you to that simple fact. You acted as though he were another Michael, but he wasn't even close. His desire for his own cousin brought the City to its knees.'

'Don't make me cross, Amber. I am aware that Marcus was far from perfect, but one has to work with the tools one is given. If you and your father had shown me a little more support, then perhaps I would still be on the throne.'

Amber stared at her. 'You opened the gates in the Middle Walls.'

'Yes. Medio was brim-full with my enemies. I would have saved Auldan, and I would have retaken the City once my enemies were dead. This City has a very short memory – has everyone forgotten the hundreds of thousands of greenhides I killed in my first thousand years here? Were it not for me, there wouldn't have been a Medio, or a Bulwark. How do you think the mortals were able to build those walls? Because of me. Day after day for centuries, it was me who went out to drive back the Eternal Enemy. Was I wrong to wish for a little respite after that? Was I wrong to try to groom Michael and then Marcus in the arts of ruling? My dear husband had given up by that point, and spent his days bathing in salve and chasing after the poor wretches of his harem. At least I tried.'

Amber said nothing for a long while, and Kagan watched as the god and the demigod stared at each other.

Eventually, Amber stood. 'If I were to give you some anti-salve, would you go back to wherever you are hiding and never bother me again?'

'As long as you give me a sufficient supply.'

'Wait here.'

Amber strode from the room, leaving Sofia and Kagan alone.

She turned to him. 'There you have it; the first time you have seen me with a member of my family. What do you think of Amber?'

'She seems scared of you.'

'I would hope so.'

'What did she mean by "you opened the gates?"'

'She meant exactly what she said. I let the greenhides into Medio, in order to destroy those who were trying to overthrow my rule.'

'So, all those stories about the greenhides in Port Sanders, and in the Circuit; that was because of you?'

'Yes. Why?'

'Thousands died.'

'Oh, it was more than that, Kagan. If I recall correctly, the total death toll from Medio was in the region of one hundred and eighty thousand. Almost half the population of that part of the City. It sounds harsh, but I had decided that it was time for a cull. I would have restored the City; rebuilt it out of the ashes, but there was so much going wrong at the time. If I could do it all again, I would have used a different strategy.'

'Do you mean that you regret it?'

'Regret what? The deaths? No, Kagan. You have to understand something; when you are immortal, you start to see things in a longer perspective. Mortals come and go so fast that you can blink and several generations of them will have passed. And when you are a ruler, you have to make decisions that will shorten, or lengthen, the lives of many thousands of your mortal subjects. If one was to have empathy for every single mortal that breathed the air of the City, then one would succumb to depression and enter a state of hopelessness. Instead, one has to concentrate on the bigger picture, and look at the masses of the ordinary citizens as a collective. And, sometimes, in order to save a patient, one must cut out an infection, even though it hurts.'

Kagan glanced away, recoiling from the logic of amorality espoused by Sofia. In Alea Tanton, many people had believed that the gods were uncaring and ruthless, but it still came as a shock to him to hear the words leave her lips. A hundred and eighty thousand men, women and children, ripped to shreds by greenhides, and she thought nothing of it.

He tried to look beyond her words. He thought he had got to know her well, sharing each day and night together for nearly two years. He knew her as generous, and loyal to those who were loyal to her. She cared about him, he was sure of it, so how could the woman he loved also be the heartless god that had killed so many? Perhaps he could be a good influence on her; and maybe he already had been, tempering the savage nature caused by her immortality. Perhaps her love for Maxwell would have the same effect.

'What's wrong, Kagan?' she said.

He looked at her. 'I'm finding it hard to reconcile the Lady Sofia I know, with someone who could open the gates to the greenhides.'

She frowned. 'Weren't you listening to me? I was the God-Queen. Did I make mistakes? Yes. I'm not perfect. You saw me kill Dizzler and the others; you must have guessed that I had killed before.'

'Dizzler deserved what he got; that's the difference.'

'I've had enough of this conversation. We can continue it back in Port Sanders; let's not argue here, while we wait for Amber to return.' She glanced at the door. 'Where is she? She's been gone too long. We may have to depart in a hurry, Kagan, so be ready.'

She got up, and paced the threadbare carpet, glancing at the soot-darkened paintings and faded tapestries adorning the walls.

'This place could really do with a decent decorator,' she said, shaking her head, 'and a good clean. There are cobwebs in every corner.'

The door opened, and Amber walked in.

Sofia marched over to her and extended her hand. Amber frowned, and passed over a small collection of vials. Sofia held one up to the light of a lamp and swirled the contents.

'This should last a few decades,' she said. 'Good job, granddaughter. Now, should Kagan and I leave immediately? I assume you have sent a messenger to Pella to notify the King and Queen about my presence here?'

Amber bowed her head. 'It's what you would have done, grandmother.'

'Really; I would have betrayed my own flesh and blood?'

'You forced Aila to marry Marcus.'

'Yes, well, you have me there. And I suppose that you need to protect yourself, especially if Vana or Silva have already noticed that I'm here.' She walked back to where Kagan was sitting, and placed the vials into her bag. 'Come,' she said to him; 'it's time to leave.'

He stood, and started to walk for the door.

'Kagan, wait,' Sofia said. 'We're not going by carriage. The militia will stop us before we've left Auldan, and besides, I told Saul to leave as soon as we entered the palace.' She took the copper-coloured device from the bag, and turned back to Amber. 'I hope a long time elapses before we meet again, granddaughter.'

She swept her fingers over the surface of the metal device and Kagan saw the air around him dissolve, and in an instant, they were standing inside Sofia's bedroom in Port Sanders.

Kagan cried out, his eyes wide.

Sofia laughed. 'Your first time travelling by Quadrant, I assume?'

'That... thing transported us here?'

'Indeed. It also brought me all the way from Lostwell.'

'Could it take us back there?'

'It could, if Lostwell still existed; alas, it doesn't. I checked. The world ripped itself to pieces.'

She extracted the set of vials from the bag and studied them.

'Is that anti-salve?' he said. 'Is that how you've been masking your powers?'

'So, you were listening to me and Amber talk? Good. Yes, a small dose suppresses my powers, rendering me invisible to any demigods with the ability to track us.'

'Don't you need to take some? I mean, if it's worn off?'

'It hasn't worn off, dear Kagan.'

'But, what you said to Amber...'

'I was bluffing. If she had tried to kill me, I would be dead. Did you seriously think I was going to travel through the City with my powers shining like a beacon? I meant what I said before; I intend to stay hidden for a long time to come.'

'But the King and Queen will know that you're back in the City.'

'If I hadn't gone to see Amber, then they would have discovered that when my last dose of anti-salve ran out; in other words, in a couple of days. The only person hurt by this is Amber, who has brought upon herself nothing but more suspicion. She would have done far better by helping me, as her father did in the desperate days when I first arrived back in the City.' She slid the Quadrant into a drawer by the bed and locked it. 'I won't be needing that for a while. In fact, I don't think I'll be leaving the mansion again for at least a year.'

The sound of a baby crying came through from the adjoining room.

Sofia smiled. 'I hear that a certain little demigod is awake. Come; let us see our son.' She walked towards the nursery. 'Do you know the best thing about being rich?' she said, as she put her hand on the door. 'Having a child, but never having to change a nappy or get up in the middle of the night; don't you think, Kagan?'

He watched her as she disappeared through the doorway. A sudden urge to run rushed through him like a shiver, and his mouth went dry. He couldn't run; his son was in the next room, and even if he did run, where would he go? The urge drained away, and he shook his head to clear it. How could he have even considered running? His life was as close to perfect as it was possible to get; only a fool would throw it all away.

He pushed the hundred and eighty thousand torn bodies to the back of his mind, and walked through the door.

CHAPTER 4

POPPY, GINGER, TAB-TAB AND FLUFFY

F ortress of the Lifegiver, The Bulwark, The City – 21st Marcalis 3422

'Poppy!' said Jade, patting her lap.

The sleek black cat continued to lick her paw, ignoring her.

'Poppy, get up here; that's an order.'

The cat peered out of the window.

'Stop looking at the greenhides and get onto my knee. Bad cat.'

Poppy turned, her green eyes scanning Jade's lap. She drew down, as if to leap across the gap to where Jade was sitting. As she was about to jump, a huge ginger tom leapt up from the floor and landed on Jade's knee. He began circling on her lap, digging his claws in.

'Oh, Ginger,' said Jade; 'was I asking you?' She stroked him, and his head butted her hand as he started to purr loudly. Poppy decided that she would join him, and a second later, Jade had two cats vying for attention on her lap, each trying to claim the larger space. Jade laughed, and stroked them both.

'Who's my lovely little kittens?' she said, a broad smile on her face. 'Oh, you're a heavy boy, Ginger, my handsome Prince of the Bulwark. Don't get jealous, Poppy; you can be a princess when I take over the City and get rid of all the stupid mortals. What's that? Yendra wouldn't want me to kill all the mortals? Well, Poppy, that doesn't matter any more, as dear old Yendra is as dead as a... dead greenhide.' Jade paused, noticing the awful sense of guilt that she always felt when she thought of Yendra. Stupid guilt. Jade had nothing to feel guilty about – she hadn't been anywhere near Yendra when her father had killed her; she had been in Jezra, obeying orders. It wasn't her fault that Yendra was dead, and it wasn't her fault that Yendra's last words had been inside Jade's head; her final, desperate cry for help before the end.

'Don't make me cry, Poppy,' she said. 'I'll be angry with you if you make me cry again.'

The black cat lifted her head and butted Jade's face, then let out a loud meow. Ginger was curled up on her lap, feigning sleep, having occupied the larger portion of her knee. Another meow came from the floor, and Jade glanced down to see Tab-Tab and Fluffy sitting on the floor, their paws arranged neatly as they begged for food and attention.

'I can't fit you all onto my lap at once,' she said. 'No, Fluffy, I don't have any favourites, I promise; I love my babies all the same. What kind of mother would have favourites? Well, apart from my grandmother – she had favourites. She liked Michael best, and didn't like Yendra one little bit. She must have liked my father too; at least I think she did. But, what I'm trying to say is that I'm not like that; I love you all equally. Even when you poop on the floor.'

A soft knock rapped on the door to her rooms.

Jade scowled. 'What?'

The door opened a crack, and Jade saw Commander Quill's stupid mortal face appear.

'My lady, may I come in?' the mortal said.

Jade narrowed her eyes, then glanced at the window-clock set in the sunward wall of her sitting room.

'It's not time for work,' she said. 'Go away.'

'I have urgent news from Pella, ma'am.'

'It had better be urgent, Quinn,' Jade said, getting the woman's name wrong to annoy her.

The commander walked into the room. She closed the door behind her, then glanced around, as if checking that no one else was present.

'Who are you looking for, Quinn?'

The Blade officer frowned. Jade knew that she hated being called 'Quinn', but her sense of duty prevented her from complaining about it.

'No one, ma'am,' she said; 'it's just that I heard voices.'

'You're hearing voices, eh? You should get that checked, Quinn. Hearing voices is a sign of madness; well, that's what my father used to say.'

Quill looked down as Tab-Tab wound her way past her legs.

'Look at that little traitor,' said Jade. 'I'm the one that feeds her, yet she goes straight to you when you walk in. You may stroke her if you like.'

'No, thanks, ma'am,' said Quill.

'Why not?'

'I'm here to deliver some news that has just arrived from Cuidrach Palace, ma'am.'

'So you said.'

'The God-Queen has returned to the City.'

Jade blinked, then her eyes bored into Quill. 'Repeat that, Quinn. What I thought you said cannot be true.'

'It is true, unfortunately, ma'am. Lord Naxor has been arrested...'

'Good.'

Quill hesitated, then carried on. 'He has been arrested because he was hiding the fact that Queen Amalia is currently in the City. He refuses to say where, and Lord Salvor has been unable to read it from his mind. The other demigods in Cuidrach have been questioned, but none seem to have been aware that Queen Amalia was back. Then, this morning, your sister reported that the former God-Queen had visited her in Greylin Palace, to pick up supplies of anti-salve. She claims that your father assisted Amalia. The Queen wants you to question Prince Montieth.'

Jade said nothing, her mind still trying to cope with the news that Amalia might be in the City.

'Are you willing to do so, ma'am?'

'What?'

'The Queen wishes to know if you are willing to question your own father regarding this. Lord Salvor does not have the strength to force his way into the prince's mind, just as he cannot access Lord Naxor's thoughts.'

'He's not very good, is he, Poppy? Yendra could have read their minds without any problem.'

Quill waited, her eyes uncertain.

Jade glanced up at her. 'Lord Naxor must be lying. My grandmother can't be in the City. If she were, then she would be killing mortals everywhere you looked. The bodies would be piled high on every street; bloated, green corpses, all covered in wriggling maggots.'

'Nevertheless, it appears that she is back, ma'am. Even if Naxor was lying, why would your sister invent such a story?'

'Amber's a horrible little liar too,' she said; 'and a bully. Pay no attention to anything she says.'

'Then, perhaps it would be wise to see what your father has to say on the subject?'

Jade's temper flared. 'But I don't like talking to him. He makes me feel... bad. I don't like feeling bad. He says the most awful things to me.'

'I can come with you, if you like, ma'am.'

'And what good would you do, Quinn? Eh? Tell me.'

'I don't know; I could give you some moral support?'

Jade sighed. 'Stupid mortal. I don't need your assistance, Quinn; I exist on a far higher plane than you can even imagine. I am nine hundred and nine years old. How old are you?'

'Thirty-one, ma'am.'

'See? I have lived almost thirty of your lives. How could you possibly be of use to me? Except as a servant, obviously.'

'Lord Salvor is due to check in with me in a few minutes, ma'am, and he will require a response from you that he can relay to the Queen. What shall I tell him?'

Jade simmered, her anger sending her mind to cruel places. She imagined melting Quill's face, then remembered that Yendra would have disapproved.

'Fine,' she muttered; 'but this is a waste of time. My grandmother would never dare to set foot in the City again. But, I'll do it after I've been up on the battlements. If I absolutely have to speak to my father, I'm going to need to kill something first.'

Quill nodded, a look of relief on her face. 'Thank you, ma'am.'

Jade stared at her. 'Why are you still here? Go away.'

Quill saluted. 'Yes, ma'am.'

She turned and left the room, leaving Jade feeling more alone than she had expected. She frowned, then gently removed the two cats from her lap, setting them down onto the polished floorboards.

'Don't blame me,' she said; 'It's Quill's fault. Blame her.'

She walked into her bedroom, and pulled off her black dressing gown. She had washed when she had awoken that day at noon, so she dressed in the dark green robes that she liked to wear whenever she was going to kill greenhides. They suited her name, and made her feel dark and sinister, which she enjoyed. She sat by her dresser and put on some make up, choosing dark colours to line her eyes, and a lipstick that was more purple than red. She gazed at her reflection.

'I am so much more attractive than Amber,' she said to Fluffy, who was sitting by her legs. 'Say nothing if you agree.' The cat stared at her. 'Good boy.'

She laced up her black leather boots, and placed a slender silver tiara onto her brow, attaching it to her dark hair with a couple of little butterfly-shaped clasps. The Royal Family was no longer in power, but she still wanted the mortals to know that she was better than them.

She stood, and made her way to her little study. It was filled with the books from Yendra's collection, but Jade only used the room as a place to keep the cats' food bowls. She unwrapped some fish from a cupboard and the four cats seemed to appear from nowhere, meowing and rubbing their faces against her legs.

'Settle down, children,' she said. 'Mummy has fish for all the good cats.'

She leaned down and filled their bowls, and the cats tore into the food. Jade watched them for a moment, then went to the bathroom and washed her hands to get rid of the smell. She glanced into the wall mirror, took a long breath, then walked to her front door and opened it. The two soldiers outside stood to attention, their steel breastplates glimmering in the sunlight that came into the hall through a slit window. Jade walked between the soldiers and began to descend the stairs from the upper floors of the Duke's Tower. She passed a few other servants and guards as she went all the way down to the ground floor, but she ignored them.

Her permanent squad of personal guards was waiting for her at the entrance to the tower. Commander Quill was also there, speaking to a sergeant.

'Ma'am,' said Quill, bowing. 'I have delivered the message to Lord Salvor.'

'What message?' said Jade. 'Oh, yes. That. Well done, Quinn. I think that you should come with me when I question my father. It'll save me having to tell you what happens.'

'Of course, ma'am. When shall we go to the dungeons?'

Jade glanced up at the high battlements atop the curtain wall of the fortress. 'After I kill some greenhides. You know, I really do hate repeating myself, so don't ask me any more stupid questions, alright?'

'Yes, ma'am.'

Jade glanced at the faces of her personal guard. Not one of the mortals would look her in the eye. That meant they were scared of her, which was good, she reckoned. She was a mighty demigod, wise and noble; they probably worshipped her when she wasn't looking. She saw a face that seemed unfamiliar.

'Who are you? Why are you here?' she said.

'This is the replacement for Albets,' said Quill.

'Albets needed a replacement? Why? Did he die?'

'No, ma'am. He was transferred to a different unit.'

'Did I give my permission for this to happen?'

'If I may have a quiet word, ma'am?'

Jade sighed. 'Very well.'

They walked away from the soldiers until they were out of earshot.

'Albets complained that you kept harassing him, ma'am,' said Quill.

'How ridiculous. Wait, which one was Albets? All mortals seem similar to me.'

'He was the young man with blond hair. Do you remember? You used to proposition him relentlessly.'

'Oh, him? I wasn't harassing him; I was flirting with him; could he not tell the difference? Idiot. Most mortal men would be honoured by my attention. I am beautiful, am I not?'

'You are, ma'am,' said Quill. 'However, bearing in mind that you can be quite intimidating at times, might I suggest that you desist from flirting with the other members of your personal guard?'

'I see. Is it like me favouring Tab-Tab over Fluffy? Are the other soldiers getting jealous?'

Quill took a breath. 'Let's say yes to that.'

'Well, I wouldn't want the boys fighting over me.' She smiled at the uncomfortable look on Quill's face. 'Actually, I would; could we arrange that? They could fight to the death, and I get to keep the winner?'

'I'm afraid that's against the rules, ma'am.'

'What rules? Oh, never mind; I see that you are determined to prevent me from having any fun in this dreary old fortress. Right, where was I? Oh, yes; time to slaughter some greenhides.' She gestured to her guard. 'Follow me, boys.'

She set off towards a large stairway attached to the side of the curtain wall. Quill kept up with her, and the soldiers followed on behind. Blades turned away as she approached, pretending they were suddenly busy, or had somewhere they needed to be, and the battlements were almost deserted when she reached the top of the stairs. She gazed out at the view, and smiled. Below her, the plain stretched out endlessly, the barren ground covered in greenhides. High up on the Inner Walls, Jade could see the Outer Walls and the Moat Wall beneath her. Both were filled with Blades, though none of them seemed to be doing anything other than watching the greenhides swarm on the far side of the deep moat.

She raised her right hand, and felt her powers tingling. She was a vessel of death, never happier than when she was unleashing her powers. Her nerves sang as she flooded the area below her with her dark energy. Greenhides screamed and fell, their bodies toppling into the murky waters of the moat, or collapsing onto the rough ground. Dozens died in an instant, and she increased her pitch, flinging death out to the limits of her range, until over a hundred of the savage beasts had fallen.

Jade smiled as she gazed at the corpses, then her lips turned downwards. Already, the mass of greenhides had rushed forwards to fill the gap, and it looked as though she had achieved precisely nothing.

'Feel any better, ma'am?' said Quill.

'I did, and now I don't.'

'You killed many of them, ma'am.'

'Yes, but what's the point? No matter how many I kill, there are always more.'

'But Blackrose destroyed the closest nest, ma'am. Every greenhide that is killed cannot be replaced.'

'So, I only need to come out here every day for ten thousand days to make a difference?'

Quill frowned. 'Ten thousand days, ma'am?'

'Yes. Suppose that there are a million greenhides out there, and I kill one hundred every day – that's ten thousand days, or twenty-seven years and five months.'

'But, ma'am, according to what we know about greenhides, they only live for ten years, and two years have elapsed since the nest was destroyed. Doesn't that mean that every greenhide will be dead in eight years anyway?'

'Then what am I doing here?' Jade glared at her. 'I'm wasting my time, that's what.'

She shoved her way past Quill and strode back down the steps from the battlements. Two Blade officers were waiting for her on the flag-stones at the bottom. They saluted her, but kept their eyes averted.

'What do you want?' she snarled.

'Ma'am,' said one; 'we have been asked by the men and women under our command to request a meeting with you.'

'A meeting about what?'

'They wish us to present a list of grievances to you, ma'am.'

'Grievances? What do they have to complain about?'

'Well, ma'am,' said the officer; 'some of their grievances relate to the deteriorating conditions in the housing stock, or concerns about supplies and equipment, while other complaints are with regards to the lack of training, promotion and disciplinary matters.'

Jade stared at them. 'How dare you? Do you think my job is to pander to the trivial nonsense you mortals whine about? Get out of my sight.'

The two officers glanced at each other.

'But, ma'am...' said one.

Jade raised her hand. 'Go away, or I'll rot your eyeballs out.'

The officers bowed and hurried away.

Jade turned to Quill. 'Did you hear that? The cheek. Do those fools imagine that I have nothing better to do with my time than cater to their every whim?'

'Some of their complaints may have some substance, ma'am.'

'So, you're taking their side, eh? I might have known.'

'But, ma'am, you are the Commander of the Bulwark, and there are some decisions that only you can take. Perhaps if you were to delegate some of your responsibilities? I would be happy to address the Blades' complaints on your behalf.'

Jade narrowed her eyes at Quill. 'I know what you're up to – you're trying to siphon off some of my power for yourself. It won't work; I am the commander, not you, Quinn.'

'Yes, ma'am.'

'And now you have put me in a foul mood, right before I have to go to the dungeons to speak to my father. Remind me, why are you here, Quinn?'

'Her Majesty the Queen appointed me as your Adjutant, ma'am.'

'Hmm. So you say, though I have my doubts about that. You know what? I think you're a spy, trying to catch me out.' She pointed a finger in Quill's face. 'I don't trust you, Quinn; you'd better be very careful.'

She turned and strode off in the direction of the dungeons, then stopped as she realised that Quill wasn't following her. She glanced over her shoulder.

'Come on, Quinn; I don't have all day.'

The mortal muttered something under her breath, and walked up to Jade.

'That's better,' said Jade. 'You need to be like a little doggie, Quinn, and do what you're told.'

'Yes, ma'am.'

They entered an arched chamber dug into the side of the curtain wall, and descended into the depths of the underground dungeons, passing guards who stood to attention. They reached the heavily guarded wing where Lady Felice and Prince Montieth were being held, and a soldier unlocked the door.

'Who's there?' Felice cried out from her cell, as Jade and Quill entered the passageway.

'Shut up, Felice,' Jade said. 'Shut up, or I'll come in there and bash you over the head until your brains fall out.'

'Your time will come, Jade,' said Felice, her voice dripping with mockery. 'Edmond will tear you to pieces, and I will laugh.'

Jade stopped, and turned towards the entrance. Beyond the bars, Felice was sitting in the shadows of her prison cell, a hood over her head. Jade raised her hand, and Felice cried out in agony as a brief burst of death powers struck her. She fell onto the filthy floor, and writhed about, weeping.

'Not so talkative now, eh, Felice?' crowed Jade.

Quill coughed. 'Ma'am?'

Jade lowered her hand and shrugged. 'She started it.'

They walked on, leaving Felice gasping on the ground, and came to the cell where Prince Montieth was imprisoned. Like Felice, he had a hood over his head, but his hands were also encased in thick metal gauntlets, each padlocked and linked to shackles embedded into the wall.

Jade stared at him for a moment.

'I know it's you,' Montieth whispered. 'I heard your voice. Crawl back to your hole, you dirty little traitor; or else, come in here, and remove these blasted gloves, and prove to me that you are not worthy of a horrible death.'

'Good afternoon, father.'

'I am not your father! No daughter of mine would side with my enemies. You are weak, and stupid, and unfit to stand before me. How I wish I had dashed your brains out against a rock when you were born. Did I ever tell you what became of your mother?' He laughed. 'Oh, how she screamed before the end. She was a fool, just as you are. I enjoyed killing her, just as I will enjoy killing you.'

Jade felt her spirits sink, and she gazed at the floor of the passageway. Part of her wanted to turn around and walk back out of the dungeons, but Quill was standing next to her, watching, and she didn't want to show her feelings in front of a mortal.

'Are you still there?' cried Montieth. 'Are you weeping like a child again? I remember that you were a weeper, always crying over everything. I tried to toughen you up, but your contrary nature was always at odds with my attempts to improve you. Did you know that I let your pathetic garden die after you left?' He paused. 'Are you there? Answer me, you little bitch!'

'I'm here.'

'Ha! Then listen to what I have in store for you. When I escape from this place, I will hunt you down, Jade, and then I will torture you, slowly. First, I will remove your fingernails, one by one, taking exquisite care to ensure you feel the maximum pain, and then...'

'I'm here to ask you something.'

Montieth snorted. 'Well?'

'Where is your mother?'

The prince said nothing for a moment, then shrugged. 'How should I know?'

'The Crown knows that you helped her get anti-salve,' said Jade.

'The "Crown?" Don't try to elevate that pathetic mortal pretence at a monarchy.'

'Amber is in trouble. They think she helped you assist Amalia.'

'Amber? Pah. She might wish to take the credit, but she had nothing to do with any of it. Do you think I would tell her? She's loyal, unlike you, but she has a tendency to panic at times, and I wasn't going to risk everything by telling her that her grandmother was back. So, they know, do they? Good. That should inspire some fear in their mortal hearts.'

'Where is she?'

'I didn't ask, and she didn't tell. It was safer that way. Yendra would never be able to read from my head what I didn't know. Of course, now that Yendra is dead, there will be no one capable of stopping the God-Queen this time. Her vengeance will be terrible, let me assure you; she will annihilate the traitors and the pretenders, and all those who follow them. That includes you, Jade, although I will ask my dear mother to allow me to be the one who kills you. As her only surviving child, I'm sure she will oblige.'

Jade continued to suppress her tears, but knew she would have to leave the dungeons soon. Every second spent in her father's company made her feel sick, and useless.

'Where do you think she might be hiding?'

Montieth laughed. 'What makes you think I would tell you that? If there were any gods in the City who could read my mind, then you wouldn't be standing outside my cell door, asking me these stupid questions. Take a map of the City, and stick a pin into it, or, if you're looking for a more constructive suggestion, then climb up to the tallest tower of this fortress and throw yourself down to the greenhides. Actually, don't do that – it would give you a quick death, and you do not deserve such mercies. Let me tell you what you do deserve...'

'Goodbye, father,' said Jade, turning and walking away.

Quill followed her past Felice's cell, and they left the dungeons.

'Are you alright?' said Quill. 'Don't listen to him, ma'am; he was just trying to upset you.'

'Shut up, Quinn,' muttered Jade. She walked another pace, then started to cry. 'Don't look at me.'

Quill backed away as Jade wept, her hands covering her face. Anger fought with sorrow inside her, and she felt an urge to lash out at everything and everyone. For nine centuries she had obeyed her father. He had ordered her to never leave Greylin Palace, and so she hadn't. He had ordered her to assist in his horrible experiments, and so she had. Nine hundred years of unhappiness threatened to fell her like she had felled the greenhides beyond the walls. She sank down to her knees, oblivious to who might be watching, cursing her weakness. Only her father could induce such despair in her, and she wished she could crawl into a dark cave and hide there forever.

She felt a hand on her shoulder.

'It's over,' whispered Quill. 'Everything's going to be alright.'

Without knowing what she was doing, Jade threw her arms around the tall Blade officer, and wept into her shoulder. Quill put her arms round her back and held her.

Jade started. 'Get off me!' she cried, pushing Quill away. 'Don't touch me.' She wiped her face, but the tears kept coming. 'I just need a minute.'

She sat on the cold stone floor, while Quill watched her from a few feet away, her eyes wary, but filled with compassion. The tears stopped, and Jade took a long breath. She stood, and wiped her face again.

'I'm going back to my rooms,' she said. 'At least my cats don't want to torture me to death.'

Quill got to her feet and nodded.

Jade strode towards the door, then paused. She turned. 'Thank you, Quill. For the moral support, I mean. I guess you were right. You know, you're not completely useless, for a mortal.'

She hurried through the door, before Quill could ruin everything by replying.

CHAPTER 5

HAIRLINE FRACTURE

Pella, Auldan, The City – 21st Marcalis 3422

Kelsey watched as Frostback soared up into the red skies above Cuidrach Palace. The silver dragon circled once, then banked and sped off in the direction of Jezra. She was due to assist the Brigades, while Kelsey had been summoned to Pella.

'Good afternoon, Miss Holdfast.'

Kelsey turned, and saw Silva approach across the flagstones of the palace courtyard.

'Hi, Silva. How have you been?'

'Very well, thank you, although the news has distracted me a little.'

'Are you coming along today?'

'Yes. As I knew Lady Amalia in Lostwell, her Majesty has asked me to accompany you.'

'Remember to go a hundred yards away from me if you want to use your powers.'

Silva smiled. 'Oh, I'm unlikely to forget how your powers work, Miss Holdfast. I still remember when I first felt you block my abilities – a most strange sensation. In fact, I could tell you were out here before I left the palace.'

'I assume the Queen has asked you tons of questions about Amalia?'

'Indeed. I appear to be one of the few here in the City who isn't terrified of her. I hope we find her, of course, but perhaps not for the same reasons as everyone else.'

'Why?'

'I wish to ask Lady Amalia if she knows what happened to Queen Belinda. She might be the only person who knows where my beloved Queen might be.'

'Oh, Silva; I've already told you everything I saw up in Old Alea. Belinda was there, using the Sextant, while Amalia was nowhere to be seen.'

'But what occurred after we were all sent here? That's the question I'm interested in, and Lady Amalia might be able to fill in the gaps. I know it's a slim hope, Miss Holdfast, but it's all I have to cling onto. Don't get me wrong; I am loyal to Queen Emily and King Daniel, but you know where my heart truly lies.' She leaned in closer. 'Also, if Lady Amalia came here separately from the rest of us, then she may possess a Quadrant.'

Kelsey nodded. 'And?'

'You might wish to live out the rest of your life here, Miss Holdfast, but if there's even a small chance that I could be reunited with my true Queen, then I will take it. I informed their Majesties of this; they seemed interested in obtaining a Quadrant, if one is available.'

Kelsey said nothing. It hadn't occurred to her that there might be a Quadrant somewhere in the City, and she didn't know how she felt about it. On the one hand, she loved living in the City; she was getting on well with Van, Frostback and the people in her dragon crew, and got a great deal of satisfaction from helping to expand the territory of Jezra, but... did she intend to live there forever? Without a Quadrant, there would have been no choice about it, and she had been content with that, or, at least, she thought that was the case, but if the chance arose to return to her home in the Star Continent, would she take it?

'Here come the others,' said Silva.

Kelsey turned, and saw Salvor, Van and Cardova emerge from the palace, along with a squad of Banner soldiers, all dressed as servants or carriage drivers. Van and Cardova had taken a ship from Jezra that dawn to confer with the Royal Court, and had called for Kelsey when they had decided upon a plan.

Salvor inclined his head towards Silva and Kelsey. 'Good day to you. I shall be watching you on your journey today. I had originally intended to come along, but with Kelsey Holdfast here, there would be little point.'

'I don't mind staying here,' said Kelsey.

'The Crown deems the threat from Lady Amber sufficient to warrant you going along,' said Salvor. 'Your presence will rein her in, and prevent her from doing anything... unfortunate.'

Van stepped forward. 'The carriages are ready; we'll take the middle one, and pack the other two with Banner soldiers.'

'Is Amber expecting us?' said Kelsey.

'Yes,' said Salvor. 'I have informed her that you will be visiting. I have examined the contents of her mind, and believe that she knew nothing of Amalia's return until today. However, I also discovered that she has been hiding supplies of the salve mixtures made by her father, and it is imperative that they do not fall into the wrong hands. All of it is to be confiscated, lest Amalia return to take more.'

Van glanced at the position of the low sun. 'We should be back before midnight.'

'I shall be awaiting you,' said Salvor.

They made their way to the three carriages, each one emblazoned with a royal standard. Salvor stood back as the Banner soldiers climbed up into the lead and rear carriages, while Silva, Kelsey, Van and Cardova took the central one. They sat down inside the comfortable interior, and a soldier closed the door.

The carriages got underway, their ponies drawing them out of the palace grounds and onto the main road that led to Ooste and Dalrig. The harbour of Pella stretched out on their left, and Kelsey glanced over the dozens of tall masts.

Cardova cracked his knuckles. 'What's everyone's bet for where this rogue god is hiding, then?'

'King Daniel seems to think that Tara is the most likely place,' said Silva. 'Apparently, Lady Amalia was very fond of that particular town.'

'Then it would be too obvious,' said Cardova. 'Wouldn't she hide somewhere that she won't be recognised? I reckon she's buried herself deep within the Circuit.'

'Why?' said Van.

'Because that's where I'd hide, sir. The place is like a warren.'

'Aye,' said Kelsey, 'but Amalia would hate living there, among all the poverty and grey concrete. Wherever she is, she'll be comfortable.'

'I agree,' said Silva. 'Ooste or Port Sanders might be a better bet, or even Pella. Imagine, she could be living right under our noses, and we'd never know.'

'Dalrig is also a possibility,' said Van. 'The Gloamers are so secretive, that she could probably live there openly.'

'I'm guessing that dear old Naxor isn't saying anything?' said Kelsey.

'Oh, he's talking,' said Cardova, 'but he isn't saying anything we want to hear. To be honest, I think he's enjoying all the attention. He's sitting in his cell as if he owns the place.'

'Did you speak to him?'

'We both did,' said Van. 'He was holding forth on how much the City owes him for all the good he's supposedly done. He was taking credit for bringing Corthie here, and Blackrose, and for a million other things. The only topic he wouldn't discuss was Amalia.'

'Did he read your minds?' said Silva.

Van shook his head. 'He was wearing a hood, so at least we didn't have to look at the smug grin that was probably on his face.'

'I feel like the odd one out,' said Cardova. 'You three have all met this Amalia.'

Kelsey shrugged. 'You're not missing much.' She glanced out of the window. 'Look; the beach. Next summer, I am definitely coming here.'

Van raised an eyebrow. 'You said that last year.'

'Aye, but this time I mean it. You can come along, and serve me drinks while I recline on the warm sand all day.'

'Lucky me,' he said.

The carriages came to a junction, and took the turn that led towards Dalrig. They left the houses and streets of Outer Pella behind, and began to cross the stretch of farmland that lay inside Gloamer territory. To their left, the high cliffs of the Shield Hills rose above the central plain of Auldan, blocking the view of the Clashing Seas and the Western Bank.

'I heard,' said Cardova, 'that those hills are almost hollow; so much salve has been dug out of them over the centuries. It's hard to imagine that every bit of salve I've ever seen comes from here. This is the very location that the Ascendants destroyed Lostwell to find. Can you picture their faces, if they had got here, when they realised that the salve had run out?'

The outer walls of Dalrig appeared in the distance, and the occupants of the carriage fell silent as each looked at the tall battlements. The old town of Pella had also retained its ancient walls, but several sections had been demolished, or were in disrepair, while the walls of Dalrig looked strong and well-maintained. Sitting on the battlements was an array of ballistae, all pointing upwards. The carriages slowed as they reached a huge gatehouse built into the walls. Soldiers from the Gloamer militia strode forwards, their hands cradling crossbows, and an officer raised his arm to halt the party from Pella.

'We have to consider the possibility that this is a convoluted trap,' said Van. 'Everyone needs to be on their guard when we enter Dalrig, just in case Lady Amber intends to betray us.'

'Frostback would burn the place to the ground if anything happens to me,' said Kelsey.

'Which is why we're probably going to be safe,' said Van; 'just don't take any chances.'

Cardova glanced at her. 'It must be nice having a dragon as a bodyguard.'

'It is,' she said. 'Are you jealous?'

'I've fought on Dragon Eyre. Personally, I've had enough of dragons. They're chaotic and unpredictable. I wasn't on the Grey Isle when Tarsnow got himself killed, but what happened there didn't surprise me in the slightest. Their pride always seems to overrule their common sense.'

Kelsey smirked at him. 'So, you are jealous?'

A Gloamer officer stared through the carriage window at them, his face making plain the contempt he felt for the envoys from Pella, then he turned, and raised his hand. The gates in the walls opened, and the carriages started to move again. They passed through the darkness under the arched opening, then emerged back into the sunshine on the other side. Kelsey gazed at the view. Neat rows of two-storey stone houses stretched away on either side but, unlike Pella, there were no gardens or flower boxes in sight, and the clean streets seemed lifeless. A few civilians were walking along the smart pavements, dressed in long, black winter coats, and wearing hats. Every man seemed to have the same moustache, and each woman's hair was tied up and hidden under veils or hats.

'What a cheery-looking bunch,' said Kelsey. 'Still, I guess I'd be miserable too if I had Prince Montieth as my ruler.'

'I think they look very smart,' said Silva. 'I can't abide the young women in Pella with their short skirts and bosoms hanging out for all to see.'

Cardova laughed. 'No comment.'

'For Pyre's sake, Silva,' said Kelsey; 'I hope you don't say that sort of thing in front of Queen Emily.'

'I most certainly would not,' the demigod said; 'and I'd be obliged if you didn't repeat it to her Majesty.'

Before long, the high mass of Greylin Palace came into view, and the three carriages turned left by the harbour of Dalrig, and drew up alongside the huge, forbidding structure. There didn't appear to be any court-yard attached to the palace, so the carriages came to a halt on the street opposite a closed and guarded set of tall doors. The Banner soldiers jumped down from the other two carriages, and Cardova opened the side door of the central one. Kelsey took his offered hand and climbed down, then glanced around at the empty street. When Silva and Van had also stepped down from the carriage, they crossed the moat bridge and walked up to the tall doors, where several Gloamer militia were standing.

Van spoke to one of them, and the guard disappeared into the palace.

'I'd forgotten that there were no windows,' said Cardova, his eyes scanning the building.

'How odd,' said Silva.

'And not even remotely sinister,' said Kelsey.

One of the tall doors opened, and an old woman peered out.

'Good evening, ma'am,' said Van; 'we're here to see Lady Amber. I believe she is expecting us?'

The old woman said nothing, but opened the door wider, and they filed past her. Behind Kelsey trooped the dozen Banner soldiers that they had brought with them. The old woman narrowed her eyes at them, but allowed them into the palace.

They entered a dimly-lit hallway, full of dark wood panelling and blackened old portraits. Amber was waiting for them at the bottom of a grand set of stairs, her hands by her sides.

'Welcome back to Greylin,' she said; 'at least you came in through the front door this time.'

Van smiled. 'Greetings, Lady Amber. If we had arrived at the front door last time, would your father have let us in?'

'Probably not. Is this my reward for honesty; being hounded by agents of the Crown?'

'I assume Lord Salvor informed you of the purpose of our visit, ma'am?' said Van.

'He did.' Amber's eyes flitted to Kelsey. 'You again? Do the King and Queen trust me so little that they felt you had to attend? What did they think I was going to do – kill everyone?'

'Believe me,' said Kelsey; 'the last thing I wanted to do was come back to this dump.'

'You are welcome to leave at any time, Miss Holdfast.'

'Lady Amber,' said Silva, 'do you know where Lady Amalia is hiding?'

Amber stared at her. 'Who are you?'

'This is Lady Silva,' said Van; 'from Lostwell.'

'Ahh, the one with abilities similar to those possessed by my cousin Vana? You needn't have bothered coming here; the Holdfast girl's powers will prevent you from sniffing out any traces of the former God-Queen.'

'I was a friend to Amalia in Lostwell,' Silva said. 'On that world, I knew nothing about her history here in the City, but I do know that she used to be very good friends with Queen Belinda, and any friend of my Queen is a friend of mine.'

'Then, you should know that my grandmother also spoke well of you when she was here this morning.'

'Let me ask you again, Lady Amber – do you know where she is hiding?'

'No, I do not. If I did, then Salvor would have been able to read it out of my mind, wouldn't he?'

'Does she have a Quadrant?'

Amber hesitated for a moment. 'She does.'

'If she contacts you again,' Silva went on, 'then please inform her that I am willing to act as an intermediary between her and the Crown. I am stronger than Lord Salvor, and can be trusted to keep her location a secret, if she is willing to talk to me. There may be a middle ground that would satisfy all parties.'

Amber rolled her eyes. 'If Amalia returns here, with anti-salve in her system, then she won't be leaving alive.'

'On the subject of anti-salve, ma'am,' said Van; 'I believe that you have something for us?'

'I do,' she said. 'And, I wasn't "hiding" it, no matter what Salvor says. The simple truth is that no one asked me if I had any of my father's salve mixtures.'

'No one is accusing you of anything, ma'am. Now, we would be grateful if you could take us to where these mixtures are located.'

She glanced at the dozen members of the Banner standing behind Van in the hallway. 'Your soldiers will have to remain here.'

'Soldiers?' said Van. 'You are mistaken, ma'am. They are our assistants; here to help carry the results of your father's salve experiments back to our carriages. I insist that they come along.'

Amber glared at him, then slowly nodded. She turned without a word, and strode off down a passageway. Van glanced at the others, and they followed her. Amber led them to a set of stairs, which they descended, and Kelsey recognised the basement under the palace from her previous visit. She took them to a door close to where Montieth had caged the King and Queen, and unlocked it with a long, iron key. It creaked as she pushed it open, revealing nothing but darkness. Amber disappeared into the shadows. She lit a wall lamp, and the others walked through the doorway, entering a large chamber. Human-sized cages were racked up against the right hand wall and, although they were empty, a few had bloodstains on their floors and walls. A six-foot-long table sat in the middle of the room, with shackles attached to each corner, while workbenches took up the wall on the left.

'Pyre's tits,' said Kelsey, her eyes wide; 'is this where that mad bastard carried out his experiments? Did he do things to people on that table?'

'He was testing the limits of salve,' said Amber, her face expressionless; 'determining the true extent of its healing properties. To do that, he necessarily had to first cause injury.'

Cardova whistled as he picked up a jagged steel saw from a workbench. 'This looks like it could "cause injury."'

Amber gave him a cold smile. 'It has probably been used to maim hundreds of mortals over the years; maybe thousands.'

Cardova grimaced and placed the saw back onto the counter. He glanced along the bench and gestured towards a row of glass vials, sitting in an iron rack.

'Those look promising,' said Van. He turned to Amber. 'What types of mixtures are here, ma'am?'

'Silver, red and green,' said Amber. 'Take great care with them, as all three can easily kill mortals. The silver ones are concentrated salve; the red one is anti-salve, and the green ones are death-salve. That is the entire stock; please, take it all.'

Van nodded to the soldiers. Two approached the workbench, and began to load the vials into a straw-filled crate.

'Why is there only one vial of anti-salve?' said Van. 'Did you give the rest to Amalia?'

'Yes,' said Amber. 'She threatened to kill me. I meant to give her all of it, but I found that last vial later on, after she had gone.'

'Was she alone?' said Kelsey.

Amber turned to her. 'No. She came with a mortal man.'

'Who?' said Van.

Amber shrugged. 'A young Exile from Lostwell. Kagan, I think his name was.'

'Kagan from Lostwell?' said Van. 'Thank you, ma'am.' He glanced at Cardova.

'I'll check the records of the known Exiles, sir,' he said; 'and see if that name comes up.'

The two soldiers who were filling the crate turned, and nodded towards Van.

'All ready, sir.'

'Leaving so soon?' said Amber. 'What a pity.'

'Shouldn't we destroy Montieth's laboratories?' said Kelsey.

'It would accomplish nothing,' said Van. 'Even if he were somehow to escape, he has no salve left.'

They withdrew from the cold chamber, and the soldiers carried the crate back up the stairs.

Van turned to Amber. 'I'll be sure to tell their Majesties that you cooperated, ma'am.'

'You do that, little mortal man.'

The old woman from before opened the tall doors at the front of the palace, and the royal party left Greylin.

Kelsey glowered at the forbidding stone building. 'Is it wrong of me to want to burn this place to the ground?'

'No,' said Van. 'That's exactly what I'd like to do, but the Gloamers would never let us leave Dalrig alive if we destroyed their palace.'

They boarded the three carriages, and they began to move off. They turned the corner at the sunward end of Greylin, and were confronted by a large mob of civilians. They were marching through the marketplace by the waterfront, chanting anti-Pellan slogans.

Cardova frowned as he glanced out of the window. 'Someone has alerted them to our presence, I see.'

A stone flew through the air, and bounced of the side of the lead carriage.

'Keep moving,' cried Van up to the drivers, 'but do not retaliate.'

'Yes, sir,' came the reply from the driver's bench.

Another stone came at them, scuffing off the cobbles by the carriage wheels, then a torrent of them hurtled over from the direction of the mob. Van ordered Kelsey and Silva to shelter on the floor as rocks battered the side and top of their carriage.

The lead carriage picked up speed, and headed straight towards the mob. At the last moment, the Gloamers cleared a path, and then the three carriages were surrounded by a baying mass of civilians. They banged on the sides of the carriages with their fists, and continued to hurl rocks at the soldiers up on the driver's benches. Kelsey tried to look up to see what was happening, but Van had a hand on her shoulder, and was keeping her down on the carriage floor, while Cardova was shielding Silva.

The chaos seemed to last an eternity. Glass from the shattered carriage window rained down on them, but the carriage kept moving forwards, and, eventually, they pulled away from the crowds by the harbour. Van glanced out of the broken window, and took a breath.

'We're clear,' he said. 'Everyone alright?'

'Fine, boss,' said Cardova, who was picking shards of glass out of his clothes.

Van released his grip on Kelsey, and she clambered back into her seat. Silva brushed down the front of her dress and sat next to her. She had a deep scratch on her face from a piece of glass, and Kelsey watched as the demigod healed herself.

Silva smiled. 'I am exceedingly grateful that your blocking abilities do not encompass self-healing, Kelsey.'

'And,' said Cardova, 'at least we don't have to wonder what the Gloamers think of the mortal monarchy.'

The journey back to Pella was uneventful, and the three battered carriages pulled into the courtyard by the iceward flank of Cuidrach Palace. They dismounted, and Kelsey stared at the damage that had been done. A couple of the ponies had injuries, and four of the Banner soldiers who had been driving the carriages had cuts and bruises from the welter of rocks that had been thrown at them. Van made sure that they were taken away to the palace infirmary, then he went into the building. Kelsey, Cardova and Silva followed him inside, along with two soldiers, who were carrying the crate filled with Montieth's salve.

The Queen was waiting for them in Salvor's office, the demigod sitting across from her. Van and the others entered, and bowed before the Queen.

'Salvor told me what happened,' said Emily, shaking her head. 'Damn Gloamers.'

'We were in a tight spot for a moment, your Majesty,' said Van, 'but I think they just wanted to demonstrate their feelings.' He gestured to the soldiers to place the crate onto the long wooden meeting table.

Emily stood, and walked over to the open crate. She peered inside. 'I remember these colours from Maeladh Palace. The death-salve needs to be locked away securely.'

'Should we destroy it, your Majesty?' said Salvor.

'Most likely,' said Emily, 'although I'll need to get the King's agreement. His Majesty is currently dealing with an outbreak of trouble in the Circuit. Only one vial of anti-salve?'

'Lady Amber gave the rest to Lady Amalia,' said Silva.

Emily nodded. 'In that case, she'll be able to continue hiding from us indefinitely. How did Amber take your offer to act as an intermediary?'

'She affected to be uninterested, your Majesty,' said Silva, 'but I believe that she will pass on the message if the opportunity arises.'

'Alright. Keep the anti-salve handy; it might come in useful. These last vials – the concentrated salve – is there any way to dilute the mixture? It would be far more useful if it could be rendered into a state that won't poison mortals.'

'I don't know,' your Majesty,' said Van. 'Possibly, only Prince Montieth might have the answer to that, and I doubt he will be forthcoming with the information. Naxor might also know, as it was he who used to prepare the salve mixtures that were taken to Lostwell.'

Emily reached into the crate and picked up a vial of concentrated salve. The silver contents gleamed as she swirled the mixture.

Kelsey frowned. 'Be careful,' she said; 'that vial has a crack in it.'

Emily glanced at the vial just as a cloud of vapours burst from its side. Van leapt at the Queen, grabbing the shattered vial and pushing her back a yard as the vapours hissed around his hand. He cried out, dropping the vial, the skin on his right hand blistering. He fell to his knees, grasping his wounded fingers, then collapsed to the floor, convulsing.

Kelsey stared, her mouth open, as Cardova threw his coat over the pieces of the broken vial, smothering the vapours. He called for guards, and Banner soldiers bounded into the room.

'Hold the major-general down,' snapped Cardova. 'Gloves only.'

Burly soldiers grabbed Van's arms and legs, pinning him to the ground as he continued to shake violently. Foam was coming from his mouth, which was twisted into an expression of sheer agony. He shuddered one last time, then his eyes closed and he lay still. Kelsey pushed her way to his side, and knelt by him. She reached for his hand, but Cardova blocked her.

'Don't touch his skin, ma'am,' he said; 'there might still be residue on his hands.'

'Is he going to be alright?' said the Queen, her eyes wide with fear.

Cardova glanced up at her. 'I don't know, your Majesty. He's had a massive dose of salve.' He turned to a sergeant. 'We'll have to wash off any excess that might be on his skin. Get a bath ready, filled with hot water. We'll burn his clothes.'

'Yes, sir,' barked the sergeant, before running for the door.

'And, after the bath?' said Emily.

'Then, your Majesty,' said Cardova, 'we'll have to wait and see. I don't want to dispirit you, but I've known soldiers in the Banners who have over-dosed on salve. About half make it; the other half don't.'

Kelsey raised a hand to her mouth. She knew that Van wouldn't die; after all, the vision she had seen of them sitting with a baby had yet to come to pass, but the sight of him lying unconscious, his face a mask of pain, was like a knife in her heart.

The sergeant returned, with more soldiers and a stretcher.

'The bath is being prepared, sir,' he said to Cardova.

'Thank you, Sergeant.'

The soldiers moved Van onto the stretcher, being careful not to touch his skin.

'I'm coming with you,' said Kelsey. 'I'll help.'

Cardova opened his mouth to say something, then nodded.

'Do everything you can, Captain,' said Emily, her voice a little shaky.

Cardova bowed his head. 'We will, your Majesty.'

The soldiers lifted the stretcher off the floor, and Kelsey joined them as they walked across Salvor's office.

'He's strong,' Cardova said to her, as they followed the stretcher out into the palace hallway. 'If anyone can survive a salve overdose, it's the major-general.'

Kelsey said nothing, her eyes fixed on Van's sickly face, and on the severe burns covering his hands.

Damn Amber and the Gloamers, she thought, wishing they had reduced Greylin, and its resident demigod, to ashes.

CHAPTER 6

COMING FORWARD

Pella, Auldan, The City – 28th Marcalis 3422

Van looked terrible. His face was pale and drawn, his eyes bloodshot, and thick rolls of bandages covered both of his hands.

'You're looking much healthier,' Emily said, smiling from her seat next to his hospital bed. 'And it's good to see you sitting up again. How are you feeling today?'

'A little better, your Majesty,' Van gasped, his voice weak.

'Good; that's good.' She caught Kelsey's glance from the other side of the bed, and stood. 'I'll let you rest; that's what you need.'

'Thank you for coming to see me, your Majesty.'

'Of course. I'll pop by tomorrow.'

'I'll walk you to the door,' said Kelsey, getting to her feet.

They strode towards the entrance to Van's private room.

'It pains me to see him like that,' Emily said, her voice low; 'so one can only imagine how you are feeling, Kelsey.'

'You were right, though – he is looking better. For the first few days, he seemed to be withering away in front of us. Look, I know I've been a bit bad-tempered on some of your visits, but Van really appreciates you taking the time to see him every day.'

'He saved my life, Kelsey. It was so stupid, picking up that vial.' She lowered her gaze. 'Thank Malik that he's starting to recover.'

'It wasn't your fault, Queenie.'

'You say that, but I've noticed the way you look at me sometimes.'

'I can't help it,' she said. 'Part of me does maybe blame you, even though I know that it could have happened to anyone. Perhaps I'm also a wee bit jealous that he was so willing to give up his life for you; but, you know, that's his job.'

'He signed a contract, that's why he's loyal to me, Kelsey. With you, it's different – he loves you.'

Kelsey said nothing.

'I'll be back here tomorrow at the same time,' Emily went on. 'Will you still be here?'

'Aye, though I might nip over to Jezra for a few hours to pick up some clothes, and to check in with my crew.'

'Alright. Well, if you need anything, you know who to ask. The City owes you and Van a great debt, so don't hesitate to let me know what else you require.'

'Thanks, Queenie.'

Emily smiled, then left the room. Outside, a squad of Banner soldiers were posted by the door, guarding their commander, and Emily's own team of Royal Guards were standing next to them in the hallway. Their sergeant saluted her, and they followed Emily as she made her way to Salvor's grand offices. She left the soldiers at the entrance of the room and strode inside, where Salvor and her husband were sitting by a roaring hearth.

Daniel glanced at her. 'How is he?'

'Better than yesterday,' said Emily, walking over to them, 'though it'll be a while before he's back on his feet again.'

Salvor stood. 'Would you like a drink, your Majesty? The King and I have been discussing today's agenda.'

'Just a glass of water, please,' said Emily; 'with some lime in it.'

Salvor bowed. 'At once, your Majesty.'

Emily sat as Salvor walked to the corner of the room. She glanced at the King. 'Anything new?'

He shook his head. 'Just the same litany of emerging disasters. The Circuit, well, you know how bad it is there. Separatist gangs are battling the local militia, and they're no closer to agreeing to a new set of leaders. And, well, there's Jade.'

Emily smiled as Salvor handed her a glass of water.

'It can't go on like this,' said Daniel. 'We have to do something about Jade. She's been Commander of the Bulwark for eighteen months, and she doesn't seem to have done any administrative work at all, and she refuses to delegate it to her officers. Sometimes, she emerges from her rooms for only a few minutes each day, to kill some greenhides, and then she hides herself away again.'

'The Blades have a solid set of rules,' said Salvor, taking his seat by the fire once more, 'and a clear chain of command, so their institutions can cope with a certain level of neglect. However, as his Majesty stated, things cannot continue in this state forever. Half of the housing stock is rotting away, and the cells are full of Blades awaiting judgement for a whole range of misdemeanours that require Lady Jade's attention.'

Daniel nodded. 'She might have been great at helping repel the greenhides from the City, but she's hopeless at running the Blades.'

'We knew that,' said Emily. 'We discussed this before we appointed her. The threat from the greenhides upon our eastern flank is diminishing by the year. In a decade, the plains in front of the Great Walls will be empty.'

'I fear that there might be a mutiny before then,' said Daniel. 'We know that there are Blade officers whose hearts were solidly behind Duke Marcus, and the God-Queen. They fear Jade, just as they feared Yendra. The only difference is that they also respected Yendra.'

Emily sighed. 'Then, what do we do?'

'I don't know,' said Daniel. 'I was hoping that you'd have a suggestion.'

'We can't demote her,' she said; 'she might take it very badly indeed. Therefore, if we want her out of that position, then we'll have to find something else for her to do; something with equal prestige. Like, for example, Governor of Jezra. Secondly, we'd need to find a replacement.

Would we pick a mortal or a demigod? Are there any demigods that we trust enough to hold that position? They would have an army under their control. I would be happy if Salvor did it, but he's too useful to us here.'

The demigod bowed. 'Thank you, your Majesty.'

'Who else?' said Emily. 'Mona? Silva?'

Daniel laughed. 'I'm still picturing Jade as Governor of Jezra. You can't possibly be serious.'

'You asked for my suggestions.'

Daniel frowned. 'Yes, but Jade in charge of Jezra?'

Emily shrugged. She didn't say it, but part of her wanted to keep Jade as Commander of the Bulwark, thinking that it might be wise to allow the Blades to weaken a little under the demigod's rule. They were the only tribe capable of flooding the rest of the City with soldiers, and could become dangerous if led by anyone disloyal. Jade might be incompetent, but at least she was loyal.

'There's another reason to move her,' said Daniel. 'She's done absolutely nothing to prepare the territory of the Blades for the elections and, with only two months to go, it'll soon be too late. At the very least, we should appoint someone else to look after that aspect of her administration.'

Emily caught Salvor's eye.

'Darling,' she said to Daniel, 'maybe it's time to think about a possible postponement of the elections.'

The King's face hardened, and he narrowed his eyes. 'No.'

'But, Danny, five of the tribes have yet to pass the necessary agreements for the elections to go ahead. If we postponed for a year, then...'

'If we postponed for a year, then we may as well give up,' spat Daniel. 'The courts have delayed or blocked half of the constitutional laws, and, without elections, the rest of my reforms will collapse, and we'll be back where we started. We must press on.'

'What if five of the tribes refuse to hold the election? We cannot force people to vote, Danny. The Rosers, Gloamers and Sanders are set to boycott polling day, while the Evaders and Blades are not in a fit state to even conduct elections. Having only four tribes actually vote would be worse than none at all.'

'But if we miss this opportunity, it may never come again,' said Daniel. 'I have meetings scheduled with the Roser delegation – they are the key. If I can persuade them to change their minds, then the Sanders will follow, and we'll have a majority of six tribes. Seven, if the Evaders can hold even a partial vote; and eight, if we replace Jade with someone competent to govern the Blades.'

'Very well,' said Emily, 'but if the Rosers continue to hold out, will you reconsider?'

Daniel stared at the surface of the table. 'What about the Banner forces?'

'What about them?'

'You're always telling me how useful they are; like our own private army, you said. Couldn't we use them to enforce the election in the territories that are being obstructive?'

'Use soldiers to force people to vote?'

'No,' he said. 'Use soldiers to force the local authorities to allow people to vote. The Rosers are governed by a tiny clique of extremely wealthy landowners, aristocrats and merchants; why should they get to decide if the people of their tribe can vote? The sight of Banner soldiers on the streets of Tara would wake them up.'

'Yes, and unite every Roser against us. No, Danny, I will not agree to that. The City needs to change, but not through violence and oppression. If the God-Queen is biding her time, waiting for an opportunity to strike, then this would be the perfect moment for her to do so. She would paint us as the tyrants.'

'But, without elections, we are tyrants.'

Emily grappled with her temper. 'We are the appointed monarchs of the City.'

'What's the difference?'

'We obey the law, Danny; that's the difference. If we throw the laws away and start sending Banner soldiers to areas that oppose us, we'll be no better than the God-Queen.'

'Then we shall fail,' Daniel said, his voice rising; 'thanks to your timidity. You want us to rule with one hand tied behind our backs.'

'I want us to rule within the law.'

'What about the Grey Isle? You sent soldiers, and dragons, to illegally seize part of Gloamer territory, and you didn't even bother consulting me. You want to have it both ways – you can break the law, but I can't.'

'The Grey Isle was a mistake.'

'Then why haven't we handed it back to the Gloamers?'

'Don't shout at me, Danny.'

'That means you don't have an answer; you know I'm right. I can't believe this. We're so close to success, and your nerve has failed. What happened to our dreams to reform the City? When did you decide to abandon the very people we are supposed to rule?'

Emily stood. 'I don't wish to discuss this any further.'

'Your Majesty,' said Salvor; 'there is still much on the agenda to go through.'

'You'll have to do it without me,' she said. 'I don't intend to stay here and be shouted at.'

She walked to a side entrance and strode through it, and a small group of guards hurried to keep up. Her anger simmered as she made her way towards the royal quarters, her heels clacking off the marble floor. She reached her rooms and left the soldiers at the door. Inside her living room, her mother was sitting on a couch, reading.

She glanced up. 'Good morning, Emily. I wasn't expecting you back so soon.' Her eyes narrowed as she caught her daughter's expression. 'Is everything alright, dear?'

'No. Everything is not alright. Where's Elspeth?'

'I've just got her to sleep, dear, so please keep your voice down.'

Emily sat.

'Have you and Daniel had a disagreement?'

'Yes.'

Her mother nodded. 'Can I help?'

'I suggested postponing the elections.'

'Ah, I see. Was that wise, dear? You know that this is the King's passion.'

'I know. That's why I haven't brought it up before. Perhaps I should have. His passion has blinded him to the cold reality of what will happen if the elections are a failure, which, they will be. Our authority will be in tatters.' She stood again. 'I want to see Elspeth.'

'Please don't wake her, dear.'

Emily walked to the door of the nursery and edged it open. The small room was in semi-darkness, its shutters drawn, and she could see the peaceful form of the child, asleep in her cot. Emily stole across the carpeted floor, and rested her hands on the railing of the cot. She watched the infant's chest rise and fall, and smiled at the expression on her sleeping face. She felt an urge to pick her up for a cuddle, but her mother would be annoyed if she disturbed the child's morning nap. She had been back at work for nine days, and she was missing spending time with her baby daughter. Her anger with Daniel started to fade as she watched the child sleep. His point about the Grey Isle had been accurate; she had broken the rules to occupy the small island, and was breaking them further with every day that she refused to withdraw the Exile forces from the territory. But the Grey Isle was remote, and isolated – sending Banner forces into Tara would be a disaster; surely Daniel realised that?

She crept back out of the nursery and closed the door. Her mother let out a sigh of relief.

'Thank you for resisting the temptation to wake her,' she said. 'She gets tetchy if she misses her morning nap.'

Emily sat back down.

'Are you feeling the burden, my dear?'

'Yes, mother.'

'I always knew it would be a strain. As proud as I am of you, bearing that amount of responsibility will exact a heavy price. Try not to worry about the things over which you have no control.'

'That's easy to say.'

'And, not so easy to do. I understand, dear, but how else are you expected to cope?'

There was a soft knock upon the door.

Emily frowned, her eyes narrowing as Quill entered the room.

'I asked not to be disturbed,' said Emily; 'and why aren't you in the Bulwark?'

Quill escorted a hooded figure into the room, then she closed the door behind them.

'Sorry, your Majesty; I had to speak to you in person. It's rather urgent.'

'Is this about Jade?'

'No, your Majesty, and her ladyship is unaware that I have travelled here today. I have brought someone that I think you need to speak to.' She nodded to the hooded figure. 'Show yourself.'

The figure removed her hood, revealing a young woman.

Emily squinted. 'Rosie? Rosie Jackdaw, is that you?'

The young woman smiled. 'You remembered my name, your Majesty,' she said, curtseying.

'Come and have a seat,' Emily said; 'Rosie, this is my mother, Lady Omertia. Mother, this is Rosie Jackdaw, the younger sister of Maddie. How is your brother? Tom, was it?'

Rosie sat. 'Yes, your Majesty. Tom's fine; he's still posted at Stormshield, but he's liking it there.'

'And, what are you doing with yourself?'

'I'm with the Twenty-Seventh Ballistics Battalion. Designing and building ballistae and catapults, basically. I'm a Junior Artificer, your Majesty.'

'Excellent. Are you here to ask about your sister?'

'I wasn't, but do you know anything about how Maddie is doing on Dragon Eyre? I mean, your Majesty?'

'There is nothing new to tell, I'm afraid,' Emily said; 'although, Kelsey Holdfast happens to be in the palace, and she spent time with your sister on Lostwell. Would you like me to summon her? She probably has a few stories she could share.'

'Perhaps later?' said Quill. 'Rosie, tell the Queen what you told me.'

'Well,' said Rosie; 'I heard something a while ago that I know isn't true. I didn't say anything to anyone about it, because I assumed that you would know, your Majesty. But, when I told Commander Quill, she didn't know, and she said that you didn't know, either.'

Emily smiled. 'I see, or at least I think I do. What is it that I don't know?'

'Do you remember, a few years ago, Blackrose took me and Maddie away, to the Eastern Mountains?'

'Yes. Corthie, Belinda and Naxor were there also, weren't they?'

'Yeah, that's right. Well, Maddie and I lived there for a bit, and there were caverns next to the valley where Blackrose slept. Maddie and I took shelter in the caves, and we found something there.'

Emily's smile faded. 'What did you find?'

'Salve, your Majesty. Tons of it. Whole caverns filled with the stuff.'

'Amalia's breath,' Emily gasped.

Rosie shook her head. 'I can't believe you didn't know. I always assumed that someone would have told you about it, especially if the salve mines here have run out.'

'The only person who could have told me is Naxor, as the others are no longer in the City; and Naxor, for some reason, has neglected to inform me.'

'Then, I should have come forward before,' said Rosie. 'Sorry. Like I said, I just assumed that you knew. It was only when I happened to bump into Commander Quill, and we ended up having a chat, that I mentioned it to her.'

'That was early this morning,' said Quill. 'I brought her straight here, your Majesty.'

Emily studied the young Jackdaw sister. 'You said you have told no one else of this?'

'That's right, your Majesty. Not even Tom.'

'That was remarkably discreet of you, Rosie.'

'The way I figure it, your Majesty, is that salve has been nothing but bad for the City. It can heal wounds, which is great and everything, but

I heard that there are gods out there who want to find us and destroy us because of it. And, it keeps the gods young; but, do we really want that? Maybe without salve, they'd age and eventually die off.'

'Some of those gods are my friends.'

'Yeah, but let's be honest here – for every decent god, there are a dozen bad ones. Anyway, that's why I didn't say anything. The fewer people who know about the salve in the mountains, the better, in my opinion. But, of course, you're the Queen, so I guess that you should know.'

'Whatever the reason, I am very glad that you didn't spread the news of this around. I'm going to have to ask you to swear that you'll continue to keep your silence regarding it.'

'Sure. I'm happy to do that, your Majesty.'

'Now, do you think you could remember how to get to that location?'

'Maybe, but it would be easier to ask Naxor. He made a Quadrant take him there, so he must know how to find it.'

'Unfortunately, Naxor is not being very cooperative at the moment.'

Rosie frowned. 'I don't understand. Could you not just order him to tell you?'

'I could, but he would defy me. Also, I feel it might be better if he doesn't discover that I know.'

'There's a rumour going around the Bulwark that he's been arrested.'

Emily glanced at Quill.

'There are always rumours in the Bulwark,' said the officer.

'Is this one true?' said Rosie.

'Yes,' said Emily. 'Lord Naxor is currently in a cell beneath Cuidrach Palace.'

'What did you catch him doing this time? Or, is that a secret?'

Emily considered for a moment. 'Would you like to work for me, Rosie?'

Rosie blinked. 'Wow. I mean, I'm flattered and everything, but what would I do? You don't even know me, your Majesty.'

'No, but you seem like a capable young woman.'

'But, why?'

Emily smiled. 'I guess that was my polite way of saying that you won't be returning to the Bulwark, Rosie. I can't risk any word of this getting out, and I'll need you to assist with a team I'm going to put together to investigate this new salve mine. If you say yes, then I won't have to order Quill to make sure that you are prevented from leaving the building.'

'Oh. Well, in that case, I would be delighted to work for you, your Majesty.'

'Excellent. We'll find you some rooms in the palace for the foreseeable future; Quill can sort out the transfer from your Blade battalion, and she can organise your new quarters.' She turned to the officer. 'Have her assigned to me personally, as an aide, but keep it quiet for now.'

'Yes, your Majesty.'

Rosie pursed her lips. 'Am I your aide now, your Majesty?'

'Yes, you are.'

'Does that mean you can tell me why Naxor was arrested?'

'Let's see how you get on, first. How old are you Rosie?'

'I just turned eighteen, your Majesty.'

Emily nodded. 'Assign her someone you trust, Quill. A sergeant, or suchlike. Someone to keep an eye on her in the palace, and to make sure no harm comes to her. Also, to keep her presence here a secret, for now.'

Quill bowed. 'I shall, your Majesty; and then, I'll have to return to the Bulwark. Lady Jade will be rising from her bed shortly.'

'Am I right in saying, Quill, that if the Commander of the Bulwark, that is, Lady Jade, is called away from the Bulwark for any reason, then that leaves the Adjutant in charge?'

'That is indeed so, your Majesty.'

'Then, keep this to yourself, but prepare to be in charge of the Bulwark. I have an idea that might keep Lady Jade away from her post for a while.' She turned to Rosie. 'Thank you so much for coming today,

Miss Jackdaw; I'm sure I'll be seeing a lot of you over the next few days. Quill will show you out, and take you to where you'll be staying.'

Rosie got up from the couch, and Quill escorted her out of the royal chambers. Emily let out a long breath as soon as they had left.

'Your new aide seems like a nice young lady,' said her mother.

Emily frowned.

'What jobs are you going to get her to do?' her mother went on.

'I have no idea; I only did it to stop her leaving the palace, and I didn't want to put her in a prison cell. Oh mother, this is a nightmare.'

Lady Omertia raised an eyebrow. 'I don't follow, dear.'

'Everything I dreaded is coming true. When we ran out of salve, I was disappointed at first, but then I realised that it was actually a good thing. With no salve, then if the gods who are hunting us ever found us, then maybe they'd leave us alone. And now, we have a mountain of salve, just on our doorstep. Worse, Naxor knew about it and didn't tell me. Secondly, the Ascendant gods had no way of getting here, but then I discover that Amalia has a Quadrant in her possession. She could betray us to Implacatus in a heartbeat, if she wanted to. But, Amalia being back is the biggest disaster of all. Now, we have a powerful enemy, a means for an even greater enemy to get here, and a reason for them to come. For the good of the City, it should have been me who died in Maeladh, not Yendra. She would have been able to face these odds.'

'Don't say that, dear. Never once in your life have you conceded defeat, regardless of the odds. Giving up is not in your nature.'

Emily glanced out of the window at the pink sky. She felt drained, and the burdens she bore upon her shoulders seemed to be pinning her to where she sat. Amalia, Naxor, Jade, and now a new salve mine had been added to the weight.

She stood.

'Where are you going, dear?' said her mother.

Emily glanced at the door leading to the cot where her daughter was sleeping. That's where she wanted to go; instead, she turned for the door that led to Salvor's office.

She steeled herself. 'I'm going back to work.'

CHAPTER 7

WINTER BREAK

S unward Range, Roser Territory, Auldan, The City – 3rd Monan 3422

Kagan and Sofia stopped on the path to take a look at the view. The hillside sloped away from them, revealing the lush, green expanse of Roser territory, from the rounded peaks of the Sunward Range, all the way down to the plains where the Union Walls lay. To their left, in the distance, were the suburbs of Outer Pella, while the Warm Sea was invisible over a high ridge to their right.

'When Malik and I first arrived here,' Sofia said, 'these hills were covered in greenhides.' She glanced at Kagan, a light smile playing on her lips. 'We were almost too late. The four towns – Tara, Pella, Dalrig and Ooste – had been under siege for over a year, and were on the verge of collapse. The people huddling behind the walls were starving and desperate; our coming was like a storm. I killed many thousands of greenhides that first day, starting here on these very slopes. That night, Malik and I entered Tara as hero gods; deliverers. Crowds of mortals threw themselves to their knees in front of us, begging us to save them.'

'Did it only take one day to beat the greenhides?' said Kagan.

Sofia laughed. 'No, Kagan. Every morning, I would awaken within Maeladh Palace – the frightened inhabitants of the town had already given us the home of their prince to live in – and then I would go out and drive the greenhides back once again. It was never enough. No matter how many I slaughtered, there were always more the following dawn. So, I travelled further east one day, and found the closest nest. It was in the centre of the great plain between the City and the Eastern Mountains. There, I single-handedly slew the greenhide queen, and all of her daughters, and burnt the nest to ashes. I had to use my Quadrant to escape the cataclysm I had caused, and I can still recall the smell. After that, the greenhide attacks lessened, and, within fifty years, we had constructed the Union Walls, uniting the four towns into one City, and I was able to rest, at last.'

Kagan nodded. 'Is that when you became the God-Queen?'

'Yes. The people here were backward. Malik and I gifted them much to ease their lives – schools, printing presses, heating, plumbing, farming techniques, ship-building. We taught them how to dig out the huge cisterns under the City, to store the flood waters from Freshmist and Sweetmist, and we showed them how to construct ballistae and crossbows. In return, they worshipped us, and gave us salve. We didn't know what it was, naturally. The mortals used it to heal wounds, but its effects on Malik and I were... surprising, to say the least. We both looked old when we got here; all of the gods of our generation did, but after a few doses, we appeared as fresh faced and youthful as I do now. For several centuries we lived our best lives; we were happy, and the people of the City prospered.'

'What happened then?'

'Two things came along to ruin our tranquillity. First, the blasted Aurelians staged a rebellion against our rule. They wanted mortals to be in charge, after everything Malik and I had done for them. For this betrayal, we stripped the last vestiges of power from the four towns, and abolished the mortal royal houses, from which the princes were descended. Secondly, the greenhides returned, pushing a great mass of fleeing civilians in front of them – the Evaders. We opened the gates in the Union Walls to allow them in, and the City became terribly over-crowded; and worse, it was under siege again, and I had to go back out and do it all over again. Untold numbers of greenhides, and another nest, on my own. After that, when the Middle Walls were constructed, I wearied of it all. The endless death and slaughter ground me down, and so Malik and I decided to have children, so that we could start to share the great burden that had fallen upon our shoulders. Michael was first, then Montieth and Isra. The twins Niomi and Khora followed, and finally Yendra. With six God-Children, Malik and I could afford to step back, and enjoy some peace and quiet; could anyone say that I didn't deserve that, after all I had done?'

She quietened for a moment, her eyes gazing out over the terraced slopes of the hills.

'No one remembers any of this,' she said. 'All they remember are the mistakes I made towards the end of my reign. By that point, both Michael and Malik were dead, and my dreams were in tatters. Is it any wonder that I bear a grievance towards the ungrateful mortals who now live here? There would be no City were it not for me.'

A chill winter breeze gusted across the slopes, and Kagan pulled his coat tighter around him. Twelve days had passed since their visit to Greylin Palace, and he was still struggling to reconcile the Sofia he thought he knew with the shadowy figure of the hated and feared God-Queen. The meeting with Lady Amber had affected Sofia too, and she had been restless and distracted in the days following. Despite promising not to leave the mansion for a year, she had announced that they were going to stay on the small estate that she had purchased in Roser territory, for a holiday. Kagan had been worried at first that she might be recognised, but the villa in the heart of the estate was isolated and quiet.

'Ruling is a burden that I do not care for any more,' she said. 'If only Belinda were here; she could have been queen, and I would have been happy to sink into obscurity; without her, I have no desire to try to wrest my powers back.' She smiled. 'It feels quite liberating to say that out loud.'

'Do you mean it?'

'Yes, I believe so. You and little Maxwell have given me something other than power to think about, and, for the first time in a very long time, I am content. You know, if you were to propose to me, I wouldn't say no.'

Kagan's eyes widened. 'You want to get married?'

'Why not? We've been living together for a year and a half, and we have a child. Besides, if I want to pass myself off as a young aristocrat, people will think it odd that my son was fathered by a mere servant. Marriage would lend us a little more respectability.'

Kagan lowered himself to one knee on the gravel path. 'Sofia,' he said; 'I adore you more than words can say; will you marry me?'

She smiled. 'I will.'

He stood, grinning, and they kissed.

'You are aware,' she said, 'that by tying yourself to me, you put your-self at great risk? If I am discovered, you will be punished next to me.'

'I don't care; you have my heart, Sofia. I would risk anything for you.'

'What about your doubts?'

'What doubts?'

'The doubts you feel regarding some of the acts I committed as God-Queen? Things have been a little different between us since Greylin, when you discovered that I had opened the gates in the Middle Walls to the greenhides. Does that no longer trouble your conscience?'

'That was something the old God-Queen did, not Lady Sofia.'

She narrowed her eyes a little, then shook her head.

He shrugged. 'That's how I'm coping with it. You've lived the equiva-lent of a hundred lives, maybe more, and I've only known you a short time in comparison. Anything you did before we met belongs to the past, and I'm not blameless either. I got the job working in the mansion in order to rob you, if you recall. People can change.'

'Maybe mortals can; I'm not sure I'm capable of change. However, if you are sure, then we shall press ahead. I'll ask Gellie to start the prepa-rations. It'll be a small ceremony, of course, but people will assume that we are choosing to marry quietly because we already have a child.' She smiled again. 'This makes me happy, Kagan; you make me happy.'

He took her hand, and they set off down the path, heading towards the villa. At the bottom of the slope, they passed the buildings where the local brandy was made, and Sofia waved at the workers standing outside. Beyond that was the villa she had purchased, a neat sandstone structure that perched on the edge of a wide terrace, positioned to get as much sunlight as possible. They walked round to the side of the villa, where Gellie was supervising a few servants. Maxwell was being looked after by a young Sander woman, who was sitting on a rug that had been spread out on the grass, the baby in her arms.

'Gellie!' Sofia called, as they approached.

The housekeeper bowed. 'Ma'am. Did you enjoy your walk?'

She beamed. 'Kagan has just proposed to me, and I said yes.'

If the Fordian housekeeper harboured any concerns, she kept them well hidden behind her features. Her face opened up into a large smile. 'Congratulations, ma'am; that is splendid news.'

'Thank you, Gellie. How do you feel about handling it all? I would like the wedding to take place here, on our little estate, but in the summer time. Make sure there are lots of flowers.'

'Leave it to me, ma'am,' said Gellie. She glanced at Kagan, but said nothing.

He walked over to the rug and crouched down by the Sander woman. She bowed her head to him, and passed over the baby. Kagan sat, and balanced Maxwell on his knees. The eight-month-old child smiled up at him, then tried to wriggle away.

'He's been crawling again this morning, sir,' said the Sander woman.

'He's so big already,' Kagan said; 'aren't you, little Max?'

Sofia smiled down at them.

A servant appeared through a side door. He bowed low in front of Sofia.

'Ma'am,' he said; 'a carriage has arrived at the front of the villa.'

'Visitors?' said Sofia.

'Yes, ma'am. Lord and Lady Aurelian.'

Sofia blinked. 'The Aurelians are here?'

'Yes, ma'am. Apparently, they own the next estate along, and have come to greet their new neighbours.'

'What? Where are they?'

'I let them in, ma'am. They are currently waiting in the drawing room. Did I err?'

Sofia put a hand to her face.

'I apologise if I did something wrong, ma'am,' said the servant. 'They are the parents of the King; I wasn't aware that I should turn them away.'

'Gellie,' said Sofia, 'get everyone indoors. Unfortunately, I am feeling a little sick, and will have to lie down. I am not to be disturbed, under any circumstances. Kagan, bring Maxwell and come with me.'

She strode into the villa, and Kagan stood, the child in his arms, and followed her into the house. They walked into their bedroom, and Sofia went round the windows, closing the shutters.

'The Aurelians?' he said. 'Why is that name familiar? Wait; are they the same family that staged the rebellion all those years ago?'

'Yes, but that's hardly relevant now, Kagan. Rather more pertinently, Lady Aurelian is one of the few people in the City who would recognise me instantly. The last time I saw her, she was my prisoner, in Maeladh Palace. I should have executed her when I had the chance, but I was too busy gloating over my imagined victory. Damn it. You will have to speak to them. Tell them I'm sorry, but I'm too ill to leave this room. Tell them I have a severe headache or something. Oh, and make sure you tell them that we are betrothed, otherwise they might assume that you are a servant and refuse to talk to you.'

'Alright. What are they like?'

'Lord Aurelian is a typical Roser landowner and aristocrat; keeps himself to himself, and stays as far away from politics as it's possible to do.'

'And Lady Aurelian?'

'Lady Aurelian is a bitch of the highest order.' She reached out with her arms. 'Give me Maxwell and go.'

He passed her the baby.

'You'll be fine,' said Sofia; 'go.'

Kagan took a breath, then left the room. Gellie was waiting outside, and escorted him to the large drawing room at the sunward end of the villa. One entire wall of the room was made up of huge windows that reached from the floor to the ceiling, and the chamber was filled with light. Sitting on a long couch by the windows was a man and a woman, who stood when Gellie and Kagan entered.

'My lord and lady,' said Gellie, bowing.

Lady Aurelian raised an eyebrow.

'My humble apologies,' Gellie went on, 'but I am afraid that you have arrived at an inopportune moment, as Lady Sofia of the Southern Cape is presently ill.'

'Oh dear,' said Lady Aurelian; 'how terrible.'

Gellie gestured to Kagan. 'This is Lady Sofia's betrothed, Lord Kagan of Alea Tanton.'

'Good morning,' said Kagan, inclining his head a little.

'Nice to meet you, old chap,' said Lord Aurelian, extending his hand.

Kagan strode forwards and shook the lord's hand. Lady Aurelian reached out with her hand, and Kagan kissed it.

'I shall bring refreshments,' said Gellie; 'please make yourselves at home.'

The Fordian housekeeper left the room, and Kagan attempted a smile.

'Please sit,' he said.

'So, it's true?' said Lady Aurelian, as they took their seats. 'There really are green-skinned people from Lostwell now living in the City?'

'Gellie is a Fordian,' said Kagan; 'one of the few who survived the destruction of Lostwell.'

She smiled. 'What an accent you have! Most rustic and charming. It's such a shame that Lady Sofia is ill; I had been looking forward to making her acquaintance. I hear that you have a young son?'

'That's right. Maxwell.'

'How lovely. I recall when my son was only a baby, and now he's the

King of the entire City. Being an Aurelian is a blessing, but it also carries its burdens.'

Kagan nodded. 'Do you live in the neighbouring estate?'

'We own it,' she said, 'though I'd hardly say that we lived there. My husband runs the family businesses from our home in Tara, while I am often to be found advising the King and Queen in Pella. We get to spend very little time at our villa. You must come and visit us there for dinner one evening.'

'Thank you.'

'So, how are you finding the City?'

'I've yet to visit much of it,' he said, 'but I love Port Sanders, and the villa here is beautiful.'

'Might I ask,' said Lord Aurelian, 'what you intend to do with the brandy facility on the estate?'

Lady Aurelian shot her husband a look. 'Really, darling?'

The lord shrugged. 'Lady Sofia happens to have bought my favourite brandy distillery. I'm merely enquiring about its future. It would be a tragedy if it were to be closed.'

'We intend to keep it running,' said Kagan. 'It's also Sofia's favourite brandy; I think that's why she bought this particular estate.'

Lord Aurelian smiled. 'Your betrothed has excellent taste. Let me know if you need any advice on any aspect of the business; I have a lot of experience in this field.'

'Tell me more about Lady Sofia,' said Lady Aurelian. 'As far as I know, she was the only landed aristocrat to escape the devastation of your home world. What was the nature of her business on Lostwell?'

'Land, shipping and trade, mostly,' he said. 'Lostwell was a big place, and I don't have many more details, unfortunately.'

'And you?' she said. 'Were you also part of the Lostwellian aristocracy?'

'Yes, but I confess that I wasn't as rich as Lady Sofia.'

'Ahh, so you are marrying up? Good for you. Now, I did hear of one little thing that concerned me. It has come to my attention that Lady

Sofia has donated a considerable amount to a certain legal fund. Were you aware of this?'

'Yes.'

'Are you also aware that this fund is designed to obstruct and delay the constitutional proposals put forward by my son, the sovereign King of the City?'

'I'm aware of that, yes.'

'Hmmm. Perhaps you are not fully enlightened as to the consequences of such a move. I had hoped to have a little chat with Lady Sofia regarding this. It would be wise, I feel, if she were to stop her opposition to the new laws. One might say, if one were bold, that the new laws are none of her concern, being, as she is, a foreigner to the City. In fact, one could call her stance a little hypocritical.'

'Why?'

'Well, my dear Kagan, it appears that Lady Sofia is happy to accept some of the changes. Before the new land laws were passed, it was illegal for any non-Roser to purchase estates in Roser territory, and yet here we are, sitting in your villa. Does Lady Sofia only object to those portions of the law that personally disadvantage her?'

Kagan hesitated.

'It was an easy mistake to have made,' Lady Aurelian went on. 'I can imagine that poor Lady Sofia was bombarded with requests from self-serving merchants in Port Sanders, and she probably only wanted to give a good impression of herself, to fit in. Alas, I fear that she has taken advice from all of the wrong people. However, it is not too late to make amends. If Lady Sofia were to declare her support for the new laws, I imagine that my son, the King, would be exceptionally grateful.'

'I will speak to her about it.'

Lady Aurelian smiled, though her eyes remained sharp. 'You do that. I would also like to issue a general invitation to you and your betrothed, to attend the Royal Court in Pella. In fact, it surprises me that Lady Sofia has not already been to visit the King and Queen of the City. As I said, she is the sole aristocrat of any distinction from Lostwell, and I would have thought that she'd be keen to pay her respects to the rulers of your new home. Instead, she appears to be trying her best to hide herself away. Why is that, do you think?'

'Lady Sofia is a very private person.'

'Yes, but does she not feel a certain responsibility towards her thousands of fellow Exiles? She appears to be richer than the rest of them put together. Does she not aspire to a leadership role?'

'She wishes to live quietly.'

'Leave them be,' said Lord Aurelian to his wife. 'It is precisely as I guessed. Sofia merely wants a quiet life.' He glanced at Kagan. 'I can sympathise.'

'Sympathy is all very well,' said Lady Aurelian, 'but what about duty and responsibility?'

'Perhaps in time,' said Kagan. 'At the moment, we are concentrating on Maxwell, and the wedding. With the City so divided, it might be wiser to keep away from politics.'

'But, she has already intervened in politics,' she said, 'by giving all that money to the Sander's legal fund. Does Lady Sofia now see that as a mistake?'

'I wouldn't like to say.'

Lady Aurelian sighed. 'I used to find naivety charming, but perhaps I'm less patient than I used to be.'

The door opened, and Gellie walked in. She guided a pair of servants to wheel a trolley over to where the Aurelians were sitting.

'I have prepared some food and drink for you,' Gellie said, bowing.

'Thank you,' said Lord Aurelian.

'How is Lady Sofia?' said Lady Aurelian. 'Is she any better?'

'I'm afraid not, ma'am.'

'This is a little frustrating,' she said, 'but what can one do?'

Gellie and the servants bowed, and left the room. Lord Aurelian reached over to the trolley, and helped himself to a glass of wine and a plateful of food.

'I think these olives are from our estate, dear,' he said.

'About the invitation to the Royal Court,' she said, ignoring her husband, 'do you accept? Shall I tell the King and Queen to expect you?'

'No,' said Kagan.

'Excuse me? Did you say "no?"'

'It would send a signal to the City that we are happy with the new laws, which is not the case. Now, that would be hypocritical, would it not?'

Lady Aurelian glared at him. 'How disappointing. It isn't often that I have a generous offer thrown back into my face. Let us all hope that this... decision doesn't come back to bite you.'

Kagan picked up the bottle of wine. 'Would you like a glass?'

'No, thank you.'

'It's very good,' said Lord Aurelian. 'I think it's from Lord Merton's estate; a most delicate vintage.'

Lady Aurelian rolled her eyes.

Kagan poured himself half a glass and took a sip.

'There was another reason for our visit,' Lady Aurelian said. 'Now, Kagan, I don't wish to alarm you, but you must be on your lookout.'

'For what?'

'Have you ever heard of a person referred to as the God-Queen?'

Kagan's mouth went dry. He stared at Lady Aurelian for a moment, then shook his head.

'No? Well, she used to be in charge of the City before we chased her away. She is a most despicable and heartless creature, responsible for untold amounts of pain and suffering. As the name suggests, she is a god, who possesses the darkest death powers imaginable. With one flick of her fingers, she would be able to kill hundreds of people at once. During the recent conflict, she tried her best to annihilate every mortal in the City, and now she has returned.'

'She sounds very dangerous.'

Lady Aurelian laughed. 'Yes, quite. Dangerous, ruthless; a killer. She will stop at nothing to reclaim her old power here in the City, which is another reason I would encourage you and Lady Sofia to align yourself to the Crown. For, when she makes her move, which she no doubt will, the City will be riven between those who support her, and those who oppose her. Fortunately, the vast majority of people living in the City hate her, and would do anything to prevent her from retaking control. Regardless of our differences over the constitutional laws, I trust that you will support the Crown if the God-Queen re-emerges from the shadows?'

'Was she a bad ruler?'

'Haven't you been listening to a word I've said? She governed the City as if it were her plaything, and as if the mortals were nothing but expendable tools. Also, she was responsible for the greenhides coming to this world in the first place; without her, the City would have lived in peace for thousands of years, instead of existing under a state of permanent siege.'

'I'm sorry? The God-Queen brought the greenhides here?'

'Yes. Greenhides do not exist naturally upon this world. Amalia, for that is the God-Queen's name, transported them here from another world, and unleashed them upon us, only to turn up at the last second to save us, making it look as though she were the hero. The God-King was responsible too, of course, but as he is dead, there's little point in continuing to blame him for it. Ask yourself, Kagan, whose side would you be on if Amalia returned? Can the Crown count upon the support of you and Lady Sofia in this matter?'

'I'm not sure what we can do about it.'

Lady Aurelian leaned towards him. 'Keep your eyes and ears open, young man. Because Lady Sofia has donated money to the insidious forces aligned against the King and Queen, it is possible that someone might approach you, thinking that you may be receptive to the message of the God-Queen. You must not allow yourself to be taken in by their words, no matter how honeyed they may be. If you do hear such whisperings, I would be obliged if you would let me know. At once. The threat from the God-Queen can be overcome, but only if the mortals of the City are united.'

'Alright. I'm willing to do that.'

'Good boy.' She glanced at her husband. 'Time to leave, I think.'

Lord Aurelian put down his glass and plate, and stood. Kagan got to his feet, and shook the man's hand again.

'You've got a lovely little estate here,' Lord Aurelian said. 'Keep the brandy flowing.'

Lady Aurelian stood, and Kagan walked them to the door, where Gellie was waiting.

'Thank you for the visit,' said Kagan, as they reached the main entrance of the villa.

'Thank you for having us,' said Lord Aurelian. 'Until next time.'

Gellie and Kagan waited, watching through the open doorway until the Aurelians had boarded their carriage.

'You did well,' said Gellie, as she closed the door.

'Were you listening?'

'I was. Your refusal to attend Royal Court was well handled. You're continually surprising me, Kagan. Perhaps her ladyship isn't making a terrible mistake by marrying you.'

A door opened, and Sofia peered out. 'Have they gone?'

'Yes, my lady,' said Gellie. 'Their carriage is back on the road.'

Sofia puffed out her cheeks. 'That was close. Why didn't I know that this villa was right next to the Aurelian's estate?'

Kagan glanced at her. 'Did you bring the greenhides here?'

'Oh,' said Sofia. 'Let me guess; Lady Aurelian told you that?'

'Yes. She was warning me to be on the lookout for the God-Queen.'

Sofia laughed. 'Was she? How droll. I almost wish I had leapt into the room at that moment; it would have scared her half to death.'

'Did you bring the greenhides to this world?'

Sofia snuck back into the bedroom without answering, and Kagan followed her in and closed the door.

'Did you?' he repeated.

'Oh, Kagan; don't make a fuss. It's true, but it's complicated. Malik and I opened a portal, and allowed a greenhide queen and some workers to enter this world; that part's correct, but we didn't mean for them to get out of control. We over-estimated our own powers.'

Kagan stared at her. 'But, why? Why would you bring greenhides to a world where there were none?'

'We were on the run from the Ascendants at the time, and thought, mistakenly as it turned out, that they were hot on our heels. We truly expected Edmond and the others to appear at any moment, and were planning on breeding greenhides as an army to protect us. Needless to say, it all went wrong. It turns out that only the Ascendants have the power to control greenhides, and our experiment got out of hand. Before we could blink, there were millions of them, running feral across the entire world. What else did that bitch tell you about me?'

'That you were a killer.'

'Yes, well, you knew that already.'

'And you were biding your time, waiting to strike so that you could reclaim your throne.'

Sofia smiled. 'She was wrong about that part.' She took his hand. 'You told me that you believe people can change. I think I've changed. I don't want to be the God-Queen again; I just want to be Lady Sofia, living my quiet life of comfort with you and Maxwell.'

'Someone is bound to get suspicious eventually.'

'No, the opposite is true, Kagan. Eventually, there will be no mortals left alive who would recognise me. The difficult period is right now, when people like Lady Aurelian are still around.'

'Do you truthfully not want to be all-powerful again?'

'That's right. I'll swear it, if you like. Come summer, I intend to make a wedding vow to you; is that not proof enough of my intentions?'

Kagan said nothing. He wanted to believe her, but was finding it hard to shake the words spoken by Lady Aurelian.

'I know what will distract you,' she said, coming closer. She leaned up, and whispered in his ear, 'Shall we try for another child?'

He closed his eyes, feeling her breath against his neck.

'I want six in ten years. How does that sound, husband-to-be?'

He put his arms around her. 'It sounds perfect.'

CHAPTER 8

CONSTRAINED

F ortress of the Lifegiver, The Bulwark, The City – 4th Monan 3422

Jade frowned at the book. It was a seven hundred page history of the City, and, according to the index, she had a mere two mentions in it. She had looked them both up – one was a note of her birth, and the other was a bland comment saying that she lived in Greylin Palace. That was it. Worse, there were seven mentions of Amber.

She hurled the book against the wall of the study, leaned over from where she was sitting on the floor, and pulled another volume from the bookcase.

Auldan through the Ages

She opened the book at the back, and flipped through the pages until she reached the index. She had lived in Auldan for the vast majority of her life; surely she would merit a few mentions? She found a royal family tree in the book's appendices, and located her name with a smile. Then she picked up a pencil and scored out her sister's name, writing in *Ugly Cow* in its place. She laughed.

A cat meowed next to her.

'What is it, Tab-Tab? Has your mouse died again?'

She glanced at the cat, and saw the dead rodent lying on the carpet next to Tab-Tab's front paws. Jade poked it with a finger, then sent a spike of powers into the little corpse. The mouse shuddered, then its claw wounds healed and its eyes opened. It stared up at the cat and ran for it, but Tab-Tab was waiting, and tore off across the floor after it.

Jade laughed again. 'Silly Tab-Tab.' Her eyes went back to the book, and she found the index. She checked her sister's name first, and counted the mentions. Fourteen. That seemed far too many for such a stupid person, but gave her hope that she would also have several. She skipped a few pages to her name, her finger running down the paper.

Her eyes narrowed. Three mentions for Lady Jade. Three! Anger boiled over inside her, and she began tearing the pages from the book, ripping them to shreds. She yanked the back cover, trying to pull it off, but the old bindings were too strong, and she ended up throwing the entire thing against the wall with a yell of frustration.

Stupid books. She should burn them all. Or, better still, she should write her own history of the City, making sure that she was given the starring role, as she deserved. Amber would be included, of course, but Jade would be certain to show everyone how awful and mean her sister really was. She remembered a particularly nasty beating inflicted upon her by father, and how Amber had stood by and laughed as Jade had been thrashed. Afterwards, Amber had told Jade that she had deserved the beating and, since father hated her so much, it would probably be better if she killed herself. She then offered to help Jade do it.

Jade's fists clenched at the memories. Yendra had told her that she had been damaged by her life in Greylin, but that she was still redeemable. You cannot help your feelings, she used to say, but you can control your actions. A tear rolled down her cheek. What if Yendra had been right about being damaged, but wrong about being redeemable? Maybe it was too late for her; maybe her father and her sister had warped her so much, that there was no way back?

No, she said to herself. She had helped the City against the green-hides; she had proved that she was useful, and loyal. She had been promoted to Commander of the Bulwark; that must mean that the King and Queen trusted her. She cheered up a little. Yes, the King and the

Queen believed in her and, even though they were only mortals, that had to count for something.

She got to her feet and went through to her living room, pausing by the window to glance down at the hordes of greenhides swarming by the far side of the deep moat. She should probably go up onto the battlements to kill a few, but she wasn't in the mood. She noted the position of the sun, and frowned. It was well after noon, and Quill still hadn't been round to visit her. She strode to the front door of her suite of rooms and glanced out into the hallway.

'Where's Quill?' she said to the two guards standing by her door.

'Shall I go and look for her, ma'am?' said one.

Jade stared at him. 'Yes. When you find her, tell her that I want to see her, immediately.'

The guard saluted, and ran down the stairs. The other guard kept his gaze lowered.

'Do you like cats?' she said to him.

'Eh, ma'am? Cats? Yes, I suppose so.'

'Do you want to come inside and play with mine? I have four.'

The guard's face paled. 'Uh, I can't, sorry, ma'am. I've been ordered to guard your quarters. I can't leave my post.'

'Oh. Alright.'

She went back into her rooms and closed the door, feeling a strange sensation of sorrow. For a brief moment, she wished she had a friend to talk to, then she banished such foolishness from her mind, and paced the floor, waiting for Quill to arrive.

'That took twenty minutes, Quinn!' Jade shouted. 'Why did you make me wait for twenty minutes?'

The Adjutant of the Bulwark closed the door to Jade's rooms and approached. 'I apologise, ma'am. I was busy trying to deal with an angry protest outside the gates of the fortress.'

'Well, don't do it again,' Jade cried. 'I don't like waiting. And get me new guards. That one out there was looking at me in a funny way; I don't like him.'

'Certainly, ma'am. What was it that you needed me for? I have many things that require my attention.'

Jade pointed towards herself. 'I should be the sole focus of your attention, Quinn. I am Commander of the Bulwark.' She paused. 'Did you say that there were angry protests outside the fortress?'

'That's right, ma'am. A rather large mob has gathered, made up of Blades from the housing sectors close to Arrowhead and Stormshield. They're demanding to see you, to present a list of demands.'

'Demands? How dare they? What kind of demands?'

Quill reached behind her steel breastplate and produced a rolled up scroll. 'Let's see,' she said. 'Alright; firstly, they want access to their loved ones in prison, and speedy movement on the backlog of criminal cases awaiting judgement. They want repairs carried out to their houses and water supplies. Apparently, the heating systems in Sectors Four and Five have completely broken down, and their families are freezing in the cold of winter. There was a food riot in Sector Three a couple of days ago, and the killers of some innocent bystanders are still at large. Next...'

Jade sat, feeling a longing to return to her warm bed. 'I think I've heard enough.'

'There is also an issue with the payment of wages to Blade units along the Great Wall, ma'am.'

'Then, why don't you pay them?'

'I cannot, ma'am. The funds in the Blade treasury are exhausted. We need to speak to the Crown, and negotiate a loan.'

'What, and admit to them that we're bankrupt?'

'They already know, ma'am.'

Jade glared at the tall officer. 'Is that what you were doing in Pella when you snuck off there? Telling tales about me, eh?'

'No, ma'am.'

'What were you doing, then?'

'I'm not at liberty to say, ma'am.'

'But I'm your commanding officer, Quinn! This is insubordination. I demand that you tell me.'

'Perhaps we should travel to Cuidrach Palace, ma'am, and you can ask the Queen in person. And, while we're there, we can also ask her about a loan to cover the wall garrison's wages.'

Jade struggled to control her temper, the fingers of her right hand twitching.

'Or,' Quill went on, 'I can sit down with you, and we can calmly go through the protesters' list of grievances.'

'Why should I pander to those snivelling ingrates?'

'Because, ma'am, those "snivelling ingrates" are the backbone of the Blades. May I speak freely?'

'Go on.'

'The Blades are simmering over with anger and frustration, ma'am. You might not see it, hidden away up here in the top floor of the Duke's Tower, but people are suffering. Some families have gone unpaid since the middle of last month, while others are living in housing that isn't fit for rats to dwell in. The courts system has collapsed, and there's a huge backlog of cases, even for the most trivial of offences. Some suspects have been held on remand for over a year without being seen by a lawyer, let alone a judge. There have been no promotions in a year and a half, and there's a growing number of critical positions that have not been filled. In short, ma'am, if things carry on in this manner, there will be a mutiny.'

Jade's resolve nearly crumbled. She gazed up at Quill. 'Why do you hate me?'

The tall officer looked confused. 'I don't hate you, ma'am; I'm on your side. I'm trying to help.'

'What would you do if you were in charge?'

'May I sit, ma'am?'

Jade nodded.

Quill took the seat opposite Jade. 'Well, ma'am, first, I'd promote two or three officers to new positions, and give them the tasks that you don't want to do. Appoint someone to lead the courts, someone who has the authority to name new judges and issue sentences without your signature or approval. Do the same with a new promotions board, and a housing board; let others do the work if you'd rather not.'

'But, I don't trust anyone.'

'I could start the process off, ma'am. I have a few names. A couple of the Banner officers that Major-General Logos lent us are exceptionally gifted organisers, and they come without any previous Blade baggage.'

'No.'

Quill frowned. 'A leader either has to work every hour of every day, or they need to learn to delegate, ma'am. You have done neither.'

'If there's a mutiny, then the Crown will strip me of my command. I would be humiliated.'

'Your humiliation is what I'm trying to prevent, ma'am. If you don't trust the Blades, then how about those Banner officers? There are about a dozen of them altogether, but I could ask if any more might be spared.'

'They're foreigners.'

'Yes. What better way to ensure that they don't harbour any hidden loyalty to Marcus and the God-Queen? The Banner are professionals, and at the moment we're under-employing them.'

'How would the Blades take it? Not too well, I'd imagine; especially the old veterans, if they see foreign Banner soldiers taking over.'

'I suspect most would be happy to see some sort of normality return.'

Tab-Tab chose that moment to leap up onto the couch and drop a dead mouse onto Quill's lap. The Adjutant glanced down.

'Why, thank you, Tab-Tab,' she said.

'She wants you to re-animate it for her,' said Jade. 'Being a cat, she doesn't realise that you are a powerless mortal.'

Quill narrowed her eyes a little, as Jade pointed at the mouse. The small rodent wobbled, then tried to get to its feet, but fell off Quill's lap instead. The cat followed it down to the carpet, and pawed it, but it remained still.

'I think that one's done,' said Jade. 'You'll have to catch a new one,

Tab-Tab.' She sighed. 'If I agree to this Banner takeover, would that prevent a mutiny?'

'Not on its own, ma'am, but if you were to negotiate a new loan from the Crown to cover the outstanding wages as well, then I think that would suffice.'

A loud thumping came from the door. Jade scowled, as Quill got to her feet. The officer opened the door to an out-of-breath soldier.

He bowed. 'The mob have broken through into the fortress, and are ransacking the stores.'

'What?' cried Quill. 'When I left a few minutes ago, the garrison were in full control of the gates; what happened?'

The soldier glanced down. 'The guards let the protesters through, ma'am.'

Jade leaped to her feet and strode towards the soldier, her hand raised. The soldier shrank back in fear.

'You let a mob enter the Fortress of the Lifegiver?' Jade yelled. 'You should die for that!'

Quill stepped between them. 'No, my lady. This man has come here to tell us; he is not to blame.' She turned to the cowering soldier. 'Go downstairs and lock the doors of the Duke's Tower. Tell the guards on duty there to let no one in. Quickly.'

He saluted. 'Yes, ma'am.'

Jade glared at his back as he ran down the stairs.

'Remain here, ma'am,' said Quill. 'I shall ensure the tower is impregnable, and then I'll call out the entire reserve from their barracks.'

'What about my father? Are the mob likely to be able to reach his prison cell?'

'No, ma'am. There are far too many guards and locked doors between the protesters and the prince. They won't even get close to him. Don't worry; the situation will be back under control soon.'

'What are you talking about, Quinn? I could restore order in seconds; I'll kill every one of that mob, then no one will dare defy me again.'

'Please, ma'am; no. If there's a massacre, then we'll lose the entire Bulwark.'

'But they're looting the fortress! Marcus would have cut them down without hesitation.'

'Do you want to be known as a second Marcus, ma'am? He was the most reviled Commander of the Bulwark in history. They're looting the stores because they're freezing and starving, not because they're rebels. You would be slaughtering desperate men and women.'

Jade stared at her, then she sat down again, saying nothing. Quill seemed to take that as acquiescence and left her rooms, closing the door behind her. Jade gazed at the floor, where the dead mouse was still lying, ignored by the cats. Eight re-animations in quick succession had clearly been as much as the creature's body could take. She remembered watching her father get to forty-seven re-animations of a human over the course of a couple of days in his laboratory. She had seen that man die forty-eight times before his constitution gave out, her father's knife being wielded with a savage efficiency.

She leaned over, and picked the mouse up by the tail. It swung in a lazy circle under her grasp, and she watched it for a moment, peering into its dead eyes every time it spiralled round. She felt within for its life force, but it was utterly exhausted. She shuddered. It felt the same as touching Kelsey Holdfast; as if it wasn't even there. She walked to the window and dropped it out. Looking down, she could see the mob rampaging through the main courtyard of the fortress. The huge gates that led to the road connecting the fortresses on the Great Wall were lying open, and a few Blade soldiers were standing around, doing nothing to intervene.

A storehouse had been broken into, and protesters were emerging, carrying crates and kegs, or sacks of food in their arms. Others were loading jugs of heating oil onto the back of a cart, and Jade watched as a soldier helped them.

Jade's temper rose. The looters were bad enough, but to see the garrison of the premier fortress on the wall assisting them was too much to bear. She raised her fingers, tempted to send a blast of death powers down into the courtyard – if she could reach the greenhides from the battlements, she could reach the looting civilians. Then she remembered what Quill had said about Marcus. Did she want to be like that? Marcus had been ruthless, refusing to tolerate the slightest hint of insubordination. The Blades had hated him for it, but his methods had worked, and in his hands, the Blades had been obedient and loyal. So loyal, that they had followed his orders to occupy the rest of the City.

She lowered her hand, conflicted. What was wrong with her? Marcus wouldn't have hesitated, nor would her sister or father. The God-Queen would have scorned her weakness. She pulled her eyes away from the chaos in the fortress courtyard, and shut her ears to the sound of the cries and shouts echoing up to the tower. She sat down, and Ginger jumped up onto her knee and settled onto her lap, purring.

The Duke's Tower had been designed by Marcus to be the strongest point within the fortress. The mob that had broken in seemed to understand this, and they left the severe fortification alone, like an island in a sea of destruction. Jade sat with her cats, then paced the floors of her rooms, and, when she could stand it no longer, she crept out of her quarters and peered down the stairs.

She heard a few voices coming from the lower floors of the tower, and she felt a keen sense of embarrassment rise up through her body. The soldiers down there were protecting her from the mob, but she didn't need protecting – she was the most powerful being in the entire Bulwark, and the thought that mere mortals were shielding her made her feel humiliated. She started to descend the stairs, passing the empty offices on the floor beneath her rooms, and continuing down. She saw Quill's chambers, which were also deserted, then went down to the ground level. A group of about twenty Blade guards were positioned in the hallway at the foot of the stairs, close to the main entrance of the tower, which was sealed by thick, barred doors. Quill was with them, talking in a low voice as the soldiers watched her.

Jade stood on the stairs for a moment, until the first soldier saw her, and then the rest of them turned to look, and the hallway fell into silence.

Quill saluted her. 'Ma'am, I have sent a pair of runners to Arrowhead, to inform them of the situation, and to request reinforcements.'

Jade's face fell. 'Everyone will know of this shameful humiliation. The Commander of the Bulwark's own fortress – ransacked by a mob. Everyone in the City will laugh at me.'

The soldiers squirmed uncomfortably, but none spoke.

'The good news,' Quill went on, 'is that we're safe in here until the garrison from Arrowhead arrives.'

'Safe from our own soldiers and people?' said Jade. 'We should be leading them, not hiding from them. Is there nothing else we can do?'

'Duke Marcus constructed several secret tunnels beneath the tower,' said Quill; 'we can use them if things get desperate. One of them leads to a turret on the Outer Walls, and we can flee there if...'

'That's not what I meant. Running away would be worse than skulking in this tower. Maybe I should go outside and speak to the crowds.'

'I would advise against that, ma'am. The mob is in a foul mood; they might try to attack you.'

'I would slay any who tried. I could slay them all. You know this.'

'Yes, ma'am. Everyone in the Bulwark knows the powers you possess. And yet, the people are so desperate, that they're willing to risk your death powers to make their point. If you slaughter them, then every other Blade will rise up against you. You cannot kill every Blade. By not using your powers today, you will be showing the rest of the City that you are open to compromise.'

'But, I'm not open to compromise. I will never compromise with looters and hooligans. I want everyone who entered the fortress illegally to be sent to the Rats, and every soldier who helped them executed. Once that is done, then we can look at their pathetic list of grievances.'

'But...'

'Are you questioning my authority, Quill?'

The tall officer glanced away. 'No, ma'am.'

Jade glanced at the faces of the Blade guards in the hallway, but none would meet her eyes.

They loathed her, she realised with a start. They all loathed her.

'Have I killed a single Blade since I was appointed Commander of the Bulwark?' she said.

No one answered.

'Well?' she said. 'Have I?'

'No, ma'am,' said Quill.

'Marcus used to flog dissenters. Have I had anyone flogged?'

'No, ma'am.'

'Marcus had a harem, which he filled by stealing young girls from their families. Have I done anything like that?'

'No, ma'am; you haven't.'

'Then, why do you all hate me?'

The soldiers looked away. Jade saw that one had sergeant's insignia on his shoulder.

'You,' she said; 'Sergeant, why do you hate me?'

The soldier glanced up at her. 'Hate is a strong word, ma'am.'

'That didn't answer my question,' she said. 'Speak. I swear that no harm will come to you; speak.'

The sergeant glanced at Quill, who nodded.

'Well, ma'am,' the sergeant said, 'Marcus was a bastard, it's true, but with him you could tell that he wanted the Blades to be the best army in the City, and he rewarded those who were loyal to him. He made mistakes, some terrible ones, but he made you feel like you were part of something. But, with you, ma'am, it seems that you don't care at all. There are no rewards for loyalty, and no punishments for disloyalty either, so why bother? You're allowing Blade territory to fall into ruin, so what's the point of making an effort any more? Everyone knows that the greenhide threat is dwindling, and that in a few years there will be none of them left in front of the Great Walls. It should be a cause for celebration, but instead, everyone's worried that the Blades will become superfluous to the needs of the City. In fact, there's a suspicion that the Crown put you here deliberately to run us into the ground, as a punishment for everything that Marcus ordered us to do. You were put here, in other words, because they knew you'd fail, and they hope you bring us down with you. Ma'am.'

Jade stared at him, unable to shake the feeling that he was describing a reality that was accurate. Would the King and Queen have done such a thing? She had assumed that being appointed the commander had meant that they had faith in her abilities; could it be true that they had wanted her to fail? That they had known she would fail? Her self-confidence began to collapse, and she sat down heavily onto the bottom step of the flight of stairs, her head in her hands.

What was the point of it all? Had she survived the traumas of Greylin Palace only to be the butt of a cruel joke? Her family hated her, the Blades hated her, and now it seemed as though the King and Queen had been laughing at her behind her back. Anger fought with self-pity within her, and she clenched and unclenched her fists in impotent rage.

'I'll resign,' she said, her voice low.

The soldiers stared at her.

'Excuse me, ma'am?' said Quill.

'I'm resigning the command. Adjutant, you are now in charge of the Bulwark. I was wrong to imagine that I could replace Yendra – no one can replace Yendra. I'll pack my things and leave as soon as the mob has been cleared from the fortress. I'm taking the cats; I'm not leaving them here, all alone.'

No one spoke.

'This is what you all want, isn't it?' she cried. 'Are you happy now? I have been shamed and humiliated enough; stop staring at me.'

'We can discuss this again, ma'am,' said Quill, 'once things have calmed down.'

'No. It's too late for that. The sergeant spoke the truth; I can see it now, as clear as day. I was supposed to fail, because that's all anyone expects of me. My father, my sister, and now the King and Queen. They all think I'm useless; a joke. Well, I'm not going to be anyone's joke, not any more. I quit.'

She stood. For a moment she waited, to see if any of the soldiers would beg her to remain in her post. No one moved, or even met her glance. She nodded, then turned and trudged back up the stairs.

At least her cats loved her, she thought, as a tear rolled down her cheek.

CHAPTER 9

THE BABY QUEEN

Jezra, The Western Bank – 5th Monan 3422

'Good morning, sleepy-head.'

Kelsey opened her eyes, and stretched. She glanced up from the couch where she had been sleeping, and saw Captain Cardova looking down at her.

'Did I sleep in?' she mumbled.

'No, I'm early,' he said. 'Should I come back? Do you need a moment to get your clothes on?'

Kelsey sat up, her blanket wrapped round her. She gazed around Van's living quarters, her mind still fuggy with sleep. Cardova strode over to a window, and opened the shutters a little, letting the dawn light spill into the room. Kelsey's eyes fell onto the low table next to the couch, where a half-empty bottle of brandy lay. On the floor beside it was a pile of her clothes.

'Keep your back turned,' she said, as she reached down to grab them.

'Certainly, ma'am,' said Cardova. 'It's a beautiful morning in sunny Jezra; crisp and clear.'

'Stop being so bloody cheerful, Lucius,' she said, pulling her clothes on. 'It does my nut in.'

'Are you officially living here now?'

'Why?'

'No reason. I just wondered.'

'I don't know. Pyre's arse; I'd kill for a coffee.'

'And a cigarette. I had a dream about smoking a few nights ago; I almost wept when I awoke.'

'Right; you can turn round again,' she said, standing.

Cardova turned and half-smiled at her.

'I'll shower when I get back to my own house,' she said.

'I wasn't judging you. Shall we visit the patient?'

Kelsey pulled her hair back, and tied it behind her neck, then yawned.

'Late night?'

'Aye,' she muttered. 'Van was in a foul mood, and we ended up fighting. And then I drank too much brandy.'

'What were you fighting about?'

'He wants to go back to work, and I was telling him not to be so stupid, and that he needed to rest.' She frowned at the captain. 'I hope you aren't here to try to get him to do any work.'

'I just thought I'd pop over to deliver some news.'

'What news?'

'Let's go and see the major-general, and I'll tell you both at the same time.'

Kelsey walked over to the door of Van's bedroom and knocked. She listened for a moment, then opened the door a crack.

'I'm awake,' said Van from within.

Kelsey and Cardova entered the room, and the captain opened the shutters.

'Good morning, sir,' he said. 'Sleep well?'

'No.'

Kelsey sat by the bed. Van was sitting, propped up by pillows. His face looked tired and drawn, and his eyes flashed with suppressed frustration.

'Another day in this damn bed,' he muttered.

'Another day closer to your recovery, sir,' said Cardova. 'It's only been fourteen days since you were poisoned by concentrated salve; not too much longer to go.'

'I was thinking,' said Van, 'that I could hold meetings from in here. You could send the officers up, and I could start to feel useful again.'

'No chance,' said Kelsey.

'It's not your decision,' said Van. 'I'm the best judge of when I'm ready to return to work. All this lying about is driving me crazy.'

'You can go back to work when you are able to walk to the bathroom and back on your own.'

Van glared at her.

'Are you able to do that, Van?' she asked. 'No? I didn't think so. So, stop whining like a child.'

'Aren't you supposed to be at work, yourself?'

'Not yet. Lucius arrived early. I've still got twenty minutes.'

'You can leave now, if you like.'

'Aye? Maybe I should, only this time, I won't come back. Is that what you want?'

Van stared at her, but said nothing.

'Anyway,' said Cardova, 'I came here to tell you that Lady Jade has resigned as Commander of the Bulwark. Adjutant Quill has taken over as temporary commander while the Crown decides what to do.'

'Jade quit?' said Kelsey.

'There was a riot in the Fortress of the Lifegiver, and, apparently, the soldiers there stood by and allowed it to happen. Jade was besieged in her tower for hours, while the mob sacked the place from top to bottom.'

Van frowned. 'I'm not sure if this is good news or bad news. I assume Montieth remains locked up?'

'Oh yes. The mob had no desire to free a mass murderer, thankfully.'

'What's Jade going to do now?' said Kelsey.

'Who knows?' said Cardova. 'Queen Emily will no doubt think of something. Maybe she'll appoint her to Jezra, you know, if we're really lucky.'

'Don't say that, for Pyre's sake,' muttered Kelsey. 'The woman's an idiot. Jade, I mean. Obviously. Not the Queen.'

Cardova laughed. 'I don't think there was any confusion there.'

'Another disgruntled demigod is hardly what the City needs right now,' said Van. 'Yendra had a lot of faith in Jade; she can't be all bad.'

'Yendra could see the good in everyone,' said Kelsey; 'it was her biggest fault.'

Van glared at her. 'What a stupid thing to say. Yendra gave hope to the entire City; she...' He paused, his voice almost breaking. 'She did her best.'

'Some people have no good in them.' Kelsey said. 'Acknowledging that isn't stupid.'

'Maybe you should leave.'

'Fine,' she said, standing. 'Your company is insufferable anyway.'

'Lucius,' said Van; 'could you stay for a moment?'

'Yes, sir; of course. I'll just walk Kelsey out and be right back.'

Kelsey left the bedroom, then stopped by the couch to shove her things into a bag.

'He doesn't mean all that,' said Cardova, watching her. 'You being here has been crucial for his recovery.'

Kelsey snorted.

'It's true. You might drive each other crazy, but without you, I don't think he would be anywhere close to getting better.'

'Thank you for saying that, Lucius.'

'Come back after work,' he said; 'the three of us can have dinner together, and I'll referee your fights with him.'

'Why are you trying to push us together?'

'My job is to make the life of the Commander of the Exiles as easy as possible; to remove anything that hinders or obstructs him from carrying out his duties, and to encourage whatever allows him to retain his focus. He loves you, Kelsey. You challenge him, and you give him purpose.'

'What about me? What about my purpose?'

'I don't work for you; I work for him. But, at the same time, I like you, and I would never try to persuade you to do something that you were opposed to. If you truly don't want to be here, then don't come back. It would break his heart, but that's better than him being strung along indefinitely.'

'Don't you ever give a thought to your own happiness, Lucius? There are plenty of Brigade girls who would trample me to death in their haste to get a piece of Captain Cardova, yet you've never been with any of them, as far as I know.'

'I've already been married once, Kelsey. Once was enough.'

'You were married?'

'On Implacatus, yes. For two and a half years. It turned out that my bride wasn't too happy about me continuing to sign up for Banner operations, and that was the end of that. She said that I loved the Banner more than I loved her, and she wasn't wrong. I guess I'm bad husband material.'

'Children?'

'No, praise the Ascendants.'

Kelsey pulled the strap of her bag over her shoulder. 'I'll think about dinner tonight. See you later, Lucius.'

She walked from the room, passing Banner soldiers guarding the entrance corridor. They saluted her, and she headed down the stairs, conscious that she looked like she had been up all night. The walk back to her little red brick house cleared the last of the sleep from her head. She showered, changed her clothes, then hurried up to the foundations of the ancient palace. Her crew was waiting there for her, along with Frostback, who was having her wings scrubbed by workers with long soapy brushes.

'Morning, ma'am,' said Sergeant Nagel, leaning on a mop.

'Sorry I'm a bit late,' she said.

'Not to worry, ma'am. Everyone knows that you've been helping to look after the commander.'

She walked up to Frostback.

'Ahh, my rider,' said the silver dragon. 'Are you refreshed and ready for another day's toil?'

'Not really. Though, it'll take my mind off all the arguments I had with Van last night.'

'You two bicker like a married couple. It must be true love.'

'Was that an attempt at dragon sarcasm?'

'No. Dragons are incapable of sarcasm. I meant it truthfully. If you didn't care about each other, then you wouldn't argue. If you were indifferent to each other, you would walk away, instead of returning night after night for more. Did you couple with him?'

Kelsey's face flushed. 'Don't ask me that.'

'Why not? Are you embarrassed? There is nothing shameful in it, surely?'

'No, we did not "couple." We haven't since before his accident. He's too sick, and, to be honest, I was more tempted to slap him across the face than I was to jump into bed with him. He was being extremely pig-headed.'

Vadhi sidled over to them, her hands clutching onto a pail of water. 'Boss?'

'Aye?'

'How's the commander?'

'Still in bed,' she said. 'It'll be a while before he's up and about.'

Vadhi nodded. 'Were you there last night?'

'Aye.'

Vadhi nodded again.

Kelsey sighed. 'Was there something you wanted to ask me, Vadhi?'

'Did you, ah, see Captain Cardova there?'

'I did.'

Her face went red. 'Did he say anything about me?'

'I'd forget about Captain Cardova, if I were you, Vadhi. He's married to the Banner.'

'Maybe we could arrange another night out, and we could accidentally bump into him?'

Kelsey pursed her lips for a second. 'I've got a better idea. Are you free for dinner tonight?'

'Maybe. Yes. It depends.'

'Dinner with me, Van and Cardova?'

Vadhi's eyes widened. 'You would do that for me? Thanks, boss. Absolutely; I'll be there. What should I wear?'

'Something casual. Don't let on how much you fancy him. And, be prepared for arguments; Van and I aren't getting along very well.'

'Why not?'

'He's fed up being stuck in bed all day, and it's making him irritable. Though, keep that to yourself, alright?'

'Sure thing, boss.'

A Brigade officer strode over. 'There's been a change of plan,' he said. 'I've asked Halfclaw to begin a more detailed survey of the cliffs he found yesterday.'

'Aye?' said Kelsey. 'How come?'

'According to the geologists, there might be iron deposits there.'

'And if there are? Those cliffs are fifty miles away.'

'There's talk of setting up a remote mining station, surrounded by walls, with the dragons ferrying workers and materials back and forth.'

'You are assuming rather a lot, Colonel,' said Frostback. 'We are not beasts of burden.'

The Brigade officer bowed low in front of the dragon. 'We would not do anything without your complete agreement, of course. We are all very grateful for everything you do for us.'

'That's better,' said the dragon.

'That reminds me,' said the colonel; 'I need to show you some plans that have been drawn up.'

'Plans for what?' said Frostback.

'A type of wooden carriage, that can be carried by a dragon. We're working on a few prototypes at the moment. Each carriage would be able to fit eight humans, or a mixture of humans and cargo. The Crown approved the budget for it a couple of days ago.'

Frostback looked less than impressed, but said nothing.

'Shall we go?' said Kelsey.

'Yes,' said the dragon, 'before the colonel decides to deliver some more surprises.'

Kelsey clambered up the ropes to the dragon's shoulders, and strapped herself into the harness. The officer and the crew took a few steps back, and Frostback rose into the air. Kelsey smiled as she glanced around. Sometimes, she was convinced that she had the best job in the world.

The rest of the morning passed quickly, with Frostback keeping the greenhides away from the area where the Brigades were working. Trenches for wall foundations were being dug, and the stumps of the burned and broken trees were being loaded onto the backs of wagons. The greenhides had slowly learned to be wary of the region around the walls of Jezra, but several dozen still tried to break through to where the workers were toiling in the winter cold. Every time they charged, Frostback would send them screaming back down the slopes, leaving many dead and smouldering on the ground.

Halfclaw was sighted at noon, but instead of returning to Lower Jezra, he turned straight for Frostback, and the two dragons circled over the forest.

'Did you find iron?' said the silver dragon.

'I did not,' said Halfclaw; 'I found something else; something that you need to see for yourself.'

'Let me escort the workers back to safety first,' said Frostback, 'and then we shall take a look.'

Most of the Brigade workers had already passed back through the gates in the high town walls, and Frostback hovered over the stragglers until they were all through. As soon as the gates were closed, she ascended back up to where Halfclaw was waiting, and they soared to the west, crossing the vast forestland beneath them. The land was high and flat, with a few ridges and valleys. They crossed a river that tumbled down a rocky slope, where hundreds of greenhides were drinking, then veered a little to sunward. The miles rolled by, and Kelsey was staggered at the sheer size of the forest. Everywhere she looked, there was nothing but trees, interspersed with a few barren hill-tops. She frowned, as she noticed a large clearing in the distance.

'What's that?' she said.

'That's the base of the ridge I was investigating,' said Halfclaw. 'Do you see the line of cliffs above it? Keep your eyes on that.'

Kelsey squinted as they got closer to the ridge. It looked like someone had dropped a wall of rock into the middle of the forest. It stretched for over a mile, and was at least two hundred feet high. Nothing grew on its steep sides, and the area below it was barren and scrubby. Kelsey looked closer, and saw greenhides, masses of them, scuttling around at the base of the cliffs. They seemed to be spilling out from a series of dark holes along the side of the ridge. The two dragons descended to get a closer look. Hundreds of greenhides began shrieking as they noticed the dragons' approach, and the noise rose up to echo off the rocks of the cliffs. Some of the beasts were scurrying into the dark holes, while others were still coming out.

'Pyre's sweaty armpits,' Kelsey muttered. 'Look how many there are. Why are they going into the cliffside?'

'It's a nest,' said Halfclaw. 'We've found it.'

'Are you serious?'

'I think so. I have examined every yard of the ridge, and there are entrance holes on this side only. For all we know, the nest could extend for miles under the cliffs.'

'Does that mean that there's a queen down there, somewhere? Have you seen it?'

'No, but this is the first greenhide nest I have come across. I imagine that the queen stays underground.'

'We could try a little experiment,' said Frostback.

'Such as?' said Kelsey.

'Perhaps we could send some fire into those cavern holes. If thousands of greenhides rush out, then we'll know for sure that it's a nest.'

'I concur,' said Halfclaw. 'You go left, and I'll go right.'

The two dragons separated, and Kelsey clung onto the harness rail as Frostback banked. The silver dragon turned to sunward, then swept back round, opened her jaws, and unleashed a fiery torrent of flames at the dark openings marking the cliffside, while Halfclaw did the same thing from the iceward end. The effect was immediate. Within seconds, greenhides were streaming out of every dark entrance along the ridge in their thousands, each screaming and shrieking their anger at their assailants. Dozens were incinerated in the flames, but still they came, pouring out of the holes and spreading along the base of the ridge. Kelsey watched, her eyes wide at the sight. The ground trembled, and an enormous greenhide, five or six times larger than the others, crawled out into the open air. Its skin was pale, as if it had never glimpsed the sunlight, and it had long talons at the end of each limb. It pulled itself out of the ground, sending streams of earth and stones sliding down the ridge, and shrieked at the dragons, who pulled up to a safe altitude.

Kelsey stared down at the grotesque abomination below them. The creature's face was tilted upwards, and its insect-like eyes were gleaming with a savage fury. It bellowed its hatred up towards the dragons.

'Let's go back to Jezra,' said Kelsey, staring at the beast; 'just looking at that thing is making me feel queasy.'

***

The sun was setting as Kelsey and Vadhi walked along the streets of Jezra towards the harbour. Gulls were squawking over the long quay-side, and hovering above the fishing vessels that were coming in to berth.

'Captain Cardova definitely isn't going to bring someone else along to dinner, is he?' said Vadhi. 'Are you sure?'

'As sure as I can be, Vadhi,' said Kelsey.

'Will he be annoyed that you invited me without asking first?'

'If he is, then that just tells you what kind of guy he is. Look, don't get your hopes up too much; I don't think he's looking for a relationship with anyone at the moment. Try to treat this evening as an opportunity to get to know him a bit better.'

Vadhi nodded, but Kelsey could tell from her eyes that she was nervous.

'I didn't see you in the Common Rooms after work,' Vadhi said.

'No, I had to visit the Brigade Headquarters, to pass on some news about today. After that, I had to go straight home to wash and change.'

They reached the Banner Command Post, and the soldiers on duty waved them through the front doors. Lady Mona was coming out of a side door as Kelsey and Vadhi entered the building.

'Ah, Miss Holdfast,' the demigod said, her long white gown shimmering in the light. 'I was hoping to find you. I was up visiting Major-General Logos earlier, with some of the finds from under the ancient library. It's all very fascinating, and should give the Academy something to dig its teeth into.'

'Hi, Mona,' said Kelsey. 'Happy month-name, if that's a thing.'

'It isn't, luckily. But, thank you all the same. I confess that I often completely forget that I have a month named after me.'

'Does it make the other demigods jealous?'

'I wouldn't imagine so,' said Mona, 'though Naxor used to tease me about it. Come round to my office here when you have a spare moment, and I'd be happy to go over some of our findings from the excavations.'

'Maybe tomorrow? We have a dinner appointment.'

'Then, I shan't keep you any longer. Have a lovely evening.'

Kelsey smiled, and Mona strode away down the hallway.

'She has a month named after her?' whispered Vadhi.

'Aye. This is Monan, and she's Mona.'

'Wow. Are all the months named after gods?'

'Aye, but only three of the twelve months are named after gods that are still alive – Mona, Montieth, and Amalia; the rest are all dead.'

They climbed the stairs to Van's apartment, and the guards nodded when they saw Kelsey, and opened the door for them. Cardova was lounging on a couch, with his feet up on the table, reading a book. He glanced over the pages, and smiled.

'You came,' he said, swinging his feet back to the floor; 'and you brought a friend. Vadhi, was it?'

'Yes,' said Vadhi, her face flushing.

'How is life in Frostback's crew? I mean, apart from having such a terrible boss. I hear that Kelsey Holdfast is a nightmare to work for.'

'Ha ha,' said Kelsey. 'What are you reading?'

'Chancellor Mona was here earlier, and she brought round a load of books for Van to read. I purloined this one.' He glanced at the spine. '*The Building of the Great Wall*.'

'Any good?'

He shrugged.

'How's Van?'

He shrugged again.

'I'll check on him before dinner; you can entertain Vadhi.'

She walked to the bedroom door and let herself in. Van was sitting up in his bed with a face like thunder, a dozen books littering the blankets around him.

'Evening, Van.'

Van grunted back at her.

'We found a greenhide nest. *The* greenhide nest. It's fifty miles from here, so it must be the one that all of the greenhides are coming from.'

He stared at her. 'You found it?'

'Well, Halfclaw found it. He guided Frostback and me there, and we saw it with our own eyes. We also saw the queen.'

'I hesitate to call you a liar, but I doubt that you saw the queen.'

'Why?'

'How big was it?'

'As tall as a tree; it was massive. It came wriggling its way out of a tunnel entrance and shrieked up at us. Apart from you, I've never seen anything so ugly in my life.'

'It sounds like a baby queen.'

'A *baby* queen?'

'Yes. The real queen will be so large, that she would completely destroy the nest if she emerged into daylight. Most queens keep a retinue of younger queens in their nests; when they're old enough, they fly away and form a new nest.'

'Those bastards can fly?'

'Only for a single, short period of their lives. Their wings fall off after that, I think. Hang on, Lucius is the expert on this.' He turned to the door. 'Lucius!'

The door opened, and Cardova walked in, Vadhi trailing him.

'Yes, sir?'

'They found the nest.'

Cardova glanced at Kelsey. 'How far away is it?'

'About fifty miles.'

'They also saw a baby queen,' Van went on.

'Yeah?' said Cardova. 'Did the dragons attack the entrance of this nest?'

'Aye, with a ton of fire.'

Cardova nodded. 'That will explain it. Often, a queen will have one of her juniors stationed close to an entrance in case of attack.'

'Tell her about their wings; I forget the details.'

'Sure.' Cardova sat on a chair by the bed. 'By the way, sir, this is Vadhi.'

'Hello, Vadhi.'

'You met her one night a while back,' Cardova went on; 'she's in Frostback's crew. The new girl. Anyway, junior queens usually stay in their mother's nest for thirty-odd years, then they start to grow their wings. At that point, the main queen starts to see them as a threat to her rule, and kicks them out of the nest. The juniors fly off, find a suitable location, and start their own nest. However, on this world, as there is no space for any more nests, I imagine that the juniors are all killed by their mothers, until, eventually, one of those juniors is too strong, and defeats her, becoming the new queen in her place.' He grinned. 'See? All those years at college weren't wasted; well, not completely. And it was only one year, technically.'

'And,' said Kelsey, 'what happens to their wings?'

'They fall off, and the new queen eats them.'

'Eww.'

'No one ever said they were charming creatures.' He rubbed his hands together. 'A nest, eh?'

Van gestured for Vadhi to sit down. 'The captain here has experience of destroying a nest.'

'Is that right?' said Kelsey.

'Yes,' said Cardova, 'though, needless to say, I was hardly alone. It was on Dragon Eyre. We cleared the island of the soldier-types first; we sat offshore on a fleet of ships and bombarded them for days before we landed. After that, we dropped tons of flammable tar down the entrance hole of the nest, lit it, then stood well back. It was still smoking when we happened to sail by ten days later.'

'I want you to come up with a plan, Lucius, for getting rid of this one,' said Van. 'If we can knock it out, then in a decade, we'll be able to extend the walls of Jezra for miles, without any fear of being attacked. In fact, we'd have peace on both sides of the City.'

Cardova leaned forward, resting his elbows on his knees. 'I'll think of something, sir.' He glanced at Kelsey and Vadhi. 'Naturally, it'll involve dragons.'

'I thought it might,' said Kelsey.

'Send Cuidrach a message in the morning, Lucius, to let them know,' said Van. He seemed to brighten up. 'This is good news. Well done, the dragon team. Please deliver a live goat to Halfclaw as a token of my appreciation.'

'Will do, sir,' said Cardova. He glanced at Vadhi. 'Do you want to help me set the table? A porter should be arriving with our dinner soon.'

'Absolutely,' said Vadhi, getting to her feet.

Van watched them leave the room, then turned to Kelsey. 'I'd like you to ask first before you bring guests round.'

'Vadhi's nice; I like her.'

'I'm sure she's wonderful, but don't I get a say? This is not a tavern; it's my bedroom.'

'I didn't think you'd mind. But, I take your point. I'll ask next time.'

Van opened his mouth to speak, then closed it again, his eyes catching Kelsey's glance.

'I know I've been a right pain in the ass these last few days,' he said. 'I hate being powerless, and feeling weak. It's stupid, but nothing bothers me more than lying around doing nothing. My mind can't handle inactivity; I need to be busy. Every time I got into trouble on Implacatus, it was because I was idle; waiting around in between operations.' He paused. 'The next thing I say is going to annoy you, but here goes – I'm starting work tomorrow. Don't say anything. At first, I'll just do a couple of hours a day, to ease myself back in.'

Kelsey said nothing.

'If you know me, Kelsey,' he went on, 'then you'll understand that this is what I need.'

'Alright.'

Van frowned. 'Is that it? No lectures about how stupid I'm being? No calling me a "numpty?"'

'You are a numpty,' she said. 'I have one condition.'

'Oh yeah? Let's hear it.'

She leaned in, and kissed him. 'I want to move in.'

'What? I mean, yes; but why? Why now?'

'I practically live here anyway. It's time.'

He smiled. 'So, is this it? Are we actually starting a relationship?'

'Don't over-analyse it, Van,' she said, a slight smirk on her lips. 'Let's just say that you've grown on me, for a numpty.'

CHAPTER 10

BEST LAID PLANS

Pella, Auldan, The City – 6th Monan 3422

Pella, Auldan, The City – 6th Monan 3422

The two women walked through the carefully-tended gardens, their squad of guards remaining a few paces behind them. The sun had not long risen, and the sky was a deep red.

'It's nice to get out of my new rooms,' said Rosie.

'Are they comfortable?' said Emily.

'Yes. The rooms are great; a big improvement on my quarters in the Bulwark, and I have tall windows, from where I can look out over Pella; but I do miss getting outside.'

Emily nodded. They paused for a moment so that Emily could check the progress of her new rose garden.

'I am sorry, you know,' Emily said, her breath misting in front of her face. 'I realise that being confined to your rooms must make you feel like a prisoner. And that's not fair, because you've done nothing wrong.'

'I understand, your Majesty. I don't like it, but I understand.'

'Everything should become clearer today,' Emily said, 'once the dragons have been, though I admit I'm a little nervous about the whole thing. Deathfang hasn't visited the City since Tarsnow was killed.'

'I haven't even seen a dragon since Blackrose left,' said Rosie. 'I'm looking forward to it.'

'Remember that these dragons are a little less... sophisticated than Blackrose; though, for Malik's sake, don't tell them I said that. Frostback and Halfclaw are the friendliest, but I'm not sure if they're even speaking to Deathfang and the others in the colony over in the Eastern Mountains. We'll have to be very careful, very diplomatic, when they get here. One wrong word, and their pride will take over.'

Rosie narrowed her eyes. 'Are you sure you want me at this meeting, your Majesty?'

'Yes. They know Maddie, so you being there might help with things. Also, I want you to be closely involved with the expedition to survey the salve mine; after all, you have already been there. Is that something you would be willing to do?'

'You mean, you want me to actually go back to the mountains?'

'Just for a little while. Once the location has been mapped, and the route charted, then we can take another look at your situation. What do you think?'

'Alright. Who else will be going?'

'That brings us to our little walk this morning, Rosie. I have been giving a lot of careful consideration to the make-up of a small team. There will be you, naturally, and also the two sergeants that Quill assigned to look after you.'

Rosie glanced over her shoulder at the squad of soldiers following them. Among the group, were two veteran Reaper sergeants from the Royal Guard.

'My shadows?' Rosie said.

Emily smiled. 'Yes. Is that fine with you?'

'Darvi's alright; he's a good laugh, but Inmara treats me like I'm her wayward daughter.'

'Her heart's in the right place. She's one of my most experienced sergeants.'

'She needs to remember that I'm eighteen, not fourteen. Who else?'

'I've found a cartographer from the Banner of the Lostwell Exiles,' Emily said. 'He's surveyed maps for the Banner before, so I think he will be useful. He's a lieutenant.'

'Will he be in charge?'

'No. I have someone else in mind for that role.'

They reached a crossroads in the gardens, their winter boots crunching off the frost-bound gravel. To their left was a brightly-painted gardener's cottage, a small, one-storey building nestled amid a stand of cedar trees.

'Will I know this person?' said Rosie.

'You will certainly know of them. In fact, I think you might have met, when everyone gathered to say goodbye to Corthie, Blackrose and your sister.'

They took the path towards the cottage.

'She's living in here, for the moment,' Emily said.

'She?'

'Yes.' They paused by the front door. 'I'm going to tell you who it is before we go in. Don't be alarmed. I know that the Bulwark has been filled with rumour and speculation, but I am of the opinion that Lady Jade is misunderstood.'

Rosie's mouth fell open. 'Jade? Please tell me that this is a joke, your Majesty.'

'It's not a joke. You might not have heard, but Lady Jade resigned from her position as Commander of the Bulwark a couple of days ago.'

'Thank Malik for that; she was an utter disaster.'

'And yet, I have appointed her to lead the expedition to locate and survey the salve mine. I am going to ask you to be kind, Rosie. Lady Jade has been badly hurt by her experiences. Some of this is my fault. I thought that she would grow into the role as commander, but some people are simply not suited for such administrative roles.'

'Has she accepted this new position?'

'She doesn't know about it yet. That is why we are here.'

Emily knocked on the door, and pushed it open.

'Jade?' she called out.

'We're in here, your Majesty,' came a voice from the room to the right.

Emily and Rosie entered the cottage, and closed the door. They took off their winter coats and went into a small kitchen, where Jade was sitting at a table, her eyes red. Across from her sat Lady Silva, who was keeping half an eye on Jade.

'Your Majesty,' said Silva, rising to her feet and bowing.

'Good morning, Silva; good morning, Jade,' said the Queen. 'I've brought someone with me – Rosie Jackdaw, Maddie's younger sister.'

'How do you do, Miss Jackdaw?' said Silva. 'I have made some mulled wine; would you like some?'

'Yes, please,' said Rosie.

'Thank you,' said Emily, taking a seat.

Jade said nothing, her gaze fixed on the surface of the table.

'How are you finding the cottage, Jade?' said Emily, as Silva prepared the wine. 'Rosie, please sit.'

Jade didn't respond.

Rosie sat down, her eyes wary as she glanced at the sullen demigod.

'I have a few things to say,' Emily went on, 'and I need you to listen to me, Jade. Are you listening?'

Jade slowly turned her face towards the Queen. 'Are you going to arrest me?'

'Of course not,' said Emily, her eyebrows crinkling. 'Whatever gave you that idea?'

'Everyone hates me.'

'That's not true. I certainly don't hate you.'

'You set me up to fail. You humiliated me. You wanted me to fail, didn't you? You hate the Blades, and you were using me to bring them down.'

'That rumour has no truth to it, Jade. I wanted you to succeed, and I still have faith in you.'

Silva returned to the table and set down four mugs of mulled wine.

'That's what I've been telling her, your Majesty,' she said, sitting. A ginger cat leapt up onto her knee. Silva frowned and raised her hand to push it off, but stopped when Jade glared at her.

'You have cats here?' said Rosie.

Jade stared at her. 'They're mine. They hated the journey from the

Bulwark. I had to lock them up in little cages and put them onto a wagon. They cried the whole way. If you are mean to them, I will kill you.'

'I'm not going to be mean to them; I like cats.'

Jade narrowed her eyes, as if trying to detect if Rosie was lying.

'Let's not threaten to kill anyone,' said Emily. 'I want to return to the things I need to say. Firstly, Jade, and this is official, but you are not being blamed for anything that occurred in the Bulwark. That slate is being wiped clean. Adjutant Quill has sent in a full report, and she held you to be blameless for the riot that resulted in the sacking of the Fortress of the Lifegiver. On the contrary, Quill stated that you behaved with admirable restraint, under severe provocation. Secondly, with regret, we accept your resignation.'

Jade frowned. 'Quill said nice things about me?'

'Yes. Quill is a good soldier, one of my best, and I trust her judgement. I now need to ask you, Jade, if you are willing to take on another role for the City. I have an important position that needs filled, and I can think of no one who is better suited.'

'Why would you want me?' said Jade. 'I've failed at everything.'

'That's not true. Do you remember when you first pledged your allegiance to me?'

'Yes. Yendra forced me to do it.'

'I know. But, since that day, you have shown me nothing but loyalty. When the greenhides broke through the Middle Walls, you could have fled, but you didn't. You saved my life that day, and the lives of many others. I do not forget these things, Jade; I will never forget them. Everyone makes mistakes. Perhaps I made a mistake in placing you into a role that did not suit your talents. If so, then I apologise to you. I also apologise for asking you to question your own father. I put you in a difficult position, and yet you obeyed my orders without question. Thank you. Yendra had faith in you, Jade, and so do I. Are you ready to try again?'

'I don't know,' said Jade. 'I can't think of anything I'm good at, except for killing greenhides. What if I make a mess of it?'

'Let me tell you about the role first,' said Emily, 'and then you can decide. However, what I am about to say is a secret, and must not be spread around; at least, not yet. Silva, the same applies to you, naturally.'

'Of course, your Majesty.'

'Right. You are aware that the City has run out of salve? Well, that might not be strictly accurate. Within the Eastern Mountains a couple of years ago, Blackrose, Maddie, and Rosie, made a discovery. It appears that there is a very large deposit of salve in the mountains.'

Silva gasped, and put a hand to her mouth.

Emily nodded. 'I see that you grasp the significance of this. It is, in fact, the worst news possible. If there were no salve, then we would cease being a target for the Ascendants. However, that is immaterial, and we have to accept reality as it is, not as we would wish it to be. Jade, I want you to lead a team to the mountains, under the strictest secrecy, to chart and examine the new mine. You will be required to liaise with the dragons, whose colony exists in the same mountain range. This is unavoidable, for we need the dragons to transport the team to the mountains. I have arranged for the dragons to visit Cuidrach Palace this afternoon, to discuss the practical arrangements. As of this moment, they too are unaware of the existence of the new salve deposit. I will tell them all about it, as there is no point in trying to deceive dragons. Their agreement will be necessary.'

'They might say no,' said Rosie. 'What will we do if that happens?'

'If Deathfang says no, then we can appeal directly to Halfclaw and Frostback. However, that is a road paved with potential danger, as I would not be eager to drive a wedge between the two groups. Let us all hope that Deathfang says yes.'

'If my father discovers that there is more salve,' said Jade, 'then he will try to escape.'

Emily frowned. 'Hasn't he tried already?'

'No. Not seriously. He doesn't see the point, as he believes that his days of experimenting with salve are over. Once he learns that there is more, then his spirit will be reinvigorated. And what about the God-Queen? What if she learns the truth?'

'What do you mean?' said Rosie. 'What's the God-Queen got to do with anything?'

'Time to reveal another secret,' said Emily. 'The God-Queen has returned to the City, Rosie. That's why Naxor was arrested, because he had been hiding that knowledge.'

Rosie stared at her. 'Malik's ass. The God-Queen is back? Where is she?'

'We don't know. She's been using a substance known as anti-salve to mask her powers from us. So far, she hasn't made any aggressive moves, but we believe that it is only a matter of time.'

'Are you looking for her?'

'Of course. Lord Salvor has been spending his days doing little else.'

'But, doesn't she only have one arm? That's what I heard.'

'Kelsey Holdfast is the most recent person to see her, and she has informed me that her arm has grown back. Indubitably, she will have taken other steps to hide her appearance, such as dosing herself with salve to look younger, or older. If she has the same abilities as Montieth, then she might look like a little old lady, or even as a young teenager; we simply have no idea.'

'She wasn't in Alea Tanton when Lostwell was destroyed,' said Silva, 'and Lady Amber has confirmed that she is in possession of a Quadrant.'

'That means she might have been hiding in the City for quite some time,' said Emily, 'longer than the Exiles have been here. She will probably be living under an alias, buried deep out of sight.'

'If she has a Quadrant,' said Rosie, 'and she finds out about the salve…'

'Indeed,' said Emily. 'That remains my greatest fear. What would Amalia do to regain control? Would she sell us out to the Ascendants – offer them salve in return for military assistance? I believe she would. That is why it is critical to keep a veil of secrecy over the entire operation.'

'Why don't we destroy the mine when we find it?' said Jade.

'That thought has occurred to me also,' said Emily. 'Can dragon fire destroy salve? Or, at least, render it unusable? What if the mountains are riddled with salve deposits? It might be a coincidence that the very valley chosen by Blackrose contained salve, or it might be that salve is common. This is another thing that I need you to find out, Jade, if you are willing to take on this new role.'

'Will I be in charge of the expedition?'

'Yes, Jade. You will have Rosie, a pair of Reaper sergeants from the Royal Guard, and a Banner cartographer.'

'That's a very small team.'

'I know. The numbers will be kept small to reduce the chance that the secret gets out. The two sergeants, and the cartographer, have not yet been told the true extent of the operation. You will tell them on the journey there, and not a minute before. You will take enough supplies to cover a month, but the expedition might not last as long as that.'

'Who will look after my cats?'

'I'll find a trooper who loves animals, and place them here in this cottage. Their entire job will revolve around caring for them.'

The door to the kitchen opened, and a soldier peered into the room.

'Apologies for disturbing you, your Majesty, but Captain Cardova from the Banner has arrived off the first boat from Jezra. He says that he has an urgent matter to discuss with you.'

Emily narrowed her eyes. 'How urgent?'

'He didn't say, exactly, ma'am.'

'Is he outside the cottage?'

'Yes, ma'am. Shall I tell him to wait in the palace?'

'No, send him in. I'd better hear his news right away.'

'Yes, ma'am.'

Emily turned to the others as soon as the soldier had disappeared. 'Not a word of what we've been discussing, alright?'

The door opened again, and Cardova entered, a smile on his lips. He bowed.

'Your Majesty. Good morning, all. Thank you for seeing me at short notice.'

'Everyone,' said Emily, 'this is Captain Cardova, Major-General Logos' aide. How is Van doing?'

'He's getting there, ma'am; slowly. Kelsey Holdfast has been a rock.'

'Good. Now, your news?'

'Yes, ma'am. We have located the western greenhide nest. I've been working on a plan all night, and it needs royal assent.'

'I see. That's very good news, Captain. Does your plan involve dragons?'

He smiled. 'It does indeed, ma'am.'

'Were you aware that I summoned Halfclaw and Frostback to the palace today?'

'Eh, no, ma'am. I didn't see any summons before I left Jezra.'

'I have not long asked Lord Salvor to send a message to them. It probably arrived while you were crossing the Straits. Do you have a copy of your plan with you?'

He reached behind his armour and withdrew a rolled-up document.

She took it. 'Thank you, Captain. Please go to the palace and await me there; I need to finish this present discussion before I can turn my full attention to the nest.'

Cardova saluted, then left the cottage.

'He's Banner?' said Rosie. 'He's almost as tall as Corthie.'

'Captain Cardova is an extremely competent officer.'

Rosie grinned. 'I'm sure he is.'

'Try to remain focussed, Rosie.' She tucked the captain's plan into her robes.

'I'll do it,' said Jade. 'I'll lead the expedition, if the dragons agree.'

'Thank you, Jade. I'll leave Rosie here with you, so that you can get to know each other.' She stood. 'I'll expect to see you all on the palace roof when the dragons arrive in a few hours.'

Silva and Rosie bowed, while Jade kept her glance down.

Emily smiled, then left the cottage.

The Queen spent the next two hours going over the plan to destroy the nest with Captain Cardova in the palace. The captain was easy to get on with, and she learned through him that Kelsey had moved in with Van in Jezra, a fact which pleased Emily.

They had just finished lunch, when they were informed that Frostback and Halfclaw had arrived. They made their way up to the roof, after sending a messenger to Jade's cottage to let them know.

Up on the roof, Kelsey was standing, talking to the two dragons, who had landed onto the flat, open space. Her eyes did a double-take when she saw Cardova walking by Emily's side.

'I can't seem to get away from you, Lucius,' she smirked. 'Are you following me?'

He laughed. 'Stalking would be a more accurate term.'

'How did you get on with Vadhi last night?'

'Who's Vadhi?' said Emily.

'She's in Frostback's crew,' said Cardova, 'and I got on well with her, thank you very much. Nothing happened, though, so you can forget about hearing any gossip.'

Kelsey frowned. 'Do you not like her?'

'I like her,' he said, 'but I'm not interested in getting involved with anyone. Remember that, the next time you think about trying to set me up.'

The silver dragon lowered her head. 'Kelsey loves to interfere in the lives of others.'

'I do not,' Kelsey said.

'Then, why do you do it?' said Frostback. She turned to the Queen. 'I assume that you have asked us here because of the nest that Halfclaw found yesterday?'

'Partly,' said Emily, 'although the truth is that I summoned you before I even knew about the nest. Your father is arriving soon, Frostback. He asked that you be here. Now, I understand if you don't want to see him, and you are free to return to Jezra if that is the case.'

'Deathfang is coming?' said Halfclaw, his eyes gleaming.

'Yes. He asked that you also be present,' said the Queen.

'Why is he coming here?' said Frostback.

'Burntskull visited Icehaven a few days ago, and passed on a message from your father. I think he wants to discuss how the City and the dragons can be of mutual assistance to each other.'

Halfclaw tilted his head, as if amused. 'I see. It took two winters in those leaky caverns for them to see some sense on this matter.'

'Deathfang proposed this some time ago,' said Frostback, 'but the others disagreed. It was one of the reasons we had to leave the colony in the mountains. It is good news indeed, if the others have finally changed their minds.'

'Do you think he wants a reconciliation?' said Kelsey.

'I hope so,' said Frostback. 'We have gone too long without speaking to each other. However, no matter what happens, I shall not be leaving Jezra.'

'It cheers me to hear that,' said Emily.

'And me,' said Cardova. 'Frostback and Halfclaw are the true heroes of Jezra. We would have accomplished very little without them.'

'I appreciate that comment,' said Halfclaw. 'I, too, shall stay.'

'Actually, Halfclaw,' said the Queen; 'I may have a special job for you, one that might take you away from Jezra, but only for a few days.'

Cardova nodded towards the stairwell, and Emily turned to see Jade and Rosie emerge onto the roof, followed by the two Reaper sergeants, who remained by the stairs.

'Thank you for coming,' said the Queen. 'Everyone, you all know Lady Jade, of course. With her is Rosie Jackdaw. Rosie, this is Frostback and Halfclaw, and this is Kelsey Holdfast, Corthie's sister.'

Rosie's eyes went from the dragons to Kelsey. She frowned. 'You don't look anything like Corthie.'

'Thank Pyre for that,' said Kelsey. 'Are you Maddie's sister?'

'Yeah. How did you know?'

'I can tell from your face. What are you doing here? Are you looking to follow in your sister's footsteps?'

'No. I'm here because, well, I can't say.'

'All will become clear soon,' said the Queen. She glanced up, and saw two dark specks approaching in the pink sky. She took a breath. 'Here they come.'

Frostback and Halfclaw moved to the side of the wide roof to clear a space, and the others gathered by their gigantic forelimbs.

Cardova nudged Kelsey. 'Why are you and Corthie so dissimilar? Do you have different fathers?'

'No. My mother was Holdings, which is what I look like, but my father was a Kellach Brigdomin, who are all pale-skinned and tall. A bit like you, in fact. You could actually pass for a Kellach on my world. Why are you so tall?'

He shrugged. 'My little brother's even taller.'

Emily turned from them to watch Deathfang and Burntskull descend. The enormous grey dragon landed first, then pulled in his wings while the smaller form of Burntskull touched down next to him. The roof trembled under the weight of four dragons and, for a moment, no one spoke.

Emily stepped forward. 'Welcome back to Pella, Deathfang, Burntskull. I am truly delighted that you have seen fit to re-establish a line of communication between us.'

Deathfang tilted his great head. 'Queen. It has indeed been too long. However, it has taken time for the dragons in the mountain colony to reach a consensus.' He turned to face his daughter. 'Frostback, my heart is gladdened by the sight of you. How have you fared, daughter?'

'Very well, father,' she said. 'I have missed you, but Halfclaw and I have been busy, assisting the humans to expand their territories on the Western Bank.'

Deathfang turned to Halfclaw. 'I hope you have been treating my daughter with the respect she deserves.'

'He has behaved most honourably,' said Frostback. 'I am very pleased with him.'

'Good,' said Deathfang. He noticed Kelsey. 'And you, my daughter's rider, I also hope that you are well. My debt of gratitude to you burns as brightly within my heart as it ever did.' He glanced at the three other humans. 'I do not know you, although this tall one is a Banner soldier; this other one has the air of a god or demigod about her; and this last one reminds me of Maddie Jackdaw.'

'I'm her sister,' said Rosie.

'This cannot be a coincidence,' said Burntskull. 'What plans have you been cooking up, Queen?'

'I'll get to that,' said Emily. 'You were correct in your assumptions, Deathfang. This is Lady Jade, and the Banner officer is Captain Cardova. Now, I would like to hear what you and Deathfang propose.'

'Very well,' said the grey dragon. 'I shall speak first. The colony that we have established is in a wonderful location, with fresh water, and easy access to the hunting grounds on the higher slopes of the mountains. It is perfect in almost every regard, but, as Frostback and Halfclaw know, it remains cramped, and is prone to leaking. During the recent months of Sweetmist, the caverns flooded, and we had to spend many miserable days and nights exposed to the winds, rain and storms. We wish to ask if you could spare a company of human workers, equipped with all manner of the tools that your kind use. The caverns need to be extended, and made water-proof, and I also require the excavation of a series of tunnels to link the various living spaces. Is this something that you could do for us, Queen?'

'Yes.'

Deathfang looked wary. 'You do not wish to negotiate first?'

'There's no need. I agree to your request, without any conditions attached. I can have workers sent there at your convenience, and the work will be completed by the start of Freshmist. I cannot bear the thought of your little ones shivering in the cold and wet for another rainy season.'

'You are too kind, Queen; thank you.'

'It is easy to make promises,' said Burntskull, 'but these are just words. How will the workers and materials be transported from the City to the mountains?'

'We are currently constructing a new type of carriage,' said Emily;

'one designed to be carried by a dragon. Each carriage will be able to hold several workers, and their tools and supplies.'

'What, and you just happened to be building these?' said Burntskull. 'Is this another coincidence?'

'No. I ordered them to be made when I heard you were coming. I was able to anticipate your request, as Frostback had already made me aware that you might require workers. I also intend to use one of these carriages to transport Rosie Jackdaw and Lady Jade to the mountains.' She glanced around at the faces of those gathered on the roof. 'Half-claw, would you be willing to take this carriage to the Eastern Mountains?'

The green dragon lowered his head. 'To what end, Queen?'

'Do you wish to tell them, Rosie?'

The young Jackdaw woman gazed up at the dragons. 'There are salve deposits in those mountains. I know, because I saw one.'

'Salve deposits?' said Cardova.

'That's right, Captain,' said Emily. 'You can let Van know of this, but it must not go any further. I am trusting each one of you to keep this a secret.'

'So, this is the real reason we are all here?' said Kelsey. 'We found salve, *and* a greenhide nest? Pyre's arse.'

'Pyre's arse, indeed, Kelsey,' said the Queen.

Cardova laughed.

'Please don't say that,' said Kelsey. 'Only I get to say that.'

'Let me see if I understand this,' said Deathfang. 'Firstly, you have found salve in the same mountains as our colony?'

'Yes,' said Emily. 'We're not sure where it is exactly in relation to the colony, but we'll discover that when the survey team arrives.'

'I'm in charge of that team,' said Jade; 'and I would like to see this colony.'

'Are you a demigod?' said Burntskull.

'I am. I would show you, but Kelsey Holdfast is blocking my powers.'

'I'm sure we can arrange a visit,' said Deathfang. 'Secondly, you also found a new greenhide nest? Where?'

'An hour's flight to the west of Jezra,' said Halfclaw. 'We're going to destroy it.'

'Captain Cardova has a plan for this,' said Emily.

Deathfang's eyes blazed. 'Why didn't you use this to bargain, Queen? A skilled negotiator would have demanded assistance in dealing with this nest in exchange for sending workers. If I refuse to help, will you still send us aid?'

'Of course. I said that my help was unconditional, and I meant it. If you decide to help us destroy the nest, then I would be grateful, but you are not under any obligation to do so.'

Burntskull tilted his head a fraction. 'You have more pride than the average insect, Queen.'

'Don't call me an insect; at least, not to my face.'

'She's right,' said Deathfang; 'show her more manners, Burntskull. Queen, I will take your words back to the colony. If everything goes well, then one of us shall return in a few days to arrange the transportation of the workers and their supplies.'

'Thank you.'

'Daughter,' Deathfang went on, 'it has made me happy to see you again. I assume, however, that you will not be returning with us to the mountains?'

'Would I be welcome there, father?'

'You would be welcomed by me.'

'But not the others? I see. Thank you, but I will stay here. I do hope that I will see you more often from now on, though.'

'I'm sure we will. Farewell, all.'

The enormous dragon extended his wings and lifted into the sky, and Emily shielded her eyes from the gust of air. Burntskull ascended a moment later, and the two dragons soared off into the east.

'That seemed to go well,' said Rosie.

'I think so,' said Emily. 'However, we have yet to hear if Halfclaw is willing to transport Lady Jade's team to the mountains.'

'I will do it,' said the green dragon, 'but I also want to be involved in the plan to destroy the nest. After all, it was I who found it.'

'I'm sure that can be arranged,' said Emily. 'I will send a message when the first of the new carriages is ready to be tested.'

'Then,' said Frostback, 'if this meeting is concluded, we shall return to Jezra. Lucius, do you wish me to carry you there?'

'If the Queen is prepared to release me?'

'Of course,' said Emily. 'We will discuss your plan again soon, but for now, carry on with the arrangements.'

Cardova bowed, then he and Kelsey clambered up the harness onto Frostback's shoulders. Emily and the others stood back, and watched as the two dragons took off, and flew away to the west.

Emily, Jade and Rosie headed for the stairs, and descended into the palace.

'Thank you very much for today,' the Queen said, as they walked towards Salvor's office. 'I confess that I'm feeling quite pleased with myself.'

Ahead of them, a door opened, and a soldier ran through. He skidded to a halt in front of the Queen, his eyes wide.

'Your Majesty!'

'Yes?' said Emily, her chest tightening as she braced herself for whatever the soldier was about to say.

'There's been a break out from the palace dungeons, your Majesty,' the soldier said. 'Naxor's gone.'

CHAPTER 11

BLACKMAIL

Port Sanders, Medio, The City – 7th Monan 3422

The fine carriage rolled through the streets of Port Sanders, its wheels still spattered with mud from the countryside.

'I enjoyed that holiday,' Sofia said, as she gazed out of the window, 'but it feels good to be home again.'

Kagan looked up from Maxwell, who was sitting on his knee. 'I think Maxwell liked it too; all that fresh air must have been good for him.'

'I do hope that Gellie has put the heating on in the mansion,' Sofia said. 'I do not want to come back to a cold house.'

'You know what Gellie's like. I'd be willing to put money on her having done every last job on that list you gave her. I've never met anyone more conscientious. Where did you meet her?'

'In Northern Kinell. I was hiding out in a small town called Stoneship, and hired her to look after the house for me. She was so useful, that when I decided to return to the City, I brought her with me.'

'Has she always known your real identity?'

'Yes, but it meant nothing to her at first. In fact, she probably thought I was making it up. Of course, that changed after we arrived here. It was terrible at first; I had nowhere to live, and couldn't get my hands on my money without raising suspicion. Worse, Gellie is Fordian. Can you imagine how hard it was to hide a green-skinned woman in the City? She barely left the tunnels under the Circuit. To say I was relieved when Belinda sent the Exiles here would be an understatement. Do you know that you're a good listener?'

'I've been told that a few times. By Dizzler, mostly.'

Sofia raised an eyebrow. 'That awful thug?'

'I was his second in command for years, and had to listen to him telling me all of his problems. It was one of my main jobs; that, and beating people up. I was his fist.' He laughed. 'Look at me now; I haven't punched anyone in a long time.'

The carriage turned a corner, and entered the street where they lived. It edged along the pavement, then pulled into a lane that ran by the side of the mansion. At the rear were mews and a small courtyard, and a kitchen door led out from the back of the mansion. The carriage came to a halt on the cobbles, their driver jumped down, and the side door was opened.

Kagan emerged first. He held a hand out for Sofia, and she stepped down, Maxwell held over her right shoulder. The kitchen door opened, and Saul, Gellie, and the two Sander nursemaids came outside, and formed a line.

'Welcome home, my lady and lord,' said Gellie.

The servants bowed.

Sofia handed the child to a nursemaid, and they went inside. The kitchen was warm, and several pots were steaming and bubbling. They walked through into the ground floor atrium, and removed their coats.

'The house is lovely and warm, Gellie. Thank you,' said Sofia.

The housekeeper bowed. 'I had the servants up all night to make sure the mansion was comfortable for you, ma'am. Also, a visitor arrived for you early this morning. At dawn, to be precise.'

'A visitor? Who?'

'A Sander merchant by the name of Tanto, ma'am. I told him that you weren't due back until now, and he asked if he could wait. He's currently sitting in the front room.'

Sofia sighed. 'What does he want? I can't be bothered having to deal with people asking for money for their pet political causes. Sometimes, I regret giving that money to the legal fund; it's done nothing but inspire people to come here and beg.'

'He said that he had a business proposition to make, but he wouldn't be drawn on the details.'

'I could see him, if you want,' said Kagan. 'You can go upstairs and relax. I'll fob him off.'

'Would you? Thank you, Kagan. Three hours in a bumpy carriage has worn me out.'

They kissed, then Sofia started to climb the stairs. Gellie gestured towards the front room, and Kagan followed her to the door.

'Let me introduce you,' she said, and then pushed the door open.

A well-dressed man was sitting in a plush armchair, a glass of brandy in his hand, and a crooked smile on his lips.

'Mister Tanto,' said Gellie, 'may I introduce the man of the house, Kagan of Alea Tanton, betrothed to Lady Sofia of the Southern Cape.'

The man remained sitting. 'Where's Sofia?'

'She is resting,' said Gellie, 'after a long journey.'

'It's only a few hours to the Sunward Range. It was hardly a "long journey." I came here to see her, and I'm not leaving until I do.'

Kagan clenched his fists and stepped forward, but Gellie gave him a sharp glare.

'Perhaps if you were to tell me what you wish to discuss with her ladyship?' the housekeeper said. 'Otherwise, I might have to ask you to come back another time.'

The man sighed. 'This is ridiculous. I can't believe I have been reduced to this. Look here, I'm not about to divulge anything to you, but you must ask Sofia to come and see me. Now, you stupid old woman.'

Gellie frowned. 'Alright, Kagan,' she said. 'Throw him out.'

'With pleasure, Gellie.'

'Wait!' cried the man. 'There's no need for violence.'

'You should have thought of that before being so rude,' said Kagan, striding towards him.

The door to the room swung open. Sofia was standing there, her face crinkled with fury.

'Stop, Kagan,' she said. 'Don't throw this man out. Kill him.'

Kagan hesitated. 'What?'

'You heard me, Kagan. He knows. He can't be allowed to leave this mansion alive.'

The man sprang to his feet. 'Come now; is that any way to greet your grandson?'

Gellie pulled out a knife from under her robes, while Kagan closed in from the other side.

The man raised his hands, backing away. 'You can't kill me, grandmother; you owe me.'

'Really, Naxor?' said Sofia. 'What could I possibly owe you for?'

'Why do you think I was locked up in a prison cell? You must have heard about that.'

'I heard you had been arrested.'

'It was because of you,' the man cried; 'I was arrested because I wouldn't reveal your location to the King and Queen. I was protecting you.'

Sofia laughed. 'I don't believe you. Kagan, Gellie – hold him down, and I'll cut his head off. We need to be sure.'

'Is he really your grandson?' said Kagan, keeping his eyes on the man.

'He is,' said Sofia, 'which is why he must die. Otherwise, he'll tell the entire City who I am.'

'I could have done that already,' said Naxor, as he backed into the corner of the room. 'If I had, then you would have Kelsey Holdfast, two dragons, and a rather large number of Banner soldiers at your door, instead of little old me. Also, I have to warn you, that if I don't make contact with certain demigods later today, then they will deliver a letter I wrote directly to the Queen. The letter spells out the address of this mansion, and of your villa in the Sunward Range, with details about who you have been pretending to be. If you kill me, then that letter will be sent.'

'You're bluffing,' said Sofia.

Naxor smirked. 'Am I? You know me, grandmother. I can be reckless, but I'm never unprepared.'

Sofia raised her hand. 'I should kill you myself.'

Naxor laughed. 'Oh, come on; who's bluffing now? If you had your death powers, then I'd already be lying in a smouldering heap of blood and bone. I know you've taken anti-salve; so have I.'

'Why?'

'So that they wouldn't be able to track me here. You have to listen to me, grandmother – I'm on your side.'

'Lies,' spat Sofia; 'you have never been on my side, Naxor. You have betrayed me over and over again; do you think I have forgotten what you did in the cavern of Fordamere? Or before that, when you tried to kill me and Marcus in the Royal Palace? You are a snake, grandson.'

'Yeah, well, that was before Emily and Daniel put me in chains and locked me in a dungeon. They don't know what they're doing. This whole letting-the-mortals-rule thing has been an utter calamity from start to finish. It needs to end, before the City destroys itself.' He reached into a pocket, and withdrew a small vial, with red-coloured liquid swirling inside. 'See? My anti-salve; freshly stolen from the stocks that the Banner forces took from Amber. Now, why would I have taken this, if I was here to betray you?'

Gellie glanced at Sofia, the knife gripped in the housekeeper's hand.

'Just listen to what I have to say,' said Naxor; 'maybe over a brandy or two. And, perhaps some breakfast? I've been on the run since yesterday, and I've worked up a considerable appetite.'

Sofia folded her arms across her chest. 'Punch him in the face, Kagan.'

Kagan pulled back his fist, then rammed it into the man's nose. It made a crunching noise, and blood spattered over Naxor's face. He cried out, clutching his bloody nose, then sank to his knees.

'That hurt, damn it!' he yelled.

Sofia walked closer to him, her gaze fixed on the blood streaming from Naxor's nose. She narrowed her eyes, then nodded.

'Alright. Put him back into his chair, Kagan, then tie his wrists behind him. Let's imagine for a moment that my worthless grandson has something useful to say.'

Kagan reached down and hauled Naxor up by the shoulders. He dragged him back to the armchair, and pushed him down into it. Gellie passed him some cord from within her robes, and Kagan tied the demigod's hands together behind his back.

'Ow!' Naxor cried. 'There's no need to be so rough.'

Sofia slapped him across the face. 'Stop whining. Kagan, punch him every time he complains.'

'But... he'll knock me out,' said Naxor. 'I have no self-healing.'

A cruel smile danced across Sofia's lips. 'I might actually enjoy this. Alright, Naxor; talk.'

'Where will I start?'

She shrugged. 'Wherever you like. Gellie, pour me a large brandy. Kagan, bring a chair over for me; I like to sit while watching my enemies being tortured.'

'I am not your enemy,' said Naxor. 'I hate you, yes, it's true, but circumstances have conspired to make us allies.'

Sofia snorted, then sat in the seat that Kagan carried over for her. 'Speak.'

'Fine,' said Naxor. 'I've known who you really are for months. Months, grandmother, and yet I have told no one. However, I was tricked by Salvor and Mona, and they managed to read from my mind that you were back. I was able to block my thoughts before they could discover the location of this mansion, or any other details.'

'You've known I was here for months?'

'Yes. I was assigned to liaise with the Circuit, if you can believe that. The Queen wanted rid of me, that was the real reason; she's been sidelining all of the demigods. Well, not all of us, but most. Anyway, I ended up idle for months, sitting in my old mansion here in Port Sanders with nothing to do, but plenty of time on my hands. So, I started reading people's minds. I was bored. I soon learned that a rich aristocrat from Lostwell had arrived, but I didn't pay any attention. It's a good disguise, I have to admit. I discovered you by chance. I saw Kagan in the market one day, and heard his accent. I went into his head, just as I had gone into the heads of hundreds of other inhabitants of Port Sanders. Imagine my surprise, when I discovered who young Kagan really worked for. After that, I kept an eye on you, to see what you would do.'

'You've been spying on us?'

'Yes.'

She slapped him again.

'Would you stop doing that?' he yelled.

'If you were spying on me, then you would have seen the truth.'

'What truth?'

'The truth that I have no intention of trying to reclaim my previous position as God-Queen.'

He narrowed his eyes.

'Disbelieve me all you like, grandson. If your powers were working, then you would know that I wasn't lying.'

Gellie passed her a full glass of brandy, and she took a sip.

'Can I have some?' said Naxor.

'No. Not until I understand something, Naxor.'

'What?'

'Why didn't you tell the new rulers of the City that I was here?'

'Honestly? I was hedging my bets. At the time, I thought, well, I could hand you over to the authorities whenever I wished. For a while, I toyed with the notion, but I was curious to see what you would do. I even imagined that I could twist the situation to become the hero; you know, the man who saved the City from the evil God-Queen; that sort of thing. But, as time passed, I became more and more disillusioned with the idiots sitting upon the throne, and I started to wonder – maybe it would be better if things went back to the way they had been.'

Sofia laughed. 'You were a rebel under my regime.'

'You forced my hand, grandmother. I was loyal under my mother's rule, but you had her executed. That was a step too far. As was elevating the brainless Marcus to prince – what were you thinking? That clown should never have been allowed anywhere near a position of power. You have to admit it, grandmother – you made many mistakes towards the end. I still haven't forgiven you for killing my mother, and I never will.'

Sofia fell silent, her expression darkening. 'Killing Khora was a mistake.'

Naxor blinked. 'What did you say?'

'You heard me.'

'Malik's ass. You're admitting that you made a mistake? I need a brandy, now.'

'Your mother conspired with Yendra at the end of the Civil War. I never forgave her for that. When Marcus and Kano came to me with their plan for overthrowing her rule, I should have said no. But, I didn't. I saw Khora as weak; unfit to rule, but I should have stopped them. You won't believe me, but I wept when I got the news that she was dead, just as I wept for Yendra. I hated them, but they were still my daughters. Naxor, I'm sorry for your mother's death.'

The demigod stared at her, his eyes tight.

'Kagan,' she said, 'untie his wrists. Gellie, give my grandson a brandy.'

She stood, and walked over to a window, gazing out onto the streets of Port Sanders as Kagan removed the cords from Naxor's wrists, and Gellie handed him a glass of brandy. Naxor rubbed his wrists, then took a large slurp from the glass.

'Nice,' he said, nodding. 'You own the distillery where this is made, don't you?'

'Yes,' said Sofia, not turning from the window. 'It's part of my new life.'

He shrugged. 'You can keep a hold of it when you become God-Queen again.'

She turned. 'I don't think you fully understand me, Naxor. I will not become the God-Queen again. Those days are over.'

'No, they're not.'

'Yes, Naxor, they are. I have no desire to rule.'

'That's immaterial. You are who you are, grandmother; you cannot escape that.'

'I have escaped it. For the first time in a very long time, I am happy. I am content with what I have.'

'Rubbish.'

'You may mock, but it won't change my mind.'

'You're being frightfully naïve, grandmother. The King and Queen know you have returned. Perhaps, if you had managed to remain hidden for a century or so, then your little scheme would have succeeded, but it's too late for that. They're hunting you; Salvor's searching every corner of the City, and you know how methodical that old plodder can be. It'll take him a while, but he'll find you. And when he does, it'll be time for Kelsey, dragons and the Banner to make their appearance.'

'Who is this Kelsey?' said Kagan.

Naxor turned to him. 'She's a dragon rider. She flies around on this big, silver dragon, but she can also block the powers of the gods. She's the reason they were able to capture Montieth.'

'She's a god?'

'No,' said Sofia; 'she's a mortal. I know Kelsey quite well; she was my prisoner in Stoneship. I was using her unique blocking abilities to hide from the Ascendants. Gellie remembers her too.'

'They've already used her to raid Greylin Palace, twice,' said Naxor; 'she's like a military asset.' He turned back to Sofia. 'So, you can clearly see that your new life cannot last. And, that being the case, you should act when the time suits you, while you still have the luxury of that choice.'

'No.'

Naxor smiled. 'Do you recall the time I snatched Vana from the grounds of Maeladh Palace?'

'Yes. Marcus was beside himself with rage. You also killed many Roser officers.'

'And, you must remember how much Vana feared and loathed you?'

'I do.'

'Well, even she is prepared to join us. Yes, even Vana would rather you returned to power than allow the stupid mortals to destroy the City. Aside from her, we also have Ikara, Collo and Lydia.'

'The dregs, in other words?' said Sofia. 'Vana is a nervous wreck; Ikara is a vain fool; Collo is utterly useless, and an opium addict; while Lydia hates me more than all the others combined.'

'Perhaps, but look at who that leaves on the side of the mortals – Salvor, Mona, Jade and Silva. We have little to fear from any of them. They'd fall to their knees begging your forgiveness if you took over; you know they would.'

'I don't want this, Naxor; I don't want any of it.'

'Then, just be our figurehead. Reveal yourself, and give us your blessing, and we'll take over and do the rest. Once we're back in power, you can have Maeladh; that's all you really want, isn't it? Your old palace. You could live there in peace and comfort, and we'd run the City.'

'What about Montieth?'

'He can go back to Greylin and do whatever he feels like doing. Amber will come round if things go back to the way they were. Her loyalty to the mortals is wafer thin, as is Yvona's in Icehaven. All they truly desire is a return to the old days, and to be left alone to rule their little fiefdoms. Daniel's stupid new laws will ruin all of that. The elections are due at the end of next month, but they can be easily sabotaged. I have all manner of tricks ready to be deployed regarding the ballot counts...'

'I'm not interested, Naxor.'

'You don't care about the new constitution?'

'No.'

'But, didn't you donate money to the legal fund fighting the laws?'

'Yes, but that was also a mistake. I should never have attracted that kind of attention; it was vain and foolish. Lady Aurelian turned up at the villa to berate me about it, and I had to hide in the bedroom and pretend I was sick.'

Naxor laughed. 'That amuses me. Malik's ass; I hate that woman. She almost makes me pity Emily. She's on my list, near the top.'

'You have a list?'

'Of course. It contains all of the people who will need to die when we take over. Lady Aurelian, the King and Queen, naturally; possibly Jade; definitely Kelsey Holdfast and the leadership of the Banner, and maybe a dragon or two. Oh, and the infant princess.'

'But she's only a baby,' said Kagan.

Naxor shrugged. 'So? I'll make it quick and painless. I'll snap her little neck.'

Kagan felt sick. He glanced at Sofia, and could see the anger in her eyes.

'That will not be happening,' she said.

Naxor looked at her as if she were stupid. 'You would leave the Aurelian heir to the throne alive? What, and give hope to the fools who believe that they are destined to rule? Have you gone soft, grandmother?'

'You are an unpleasant person, Naxor.'

He laughed again. 'Sorry, but did you really just say that? The woman who opened the gates to the greenhides calls me unpleasant? I don't know how I'll ever recover from such an insult. Hang on, is this because you also have a child?'

'You know that?' said Sofia.

'Of course I do. I've been spying on you, or had you forgotten? A lovely little bouncing baby. Maxwell, is it? Wait, I have an idea. A compromise. The infant princess can stay alive, if she is married off to your Maxwell. Yes, that might work. That way, their offspring would have your blood, and the Aurelian's blood too. Malik's ass; I am a genius. We could rule as regents of the new royal line, and then Maxwell could take over when he's old enough.'

'It's not going to happen, Naxor. I'm getting married. Kagan and I want to have more children. After everything I've done for this City, do I not deserve some peace?'

'And you'll get it. In Maeladh, when you're the God-Queen again.'

'No, Naxor. How many times do I need to say it?'

'But, it's not an option. If you kill me, the other demigods will send the letter to the Queen. If you kick me out, then I will tell them where you are, in person. Even if I didn't, then Salvor will find you. It's over. Your silly little dream of being able to hide away forever is over, your Majesty.'

She glared at him. 'Don't call me that.'

'Why not? It's true; you are the legitimate God-Queen of the City. The Aurelians are usurpers.'

Sofia hung her head.

'Am I finally getting through to you?' Naxor said. 'Look, I'm not asking you to like me. We hate each other; that will never change, but you must see the sense in my words. You cannot hide any longer. Therefore, you have to act, and as soon as possible. I have a plan. None of the other demigods know it, of course, as Salvor would be able to read it out of their minds, but it will work. A few short months of toil, and you'll be safely ensconced back in Maeladh, where you belong, with Kagan and Maxwell, and as many other little sprogs as you fancy pushing out.'

'Where will you be?' said Kagan.

'In Cuidrach, running the City, with Lydia and Vana by my side. Ikara can take the Circuit again, and Collo can smoke opium to his little heart's content. Mona will go back to Ooste and do nothing, and even Salvor will submit, once he faces up to the new reality. If he doesn't, then maybe a spell in a god-restrainer mask will make him see sense. Do you still have that old mask?'

'No,' said Sofia.

'What mask?' said Kagan.

'It's a device that incapacitates gods and demigods,' said Naxor. 'A delightful contraption. My grandmother once placed it onto my head; an experience I'll never forget.'

'You deserved it,' she said. 'You were a traitor. You were a friend of that beast, Corthie Holdfast.'

Naxor smirked. 'Was I? I think even Corthie might be offended by that suggestion. I loathed him, and he utterly despised me. Malik knows what he would have done if he had found out some of the things I was up to. Do you remember that botched assassination attempt on him in the Circuit? The one when Aila jumped in front of him, and took the crossbow bolts that were supposed to end his life?' He grinned. 'That was me.'

Sofia frowned. 'You ordered that?'

'Yes. It didn't work, obviously; but luckily for me, Aila and Corthie were convinced that Marcus was behind it. Khora didn't know, of course; she wouldn't have approved. I felt that Corthie was becoming too much of a risk. He was too strong, and unpredictable. I would have got him too, if Aila hadn't loved him.'

'You really are a conniving little shit, aren't you, Naxor?'

'Eh, yes. But, so are you, dear grandmother. That's why we'll make a great team.'

Sofia lowered her eyes, and said nothing for a long time. Kagan glanced at Gellie, but the Fordian woman's face was unreadable. He turned back to Naxor, who winked at him, a smirk on his lips. Kagan felt the rage within him bubble to the surface. Everything had been going well, until Naxor's arrival. He felt a strong urge to punch him again, and not stop punching him until the demigod was dead.

Naxor laughed again. 'Grandmother, your betrothed is looking at me like he wants to kill me.'

'I do want to kill you,' said Kagan. 'You're ruining everything, and you're upsetting Sofia.'

'You could at least call her by her correct name. Do you even know it?' He glanced at Gellie. 'And you, Miss Fordian, prepare a nice room in the mansion for me; I'll be staying here for a while. Make sure I have a view of the harbour; I like that.'

The housekeeper looked at Sofia. 'Ma'am?'

'She's thinking,' said Naxor. 'She's mulling over my words, trying to see if there is any way around them. There isn't. It's over, and all we need to do is wait until she accepts the truth.'

Sofia glanced up, her eyes red. 'I hate you.'

'So what? I hate you too, grandmother. Now, shall we get to work?'

Sofia glanced at Kagan. 'Go to Maxwell. I need to speak to my grandson alone.'

'Why?' said Kagan. 'You can't be thinking of agreeing to this.'

'What will happen to Maxwell if Kelsey and the Banner come for me? I have no choice, Kagan; I'm sorry. Go. There are things I need to discuss with Naxor that I would be ashamed for you to hear.'

'We should kill him,' Kagan said. 'There's no letter; he's bluffing.'

'Unfortunately, I understand my grandson well enough to know when he isn't bluffing. He's right. If I cannot hide, then, to save Maxwell, I must act.'

Naxor grinned at Kagan. 'Run along, boy. The God-Queen's back.'

Amalia lowered her head, and wept.

CHAPTER 12

CORRECT ADDRESS

Pella, Auldan, The City – 11th Monan 3422

Jade sat with Poppy and Fluffy vying for space on her lap. It was so unfair. The cats were only just getting settled into the cottage, and already Jade was having to leave.

'You'll be good while I'm away, won't you?' she said to them. 'Someone will feed you every day; twice a day, and make sure that you get all the strokes you want. They won't be able to bring your little mouses back to life; only mummy can do that, because she's very clever. But, apart from that, I'm sure they will treat you like princes and princesses. Well, they'd better. If they don't, then mummy will melt their faces off.'

She saw a figure pass in front of the room's window, and a moment later there was a knock on the door. It was that girl Rosie again, a mortal so young she was practically a child.

'Come in,' Jade yelled.

The door opened and Rosie walked in. She had been coming round to the cottage every day, and seemed to have lost her initial apprehension at being in the presence of a mighty demigod.

'Morning, Jade,' she said, smiling.

'You're supposed to call me "ma'am." I am the leader of the

expedition.'

'Sure thing. Do you mind if I get a glass of water?'

She walked off to the kitchen without waiting for Jade to respond.

'Hi, Ginger,' Jade heard the girl say; 'who's a good boy?'

Jade scowled.

Rosie walked back into the living-room carrying a glass, and sat down on a chair.

'Where are your two sergeants?' said Jade.

'Outside,' said Rosie. 'They don't always have to come in, do they? I mean, my life's not in danger.'

'It might be. Who knows? I may decide to kill you today.'

Rosie laughed. 'I never knew you had such a good sense of humour.'

Ginger strolled in from the kitchen, and jumped up onto Rosie's lap. She scratched behind his ears.

'So,' the girl said; 'are you all packed up and ready to go?'

'No. Am I supposed to be?'

'Eh, yes. We're leaving in an hour.'

'You can pack for me.'

'Sure, if you don't mind me raking through all your stuff. Let me guess – you're going to be wearing dark green?'

'It suits me.'

'You know, I'd like to see you in nice flowery summer dress; I think you'd brighten up well.'

'Shut up.'

Rosie laughed. 'You're a bit grumpy today. Are you going to miss the cats?'

'Of course I'm going to miss them,' she said. 'They're my babies. How can we be leaving in an hour if I haven't even met the Banner cartographer yet? He was supposed to be at the demonstration of the new carriage yesterday, but I didn't see him there.'

'I think they want him kept in the dark, so that he has no clue what's happening until we're airborne. You know, in case he tells anyone where we're going.' She stood. 'Shall we pack your things together?'

'I suppose I should supervise your packing,' Jade said. She gently removed Poppy and Fluffy from her lap and set them down on the couch, before standing.

They went through to the back room, and Jade sat by the bed, while Rosie starting folding clothes and placing them into an open trunk.

'That demonstration yesterday was fascinating,' Rosie said, as she packed away a pile of dresses. 'Did you know that I've been asked to make notes on its performance? They want me to suggest improvements when we get back. I might even switch specialties from ballistae to dragon carriages; I've already got some good ideas about refinements we could make to the design. I...'

'I don't care,' said Jade. 'It's a wooden box.'

Rosie nodded. 'What do you like doing? Every day when I've been over here, we've talked about the expedition, but once we're actually there, what will you do in your spare time? Do you like reading?'

'I am *in* the history books; I don't need to read them.'

'What about fiction? I'm taking some books that I've borrowed from the palace library. We can share them, if you like. Do you like romance?'

Jade pulled a face.

'Um, right. What about adventure stories?'

'I don't like reading, but maybe you could read to me?'

'I guess. Will we be taking some wine along, do you think?'

'Do you ever stop talking?'

'Sometimes. I'm going to smuggle a bottle of gin along. Or, maybe two. Don't tell the sergeants, alright?'

Jade stared at her. 'I'm in charge, not the sergeants.'

'I know, but they're so much older than me, and...'

'They're older than you? Girl, I am nearly nine centuries older than you. You speak to me as if you imagine that we're the same age – we're not.'

Rosie's face flushed. 'I hadn't realised I was doing that, but you're right. It's because you look the same age as me. I mean, I know how old you are, but my brain sees something else. I have a question for you, Jade. Do you think that you'd be taken more seriously if you looked forty, rather than twenty?'

Jade frowned. 'I don't know; I've never thought about it. I was given salve by my father from a young age; so much, in fact, that I hardly ever need to take any nowadays. I haven't had any in fifty years, and I don't think I've aged at all since then.'

'That's weird. Princess Yendra looked older than the demigods, but couldn't she have taken more salve and looked the same age; you know, if she'd wanted to?'

'Yes. She chose that appearance deliberately, to show that she was older than the generation of demigods. The God-Queen did the same, and Princess Khora too. My father, on the other hand, used to change his age on a whim, sometimes several times a day. I thought it was normal to do that. It was only later that I realised that there was nothing normal about father.'

'Are you glad you're not still in Greylin Palace?'

Jade glanced at the floor. 'I'm still getting used to it. I love the freedom, but it terrifies me at the same time.' Her face went red. 'I didn't mean that,' she said, raising her chin. 'I'm not scared of anything.'

'It's alright to be scared, especially if you were locked up in a palace for nine hundred years. I'd be scared too.'

'Didn't you hear me? I'm not scared.'

Rosie nodded. 'That's your trunk packed. You don't have much stuff. Are you taking anything else?'

'No. Everything I own is in there.'

'Then, maybe we should leave some things here, in case something happens to the trunk.'

'I don't care about any of it. The only thing I care about are the cats.'

'Oh. Alright. Grab that end, and we'll carry it outside.'

Jade stared at her. 'You want me to help carry the trunk?'

'Yes. Just outside; we'll ask the sergeants if they can take it from there.'

She eyed the trunk. 'It looks heavy.'

'You're a demigod.'

'So? That doesn't mean I have big muscles.'

'I suppose not. Let's try, anyway.'

Rosie took hold of one of the handles, and lifted her end with ease. Jade frowned, then reached out with both hands and tried to lift the other end. She strained, and managed to raise it an inch off the ground.

'Hurry!' she gasped. 'I can't hold it for long.'

They edged out of the bedroom, Jade puffing and groaning with every step. Her arms were aching, and she could feel her self-healing start to soothe the pain. They made it to the front door, and half-carried, half-dragged the trunk out onto the gravel path. The two sergeants rushed over.

'Let us take that for you, ma'am,' said Sergeant Inmara, her eyes wide, as if she couldn't believe that a demigod was carrying her own luggage.

Jade released her grip on the case, and let the sergeants take over. She walked back into the cottage, and spent a moment with each of the four cats she was leaving behind, assuring them that she would return soon. They seemed to take it well, and she returned outside.

'Where's your luggage?' she asked Rosie, as they set off down the path, the two sergeants following with the trunk.

'It's already up on the roof where Halfclaw is meeting us. I awoke pretty early this morning. I could hardly sleep from the excitement.'

Jade frowned. 'What parts do you think will be exciting?'

'Getting to ride on a dragon – I haven't done that since Blackrose was here; and going back to the valley where we stayed; and investigating the salve caverns; and just generally being away from the City for a while. I've been to Tarstation, and the icefields, and also the desert, as well as the Eastern Mountains. I'm actually pretty well-travelled, come to think of it. Not as well-travelled as Maddie, obviously. What are you looking forward to?'

'I heard that there are a lot of greenhides there, so I might get to kill some.'

'Each to their own, I guess.'

They reached the edge of the palace and entered through an open side door. It was a five minute walk to the wing that bore the large, flat roof where the dragons landed, and Jade fell into silence as they made their way along the marble corridors. Her confidence was still at a low ebb after resigning from her position in the Bulwark, and part of her shared the girl's desire to get out of the City for a while. All the same, the thought made her feel a little queasy. Up until a few years before, she had never left Greylin Palace, let alone the City. The Eastern Mountains were two hundred miles away; a distance almost beyond her imagination. The City occupied a huge place in her mind, but it measured only twenty miles from east to west, and that was at its widest point, where the Fortress of the Lifegiver lay. Her spirits fell as she thought about her old home in the Duke's Tower. She had never been happy there, not since Yendra had died, and her memories were poisoned by her father's presence in the dungeons, and by her humiliation when the fortress had been looted. Compared to that, her stay in the little cottage had been idyllic, especially after the Queen had told her that she was being held blameless. That had surprised her; she had expected to be punished, not forgiven. Maybe the Queen didn't hate her. She glanced at the young woman walking by her side. Rosie didn't seem to hate her either.

They climbed the stairs to the roof, and emerged back into the pink sunlight of the morning. Sitting on the middle of the roof was a wooden carriage, framed with bands of grey steel. It had sturdy feet at each corner, and sloping sides that terminated in an iron cone at either end. On the top were a series of grips and straps designed to be held within the grasp of a dragon's forelimbs. Its side door was lying open, and soldiers were packing crates into the interior, which also had a small number of seats. A few yards away, a man dressed in a Banner uniform was gazing at the carriage, an eyebrow raised. By his feet sat a pile of luggage. He turned when he saw Jade and Rosie approach.

'Are you the cartographer?' said Jade.

'I am *a* cartographer,' the man said, his expression guarded. 'My name is Lieutenant Flavus, a Scout in the Second Regiment of the Banner of the Lostwell Exiles. Are you Lady Jade, by any chance?'

'Yes.'

'Nice to make your acquaintance, ma'am. Perhaps you can tell me why I am here? I was told to report to you upon this roof, and to be prepared for a month-long expedition, but no other details were forthcoming. I assume, ma'am, that you will be able to enlighten me?'

'I'll tell you when we're in the air. This is Rosie Jackdaw. She will be our guide on the expedition.'

The lieutenant bowed his head towards Rosie. 'Are you military?'

'Eh, yes. I suppose,' said Rosie. 'I'm a Junior Artificer. Have you come here from Jezra?'

'Yes. I have been surveying the upper cliffs; in fact, my work there has been interrupted by these new orders. I was hoping to have finished the charts by the end of winter. One can only assume that this new operation is of a higher priority.'

The two sergeants reached the roof, carrying Jade's trunk. They took it to the carriage, and other soldiers placed it inside with the rest of the crates and supplies.

Jade beckoned them over.

'This is Lieutenant Flavus, our cartographer. And this is Sergeant Inmara and Sergeant Darvi, who will be accompanying us on the trip. Inmara is the senior of the two, so the chain of command goes – me, Flavus, Inmara, Darvi, and then Rosie at the bottom. Alright?'

Rosie narrowed her eyes and frowned.

Darvi nudged her, smiling. 'At least I get to order someone about, eh, Rosie?'

Flavus eyed the sergeant with the air of a professional looking down at a mere amateur, but said nothing.

'We'll be leaving as soon as the dragon arrives,' Jade went on. 'Rosie and I have both ridden on dragons before; it's nothing to worry about.'

'I spent three years on Dragon Eyre, ma'am,' said Flavus; 'I am familiar with the beasts.'

'Yes, well, don't call Halfclaw a beast to his face. He's more like a giant, friendly cat that can breathe fire.'

Flavus's eyes tightened, but he said nothing.

Rosie glanced towards the stairs. 'The King,' she whispered.

Jade and the others turned, and they all bowed as King Daniel strode across the roof in their direction, Lord Salvor a pace behind.

'Good morning,' the King said. He was smiling, but his eyes were troubled.

'Your Majesty,' said Jade, lowering her gaze. Why was the King there? She had been expecting the Queen. She liked Emily, but somehow felt a little intimidated by the King. He was only a mortal, she told herself.

'We thought we'd come to bid you good luck on your expedition,' the King said. 'It shouldn't take more than a month, or so I'm told. Still, you will be travelling outwith the confines of the City, and I realise that this might be the first time that some of you will have ever stepped foot beyond the walls that protect us. The Queen and I wish you to know that you will be in our thoughts, and that we are looking forward to welcoming you upon your return.'

'Thank you, your Majesty,' said Jade. 'For our part, we will strive to carry out our objectives to the best of our abilities.'

The King smiled again. 'I know you will, Lady Jade; you have our complete faith.'

Lord Salvor gestured towards the sky. 'Your Majesty; the dragon approaches.'

'Right on time,' said the King, glancing upwards. He turned back to Jade. 'Let's speak alone for a quick moment.'

They walked to the edge of the roof, out of earshot of the others.

'The Queen apologises for not being able to see you all off this morning,' the King said. 'She is busy with the search for your errant cousin.'

'Naxor?' said Jade. 'He hasn't been found, then?'

'No. He had help to escape; that seems certain. He also stole much of the supplies of your father's salve mixtures, and is presumably using the anti-salve to mask his presence from Lady Silva.'

Jade nodded.

'I also have a final order for you, Jade,' he said. 'The Queen and I feel that the destruction of the salve mine in the mountains might be the best possible outcome of this expedition. However, that will depend on various factors. If, for example, this new mine is unique, then destroy it, Jade, if such a thing is possible. If it turns out that the mountains have many such deposits, then the destruction of one would be futile. Return here after mapping it, and we'll decide what to do, if that is the case. Ultimately, we want you to take the decision based upon what you find. Is that understood?'

'Yes, your Majesty.'

The King nodded. 'Thank you, Jade; and good luck.'

They walked back to the carriage. Halfclaw was descending in lazy circles, and alighted onto the flat surface a few yards away. He lowered his head, his eyes scanning the people on the roof.

'King,' he said, tilting his head.

'Greetings, Halfclaw,' said Daniel.

'Is the carriage ready?' said the green dragon.

'Almost,' said Jade. 'How many can sit up on your harness?'

'I can carry three humans upon my shoulders,' he said. 'If five are coming, then two will have to be placed within the carriage.'

Jade glanced at her small team. 'Sergeants, you will be going in the carriage. Rosie and Flavus will ride with me on Halfclaw.'

Darvi looked disappointed, but Inmara's features remained impassive. They saluted, and walked over to the carriage. They climbed in, and the hatch was closed by the waiting soldiers. One gave a thumbs-up to Jade.

'We shall stand well back, I think,' said the King.

Jade bowed her head towards him, then climbed up the harness straps onto Halfclaw's shoulders.

'I hope that, this time, I will enjoy flying, Halfclaw,' she said. 'The last time, I was too upset by Yendra's death to pay attention.'

'That was a grim day,' said the dragon, his neck turning so that he could look at the demigod. 'Today will be better.'

Rosie reached the harness and sat to Jade's left, strapping herself in. Moments later, Flavus appeared, and he took up position to Jade's right.

'This reminds me of Dragon Eyre,' he said.

'You have been there?' said Halfclaw. 'Did you fight my kin?'

'I'm a Banner Scout, dragon,' he said; 'we tend to leave the fighting to the others. I used to survey and map the various island chains. However, I witnessed much that has been seared into my soul, and would never wish to return there.'

'I hope Maddie and Blackrose are all right,' said Rosie.

Jade turned, and waved down to the King and Lord Salvor, then Halfclaw beat his blue-streaked wings, and they ascended. He hovered over the wooden carriage, then picked it up with his forelimbs and raised it into the sky. Jade stared down at the view of the red roofs of Pella stretching out beneath them. The boats in the harbour shrank as they climbed higher, and even the sprawling complex of Cuidrach Palace dwindled into the distance. Halfclaw circled once, and Jade saw the glittering bay, and the towns of Tara and Ooste in the distance, then the dragon put on a burst of speed towards the east.

They raced over the red sandstone of Outer Pella, then the reds turned to greys as they crossed the Union Walls. Jade frowned at the endless labyrinth of concrete that made up the Circuit. The enormous bulk of the Great Racecourse rose above the grey tenements to their left.

'That gargantuan statue,' said Flavus, pointing; 'it looks the same as the one on the promontory outside Tara.'

'It's Prince Michael,' said Rosie; 'a tyrant from the olden days.'

'My uncle,' said Jade. 'I used to hide whenever he came to visit my father in Dalrig.'

They soared over the Middle Walls. Below them were the spread-out housing estates of the Blades, while to their right loomed the high walls surrounding the Hammer and Scythe territories.

'I remember that location well,' said Flavus, pointing towards the fields of the Scythes.

'I used to live directly below us,' said Rosie, 'in a little Blade house; and there, up on our left, is Stormshield Fortress, where my brother works.'

'Are you a member of the Blade tribe, Private Jackdaw?' said Flavus.

'Yeah.'

'And the militia sergeants?'

'They're both Reapers.'

Flavus nodded, then his attention was drawn by the sight of the approaching Great Walls. The tall Inner Walls reared up, followed by the lower Outer Walls, then the moat, with the smallest of the three walls.

'A fine construction,' said the Banner officer. 'I believe it has stood for over a thousand years?'

'Yes,' said Jade; 'it's two centuries older than me.'

They fell silent as the dragon carried them over the walls. The entire plain beyond the moat was crawling with a thick carpet of greenhides.

'Malik's ass, I remember this,' said Rosie. 'I never thought I'd see it again. It makes me feel... tiny.'

Jade pointed a finger at the mass of greenhides, and one shrieked and fell over, dead.

'One down,' said Rosie; 'only three hundred million to go.'

Jade frowned at her. 'Are there three hundred million of them?'

'I don't know,' said Rosie; 'it's just something that the Blades say.'

'But is it true or not?'

'You can make up any number you like for the second part, and I just fancied saying three hundred million.' She laughed. 'Don't think about it too deeply.'

Flavus raised an eyebrow. 'Are all Blades so freely-spoken whilst in the company of their superior officers? I have yet to see you salute, nor have I heard you address the commander of the expedition as "ma'am," Private Jackdaw.'

Rosie blushed.

Flavus turned to Jade. 'Now, ma'am, I would be obliged if you would inform me as to the purpose and destination of this expedition.'

Jade hesitated. Part of her was angry that he had been mean to Rosie, but another part thought that he might be right. Rosie was over-familiar, but Jade had become used to her ways over the previous few days, and enjoyed the informality the young woman exuded. At times, Jade even thought of her as a potential friend, which was a ridiculous notion, of course. A demigod could never be true friends with a mortal.

'Ma'am?' said Flavus.

'As long as Rosie does what she is told,' she said, 'then I will forgive any lapses in protocol. We are going to the Eastern Mountains, Lieutenant, to survey a salve mine that Rosie discovered a few years ago.'

'A salve mine?' he said, his eyes lighting up. He smiled. 'A real salve mine? I must say, ma'am, this is a tremendous honour.' He glanced at Rosie. 'And you discovered it, Private? Outstanding.'

Rosie beamed. 'Thanks, sir. Do I call you "sir?" I mean, you're Banner, and I'm a Blade. How does it work? I can tell you're keen on that sort of thing, so I'll try to get it right.'

'The Banner are sticklers for using the correct address, Private. It's one of the things that make us the best soldiers in the known worlds. If I had spoken to my commanding officer the way you spoke to Lady Jade, then I would have been flogged, and then probably dismissed from the Banner in disgrace. Discipline is everything. You can forget fancy new weapons, or shiny armour, or elaborate plans; without discipline, you will achieve nothing. Militarily speaking, of course.'

Rosie nodded. 'Does that mean I should call you "sir?"'

'Yes, Private; it does.'

'I'll try to remember, sir.'

'Thank you, Private. Now, tell me all about this mine; everything you can remember.' He rubbed his hands together. 'My, I can't recall being this excited.'

'That Naxor chap sounds like a tricky fellow,' said Flavus, as he listened to Rosie. The young Jackdaw woman had filled the time with stories about the valley in the mountains, while they had flown over the two hundred miles of greenhide-filled plains. The mountains had grown steadily larger on the horizon in front of them, and Jade had been keeping most of her attention on what she could see, only half-listening to Rosie.

'We're approaching the foothills,' she said. 'Rosie, do you recognise anything?'

Rosie broke off from the story to peer into the distance. 'Um; I'm not sure.'

'Halfclaw,' said Jade; 'where is the dragon colony in relation to here?'

'About fifty miles to sunward,' the dragon said, 'where it is a little warmer.'

'If I remember right,' said Rosie, 'the valley was only five or six miles from the edge of the plain, and it's slightly iceward of a pass through the mountains that the greenhides use to cross the range.'

'I can see such a pass ahead of us,' said Halfclaw. 'We shall start by following it, and search the left flank.'

'How's the weight of the carriage?' said Jade.

'My forelimbs are strong,' he said. 'I can easily manage a search of the mountains.'

Flavus reached into his shoulder bag and withdrew a wooden board with paper pinned to it, and a pencil. He gazed at the mountains, and began to sketch, and scribble down notes and distances. Jade watched him for a moment, then turned back to the mountains. They were flying over the low foothills, veering a little sunward as Halfclaw headed toward a cleft in the slopes, from where a line of greenhides was streaming.

'There's the pass,' the dragon said. 'Is it the same one, Rosie?'

'I'm not sure yet. It might be. I'm sorry; I only passed over it twice; once on the way in, and once on the way out.'

'We have all day,' said Jade, checking the position of the sun. 'It's only noon; we have time.'

In the end, it took several more hours of flying to locate the valley. Half-claw remained patient, while Rosie kept apologising for her patchy memories. Flavus said nothing during the search, but filled several sheets of paper with his drawings and notes, his eyes focussed like a hawk on the landscape around them.

Rosie was the most relieved, when she finally spotted the high, green valley below them. She yelled out in triumph to Halfclaw, and the dragon started to descend. The valley was small, and almost hidden between high ridges of bare rock. Grass grew on the valley floor, and there were trees around a large pool, formed by a waterfall that tumbled from the steep cliffside. At the other end of the pool, a stream flowed down the gentle slope, dividing the valley in two.

Halfclaw set the wooden carriage down onto the grassy bank next to the pool, and landed beside it.

Rosie beamed in delight. 'This is it.' She pointed. 'That's where Blackrose slept, by the little stream, and over there are the caves where Maddie and I stayed.'

Jade unbuckled her straps, and slid down to the ground to stretch her legs. She heard a banging from the carriage and walked over to see the hatch opening. Darvi staggered out, as if drunk, while Inmara's face had a green tinge to it.

'How was the journey?' said Jade.

Darvi fell to his knees and groaned. 'Not recommended, ma'am.'

'If you're going to vomit, please do it out of sight; I can't abide people being sick.'

'We'll be fine, ma'am,' said Inmara. 'Come on, Darvi; let's get the luggage unpacked, and the tents put up before it gets dark. Then you can fetch some firewood.'

Darvi muttered something under his breath, then got to his feet. Jade turned, and saw Rosie and Flavus by the dragon's head.

'I will leave you now,' said Halfclaw. 'I want to announce my presence here to Deathfang and the others in the colony. I shall return at dawn.'

'Thank you for bringing us, Halfclaw,' said Jade.

'My pleasure, demigod.'

He extended his wings and soared away into the sky.

'Let's help the sergeants,' said Rosie.

Flavus looked like he was going to object, then he nodded. 'Good idea, Private. The sooner we have the tents up, the sooner we can investigate the salve mine.'

'I was actually thinking about dinner, sir,' she said. 'I'm absolutely starving. I'll cook; I'm good at that. I also might have a bottle of gin for later.'

Flavus rolled his eyes. 'This is not a holiday, Private.'

'No, sir; but that doesn't mean we're not allowed to have fun. Does it, sir?'

'I should have brought the cats after all,' said Jade, glancing around. 'They would love it here; it's very pretty, with all of the wild flowers. Very peaceful.'

Flavus glanced from Jade to Rosie. 'I suppose we might have a little time to relax.'

'Excellent decision, sir,' said Rosie.

'But only once we have finished all of our tasks for the day,' Flavus went on. 'Agreed, Private?'

'Agreed, sir.'

Jade watched as Rosie and Flavus walked down the gentle slope to where the two sergeants were unpacking the carriage, and she allowed herself a little smile.

CHAPTER 13

SURPRISE

Jezra, The Western Bank – 12th Monan 3422

A bitter wind gusted over the cemetery in Jezra, as the four slain workers from the Brigades were lowered into their graves. Despite the cold, a large crowd had gathered to pay their respects to the first workers to die from greenhide wounds in over a month. Van was still too ill to attend, but many officers and soldiers from the Banner had gone along to watch.

Kelsey stood near the back of the crowd. She hadn't known any of the four victims, but funerals in Jezra were not to be ignored. Next to her stood the crews that looked after Frostback and Halfclaw. With the green dragon seconded to assist Lady Jade, Frostback had both crews to herself, and had been spoiled with all the extra attention.

When the four bodies had been interred, the crowd began to disperse, leaving the cliffside cemetery and heading off to their day's work.

'After thirty-five days,' said Nagel, 'I had been hoping we had seen the last of these funerals.'

'Do you remember what it was like when we first arrived?' said Vadhi. 'There were dozens a day back then, and we thought it was normal. It just shows you – the greenhides are still dangerous, even with dragons and walls protecting us.'

Kelsey started to walk towards the gates of the cemetery, and the others followed her.

'How did it happen?' she said.

'A ten-yard section of palisade wall collapsed during the night,' said Nagel. 'Fortunately, there was another defensive wall close behind, but the four Exiles couldn't escape to it in time. They were ripped to shreds while half of the Fourth Brigade were watching helplessly from the battlements. A nasty business.'

'I know that it's a tragedy,' said Vadhi, 'but thirty-five days without a single death is a new record. It gives me hope that we're past the worst. One day, all of the wooden palisades will be gone, replaced by those huge stone walls that we've started building.'

'That's true,' said Kelsey, 'but the stone walls won't be finished until we've conquered a lot more territory. We're still expanding, remember? The City wants another few square miles taken before we build our own version of the Great Walls.'

Vadhi frowned. 'Then, the City should send its own workers, instead of expecting us to die for them.'

'Jezra belongs to the Exiles now,' said Nagel. 'We've paid for it with our blood; it's ours by right. The City will never be able to kick us out. Major-General Logos would never allow it.' He glanced at Kelsey. 'That's right, isn't it, ma'am?'

'It certainly seems so,' said Kelsey. 'The City needs us here, to ensure its survival. We're already growing and fishing more food than we need, and we're supplying them with stone, timber and lots of other things; and that'll only increase once the new forests have had time to grow.'

Vadhi grinned. 'You and Van could be the king and queen of the Exiles in Jezra.'

'I think Queen Emily might have something to say about that.'

'Really? Sometimes, I think that they've forgotten about us. None of the royals, or the demigods, ever come here to visit; only Yendra did, and Jade, for a while. None of the others care.'

Kelsey narrowed her eyes. 'Chancellor Mona has been here for nearly a month.'

'Alright, that's true, boss; but she's only here to rummage about in the ruins looking for bits of old pottery. She doesn't care about the Exiles.'

They reached a wide set of ancient steps, and climbed up onto the top of the ruined palace foundations, where Frostback was waiting for them.

'Greetings, my rider,' the dragon said, 'and my commiserations for the loss of the four humans. Did you know them?'

'No,' she said; 'they were all Fourth Brigade.'

Frostback lowered her head. 'The colonel was here a moment ago. It seems that our work schedule has changed. They want to repair the section of wall that was breached last night, and that means no flying operations for us.'

'Oh. I see. Wait; we have a free day?'

'Yes.'

'What shall we do?'

'I was thinking of warming myself in the desert for a few hours. Do you wish to come?'

'Sorry, but lying about in the sweltering sun is not my idea of relaxing.'

'You could bring a book, and read while I bathe in the heat.'

'An oasis might be nice.'

'I'll be sure to select somewhere with both water and shade.'

'Alright then; you've convinced me. Give me a couple of minutes, and I'll be back here, and ready to go.'

She gave the crew the rest of the day off, then hurried down the steps to her brick house. She shoved a couple of books into a bag, along with some apples, bread, and a waterskin, just in case. She also changed into lighter, summer clothes, though grabbed a coat for the journey. It could get pretty cold up on Frostback's shoulders at times, and she didn't want to freeze. Despite having officially moved into Van's apartment in the Command Post, she was glad she had kept the keys to her little house. It was a lot closer to the palace foundations, for a start, but she also liked the feeling of having somewhere to call her own, if she and Van fell out.

She ran out of the house, her bag swinging from her shoulder, and jumped up the steps of the ruined palace two at a time.

'Desert, here we come,' she called out to Frostback, who was watching her approach.

'Climb up, my rider. Did you bring any books?'

'Yes,' said Kelsey, as she scrambled up the straps of the harness.

'Good. That will keep you occupied, and quiet, while I relax in the sun.'

Kelsey reached the wide saddle, and buckled herself in. 'This is nice; just the two of us for a change. Not that I don't like Halfclaw, of course; I love the scaly brute, but we've not had as much rider-dragon time recently as I'd hoped.'

'That is explained by your relationship with Van, my dear rider,' Frostback said, as she extended her wings. 'I think you'll find that Halfclaw has had very little to do with it.'

The silver dragon ascended into the cold air.

'Do you think so?' said Kelsey, frowning.

'You've been spending a lot of time with Van, especially since the accident with the salve. I don't blame you for that. It is natural to care for your mate when they are hurt. I would have regarded you as selfish and cold if you hadn't.'

Kelsey chewed her lip. The dragon soared up over the ridge at the top of the fortified cliffs, then turned towards the sun. Within moments, she had raced away across the forest, leaving the defences of Jezra behind. It was only a few miles to the Warm Sea, and they covered the tree-filled distance in minutes.

'You are being very quiet,' said Frostback.

'I'm just thinking about Van, and where it's all going. The vision I had; it hasn't happened yet.'

'Does the vision really matter any more? You seem to be very fond of each other; surely that is more important?'

'I understand that, but it still feels like a weight around my neck.'

They surged over the steep cliffs on the sunward side of the land-mass, and the forests beneath them were replaced by the still waters of the Warm Sea. Several boats were out, harvesting seafood and reeds from the marshes. There were few fish in the Warm Sea, but countless varieties of crab and lobster, and a seemingly limitless abundance of edible seaweed.

Frostback's head jerked up, and she changed direction.

'What is it?' said Kelsey.

'Other dragons,' she said; 'four of them.'

'Deathfang?'

'Yes, he is leading them.'

'Why; what's he doing so far from the Eastern Mountains?'

'Let's find out, rider.'

Kelsey scanned the heavens, until she saw four tiny specks in the sky, all rushing iceward from the direction of the desert. Frostback angled her approach to intercept them, but they saw her before she could reach them, and began to circle, awaiting her. Kelsey could make out the massive bulk of the grey Deathfang easily, and then she recog-nised the others – Burntskull, Darksky and Dawnflame.

'Greetings, father,' Frostback called out, as she joined the others circling above the waters of the Warm Sea.

'I wasn't expecting to see you today, daughter,' Deathfang said.

'Nor I, you,' said Frostback. 'What brings you so far to the west?'

'He wishes to impress the Queen,' said Burntskull.

'Not so,' said Deathfang; 'I wish to give the King and Queen of the City a measure of our strength, and I also wish to show them that they are not the only ones who can be generous. They plan to send us aid, to expand and improve our new dwelling place, and yet they ask for nothing in return. By doing this, we will show that we are the equal of such acts.'

'What are you planning, father?' said Frostback.

'We are on our way to destroy the greenhide nest that Halfclaw discovered,' said Deathfang. 'He visited us in the mountains yesterday, and gave us the location.'

'Does the City know of this plan?'

'No, it shall be a surprise.'

'But, father,' said Frostback, 'the humans have been working on their own plan for several days. We are only awaiting the return of Half-claw to put it into action.'

'Then, imagine their joy and gratitude, when they discover that we have completed the task for them. A favour for a favour; it is the honourable way. In fact, I believe that this is what the Queen was hinting at; she is a crafty ruler.'

'I fear you may be reading too much into a simple act of generosity, father.'

'You are being naïve, child,' said Darksky. 'The City wants us to feel indebted to them; insects give nothing away without expecting some-thing in return – it is in their nature to behave thus. Therefore, in order to remain free of any obligations to them, today's toil will be necessary. We are dragons; we do not need to accept the charity of mere insects – it is an insult.'

'That is some twisted logic,' muttered Kelsey in a low voice.

'Hush, rider,' said Frostback. 'We will not persuade them with such words.'

'Will you be joining us in the raid, daughter?' Deathfang said.

'I would ask you to think again, father, and inform the City of your intentions first.'

'Why?'

'Isn't it obvious?' said Darksky. 'She is in league with the insects. She honours them more than she honours her own father.'

'That is not the case,' said Frostback. 'The humans are in possession of a vast experience in dealing with greenhide nests; whereas, we are not.'

'Are you saying that it is beyond our capabilities, daughter?' said Deathfang. 'Such notions are beneath you, and are not worthy of a response. This conversation is at an end. Come with us, if you wish, or do not; it is up to you.'

He turned, and soared towards the west. Darksky, Dawnflame and Burntskull each banked, and raced off after him. Frostback's eyes flashed with anger, then she followed them.

'Cardova's going to do his nut in,' said Kelsey.

'What does that mean, rider? Sometimes, your utterings are incomprehensible to me.'

'It means he's going to be angry; he's spent days planning the attack on the nest.'

'That cannot be helped now. All we can do is ensure that my father's attack succeeds.'

They crossed the coastline again, and flew over the vast expanse of forest. Frostback stayed a few hundred yards behind the others as the miles rushed beneath them. It was a one hour flight, and Kelsey was glad she had brought the coat to shield her from the cold wind. The dragons ascended when they approached the long ridge where the nest was located, and circled high above it.

'This matches Halfclaw's description,' said Deathfang. 'There appear to be six entrances to the nest on this side of the ridge, just as he informed us. We must force the greenhide queen out into the open, and then slay her. The ordinary soldier greenhides are insignificant; ignore them. The queen is our sole target. When she is dead, we shall take her head back to the City, to show the humans what we have achieved.'

'I shall skip that part,' said Dawnflame. 'Once the creature has fallen, I intend to return to our home.'

'You are at perfect liberty to do so,' said Deathfang. 'If necessary, I shall take the head back on my own, and drop it onto the roof of Cuidrach Palace, as a gift.'

Burntskull laughed. 'I may come, just to watch that.'

Deathfang turned to his daughter. 'Are you willing to assist us, or have you come purely to stand witness?'

'I will help, father.'

'Good. You take the leftmost entrance, then Burntskull the next, followed by Dawnflame and Darksky. I shall cover the tunnel on the right flank, on the iceward side. That will leave one entrance unguarded, from where the greenhides will no doubt try to flee. Let them go! Remember, it is the queen we are here for. Keep your fires strong and steady, but do not place yourself at risk by venturing too low. A hundred greenhides can bring down even the proudest dragon, as we learned in the fighting pits of Alea Tanton.'

He tilted his head, and the dragons descended, fanning out towards the entrance to which they had been assigned. Frostback soared sunward, then banked round, hovering over the entrance tunnel on the far left, as the others got into position to her right. The greenhides began shrieking in alarm, and hundreds emerged from the tunnels, their talons clacking upwards at the enemy.

Deathfang opened his jaws, and unleashed a vast torrent of flame at the entrance on the iceward side, enveloping dozens of screaming greenhides. The other dragons followed his lead, each pouring flames down into the openings on the side of the cliff. Kelsey shielded her eyes from the glare and the heat as Frostback blasted the leftmost entrance. Greenhides spilled from the tunnel in flames, before sliding down the slope to the base of the ridge, their corpses smoking. Around the lip of the tunnel entrance, the rocks began to glow red, then the ceiling collapsed, and tons of earth and stone toppled from the cliffside. Frostback kept the flames pouring from her, despite the entrance being blocked, and Kelsey turned to watch what was happening along the rest of the ridge. The three dragons to their right were also continuing to belch flames at the cliffside, and the bodies at the bottom of the cliff were piling up in their hundreds. Greenhides were streaming out from the unguarded tunnel entrance to Darksky's right. None were attempting to fight, as the dragons were too high, and they were scattering into the forest in every direction. At the far end of the ridge, where Deathfang was stationed, the glowing earth began to shift, and a huge creature pulled itself from the fire-scorched rubble. It was as tall as a tree, and had long claws at the end of its forelimbs, which slashed through the air beneath Deathfang.

'The queen!' cried the grey dragon.

Darksky and Dawnflame broke off from burning their tunnel entrances, and rushed towards Deathfang.

'Wait,' called out Frostback. 'That is not the queen.'

The three dragons hovered over the creature, raining fire down upon it. It screamed in agony as the fires consumed its insect-like body, and collapsed to the ground, crashing into the heaps of corpses at the base of the cliff.

Deathfang roared in triumph.

'That was not the queen,' said Frostback; 'that was one of the child-queens. The queen will still be underground.'

Deathfang's eyes gleamed. 'Is this true, daughter?'

'Yes. We must burn the nest for longer; until the entire ridge has been destroyed.'

'We will follow your lead on this,' said Deathfang. He turned to the others. 'Continue.'

The dragons went back to their positions, and resumed the burning. Frostback flew to the previously unguarded entrance, and bathed it in flames. The heat increased as the five dragons persisted, each hovering over the ridge with their long necks angled down. More of the cliffside fell away, along with the incinerated corpses of hundreds more green-hides, and the acrid reek from the piles of bodies at the bottom of the ridge nearly blinded Kelsey. She gagged, the searing heat burning her throat, and pulled her coat over her face, leaving a narrow gap for her to peer out. The rocks began to melt, and the soil seemed to ignite, while the closest trees went up in flames. Still, the dragons continued, sending flames in five never-ending streams against the ridge. The ground smoked and shook, and a rift opened. Bodies and burning rocks slipped down into the dark abyss, then pale-skinned greenhides, claw-less and fangless, tried to crawl up into the open air. The dragons ignored them, allowing them to scramble up the torn ground and flee into the woods.

The earth shook again, then Kelsey realised that a monstrous form was writhing under the ground. More rifts opened, and smoke belched out as the rest of the ridge collapsed. The gargantuan beast beneath the soil reared up, rubble and bodies rolling off its back. A huge head pulled itself free of the destruction and an enormous forelimb scythed through the air. Darksky soared upwards to avoid it, while Dawnflame stared at it in horror, her flames trickling to a stop.

'Kill it!' bellowed Deathfang, then opened his jaws.

The huge queen slashed out at the grey dragon, but Deathfang swept his wings up and pulled away. He sent out a great burst of flames, striking the queen on her flank. The other dragons stopped what they were doing and joined the attack. The queen hauled its hideous bulk across the rubble of the destroyed nest, trying to swat the dragons from the air, but they remained out of its range. They darted back and forth, sending blast after blast of flames at the form of the queen, and its screams echoed off the low hills.

More of the cliffside collapsed, and Kelsey turned to watch, a flurry of movement catching her eye. She glanced down, and saw a mass of child-queens pulling themselves out from the earth.

'Frostback!' she called. 'Over there!'

'Forget them,' cried Deathfang; 'kill the queen.'

The child-queens, now numbering at least a dozen, clustered around the base of the giant queen for protection, then, at an unseen signal, they turned, and fled into the forest, scattering in every direction, and disappearing into the shadows of the thick tree cover. The dragons ignored them, concentrating on finishing off the queen. Kelsey huddled down on the harness, her head dizzy with the fumes, heat and smoke. Again and again, the dragons swooped down and unleashed a barrage of flames, but the queen was strong, and seemed to take forever to succumb. At last, it fell, and the scorched and smouldering body crashed down onto the ruined earth, smashing through dozens of fire-wracked trees and sending up a cloud of ash and dust into the sky.

The dragons circled above, saying nothing, their eyes gazing downwards at the gargantuan corpse stretching over the ground. Its head was clearly too large for any dragon to carry, and none suggested it. Instead, they circled one more time, then soared off into the east, leaving a thick pall of black smoke hanging in the air behind them.

———

Kelsey ran up the stairs of the Command Post, her clothes still reeking of smoke from the nest. The soldiers guarding the doors of Van's apartment got out of her way, and she hurried into the entrance hall.

'Van?' she said, entering the living room.

The major-general looked up from the armchair where he sat each day to work. Cardova was also there, standing by a window, a thick sheaf of papers in his hand.

'You'll never guess what's happened,' Kelsey said. 'Pyre's arsehole; I need a drink.'

Van laughed, then glanced at Cardova. 'Get her a brandy.' He sniffed. 'What's that terrible smell?'

'It's probably me,' said Kelsey, sitting on the couch opposite him.

'Maybe you should get yourself cleaned up first,' he said. 'There's hot water.'

'I will, after I tell you.' She took the offered glass from Cardova. 'Cheers, Lucius. Listen, the dragons have just destroyed the nest; they killed the queen – I saw it with my own eyes.'

Cardova stared at her, then sat. 'When? Just now? Which dragons?'

Kelsey told them the story of what had happened, while they both listened in silence. She slurped a swig of brandy as soon as she had finished, and gulped it down.

'Well, well,' said Van. 'That's excellent news.' He glanced at Cardova. 'I hope you're not too upset about being beaten to it?'

The captain shrugged. 'No; it's fine. My ego is a little bruised, but if the job's done, then it doesn't matter. Well done, the dragons.'

'Originally,' Kelsey said, 'Deathfang was going to drop off its head in Pella, but it was too big to carry, and I think the dragons were exhausted by then, anyway. They're leaving it up to us to inform the Crown. They will, of course, expect the King and Queen to be overcome with gratitude. They believe it pays back the favour given by the Queen to help improve their colony in the mountains.'

'We can certainly tell the King and Queen,' said Van. 'You and Lucius can do it in person.'

'We'll take a boat this evening, sir,' said Cardova, reclining on the couch. He glanced at Kelsey. 'The head was too big to carry?'

'Aye; far too big. The queen was the size of the entire ridge.'

He nodded. 'Then, it definitely was the queen?'

'For sure,' said Kelsey. 'It was way bigger than the baby queens.'

'And,' he went on, 'just to set my mind at ease; all of the baby queens were dealt with at the same time?'

Kelsey frowned. 'I saw one get killed.'

'Only one? What happened to the others?'

'They escaped into the forest.'

Cardova put a hand over his eyes and groaned.

'Shit,' muttered Van. 'How many?'

'I don't know; a dozen? Is that bad? Please don't tell me it's bad.'

'No,' said Cardova; 'a dozen baby queens loose in the forest is great news, Kelsey.'

She folded her arms across her chest. 'Don't be sarcastic.'

Cardova sat up, his features simmering with anger. 'I'm not blaming you for this, Kelsey, but this is exactly why the damned dragons needed to follow a proper plan. They meant well, but they didn't know what they were doing, and they've made just about the worst mistake possible. Right now, a dozen baby queens are roaming around the forest, gathering soldiers, and any workers who survived, and scouting out locations for their new nests. It was imperative that we wiped out every queen, not just the main one.'

'Bollocks,' Kelsey muttered.

'The new queens will fight among themselves,' Cardova went on, 'which will thin out their numbers a little, but it still means that there will be a continual flow of greenhides, and several new nest sites to find.' He glanced over at Van. 'Permission to get drunk, sir?'

'Denied,' said Van; 'at least until you and Kelsey come back from Pella. Then, I might join you.'

'Frostback tried to warn them,' said Kelsey; 'she tried her best to persuade them to let the City know first, but Deathfang wanted it to be a surprise.'

'Yes, well, he's succeeded there,' said Van.

'Can we recall Halfclaw, sir?' said Cardova. 'We're going to need a dragon to begin looking for the baby queens. They're still vulnerable while they're out in the open. It would be best to start the search as soon as possible, before they have time to tunnel underground.'

'Ask the King and Queen this evening, and tell them I strongly recommend it. The biggest problem will be trying to reach the salve valley in the Eastern Mountains. Salvor's range doesn't extend that far, and neither does Mona's. They might not be in a position to send any message to Halfclaw.'

Cardova nodded.

'I'd better get cleaned up,' said Kelsey, getting to her feet. 'It seems I have a boat to catch.'

CHAPTER 14

TRUST

Pella, Auldan, The City – 13th Monan 3422

Emily sat cross-legged on the rug, watching as Elspeth crawled towards her.

'That's it,' Emily said, reaching out with her arms; 'crawl to mummy.'

In the corner of her eye, she could see Daniel pacing back and forward, his face mirroring his grim mood.

'Well done,' said Emily, sweeping the baby up as she reached her; 'good girl. Danny; stop pacing. You're making me dizzy.'

He glanced over at her. 'What?'

'I said, stop pacing. Sit down. Take a breath.'

'Don't you get it?' he said. 'Everything's falling apart. We're losing control of the City, piece by piece, in front of our very eyes. As if things weren't bad enough with the riots in the Circuit, and Naxor escaping, and the God-Queen hiding somewhere; now Jezra, the one place that we'd counted as a success, is threatened by a dozen disgruntled green-hide queens, thanks to those idiot dragons.'

'They were trying their best,' said Emily.

'No, they weren't. They were letting their pride dictate their actions, just as they did when they slaughtered all those Gloamers on the Grey

Isle. They weren't doing it to be kind.' He paused, and stared at the door of their quarters. 'Where is Salvor?'

'He'll be here soon, Danny.'

'If he's not, then we should meet the Rosers without him.'

'Do you want me to come along?'

'If you wouldn't mind. Whatever they're here to tell us, it must be big news; otherwise they wouldn't have sent the entire delegation. They must know that their court case is on the verge of collapse; the final appeal should be a formality. Perhaps they've seen sense at last. With no more legal tricks at their disposal, they've run out of other options.'

'I hope you're right, Danny, but the Circuit is a bigger concern to me.'

'Those fools riot over anything.'

'Listen to us. When Marcus was in charge, we were on the side of the Evaders; but now that we rule, we think the Evaders are acting like criminals. The Evaders haven't changed – have we?'

'That was different. Marcus was oppressing them; we're trying to liberate them.'

'By forcing them to accept a constitution that they oppose?'

'It's for their own good; they just don't realise it.'

'Spoken like a true Roser.'

He glared at her. 'I don't think I like the implications of what you're saying. Are you claiming that we are the tyrants? That by giving power to the people, we are somehow exploiting them? We haven't sent the Blades or the Banner into the Circuit to restore order, nor have we rustled up the militia of the other tribes to go in, and yet the Evaders are still burning their own houses down. I remember actually hoping that Naxor had been responsible for the assassination of the delegates; at least that would have pointed to an individual who could be brought to justice. But no; it wasn't him. It was just the same old anarchy that's always blighted that damn territory; the same old cycle of violence that they can't seem to break, no matter what we do. I've had it with them.'

'With whom? The Evaders? Are you forgetting that I am one?'

'But, you're not really an Evader; you were brought up as a Roser. It's different. The people in the Circuit don't see you as one of them.'

'And the Rosers don't see me as one of them, either. I'm stuck in the middle, as if I don't have a tribe. My culture and accent offend the Evaders, and my blood offends the Rosers. Instead of representing the best of both worlds, I'm the worst.'

'Fine, I'm not going to argue with you. What should we do, then?'

'Postpone the elections, Danny. We have to.'

His face twisted in fury. 'No. We push ahead.'

'If we do that, we might push the entire City off a cliff.'

'There is no alternative.'

'There's always an alternative. We call off the elections and lay the rest of the reforms aside until the City calms down. Then, we start our search for a consensus again.'

'You don't understand, Emily. This is the greatest test of our lives. We can't fail. If we do, then the opportunity for change will never come round again. The members of the established orders – the merchants' guilds, the landowners, the aristocrats, the lawyers, the Evader anarchists – all will dig in, knowing that, when it came to it, we blinked first.'

Emily glanced down at the baby in her arms. For the first time, she felt a sense of dread for the child's future. Would Elspeth grow up feeling the same burdens as she did? The weight of responsibility seemed overwhelming; did she want her daughter to have to carry it too? She remembered the clarity with which she had begun her reign as Queen; that had long vanished, replaced by compromise and disappointment, and the feeling of hitting your head off a wall. Already, she was starting to view the ordinary citizens of the City differently, as untrustworthy and fickle; as incapable of deciding things for themselves; as people who needed to be governed with rules for their own good, whether they agreed or not. It was power that had done this to her, and to Danny; he was changing too, and not for the better.

'Where is Salvor?' the King said, his eyes glancing back at the door.

'Do you ever think about abdicating?'

He stared at her. 'What?'

'Do you ever think that we could simply return to a normal life?'

'No. It's too late for that. We might not be perfect, but we're better than those who would follow us if we ever gave up power. We would be replaced by the God-Queen and her demigods, who would force the people back into chains; and then they would come for us, even if all we wanted to do was live in peace. They couldn't allow it. We would always be a threat, and they would have to kill us, even little Elspeth. If we abdicated, they would murder us, and the City would be ripped apart.'

He paced up and down again, then stopped. 'We should go and see the Rosers.'

'Alright. Give me a minute.'

She got up, Elspeth gathered in her arms, and walked to a side door. She pushed it open with a foot, and went through into the nursery, where her mother was sitting, reading.

'Hello, dear,' her mother said. 'Are you going to work?'

'Yes, mother,' Emily said.

'What's wrong?'

'Nothing; I'm fine.'

Her mother nodded. 'Alright. I'm here, if you need to talk.'

Emily placed Elspeth into her cot. 'If you see Salvor, let him know that we've gone to speak with the Roser delegation.'

'I shall,' she said, her eyes tracking Emily's movements.

Elspeth raised her arms and began to cry. Emily's mother stood, put down her book, and walked over to the cot.

'I'll deal with this,' she said. 'You go and do what you need to do.'

Emily watched her mother pick up Elspeth, then nodded and left the room. Daniel was back to pacing the floor of the living room, his gaze lowered. Emily checked her reflection in the wall mirror, and straightened her dress. She had a few lines under her eyes from lack of sleep, and looked tired, but had no time to re-apply any make-up. It didn't matter. The Rosers usually dealt with Danny; they probably wouldn't even notice her presence.

'Are you ready?' the King said.

'Yes.'

He opened the door, and they strode out. A squad of Royal Guards immediately saluted, and formed up around them. Gone were the days when members of the public could get close to the royal quarters; dozens of soldiers now shielded them from the citizenry, and access was restricted to most areas of the palace. It had made them feel safer, but Emily knew that something had been lost.

They walked down to the wing where the meetings of the Tribal Council were held, and soldiers opened the doors for them. Inside, the large hall was mostly empty, excepting the seats at the table where the Rosers sat. The five delegates stood when the King and Queen entered, and each bowed towards them.

'Good morning,' said Daniel. 'I hope your journey from Tara was pleasant.'

'Thank you, your Majesty,' said the chief delegate, bowing again. 'Will Lord Salvor be in attendance?'

'No,' said the King. 'He is busy. The Queen and I shall hear your statement.'

Daniel and Emily took their seats on the low platform at the end of the hall. A handful of courtiers entered from another door, and took up their seats, getting ready to record the meeting. The Roser delegates sat, except for their leader, who remained on his feet, a rolled-up document in his hands.

'Speak,' said the King.

The chief delegate bowed his head. 'Thank you, your most gracious Majesties. The leaders of the Roser tribe have, after much deliberation, asked me to present to the Royal Court the following message – that, as of this day, the thirteenth of Monan, in the year Thirty-four, Twenty-two of the City, that they no longer recognise the authority of the Crown in Pella; that they are withdrawing from the Tribal Council, and from all treaties, negotiations and agreements previously made; that they are to be considered an independent entity within the bounds of the City; that...'

'Stop,' said the King.

The chief delegate glanced up at the platform, his eyes betraying his nerves.

'This is ridiculous,' said Daniel. 'The Rosers cannot leave the City.'

'Be that as it may; it is the decision of the Roser leadership. We shall no longer bow to the Aurelian Crown. Your mandate is illegitimate and your reign illegal. All aspects of the new constitutional laws that have been passed are hereby revoked, and the old customs posts around Roser territory have been re-established as of dawn this morning. We name you as usurpers, and no longer recognise your authority over us.'

He folded the document, and placed it back within his robes.

Daniel stared at him. 'You cannot do this.'

'You say that, but we have done it; so, logically, you must be incorrect.'

'You will address me by my proper title.'

'No. The time for such pretence is over.'

'I will arrest each one of you!' Daniel cried. 'You will be sent to the dungeons in chains for this act of rebellion.'

'Each of us knew that it might come to this,' said the chief delegate, 'and yet we still came here, to inform you of our decision. Do your worst.'

'I could have a thousand Banner soldiers in Tara by the end of the day,' Daniel said, his eyes burning with rage. 'Perhaps they will knock some sense into you.'

'You have the military might to do so,' said the chief delegate, 'but I would advise caution. Imagine the reaction of the rest of the City, when they learn that the so-called King has sent foreign troops into the territory of another tribe. You would need a force ten times the size of the Banner to occupy the entire City. Or, will you choose to rain down dragon fire upon the people, as you did on the Grey Isle?'

Daniel said nothing, seemingly too stunned to speak.

'What is the next step?' said Emily.

'Excuse me?' said the chief delegate. 'The next step?'

'Yes. Once you have returned to Tara, what then? The Rosers cannot seal themselves off from the rest of the City; none of us can survive in isolation. We may have our differences, but we all have to share the same, small piece of land. Is it monarchy in general that you dislike, or just us?'

'We believe that, by taking a stand, we shall initiate a chain reaction in the rest of the City. Once the other tribes see what we have done, then they will follow our lead, and you will be deposed.'

'I see. And then? Is there another leader, waiting for their opportunity? A leader whom you could bow to?'

'Are you referring to the rumours of the God-Queen's return?'

'Let's imagine that I am. Is that the kind of rule you wish to return to? Come now; be honest with us. If you are declaring rebellion against our rule, then be frank about whom you wish to replace us.'

'It is not part of my remit to discuss these matters.'

'Are you too cowardly to admit it? Too craven to confess that you prefer the certainties of oppression to the uncertainties of change? Go back to Tara, and tell them that we refuse to accept their position. The rabble who claim to lead the Rosers have no authority to secede from the City, and that is the end of the matter. Come back to us when you have something more constructive to say.'

The chief delegate frowned. 'Is that it? You refuse to accept that we can secede? If that is your message, then we shall relay it to our peers in Tara. However, the fact remains – we have already seceded, and there is nothing you can do to prevent that, short of a brutal military occupation of our territory.'

Emily studied her nails, then glanced up. 'Are you still here?'

The five delegates looked at each other, then gathered their things and strode from the hall.

'That seems to answer the question of when the God-Queen will make her move,' said Emily. 'The Rosers must have been in contact with her; they're too fearful to have acted on their own.'

She glanced at Daniel, but his eyes were downcast.

'I wonder what the God-Queen has promised them,' Emily went on, stepping down from the throne. 'I imagine a return to the old land laws and tribal courts, along with no elections, naturally. She must be eyeing up her old palace.'

Daniel got to his feet, and began walking towards the door.

'Where are you going?' she said.

'To summon the Banner,' he said. 'Tara will be ours by nightfall.'

'No, Danny,' she cried. 'That's what they want us to do. We'd be playing right into their hands.'

He turned to her, his eyes burning with anger. 'Then, what do you suggest we do?'

'Nothing. We ignore it. It's bluster, nothing more. In practical terms, it's meaningless, unless we choose to ascribe meaning to it. Let's walk to Salvor's office, and see what's been keeping him.'

'How can you be so calm?'

'Because the alternative is despair, and I refuse to despair.'

'The Rosers have betrayed us; those vile worthless bastards. They deserve to have the Banner inflicted upon them.'

'They are the same people as they were yesterday, Danny. Did you hate them then? They need time to cool off, and if that means letting them think they've won for a while, then so be it. If we ignore their silly proclamations, then they'll have no choice but to come back and negotiate. We need to be the grown-ups in this situation.'

'They aren't naughty children, Emily; they're traitors.'

'Perhaps. Let's not turn them into martyrs.'

He shook his head and walked from the hall, heading towards Salvor's office. Emily bit her tongue and followed him, their guards flanking them as they made their way through the palace. They reached the office of the demigod, and a pair of guards on duty there saluted.

'Is Salvor inside?' said the King.

'No, your Majesty,' said one of the guards. 'He hasn't been in his office all morning.'

'Go to his quarters, then, and ask him to come here.'

The guard bowed. 'Yes, your Majesty.'

The King and Queen entered the room as the guard ran off towards

Salvor's own rooms in the palace. Daniel went up to a cabinet and poured himself a brandy, and Emily took a seat by the long meeting table.

'Let's see what Salvor has to say about all this,' Daniel said.

'You trust his opinion over mine?'

'No; I just need to hear what he has to say. The chances are that he'll take your side. He has always been over-cautious.'

'Is that what you think I am?' she said.

'When it comes to my ideas – yes. When it comes to doing what you want to do, such as invade the Grey Isle, then you don't seem to hold back.'

'Are you going to cast that up at me forever? I have already admitted that I made a mistake with the Grey Isle. And, before you say it; no, I have no intention of handing it back to the Gloamers.'

'See? One rule for you, and another for me.'

'But, Danny, what possible good could come from sending the Banner into Tara?'

He shrugged. 'It would teach the Rosers a lesson. They have lorded it over the other tribes for so long, that they need their arrogance clipped. I don't think the other tribes would react badly to seeing the Rosers brought down a peg or two.'

'Sending soldiers into Tara is about the only thing that would rally the rest of the City behind the Rosers. And think; what if the God-Queen is waiting for us to do this? What if she appears in Tara, and kills the Banner soldiers? She would be treated as a returning hero. A liberator.'

Daniel frowned. 'Then, we send in Kelsey Holdfast and her dragon. The God-Queen wouldn't be able to touch them.'

'Is this the legacy we want to bequeath to Elspeth? A throne soaked in the blood of the citizens?'

'If there is no punishment for traitors, then everyone will revolt; don't you see? Sometimes, fear is the only thing that keeps the City from descending into anarchy.'

'Fear of whom? Us? I don't want people to fear us.'

'Then you shouldn't have become Queen.'

The door opened, and a member of the Royal Guard entered.

'Your Majesties, Lord Salvor is not in the palace, and...'

'What?' said the King. 'Where is he?'

'We don't know, your Majesty. However, the other...'

'Send out guards to search for him. He must be close.'

'Yes, your Majesty, but...'

'Go,' said the King. 'You are dismissed.'

'Wait,' said Emily. 'What else are you trying to tell us?'

The guard bowed. 'The other demigods are also not in the palace, your Majesty. When we looked in Lord Salvor's apartments, we also checked those belonging to Lord Collo, and Ladies Ikara and Vana. None of them are in the palace.'

'But,' said the Queen, 'someone must have seen them leave. Those apartments have guards, do they not?'

'They do, your Majesty. However, no one seems to have seen the demigods leave Cuidrach. The guards were sure at first that they were still in their rooms. It was only after we checked that we realised that they had gone. Their luggage, and much of their possessions also seem to have vanished.'

'What about Lady Silva?'

'Her rooms are in a different part of the palace, your Majesty. Should I have them checked, also?'

'Yes. No; wait. We'll come along.'

The guard bowed.

'How could this be possible?' said Daniel. 'It doesn't make any sense.' He closed his eyes. 'The Quadrant. The God-Queen has been here, in the palace, right under our noses.'

They hurried along the marble corridors of Cuidrach Palace, passing soldiers who were searching every wing and room for the missing demigods. Emily suspected that the search was futile; that the demigods had long gone, but she knew they had to be thorough. They left their own guards at the front door of Silva's small apartment, and entered. It was dark inside, with every shutter closed against the sunlight.

Emily glanced around at the thick shadows. 'Silva?'

She heard a groan coming from the demigod's bedroom, and pushed open the door. Silva was lying sprawled on the ground next to the bed. Her eyes were half-open, but her face seemed to have aged, and she looked close to death.

Emily and Daniel rushed to her side.

'What happened?' cried Emily, taking the demigod's hand. 'Can you hear me?'

'Your Majesty,' Silva groaned; 'I can't feel my self-healing powers; I can't feel any of my powers. Am I dying?'

'Help me get her onto the bed,' Emily said.

Daniel lifted the demigod's legs, and Emily took her shoulders, and they eased Silva onto the freshly-made bed, where she started to tremble and shake. Daniel's eyes went back to the floor, and he stooped down and picked something up.

'A vial,' he said. 'Anti-salve.'

'Be careful,' said Emily; 'it can kill mortals.'

'There's none left,' he said. 'Silva's been poisoned.'

Silva tried to sit up, but fell back down again. 'Naxor...' she groaned.

'Naxor was here?' said Emily. 'What can we do to help? What fixes anti-salve?'

'Only real salve,' said Daniel; 'and Naxor stole it all when he escaped.'

'Naxor...' Silva repeated; 'and Amalia. They tried to make me change sides, and when I refused, they forced me to drink from the vial. They took Salvor.'

Emily sat on the bed. 'When?'

'A few hours ago. Just after dawn. They had a Quadrant.'

'Did they tell you what they were planning?' said Daniel.

'No, your Majesty. They told me nothing like that; just that they were going to remove you from the throne, and take power for themselves. They offered me a position in their new government, but I don't work with traitors.'

'Thank you,' said Emily. 'I'm sorry that you suffered because of your loyalty.'

'What about Salvor?' Daniel said. 'Did he... turn? Is he on their side now?'

'I didn't see him, your Majesty. Naxor said that Salvor was going with them, but I don't know if he went willingly or not.'

'Our world is falling apart around us,' said the King. He frowned. 'Why didn't they kill you?'

'I don't know, your Majesty. They said that I might still be useful to them, once you have been overthrown.'

'That's not it,' said Emily; 'Amalia wants us to know that she was here. She could have sneaked in and out, and kept it all a mystery, but no; she wants us to know who did this. She wants us to be afraid.'

'It has begun,' said Daniel. 'The war has begun.'

Emily stood. 'Not yet, but it's close. We'll leave you to rest, Silva. I'll have doctors and servants come here to attend to your needs. Without salve to reverse the poison, you'll need time to recover; it's the only cure.'

'I'll try to be back on my feet as soon as possible, your Majesty.'

'Don't rush it, Silva. I don't want to lose you as well.'

She leaned over and kissed the demigod on the forehead, then she and Daniel left her rooms. Outside, Emily instructed a guard to fetch what Silva needed, and then they walked back to Salvor's office, which was still lying empty.

'What now?' said Daniel.

'We need to send a message to each of our allies – Quill, Yvona, Van. And we need to summon the Banner.'

Daniel raised an eyebrow. 'Have you come round to my way of thinking?'

'No. I still think sending soldiers into Tara is a trap; a mistake that Amalia is hoping we make. All the same, we should transfer a full regiment to Pella, and get ready to fight. Once Amalia realises that we're not going to occupy Tara, then she'll make her move. We have to be ready. We'll need the Blades on full alert, too, and every militia that's willing to fight alongside us against the God-Queen. And Frostback, as our last line of defence.'

The air in the corner of the office crackled, and two figures appeared. Emily jumped in fright, and staggered back a step. One of the figures was Salvor, who collapsed to the ground the moment he appeared. The other was a young woman with a copper-coloured device clutched in her right hand.

She smiled at the King and Queen. 'Ah, the usurpers. I hope you have been enjoying your time upon my throne.'

'Amalia?' said Daniel.

'Indeed; it is I. I know I'm looking a lot prettier these days, but it's still me on the inside. I would kill you both now, but that would be too easy, and would look bad. As Naxor is forever telling me, appearances count, and we need the City to see me as its saviour, not as a cruel murderer of the weak, and you two are nothing if not weak. Rest assured that you will see me again, and when you do, you can bid farewell to your crowns. Now, go back to your rooms, and take a good long look at your daughter. The only question I want you to ask yourselves is this – what would you do to ensure the safety of your little girl? Think about that, Aurelian traitors. Goodbye.'

The air crackled again, and Amalia vanished, leaving Salvor lying on the floor. He groaned, and raised his head.

'Are you alright?' said Emily.

'They dosed me with anti-salve,' the demigod said, his face lined with pain; 'and then they tortured me.'

She hurried to his side and crouched by him, while Daniel stood back, a wary look in his eye.

'Where are they hiding?' said Emily.

'I don't know. They took me to a dark room with no windows. My brother read my mind; they know everything. I'm sorry.'

'It's alright, Salvor,' said Emily. 'It wasn't your fault.'

'This could be another trap,' said Daniel.

Emily glanced from her husband to the injured demigod.

'We have to trust each other,' she said.

'But, he might be working for the God-Queen,' said Daniel. 'How can we trust him?'

'Because, Danny,' she said; 'trust is all we have left.'

CHAPTER 15

FAMILY REUNION

Port Sanders, Medio, The City – 13th Monan 3422

The air shimmered in the corner of the mansion's front room, and Amalia appeared. She tucked the Quadrant into her robes, and the occupants of the room fell silent, their conversations halted.

'It is done,' said Amalia; 'Salvor has been returned to Cuidrach Palace.'

Kagan glanced over at the couch, where four demigods were sitting. Apart from Naxor, they looked terrified, and were staring at the former God-Queen. Kagan could hardly bring himself to call her 'Sofia' any more.

'I also happened to bump into the King and Queen while I was there,' she said.

'Excellent,' said Naxor; 'then it's over. We've won. I mean, I assume you slew them both, and their offspring?'

'No.'

'Why not?' Naxor exclaimed, getting to his feet. 'You saw them, in the palace, and you let them go?'

Amalia walked over and sat down next to Kagan. 'Yes. What would be the point of murdering them in cold blood? The people of the City would feel nothing but sympathy for them. It would make the start of our rule dangerous.'

Naxor shook his head. 'Are you getting befuddled in your old age, grandmother? Who cares what the mortals think? How in the world did you come up with a stupid idea like that?'

Amalia smiled. 'I told them it was your idea.'

'Go back to Cuidrach, now, and kill them.'

'No, grandson. Sit down; you're getting a little hysterical.'

'The King and Queen are defenceless,' Naxor said; 'we have them. Go back and finish off the job.'

'No. But, if you really think they're defenceless, then why don't you go and do it yourself, Naxor? Why don't you go and kill them?'

'But... I, uh... fighting isn't really my sort of thing.'

Amalia turned to the other demigods. 'What about you? Any volunteers?'

No one spoke.

'I see,' said Amalia. 'Once again, my useless grandchildren expect me to do all the work. Well, I've made up my mind – if we're going to take over the City, then I want to do it with the people behind us. Or, at least not actively opposed to us. Cutting down Daniel and Emily Aurelian, and their eight-month-old child, would do nothing but turn them into martyrs. If my plan succeeds, then Banner soldiers will soon be arriving in Pella. If they enter Tara, then we shall have our excuse to start a war; a war of liberation, not a war of conquest. When I'm back in Maeladh, I don't want mobs of angry mortals at the gates; I want happy mortals toiling in the fields.'

'Grandmother,' said Ikara, 'I was wondering...'

'Hush, Ikara,' said Amalia. 'No one wants to listen to your inane nonsense.'

The demigod's face went red, while Collo laughed.

'I don't know what you're laughing about,' said Amalia, 'unless it's the realisation that you have utterly wasted your life. You could have died a hundred years ago, Collo, and no one would have noticed. Do something useful and get me a drink.'

Collo shuffled to his feet, his eyes cast down, then went over to a glass-fronted cupboard by the wall.

'Vana,' said Amalia.

The demigod's face paled. 'Yes, grandmother?'

'Don't look so nervous,' said Amalia. 'Have your powers returned?'

'Yes; the anti-salve has worn off.'

'Good. Can you sense Salvor in Pella?'

Vana closed her eyes for a moment. 'Yes. He's there. The anti-salve he took has also worn off.'

'Silva?'

Vana closed her eyes again. 'No. There's no sign of Silva.'

'Good; thank you,' said Amalia. 'Now, this is a guess, but I believe that Silva will remain powerless for at least a few days. By the time her powers return, we shall be back in control of the City. Without Silva, Salvor will not be able to find us, and so we should be able to remain hidden.'

'What did you do to Salvor?' said Kagan.

'We tortured him,' said Naxor, smirking.

Kagan glared at the demigod. 'You tortured your own brother, and now you're smiling about it?'

'Yes. It was funny. Come on; he's a damn demigod; he'll be fine. He'll have healed himself by now.'

'Then, why did you do it?'

'As part of a complex double-bluff,' Naxor said; 'you wouldn't understand, boy.'

'Don't call him "boy," Naxor,' said Amalia; 'Kagan's more of a man than you'll ever be.'

Collo returned to the centre of the room with a tray of drinks. He set it down onto the low table, then sat.

Vana reached for a glass. 'Can we trust Kagan? He's only a mortal.'

'Ahh, but Vana,' said Naxor, 'Kagan is more than a mere mortal. He's also our grandmother's conscience, because, as we all know, she hasn't got one of her own.'

Amalia raised an eyebrow. 'Says the man who wants to kill an eight-month-old baby.'

'I don't want to kill the princess any more,' said Naxor; 'she'd be far more useful as Maxwell's bride.'

'Who's Maxwell?' said Vana.

Amalia nodded over to Gellie. 'Bring him in.'

Gellie bowed. 'Yes, ma'am.'

The Fordian housekeeper left the room, and appeared a moment later, pushing a small pram.

'A baby?' cried Vana, standing. 'Whose baby?'

'Mine, obviously,' said Amalia. 'Kagan is the father. We're betrothed.'

Vana, Ikara and Collo stared at her, their mouths hanging open. Amalia shook her head at them, then stood, and walked over to the pram. She leaned inside and scooped up Maxwell, wrapped in blankets and swaddling.

'None of you will remember this, of course,' she said, 'but I was quite peaceful, for many long centuries, when I was raising my six children. I clearly didn't do a very good job, and I hope to do better this time. In fact, Kagan and I are planning on having several more children. In time, they will grow up to supplement the ranks of demigods in the City.'

'Why did you have a baby before taking back power?' said Ikara. 'That seems the wrong way round.'

'You're quite right, Ikara, which surprises me, to be honest. I had intended on remaining hidden for at least a hundred years, but that idiot Naxor ruined it all by forcing me out into the open.'

The baby awoke in Amalia's arms, and gazed around the room, his eyes wide.

Amalia smiled down at him. 'He reminds me a little of Michael. Naxor suggested that he marry Princess Elspeth, so that the Aurelian and god lines are blended in their union. It wasn't the worst idea he's ever had.'

Naxor grinned. 'It was a genius idea, from the smartest guy in the room.'

Ikara rolled her eyes, as Amalia placed the baby back into the pram.

'It makes a lot of sense,' said Vana; 'especially if we want to placate the mortals. I think they'd be more willing to accept a ruler who was connected to the Aurelians. We shouldn't forget that the current King and Queen are quite popular among certain sections of the population.'

'That is unfortunately true,' said Naxor, 'but their real support lies with the Reapers and Hammers, and neither are in a position to stop us. All the same, if something tragic were to befall the King and Queen, then little Princess Elspeth will need regents. The God-Queen could govern the regency, waiting for the day when Prince Maxwell and Princess Elspeth are wed, and come into their own.'

Kagan shook his head. 'While you control everything from behind the scenes?'

'Not just me,' said Naxor. 'All of us in this room, along with any other demigod who is willing to pledge allegiance. Lydia, for example, would join us in a flash, and many of the others will come round in time. What's important is that the government is in the hands of immortals; this crass experiment in letting the mortals take over has been little short of a disaster.'

'In some ways, it was worth trying,' said Vana, 'just to prove to them that it can't be done.'

'My,' said Amalia, 'you're brimming with wisdom this morning, Vana. It's a shame that, out of the three demigods I plucked from Cuidrach, you are the only one I don't trust. Perhaps if you hadn't been so willing to side with the Holdfasts on Lostwell, I would have more sympathy with your opinions.'

Vana blinked. 'But, none of that was my fault. I didn't even want to go to Lostwell; Naxor forced me to leave the City. And then, once I was there, what was I supposed to do? The arrival of the Holdfasts was a calamity for me, personally. First, Karalyn nearly killed me, then Corthie appeared, and behaved like an ignorant pig. I was as much a victim of them as anyone else.'

'That is true, grandmother,' said Naxor. 'Poor old Vana did the best she could. I had to listen to her many complaints about Lostwell, and about how much she wanted to return here, to her home. I'm not sure why; I quite liked Lostwell.'

Vana narrowed her eyes. 'It was a vile place. The Falls of Iron was bearable, at least until Irno was killed and the Ascendants destroyed it. As for the rest of it? Let's just say that I won't be shedding any tears over the demise of Lostwell.'

Kagan jumped to his feet, his fists clenched. 'You gods are all the same. Millions were killed on Lostwell – my friends, my family; the whole city of Alea Tanton was obliterated because some gods decided that they didn't like it. Gellie's entire people were almost completely wiped out; there's what? A thousand Fordians left alive? And you refuse to shed any tears? It's no wonder the people of the City rose up against you, if that's your attitude.'

He paused, noticing the eyes of everyone in the room boring into him. Vana, Ikara and Collo were looking at him with contempt, while Naxor was smothering a smirk.

'Let's take a short break,' said Amalia. 'Family reunions can be quite exhausting.' She stood. 'Gellie will see to your needs, and show you each to your accommodation. Kagan, let's retire to my rooms for a while, before we carry out the next step of my plan.'

She smiled, then strode from the room. Kagan glanced down at the four demigods, his features betraying what he thought of them, then followed her out. They went up the stairs to Amalia's private quarters and walked inside.

'That was quite a little speech, Kagan,' Amalia said, as she closed the door behind them. 'Am I to assume that you feel that way about every god?'

Kagan glared at her, heedless of the danger. 'You've changed. Before Naxor appeared, you were different. I was watching, and listening, to how you dealt with your family down there – is it all a bluff? An act? A few days ago, you were completely opposed to retaking power, and now you're marshalling your forces and ordering everyone around; not to mention bullying Collo and the others; not that they don't deserve it.' He sat down onto a couch and put his head in his hands. 'I don't know how I'm supposed to deal with this. I love you, Sofia; I mean, Amalia. But this? I hate this.'

Amalia kept her gaze on him, then sighed, and sat down. 'When I have to be the God-Queen; I am the God-Queen. My grandchildren are lazy, stupid and spoilt. Perhaps my loathing of them comes out as bullying, but if that's the only way to control them, then I'm not going to apologise for it.' She took his hand. 'Look, Kagan; try to see all of this as temporary. A short interlude between living here, and moving to Maeladh Palace. Once we're there, and the grandchildren are ruling the City in my name, then things can go back to the way they were. Before Khora's death, I barely left Maeladh in three hundred years; what people don't seem to understand, is that I crave a return to those days of peace and quiet. If I have to act ruthlessly to achieve that aim, then I will do so. It doesn't mean I enjoy it.'

He glanced at her. 'Is that why you didn't kill the King and Queen when you had the chance?'

'Partly. It was also to do with the shock of seeing them; I wasn't expecting them to be alone in Salvor's office. Maybe if they didn't also have a small child, then I might not have hesitated; but it made me think of Maxwell. Did I make a mistake? If I had struck them down, then perhaps we would have already won, just as Naxor said.'

'Are you expecting me to answer that?'

'Yes, Kagan; it wasn't rhetorical. Should I have killed them?'

'Are they evil?'

'Who, the King and Queen?'

'Yes. Are they selfish, uncaring rulers, who oppress the people of the City?'

'They're certainly not perfect, and have made a host of silly mistakes, but evil? Incompetent, maybe; but not evil.'

'Then, you already know the answer to your question.'

She raised an eyebrow.

'Or,' he went on, 'it is true what Naxor said – that you don't have a conscience?'

'Let me tell you a secret. It's not really a secret, but it may come as a surprise. Kagan, you know me much better than Naxor does. You know me better than any of the surviving demigods do. To them, I was always a distant, remote figure. A tyrant, perhaps, but one that remained out of reach, locked up in her palace. Whenever I emerged, such as in the last days of the Civil War, or when Khora was killed, it was always in a flurry of violence. That's what they remember, not the long centuries of peace that elapsed between each episode. I was more than happy to leave the running of the City to others, as long as my position wasn't threatened. So, knowing all that, and knowing me better than anyone else does; what do you say, Kagan? Do you think I have a conscience?'

He looked into her eyes. 'Yes. The woman I know is kind and generous; loyal and warm-hearted. The problem is, the woman I've seen over the last few days isn't like that.'

She nodded, then pulled her glance away from him. 'I know, Kagan. You're going to have to trust me. All we need to do is get through the next few days, and it will be over. I hate to admit it, but you are a restraining influence on me. Perhaps that's another reason why I didn't kill the King and Queen; I knew that you would look at me in a different way; that you would hate me for it. Stay with me, Kagan; don't leave. Be my conscience; be there to remind me of the good things – you, Maxwell, our life together; so that I don't forget myself. If you had been in Medio, I wouldn't have opened the gates.'

A tear rolled down her cheek. He reached out with a hand, and wiped it away.

'I'll never leave you, Amalia.'

It was early evening when they all gathered again in the front room of the mansion. Ikara looked bored, as if she had been expecting to lead a revolution; Collo seemed dazed, and smelled of opium; while Vana sat perched on the edge of the couch, her left leg involuntarily shaking. Only Naxor looked relaxed and at ease, his feet up on a chair as he sipped from a large brandy glass.

They turned as Kagan and Amalia strode into the room.

'I trust that your accommodation is acceptable?' Amalia said. 'If not, then there's little I can do about it. In a few days, you'll have your pick of palaces; excepting Maeladh, of course. Maeladh is mine.'

'I think I'll take Redmarket,' said Ikara.

'You'll need to renovate it first,' said Naxor. 'The Evaders have set up a commune inside it, and have made a frightful mess of the place. It'll be Cuidrach for me, I imagine. Now, grandmother; you mentioned the next stage of your plan? Is there any chance you might deign to tell us what it might be?'

'I assumed that you had read it out of my mind, dear grandson.'

He laughed. 'If I were powerful enough to read you, without you noticing, then I would have done so.' He shrugged. 'I've read Kagan's thoughts.'

'Stay out of my head,' Kagan said; 'you don't belong in there.'

'I'll do as I please, boy.'

Amalia raised her finger, and Naxor fell off the chair, writhing in agony. The other demigods fell silent, staring as Naxor's skin dissolved into discoloured boils and lesions.

'What did I warn you about?' said Amalia. 'I told you not to call him that. From now on, you will stay out of Kagan's mind. Nod if you understand.'

Naxor nodded, his face gripped by pain.

Amalia lowered her hand. 'Right. The next stage of the plan. Come on, Naxor, don't just lie there; get up. You will be coming with me, along with Kagan. The rest of you will remain here.'

'But, grandmother,' said Ikara; 'I want to do something useful. I have battle-vision; you might need that.'

'Ikara, your battle-vision is like Naxor's; often rumoured, but rarely seen.' She paused for a moment. 'Alright; I'll give you a chance to prove yourself. Gellie, fetch my granddaughter an assortment of sharp and pointy weapons; Kagan can select one also.'

The housekeeper bowed. 'Yes, ma'am.'

'Vana,' Amalia said, 'you shall stay here. Keep an eye on Collo; make sure he doesn't wander off. If he blunders his way into the kitchen, there's a good chance my cook will kill him. I assume that you have no desire to see some action?'

'None whatsoever, grandmother,' said Vana. 'I'm perfectly happy to wait here.'

'Keep your senses attuned, in case any of our enemies approach. I doubt it will happen, but Salvor might get lucky.'

Gellie came back into the room, bearing a large bundle wrapped in a blanket. She set it down on the table, and unveiled a small selection of swords, all in their sheaths. Kagan walked over, and picked one with a short, stabbing blade, then strapped it to his belt. Ikara browsed through the rest, and selected a long sword. Naxor got to his feet, a sullen expression on his face, but made no move towards the weapons.

'Where are we going?' he said.

'You'll soon see,' said Amalia. 'Gather round.'

Kagan, Ikara and Naxor moved into position by Amalia's side.

'Get ready to send people to sleep, Naxor,' she said, pulling the Quadrant from her robes. 'Let's keep the deaths to a minimum – a bloodbath is in no one's interests.' She glanced at Gellie. 'If we're not back in an hour, start to worry. After two hours, initiate the back up plan.'

'Yes, ma'am.'

'The back up plan?' said Naxor.

'Yes,' said Amalia. 'One can never be too thorough. If we are captured or killed, then I need to know that Maxwell and Gellie will be safe.'

She slid her fingers over the surface of the Quadrant, and the air shimmered. The front room of the mansion vanished, and was replaced by stone walls shrouded in shadow. Kagan glanced around. They were in a windowless passageway, lit by a couple of oil lamps.

'Where are we?' said Ikara, a hand on the hilt of her sword.

'Under the Fortress of the Lifegiver,' said Amalia. 'Naxor, find me a route to my son's cell.'

'What?' said Naxor. 'Are you serious? We're here to rescue that mad bastard? Montieth's better off locked up. We're better off if Montieth's locked up.'

'Don't be ridiculous. We need all the allies we can get, and Montieth was kind to me when I first arrived and was desperate for help. I'm not going to abandon him now. Find me the route.'

Naxor groaned, then nodded, his eyes glazing over. The others waited for a moment, then Naxor spluttered and coughed.

'Follow me,' he said.

They set off down the dark passageway, keeping quiet as they traversed the silent tunnels and cellars of the fortress. They came to a doorway, and Naxor paused.

'There are six guards on the other side of that door,' he whispered. 'One of them has the keys to the dungeon where the prince is being held. Look, is this wise? Montieth hates me.'

'Everyone hates you, Naxor,' said Amalia.

'Yes, but Montieth might take one look at me and rot my brains.'

'He probably won't even remember who you are,' said Amalia. 'He's never been good at recalling his various nephews and nieces; you'll be fine. Open the door, and send the guards to sleep.'

Naxor nodded. He placed his shoulder on the door and shoved it open, then leapt through, his hand raised. Moments later, Kagan heard several thumps, as the guards hit the ground. They went through the doorway, where Naxor was kneeling by one of the unconscious bodies, rifling through their pockets. He produced a set of keys, and they hurried to another door. Naxor unlocked it, and they came into a long hallway, with barred cells running down one wall.

They passed the first one, which contained a woman with a hood tied over her head.

'Who's there?' the woman cried.

Amalia paused, her eyes narrowing.

'That's Felice,' said Naxor; 'one of the old ruling gods from Lostwell.'

Kagan gasped. 'The patron of the Blue Thumbs?'

'Who's talking?' said Felice. 'That's right. I'm the patron of the Blue Thumbs. Are you from Lostwell?'

'Be quiet!' came a voice from the neighbouring cell. 'I am trying to rest.'

Amalia smiled, and they walked to the next cell along. She gestured to the door, and Naxor stepped forward, and unlocked it.

'It's your lucky day,' said Amalia.

The hooded and chained figure fell still. 'Mother?'

'Get those chains off him,' she said to Naxor.

'Make him promise he won't kill me first.'

'Did you hear that, son?' said Amalia. 'We are here to rescue you – no killing.'

Montieth laughed, and held up his gauntlet-enclosed hands. Naxor frowned, then walked into the cell, and began searching for the correct keys.

'Is this one of my nephews?' said Montieth.

'It's Naxor,' said Amalia; 'one of Khora's boys.'

'No; doesn't ring any bells, I'm afraid,' said Montieth.

'He's on our side, son; that's all you need to know.'

'"Our side," eh? Do we have a side now?'

'We do, indeed, son. We're taking the City back from the mortals.'

'About bloody time too.'

The gauntlets opened, and fell to the ground with a clang. Montieth flexed his fingers, while Naxor reached up to unfasten the hood.

'Who else do we have?' said Montieth. 'Is Amber here?'

'No, son. She is being watched by the mortals, and is unaware of what we're doing, as Salvor reads her mind regularly.'

'Who's Salvor?'

'Another of Khora's boys.'

Naxor released the buckle on the hood and removed it from Montieth's face, revealing a man in his forties or fifties. He grinned at Amalia, his eyes lit with a fierce cunning.

'I assume you brought the Quadrant, mother?'

'Did you think we walked here?'

Naxor stepped back a pace or two as Montieth stood. He pointed at Ikara.

'Who's that?'

'This is Ikara; one of Khora's girls.'

'Hmm. Why have so many of Khora's brats survived, eh? And, who's the mortal?'

'He's mine,' said Amalia. 'Touch him and you die.'

Montieth laughed. 'You're a little defensive, mother. I was only asking for his name.'

'I'm Kagan,' he said.

Montieth walked right up to Kagan, until he was inches from his face. 'You're not from the City. You have a funny accent.'

'I'm from Lostwell.'

'Where?'

'The world that I fled to,' said Amalia.

'Oh. Yes. I remember. Right. Shall we leave? Are you taking me back to Greylin?'

'No. As I said, Amber is being watched. We're going to my mansion in Port Sanders for now.'

'What about me?' cried Felice from the neighbouring cell. 'If you're removing the mortals from power, then I can help. I have upper vision; I could be very useful.'

Montieth and Naxor strode out of the cell, and they all walked back to look at Felice.

'Do you know her, Naxor?' said Amalia. 'Can she be trusted?'

'No,' said Naxor. 'Absolutely not.'

'He's lying,' cried Felice. 'I've never even heard of a Naxor.'

'I stole your Quadrant after Renko left Lostwell,' said Naxor.

'That was you? You bastard! You nearly got me killed. You're in league with the Holdfasts.'

'No, I was pretending to help them. Moments after I stole your Quadrant, one of the Holdfasts then stole it from me.'

'If that's true,' said Felice, 'then I can forgive that. All I want is to get out of this cell; please. I'll swear allegiance to the most powerful god in the City, if that's what it takes.'

'That would be me,' said Amalia. 'I am the God-Queen of the City.'

'I will serve you, God-Queen; I will swear any oath you like.'

'Then, get on your knees. Naxor, unlock the cell door.'

Felice slid off the bench where she had been sitting, and knelt before Amalia, as Naxor opened the barred door.

'Remove her hood.'

'But, grandmother; she'll say and do anything to get out of here. That doesn't mean she'll be loyal. Her heart will remain with the Ascendants.'

'Are there any Ascendants on this world?' said Felice.

'No,' said Amalia.

'Then, you have nothing to worry about.'

'Agreed. Remove the hood.'

Naxor muttered something under his breath, then unfastened the straps keeping the hood on. He lifted it clear of her head, and Kagan saw a young woman's face. She smiled, and laughed.

'Praise the Ascendants; I can see again.'

'Don't praise them,' said Amalia; 'praise me.'

Felice lowered her gaze and prostrated herself before the God-Queen. Kagan looked away, disgusted.

'I swear that I'll be faithful and true to you, God-Queen of the City,' Felice said; 'I have but one condition.'

'You are in no position to bargain,' said Amalia.

'Nevertheless; this one condition is essential to buying my loyalty. It will cost you nothing.'

'Name it.'

'There is a mortal from Implacatus, now living here in the City. He was a Banner officer that I had several... disagreements with. When I was locked in here, he came to mock me; to laugh at the reversal in our fortunes. The price of my loyalty is that you allow me to kill him with my own hands. I want to look into his eyes as his life slips away, and I want him to know that it was me who killed him.'

'I'm sure we can accommodate you on that. What is the man's name?'

Felice glanced up. 'Van Logos, my Queen.'

CHAPTER 16

NON-COMPLEMENTARY

The Eastern Mountains – 13th Monan 3422

The small valley was like a beautiful garden, Jade had decided. True, it needed a little pruning and tidying, but the placement of the pool was perfect, and the trees and flowers made her heart soar. Even the sound of the waterfall tumbling down the rocks felt right, and when the sun reached its zenith each day, and bathed the entire valley in light, Jade felt moved to tears. There were flowers that she had never seen before, as well as several varieties of unfamiliar trees. On the previous day, their first full day in the mountains, she had gone for a long walk up the sunward side of the valley. Sergeant Darvi had accompanied her, and they had climbed to the top of a high saddle of rock that overlooked the mountain pass. A continuous stream of greenhides was moving along the pass, though, from the width of the trampled path, it seemed as if there were far fewer than had been the case in the past.

Jade had stared at the view of the mountains for a long time, unable to describe how the sight affected her. It was beautiful, but frightening, and made her feel alive, but also alone and insignificant. The summits rose above the treeline, their bare peaks ragged and majestic, while the forests seemed to go on forever. Gazing at it all, she realised that she had been hemmed in by boundaries her entire life, from Greylin Palace to the City; a life enclosed by walls – and for the first time, she felt free.

That first day had passed in a blur, and, on the following morning, Jade wanted nothing more than to go off on another long walk.

'I'm going up the iceward side of the valley today,' she announced at breakfast, while they all sat around a small fire by the pool. 'I think there's a goat path by the end of the stream, but if not, I'll find a way up.'

Sergeant Inmara nodded to Darvi, who frowned.

'My legs aren't built for hill-climbing,' the younger sergeant muttered. 'I'm still aching from yesterday.'

Flavus shook his head. 'Don't the militia train at all?'

'We're not militia,' Darvi said; 'we're in the Royal Guard, sir.'

'Then, surely physical fitness is even more important?' said Flavus. 'After all, you are charged with the protection of the King and Queen.'

Darvi shrugged. 'I did basic training. It was a while ago, mind.'

Rosie glanced at Jade. 'Maybe you should give Darvi's legs a break today. And what about you?'

'What about me?' said Jade.

'No offence, but two days ago you were struggling to lift a trunk, and now you want to go rock climbing again? Are your legs not tired out?'

'No. You're confusing strength with stamina. I admit that I'm not very strong, but my self-healing gives me better endurance than any mortal. I could walk all day.'

'But what about the salve cave? You haven't been inside since we got here.'

'I've seen salve all my life,' said Jade; 'I don't need to see the inside of a mine – I know what they look like. My father used to make me fetch raw salve from the mine behind Greylin, until he figured out how to get dead people to do it for him.'

Flavus frowned. 'Your father made you mine the salve out, ma'am? With what, may I ask?'

'My bare hands, mostly. Although, sometimes I took a spoon from the kitchen. If I didn't return with at least a pound of salve each time, he would kill one of my cats.'

Rosie shook her head, her eyes wide. 'Wow. That does not sound like a normal childhood.'

'It was normal for me; for nine hundred years.'

'At least your father's in jail now, ma'am,' said Flavus, 'where he belongs, it seems. Private Jackdaw, I'm going to have to pull rank on you, I'm afraid.'

Rosie raised an eyebrow. 'What does that mean, sir?'

'That gin you brought; I'm going to need some.'

'It's a bit early to get drunk, isn't it? I mean, each to their own, and all that. Sir.'

Flavus smiled. 'I don't intend to drink it, Private.'

'Then, why do you want it, sir?'

'I'm going to set up a rudimentary purification process, to refine some salve; so that I can test its quality and properties.'

'Do you know how to do that?' said Jade.

'Yes, ma'am, although I am guessing that your expertise far outweighs mine on this topic. I would be grateful if you could assist me, and point out any mistakes I make. I'm always keen to learn and improve.'

'How much gin do you need, sir?' said Rosie.

'How much do you have, Private?'

'Well, we drank some last night, so that leaves me two and a half bottles.'

'Give me one bottle; you can keep the rest, Private.'

Rosie scowled. 'Thank you, sir.'

'Don't worry,' said Darvi; 'I brought some wine along.'

'What is it with mortals and alcohol?' said Jade. 'Are your lives so meaningless that you prefer oblivion?'

'Do you never drink?' said Rosie.

'Sometimes,' she said, 'but I never get drunk.'

'Not even tipsy?'

'If I start to feel the effects, I immediately power my self-healing, and then I feel better again.'

'Very sensible, ma'am,' said Flavus.

'I think you should get drunk with us, Jade,' said Rosie.

No one else around the fire spoke.

'What?' said Rosie. 'It's not a completely crazy suggestion, is it?'

'You want me,' said Jade, 'a demigod who can kill someone with a flick of my fingers, to drink so much that I lose control?'

'Oh. I never thought of it that way.'

'I don't particularly drink either, ma'am,' said Flavus. 'I shall remain sober with you. There's nothing worse than being around drunken people, when you're the only sober one.'

'Malik's ass,' said Rosie; 'I feel terrible now.'

'Why?' said Jade.

'Because I didn't try to put myself into your shoes. Are your powers a burden?'

Jade frowned. 'No. Why would they be a burden?'

'The weight of responsibility on your shoulders must get to you sometimes. Do you never wish you were normal?'

'If by that, you mean mortal, then no, of course not. Every day, when I wake up, I feel glad that I'm not mortal. Surely all mortals wish that they were gods?'

'I don't,' said Rosie. 'The things that make life worthwhile would become meaningless.'

Jade stared at her, wondering if she was telling the truth. She couldn't be; that was a ridiculous notion. All mortals were jealous of the immortality of the gods. They couldn't help it; it was in their nature.

'I shall begin work,' said Flavus. 'I shall continue mapping the valley until noon, and then I will switch to building a basic salve refinery. I'll be needing some assistance. Private Jackdaw, if you aren't busy, you can help me.'

Rosie nodded. 'Yeah, sure, sir.'

Flavus turned to Jade. 'Would you be available to assist me in constructing the refinery this afternoon, ma'am?'

'I don't want to,' said Jade. 'I hate all that. It reminds me of my father.'

'All the same, ma'am; your help would be invaluable. You probably know more about salve than anyone on Implacatus.'

'Very well. I will help you.'

'Thank you, ma'am; enjoy your walk.'

The Banner officer stood, then gestured for Rosie to follow him.

'You can stay here,' Jade said to Darvi. 'You don't need to follow me around.'

'But, ma'am,' said Inmara; 'it's our job to protect you.'

'I have death powers,' said Jade, standing; 'I don't need your help. Sergeant Darvi would be more useful down here, helping you maintain the camp.'

She walked off before either of the sergeants could respond, and was relieved when she heard no footsteps following her. She strode down the grassy bank to the edge of the stream, then followed its course as it tumbled towards the western edge of the valley. Knee-high grass was swaying in the light breeze, and a few winter flowers were adding colour to the riverside. On the left bank, trees were growing in clusters. Many had bare branches, but a few conifer and spruce trees were dotted among the others, lending a wide array of dark greens to the valley. The ridges on either side were steep, and almost completely encircled the valley, but there was a small number of goat tracks that scaled the cliffs. Near the end of the valley, where the stream disappeared into a deep gully, one such path was located. Jade left the banks of the stream, and searched among the undergrowth until she found it; then she started to climb, her spirits rising with every step.

———

That day's walk was even better than the previous day's. Without Darvi's huffing and puffing, and constant rest breaks, Jade made better time, and was free from any distractions. She paused to look at waterfalls that glistened in the morning sun, and ran her fingers through the long grass, then sat for a long time atop a high boulder at the summit of the ridge, gazing out over the view of the mountains. From the iceward flank, Jade could see snow on several of the mountain peaks, and it felt much colder on the ridge than it did down in their little valley. She wondered how her cats were doing. Then, she turned her mind to her failed career as Commander of the Bulwark, trying to work out what had gone wrong. Somehow, being up on the mountain made many of her old problems seem insignificant, and it didn't matter that the Blades had hated her. They didn't know her. No one did. Her father and sister thought they understood her well, but they were wrong. Only Yendra had come close to reaching the true Jade, and she was gone.

A longing arose within her, slowly at first, but soon it seemed to consume her. Even though she had only been in the valley for two days, she never wanted to leave. She loved it; the stream, the trees, the caves; they made her heart ache with belonging. She began to imagine what the valley might look like in early summer, when the trees would be in blossom, and the sun would be warm; and had to stop before she became dizzy.

It was a while before she realised that noon had come and gone. She hurried back down the path, clambering over the steep-sided rocks. As she descended, she caught a glimpse of something moving in the sky, and glanced up. A dragon. No, more than one. Two dragons were circling over the valley, getting lower with each revolution. Darvi and Inmara were standing next to the campsite by the pool, then Jade saw Flavus emerge from the mouth of the cave where the salve was located. Jade scrambled her way to the bottom of the path, then ran along the bank of the stream.

'What's happening?' she said, as she reached the ring of tents.

'Dragons, ma'am,' said Darvi.

'I can see that,' said Jade. 'What do they want?'

Inmara kept her eyes on the sky. 'I think we're about to find out, ma'am.'

Jade recognised the dragons as they descended, having seen them before on the roof of Cuidrach palace. The enormous grey dragon landed next to the pool, his bulk taking up half the width of the valley, then the small, yellow dragon alighted.

Deathfang gazed around the valley. Jade stopped staring, and walked towards him.

'Greetings, demigod,' said the grey dragon, his red eyes on her.

'Good morning, dragon,' said Jade.

'I believe the morning has passed,' said the dragon. 'So, this is the little valley that I have been told about? Where is the salve located?'

Jade pointed towards the cave, where Rosie was standing next to Flavus. 'In there.'

Deathfang and Burntskull twisted their long necks so that they could peer into the gloom of the cave. Rosie raised a hand, and waved at the dragons, while Flavus narrowed his eyes and edged away from the entrance to the cave.

'How much salve is in there?' said Burntskull.

'Flavus,' said Jade; 'tell them.'

'Well, ma'am,' said the Banner officer, keeping his eyes on the dragons; 'it's difficult to say without excavating it, but I would estimate somewhere in the region of a hundred tons, give or take.'

'Is that a lot?' said Burntskull.

'It is enough to keep every god on Implacatus looking young for millennia,' said Flavus.

Deathfang turned back to Jade. 'Does this mean that the Ascendants will be hunting for this world?'

'I don't know,' said Jade.

'The answer is yes,' said Flavus. 'Although, of course, the Ascendants have no way of knowing just how much salve remains on this world. All they know is that it originates here. The good news is that they cannot find this world, and, hence, the amount of salve discovered here is moot.'

'Show me some,' said Deathfang.

Flavus nodded to Rosie, who pulled a bag from her shoulder. She opened it, her hands protected by thick gloves, and held up a piece of grey rock, with silver flecked through it. Deathfang and Burntskull moved their heads closer, and Rosie took a step back, her eyes wide.

'It remains unrefined at present,' said Flavus. 'The chunk in Rosie's hands will be reduced to fit into a small vial, once all of the contaminants have been removed.'

'It is strange to imagine,' said Deathfang, 'that this lump of rock is the cause of so much strife and bloodshed. The Ascendants destroyed Lostwell in their hunt for salve, and they shall do the same to this world, if they find it.'

'How do we know they won't find it?' said Burntskull. 'Perhaps our days here are numbered.'

Flavus glanced at Jade. 'Do you wish me to answer that question, ma'am?'

Jade nodded.

'Well,' said Flavus, 'the Ascendants cannot simply use a Quadrant to get here, not if that Quadrant has never been used to travel to this world, and its owner is unsure of the exact location. There were rumours of a Sextant being on Lostwell...'

'That was not a mere rumour,' said Deathfang; 'I beheld the Sextant with my own eyes, amid the rubble of Old Alea. And then, we watched as Queen Belinda used it to send us here.'

'I bow to your knowledge,' said Flavus. 'Now, if the Ascendants were in possession of this Sextant, then they would have used it by now to travel here. It has been two years, and there has been no sign of them; therefore, we must conclude that they do not have it. Unless something changes, it would appear that we are safe enough here.'

'There are too many "ifs" in that statement,' said Deathfang. 'I dislike uncertainty.'

'There can be no certainty about such matters,' said Flavus. 'The fact is that the Ascendants will be straining every sinew in their search for this world. Without salve, they face a future of slowly aging into decrepitude, and they will do anything to avoid that.'

'You seem rather knowledgeable regarding the motivations of our enemy,' said Burntskull.

'I am from Implacatus, yellow dragon; I have spent my life among those you regard as our enemies.'

'Do you not regard them as the same, Banner soldier?' said Deathfang.

'I am contracted to serve the King and Queen of the City; and their enemies are my enemies.'

'If weasels could speak,' said Burntskull, 'that is what they would say. Is your loyalty only defined by a paid contract, mercenary?'

'I am a professional soldier.'

'Halfclaw told us that you served on Dragon Eyre,' said Deathfang; 'is that true?'

'It is.'

'Did you kill any dragons there?'

'No. I have never taken a life. I am a Scout; a trained mapmaker, and an expert in reconnaissance. I am no warrior.'

Deathfang moved his head closer to the officer, who remained where he was, his head held high.

'Do you think your hands are clean, mercenary?' said the grey dragon. 'I have heard that the Banners have carried out all manner of cruel atrocities upon Dragon Eyre, persecuting our kin.'

Flavus said nothing.

'Well?' said Deathfang. 'Is this untrue?'

'No,' said the officer. 'It is a brutal conflict. Both sides have carried out massacres of the innocent. I have witnessed dragon eggs being smashed with hammers, and I have also seen civilians incinerated by dragons. There are no winners on Dragon Eyre, only suffering.'

'His hands are tainted with the blood of our kin,' said Burntskull. 'We should kill him.'

'No,' said Jade, hurrying forward. 'This officer is under my authority.'

'It appears that the Banner of the Lostwell Exiles is riddled with those who have served on Dragon Eyre,' said Deathfang.

'Then, sire, we should kill this one,' said Burntskull, 'as an example to the others.'

Jade pushed her way in front of Flavus. 'No. I have death powers, dragons. You will not be harming any of my team.'

Burntskull's eyes glowed. 'Would your death powers work, if I bit your head off?'

'Try it, and find out.'

'We're on the same side now,' said Rosie. 'Can't we all be friends?'

Sparks and fire licked across the jaws of the yellow dragon. 'If both of us attack her at the same time,' he said, 'we shall prevail. And, there will be salve if either of us gets injured. The presence of this demigod in our mountains offends me, sire. The Queen sent her here for a reason, knowing the harm she could inflict upon us. Should we allow someone with death powers to remain so close to the young dragons in our colony? She is a threat; a provocation. It's time to teach the Queen of the City a lesson in manners, I think.'

Jade tensed, feeling for her powers. The mighty jaws of the two dragons were only a few yards from her, but she wasn't scared. Compared to the internal fears she battled every day, two dragons were nothing.

'Let's all sit down and chat instead,' said Rosie. 'Talking fixes most things.'

'Be quiet, little Jackdaw,' said Deathfang.

Rosie smiled. 'You remembered who I am? I'm touched. Wait, is that just because I'm Maddie's sister? Is she famous where you come from? What do you remember about her?'

'You ask as many questions as she does,' said Deathfang.

'You didn't eat her, did you?'

'No. She lives. Although, having travelled to Dragon Eyre with Blackrose, she might be dead by now.'

'I hope not,' said Rosie.

Deathfang gazed at her. 'There will be no killing today, Burntskull. Jade is not our enemy, and it would shame us to strike down an unarmed man who draws maps. And, this little Jackdaw amuses me. She may speak as much as Maddie, but her words contain more sense.'

'Thank you,' said Rosie. 'I always thought that was true, but it's nice to hear it.'

'Before we leave you,' said Deathfang, 'you should know that we destroyed a greenhide nest, to the west of Jezra. It was a singular triumph; a measure of the strength and honour possessed by us dragons.'

'Wow,' said Rosie. 'That's sounds amazing. Did you kill the queen? Was it absolutely huge?'

'It was extremely huge,' said Deathfang. 'It took five of us to bring it down. Though, I confess that Halfclaw is rather disappointed. He had hoped to be there, to share in our glory.'

'I wish I'd seen it,' said Rosie. 'You are all very brave.'

'The young Holdfast witch witnessed it. I imagine she will be spreading the tale of our victory all over the City. Come, Burntskull; let us return to our goat-hunt; the others are awaiting our return.'

The grey dragon extended his wings, and rose into the air. Burntskull eyed the humans for a moment, then joined Deathfang, and they flew off to iceward.

Jade exhaled, and lowered her right hand.

'That was well done, Private,' said Flavus, patting Rosie on the back. 'You handled those beasts with aplomb.'

Rosie shrugged. 'All I did was flatter them.'

'And that is exactly what they love best,' said the officer.

'I thought they were going to bite my head off,' said Jade.

'You didn't look scared,' said Rosie. 'You looked like you were ready to unleash your powers at any moment. Were you scared?'

'Not really.'

'Well, I was,' said Flavus, sitting down on the grassy bank. 'They were right, you know. The Banners have done many terrible things on Dragon Eyre. While it remains true that I personally didn't kill anyone, I was still there. I stood by, and did nothing as infant dragons, and innocent civilians, were slaughtered in front of me.' His gaze fell. 'It has tarnished my soul. Part of me thinks I deserve to die for everything we did there.'

Rosie put a hand on his shoulder. 'Everyone makes mistakes.'

Flavus broke down. He brought his hands up to his face as tears spilled down his cheeks, while Rosie rubbed his back. Jade stared at the officer, embarrassed and unsure what to do. To her right, the two Reapers sergeants were exchanging silent glances.

Jade opened her mouth to say something, but Rosie shook her head.

Flavus got to his feet. 'Apologies, ma'am; most unprofessional of me,' he said, then he strode away into the salve cave.

'Wow,' Rosie muttered. 'I wasn't expecting that. Poor old Flavus. Those dragons must have brought back too many bad memories.'

'Does he deserve forgiveness?' said Jade.

'Everyone who is sorry deserves to be forgiven,' said Rosie.

Jade nodded. 'Even though he did bad things?'

'Yes.'

'What about people who aren't sorry for the bad they've done?'

Rosie glanced at her. 'Are we talking about you now?'

'No. What do you mean?'

Rosie shrugged. 'I'm not sure I should bring it up, to be honest.'

'Then, don't.'

She walked away from Rosie, and climbed the gentle slope towards the mouth of the salve cave. Boxes and crates were piled up by the entrance, and, sitting in the shadows, was Flavus.

Jade crouched down next to him.

'Do you want me to help you refine some salve?' she said.

Flavus wiped his face with a hand. 'Yes, ma'am. Thank you. I'm sorry about... you know. It won't happen again. I should never think about Dragon Eyre.'

'It's best not to think about bad things.'

'Is that how you cope?' said Rosie.

Jade turned, and saw the young woman standing by the entrance of the cave. 'Are you following me?'

'No. Maybe. I didn't think our conversation had ended.'

'What conversation?'

'The conversation we were having about forgiveness, and regret. I want to know if you regret the things you've done.'

Jade blinked.

'That's enough, Private,' said Flavus.

'You wouldn't think that, sir, if you knew what she had done. It was before you all arrived from Lostwell. You see, I have a problem. I like Jade, but I can't reconcile that with the things I know about her.'

Flavus glanced away. 'This is none of my business.'

Rosie sat down, leaning her back against the wall of the cavern.

'I don't know what you want from me,' said Jade.

'I want to hear you say that you regret it.'

'Regret what?'

'Do you want me to spell it out?'

'I think you'll have to. Is this about the riot in the Fortress of the Lifegiver? Because, that wasn't my fault.'

'It's not about that,' said Rosie. 'It's about what you did after you escaped from Greylin Palace. You killed a few Blades at a roadblock where my sister was on duty...'

'I panicked,' said Jade. 'The soldiers stopped our wagon, and I thought they were going to send me back to Greylin Palace. Aila shouted at me for killing those soldiers. And, I healed your sister after hurting her.'

'This isn't about my sister. I can kind of understand why you acted that way at the roadblock. No, the bad things came after, when you lived in the Circuit. You raised a small army of the dead from the people you murdered, and terrorised an entire district. How many Evaders did you kill, Jade? Hundreds?'

Jade looked down. 'I don't remember.'

'But you do remember what I'm talking about?'

Jade closed her eyes. 'Yes.'

'You killed men, women, children. People fled in their thousands, to get away from the tenement where you had set up home. If Yendra and Queen Emily hadn't gone there, and stopped you, you might have ended up killing thousands.'

'Stop this,' said Jade; 'I don't want to hear any of it.'

'How did it happen? Did you think that you were entitled to act that way because you're a demigod?'

'Shut up.'

'I know that you were officially forgiven,' Rosie went on, 'but I've often wondered if you were sorry for what you did. Before I got to know you, I would have said that you had no regrets, but now I'm not so sure.'

Jade's right hand swept up, and she grabbed Rosie round the neck, then leaned in until her face was almost touching hers.

'Never mention this again,' Jade cried. 'If you do, I will kill you.'

She released her grip on Rosie's throat and got to her feet. Rosie was staring up at her, her eyes wide, while Flavus looked disgusted.

'Stupid mortals,' Jade muttered, then strode out of the cavern.

'You can run away from us, Jade,' Rosie called out after her; 'but you can't run away from yourself.'

Jade halted on the path, then turned. It would be so easy to kill them; not just Rosie and the Banner officer, but the two Reaper sergeants as well. With them all gone, Jade could live alone in the valley in peace, and no one would ever be able to remind her of the things she had done. She raised her hand, then swallowed, and let it drop back down to her side again. For better or worse, she had changed since the days following her escape from her father's palace; Yendra had seen to that. Killing the mortals in the Circuit had been something her father would have done, but she had rejected his ways, and chosen Yendra's path instead. Or, at the very least, she was trying her best.

She walked back into the cave and sat down, feeling the stares from Rosie and Flavus.

She glanced at the young Jackdaw woman. 'I'm sorry, Rosie; for everything.'

Rosie put an arm round her shoulder. 'I forgive you.'

CHAPTER 17

FULFILLED

J ezra, The Western Bank – 14th Monan 3422

Frostback lifted into the air above the foundations of the ancient palace, her forelimbs gripping onto a compact wooden carriage. It was similar to the vessel that Halfclaw had used to take the survey team to the mountains, or so Kelsey had been told. From up on the harness, she could barely see the carriage.

'I hope Nagel and the others are alright in there,' she said.

'They will be fine, rider,' said Frostback. 'If Halfclaw could carry a carriage for two hundred miles, then I can carry one to Pella. Are they the same as the carriages you talked about on your own world?'

'Those are far larger,' said Kelsey; 'they can carry a hundred soldiers in each, but they need four winged gaien to lift them – one at each corner. They can be quite hard to steer. I think the gaien need to be trained for ages first.'

'How intelligent are these gaien?'

'Oh, about the same as a horse or a dog? Quite smart, really. You can train them to circle above the position of your enemies, and things like that.'

'Their existence troubles me,' said the silver dragon, as she banked and made for the Straits. 'I do not like the idea of a dragon with the mind of an animal. If I were to travel to your world, would the humans assume that I was a dumb brute?'

'There are other differences. Colour, for example. Every gaien I've seen is a sort of brownish green; there's no variety, and certainly no beautiful silver ones. I think you'd be alright. Also, no gaien comes close to the size of Deathfang or Blackrose, and, very importantly, they can't breathe fire.'

A strong wind was gusting from the direction of the Clashing Seas to their left, and Kelsey glanced at the thick bank of fog.

'I wonder when anyone last tried to sail a boat through there,' she said.

'Halfclaw tried to fly through it. He turned back; he said that he could see nothing, and that the winds were wild and unnatural. It is a cursed place.'

Kelsey frowned, but said nothing, knowing that Frostback disliked being contradicted. She turned to glance in the other direction, and watched the mass of boats sailing from Jezra to Pella. The Crown had requested a full Banner regiment to reinforce Cuidrach Palace, along with a Brigade's worth of support staff, and so two thousand men and women were making the short crossing. Van was on one of the ships, after swearing that he felt fit enough to travel. Kelsey had decided against making a fuss about it, as it would have only served to make him more determined. It also left her with a predicament. If he was well enough to work and travel to Pella, then the ostensible reason for her living in his quarters would soon be invalidated by his recovery. If she stayed beyond that point, then it would be clear to everyone that she was no longer doing so only in order to care for him, and she wasn't sure how she felt about that.

The waters of the Straits glistened below them, reflecting the rays of the winter sun in pinks and reds. They crossed the entrance to the bay, and soared past the huge statue of Prince Michael that stood on the Taran headland. The wind dropped, and Frostback began to descend in wide circles, giving Kelsey a panoramic view of the bay, and the three towns that sat along its shores. The dragon swooped over the harbour of Pella, and hovered above the roof of Cuidrach Palace, where a small group was waiting for them. Frostback lowered the carriage, until it bumped down onto the roof, then landed next to it.

Kelsey freed herself from the harness and slid down to the roof. A couple of members of the Royal Guard saluted her, and she walked over to the carriage. Another guard was already there, opening the hatch in the side. Nagel peered out from the interior, then emerged, followed by the rest of the dragon crew.

'Set up your stuff on the roof,' said Kelsey to them; 'this'll be Frostback's base while we're staying in Pella.'

'Yes, ma'am,' said Nagel. 'You heard her,' he said to the others. 'Get all of the gear out of the carriage and onto the roof.' He turned back to Kelsey. 'Will you be heading downstairs, ma'am?'

'Aye. I've got an appointment with the Queen. I'll find out what the plans are and come back up here to let you know. You guys will be staying in the palace, so that you can be close to Frostback if she needs anything.'

'And what shall I be doing?' said the silver dragon.

'I'll find that out too. Don't stray too far for now.'

'I will remain close by, rider.'

'Thanks. See you soon.'

She walked over to the stairwell, and hurried down the steps, only becoming aware after a few moments that a pair of guards was following her. She slowed down to let them catch up.

'We're your escorts, ma'am,' said one. 'We were ordered to make sure no harm comes to you.'

'I need an armed guard, do I? Inside the palace? Things must be bad. Come on, then.'

She set off again, her escorts a couple of paces behind. She descended to the ground floor, and walked into the wing containing Salvor's office. Guards were posted at the doors, and they stepped aside and opened them for her as she approached. She strode into the large office, and glanced at the people sitting round the table.

'Miss Holdfast; welcome,' said the Queen, sitting next to her husband at the head of the table. 'Please, take a seat.'

A courtier pulled out a chair from under the table, and gestured to Kelsey.

'Would you like a drink, ma'am?' the courtier said, as she sat.

'I'm not sure yet,' she said; 'ask me again when I know what this is all about.'

The doors of the office opened again, and a group of Banner officers entered. Van led the way, using a walking stick, but looking stronger than he had since the accident. Cardova was by his side, along with half a dozen other high-ranking officers.

'Welcome,' said the Queen.

Van bowed. 'Your Majesty.'

Courtiers showed them to their seats, and the officers got settled.

Van nodded at Kelsey from across the table. 'We could see Frostback land while we were docking. How did the new carriage work?'

'Fine,' she said.

'I'm glad to hear it,' said the Queen. 'Now that everyone is here, we can begin.'

Kelsey frowned as she looked down the table. She could see Adjutant Quill, along with a sprinkling of other Blade officers, and senior officials from the local militia and Royal Guards, but there were no demigods. She glanced at the Queen.

'Yesterday,' said Emily, 'this palace was infiltrated by the God-Queen.'

The Banner officers gasped, as did Quill and the Blades, while the members of the Royal Guards shifted uncomfortably in their seats.

'Amalia was here?' said Kelsey.

'Yes. The King and I both saw her. She used a Quadrant to snatch Vana, Ikara and Collo. She also mentioned that she was in contact with Naxor. Their insurgency has begun.'

'They also poisoned Silva with anti-salve,' said the King, 'which means that we have no way of locating any of these immortals. Until she recovers, they are free to use their powers without fear of detection.

Last night, they used those powers to release Prince Montieth from the Fortress of the Lifegiver.'

'And, finally,' said the Queen, 'our mortal opponents have also been busy. The leadership council of the Rosers has declared that they no longer recognise our authority, and their militia have sealed off all roads between Roser and Reaper territory.' She paused. 'We'll give you a moment to digest all that, but don't take too long; we have a lot to do.'

Kelsey glanced at Van and the Banner officers, who had been listening attentively.

'We have summoned you all here today,' said the King, 'to discuss our military options. We have the leadership of the Reaper militia, the Royal Guards, the Blades, and the Banner. Before we can make a decision, we need to know what we are capable of achieving. As the Blades are the longest-serving force within the City, I shall now ask Adjutant Quill to speak.'

Quill chewed her lip for a moment. 'Thank you, your Majesties. I have one more detail to add – when the former God-Queen broke Prince Montieth out of the dungeons, she also freed a Lostwell god by the name of Felice. We must assume that this Felice is now working with Amalia. She has strong vision powers, possibly equalling those possessed by Naxor.' She drummed her fingers on the surface of the table. 'As for military options, the Blades are in no fit state to be redeployed to any other region of the City; nor do I believe such a redeployment to be wise. The memories of the last occupation of the City by the Blades are still fresh, and the sad truth is that the Blades are not trusted by the other tribes. The Great Walls are safe, and remain defended against the Eternal Enemy; that is the limit of what we are able to achieve.'

'Thank you, Quill,' said the Queen. 'Is there any danger of a mutiny? Does the former God-Queen retain any loyalty among the Blades?'

'Among some, yes, your Majesty. As you know, Duke Marcus structured the officer classes of the Blades to promote only those who were loyal to himself; it will take time for his influence to fade. The Banner have been generous, and have sent us fresh staff officers, but many

Blades dislike them, and resent them coming into the Bulwark. If the God-Queen goes public with her revolt, it will split the Blades. Those who fought for Marcus, and were implicated in his crimes, will side with our enemies.'

'The Blades must remain in the Bulwark,' said the King; 'that seems clear. If a new civil war breaks out, then the Blades can sit on the sidelines, as they did in the old Civil War. Above all else, we cannot risk another breach in the Great Walls. I would rather the former God-Queen regained her power than lose the City to the greenhides.'

One of the commanders of the Reaper militia leaned forward. 'If the Blades cannot do it, your Majesty, then the militia must. We cannot sit here while the Rosers block the roads and close the harbour of Tara. The food produced in the fields of Roser territory feeds half of Pella; the Reapers will starve if the Rosers aren't swiftly brought into line. It has long been a fact of history, that Pella cannot survive if both Dalrig and Tara are hostile. We can cope with one enemy on our flank, but not two. The Reaper militia stand ready, your Majesties; give the order, and we will open the roads to Tara.'

'Thank you,' said the King, 'but the militia are already stretched along the border with the Gloamers. If we move them sunward towards Tara, then there will be nothing to prevent Amber from re-taking Ooste.'

'Has Amber decided to join Amalia?' said Kelsey.

'She has made no official statement,' said the Queen, 'and we don't know if she is aware of what transpired in the Fortress of the Lifegiver last night. Lord Salvor has scanned Greylin Palace this morning, and has reported that Amber is the sole immortal in that location. However, it is not beyond the realms of possibility that she is waiting for an opportunity to side with our enemies. Withdrawing the militia from the Gloamer frontier would give her that opportunity.' She looked around the table. 'If we decide to move soldiers into Roser territory, then it will have to be the Banner. Major-General Logos, would you care to add your opinion and advice?'

'Your Majesty,' Van said; 'with Brigade support, the Banner are capable of over-running and occupying Roser territory. Neutralising the Roser militia would be the first priority, and then the occupation of key points within Tara, including Maeladh Palace and the harbour front. If the militia flee into the Sunward Range, then patrols will hunt them down. From a military point of view, this is all achievable.'

'Yes,' said the Queen, 'but would you recommend it?'

'That would be a political decision, your Majesty. The Banner of the Lostwell Exiles is an apolitical organisation. If you list your objectives, then I can assess each of them individually and present a variety of possible solutions. What we will not do, is offer political advice.'

'We want to crush the insurgency at its source,' said the King. 'If we strike at its head, the remainder of our opponents will submit.'

'If that is the case, your Majesty,' said Van, 'then the occupation of Roser territory will likely succeed in drawing out the God-Queen. It seems clear to me that this is what Amalia hopes we do. Kelsey and I do have some experience of Amalia, from our time in Lostwell. I believe that she will have thought this through as if it were a strategic game. If the Banner moves into Tara, then we would be doing what she wants; but, if you want to flush her out, then perhaps we should give her what she wants. Kelsey's presence would be essential, because if Amalia takes the bait, she will be bringing her death powers with her. Casualties will be high.'

'But,' said the Queen, 'if Kelsey goes to Tara with the Banner, there will be nothing to stop Montieth and Amber attacking from Gloamer territory. They also have death powers.'

'That is correct, your Majesty. That would most likely be their intention. Casualties in Pella would also be high.'

'What if we were to sit tight and defend Pella?'

'With our combined forces concentrated here, your Majesty,' said Van, 'then Pella would be very hard for our enemies to take. However, Amalia will also know this. I imagine that she will have a back up plan if we fail to move into Tara. If we sit tight, then I believe that she will begin to seize strategic points around the City, trying to force us out of position.'

The Queen narrowed her eyes. 'What would you do, Major-General; if you were in Amalia's shoes?'

Van glanced down for a moment. 'I would go to Icehaven, and eliminate Lady Yvona in a targeted assassination.'

The King frowned. 'But Lady Yvona hasn't declared her support for either side.'

'That is correct, your Majesty, though she has a history of opposing the God-Queen. The effect of removing her from the City would give pause to anyone thinking of supporting the Crown.' Van glanced at Quill. 'Then, I would come for you, Adjutant. You are the highest ranking Blade officer who remains loyal to the Crown. Without you, the Blade officer class might decide to declare for the God-Queen. That's what I would do, especially if I had a Quadrant and death powers.'

'We need Jade back,' said Kelsey. 'Amalia now has herself, Montieth, and probably Amber – all with death powers. Jade would even that up a little.'

'Unfortunately,' said the King, 'we are unsure if Lady Jade could be persuaded to fight against her own father and sister.'

'Where is Lady Jade?' said one of the militia commanders. 'I presumed she was in the Bulwark.'

'Lady Jade is currently carrying out an operation of the highest secrecy and importance,' said the Queen. 'Furthermore, she is out of the reach of Lord Salvor's vision powers, and cannot be contacted in any case. Whatever we decide, it will have to be done without Jade.'

'Rather than sit inactive in Pella,' said Van; 'other options are available. We could carry out our own targeted strikes, with Kelsey, Frostback, and small teams of elite Banner forces. Lady Amber would be first, followed by Lady Lydia in Port Sanders. We know their locations, and we know they are almost certainly sympathetic to Amalia's objectives. If we struck immediately, we could knock the former God-Queen's plans off course, and force her into making a mistake.'

'Are you advocating the assassination of two of the City's demigods?' said the Queen.

'Not advocating, your Majesty; just bringing the options to your attention. We could also raid Roser territory, destroying acres of vineyards and crops and bringing terror to the residents. This would obviate the need for an occupation, and also send a signal that separatists will be punished. Frostback could be employed to burn the Sunward Range, hurting the aristocratic element by destroying their villas and farms, and reducing their reserves of food. The threat of starvation, along with a liberal dose of fear, might cause the Rosers to rise up against their leaders. On the other hand, it may unify them against us. As I said, it is a political decision.'

The Queen looked queasy, and shifted in her seat.

'While conducting the raids,' Van went on, 'we could land a force in the harbour of Tara, and take the children of the leading families into custody as hostages. We could then burn Princeps Row to the ground, and destroy the harbour facilities before pulling out. If this is our decision, then it needs to be done as soon as possible.' He turned to Cardova. 'Captain, when would be the soonest time the Banner would be ready to carry out these operations?'

Cardova took a moment to sip water from a glass. 'A land raid, a dragon raid, and a ship-borne raid? Tomorrow at dawn would be the earliest, sir, if we began the planning immediately. We would require detailed maps of Roser territory, the home addresses of the aristocratic families in Tara, and enough shipping to transport several companies to the harbour. We would also need a code of conduct for the soldiers. Would they be permitted to slay civilians who resist? Should prisoners be taken, or should they be executed? If terror is the objective, then how far can the Banner go to achieve that? Symbolic measures should also be considered. We could destroy the statue of Prince Michael that overlooks the bay, for example, and scuttle the Taran fishing fleet. Also, if we are going to assassinate Amber and Lydia, then that would need to be done the following day, as Frostback would be required for the raids. '

'Pyre's arse,' said Kelsey. 'I had no idea you guys were so ruthless.'

'We are merely laying out the military options for the Crown to consider,' said Van. 'It's our duty to present them all, regardless of our personal feelings.'

'And, what are your personal feelings?' said the Queen.

'They are irrelevant to this discussion, your Majesty,' said Van.

'Are you saying,' said the King, 'that in two days, you could bring the Rosers to their knees, and also eliminate Amber and Lydia?'

'Yes, your Majesty,' said Van. 'If that is your decision, then that is what the Banner will do.'

The officers of the Blades and the Reaper militia glanced at each other, their eyes wide.

The King opened his mouth to speak, but the Queen raised a hand.

'I think we should adjourn for a short while. The King and I have much to discuss in private. Everyone; thank you for your contributions; we shall reconvene in an hour.'

The officers at the table stood as one, bowed, and began to file out of the office. Kelsey glanced at the King and Queen as she got to her feet, glad that it wasn't she who had to make the decision. Emily's face was drawn, and she looked tired, while the worry in the King's eyes was clear to discern. She followed the officers out of the doors, where they began to split into their respective forces. The Reaper militia strode off towards the dining hall, while the Banner officers were chatting together in low voices.

Van glanced at her. 'Do you want to go outside? I could do with some fresh air.'

'Sure,' she said. 'We could go for a walk in the palace gardens.'

Van nodded to Cardova, then he and Kelsey made their way along the marble corridor, Van leaning on his walking stick.

'I want to ask you something,' she said, as they walked. 'I want to know what you really think about the advice you gave in there.'

'You know me, Kelsey; you know what I think.'

'Do I? You and Cardova were suggesting massacres and murders, and the burning of crops and the kidnapping of children.'

'Why do you think we did that?'

'I don't know – you're both mad?'

He glanced down. 'Sometimes, leaders need a brutal reminder of the capabilities of an armed force such as the Banner. They need to understand the consequences of their decisions. If they want to send us into Tara, then they should realise the cost. Dead civilians, burnt crops, sunk boats, and children taken as hostages. We show them what the abyss looks like, so that they have no alternative but to face up to their own morality. It means that, if they send us in, then they can't claim that they didn't know what would follow – bloodshed, tears, and pain.'

'You said that to put them off?'

'Not exactly, but if that is the outcome, then I won't be disappointed.'

They went through an arched opening, and emerged into the pink sunlight. Several companies of Banner soldiers, and members of the Brigades, were sitting in the large gardens in small groups, talking, or going over their equipment. A few came to attention and saluted Van, as he and Kelsey strolled along a gravel path.

'That's about as much walking as my legs can take,' said Van, when they reached a low bed of flowers.

There was a bench close by, and they both sat down. Van groaned, and rubbed his knees.

'Are you in pain?' she said.

'It's fine. I'd much rather be up and about than stuck in bed all day.' He glanced at her. 'Does this mean that you'll be moving out of the Command Post?'

'Do you want me to?'

'No. I want you to stay.'

'Even though we argue?'

'We don't argue that much. Part of the reason for our quarrels has been because I'm a bad patient. I hate inactivity, and this last month has been terrible. Thanks for putting up with me through all of my moods. We should argue less as I get better.'

'I admire your optimism. But, you are getting better. If I stay, then it won't be because you're ill.'

'I know. Let's think about it again once the King and Queen have made a decision. Who knows – we might not be going back to Jezra any time soon.'

'Where are you going to be sleeping?'

'In the palace. Cardova's sorting out my quarters. Do you have your own quarters, or do you want to move in with me?'

'I have no idea where I'm staying yet. Frostback's crew are going to be living close to the roof, so, I guess I should do the same. Even if I do get my own rooms, I can still sneak into your quarters at night.'

He smiled. 'I can live with that.'

Van and Kelsey passed the time chatting on the bench, and when the hour was nearly up, they noticed a squad of Royal Guards moving through the gardens. In their midst, Queen Emily was pushing a pram, an older woman by her side.

'Who's that with the Queen?' said Kelsey.

'Her mother,' said Van; 'Lady Omertia.'

The royal party went past where Van and Kelsey were sitting, and the Queen halted.

'Don't stand,' she said, 'I know that you're still suffering from the effects of the accident with the salve.'

Van bowed his head. 'Thank you, your Majesty.'

Emily told the guards to stand back, then pushed the pram to the bench and sat next to Kelsey.

'I know we're due to restart the meeting soon,' she said, 'but I needed to get out of the palace for a minute first.'

'Have you reached a decision?' said Kelsey.

'No. The King's views differ from my own, on a few key points.'

Emily reached into the pram and picked up Elspeth, who was wrapped up in a thick blanket. She smiled at the child, then sat her down onto her lap.

'She's an exceptionally beautiful child, your Majesty,' said Van.

'Thank you. As her mother, I already knew that. Would you like to hold her, Kelsey?'

Kelsey cringed a little, but tried not to show it.

'Are you not a baby person, Kelsey?' said the Queen.

'Not particularly, I guess,' she said. 'I helped out with my sister's twins for a while, but I left the nappy-changing to my brother and his wife.'

Emily passed the baby over to her, and Kelsey placed her onto her knee. Van laughed. Kelsey looked into the infant's face, and attempted a smile.

'Hello, baby,' she said. 'Don't poop on me.'

'A baby suits you,' said Van.

Kelsey raised an eyebrow. 'You think?' She shook her head, then her mouth fell open. She glanced at Van, her eyes widening.

'What's wrong?' said Emily.

Kelsey didn't respond. Her eyes went from the palace to the red sky, then back to Van, who was gazing at her and the child.

'Shit,' she muttered.

'I'd rather you didn't use that kind of language in front of little Elspeth,' said the Queen.

Kelsey turned to her, and passed the baby back.

'I need to go,' Kelsey said. 'I feel weird.'

She stood, and hurried away down the path, leaving the Queen and Van staring at her. Kelsey carried on until she was out of sight, and sat down on the grass by a thick line of rhododendron bushes. She swallowed, then noticed that her hands were shaking. She took a breath, trying to calm herself. Once again, she had embarrassed herself in front of other people, but she didn't care.

'Hey,' said a voice.

She looked up. Van was standing on the path across from her, leaning on his stick.

'What was that about?' he said.

She stared at him. 'It's done.'

Van narrowed his eyes. 'Do you want to try that again, only this time make sense?'

'My vision,' she said. 'That was it. It's done. It's funny; I always thought that the baby was a boy, but it was a girl. It was Elspeth. '

Van crouched down by her. 'Your vision has been fulfilled?'

'That's what I said. It's over. You never have to feel that it's in the future any more. The future has happened. I feel a bit sick.'

'What do we do now?'

'Whatever we like, Van. We're free.'

CHAPTER 18

SHINING A LIGHT

Pella, Auldan, The City – 14th Monan 3422

Emily eyed Van and Kelsey as they made their way back to their seats in Salvor's grand office. Something strange was going on between them; something that had made the young Holdfast woman uncomfortable enough to run away from them in the gardens. She wondered if Kelsey had discovered she was pregnant; that might explain it; otherwise, Emily was at a loss.

'Thank you all for returning,' said the King, glancing around at the officers present. 'Before we begin, would anyone like to speak?'

Captain Cardova raised a hand.

The King nodded to him.

'Thank you, your Majesty. With your permission, I would like to steer the discussion towards Jezra for a moment. With no dragon cover, and a full regiment of Banner soldiers now in Pella, we lack the force necessary to continue the task of expanding the limits of the town, and all building work has been temporarily abandoned. Furthermore, we know that several young greenhide queens are at large in the forest to the west of the town's defences. At the moment, they will be engaged in a fight among themselves for territory, and there is a risk that some may be driven towards the walls of Jezra. Without a dragon to support the

240

ground forces, there is a chance that the defences will be breached. I would like to suggest that Lady Mona be withdrawn from her current work, and redeployed to scan the forest. If we are forewarned of a queen's approach, then we will have time to concentrate our forces.'

'That seems sensible,' said the Queen. 'Thank you, Captain; we shall ask Lord Salvor to speak to Lady Mona. Lord Salvor, as you probably know, is currently engaged in a thorough search of the City. He has examined the entirety of Roser territory, but has found no trace of Amalia or Montieth, nor of any of the runaway demigods. He has now turned his attention to Sander territory. He scanned Lord Naxor's mansion this morning, but it seems that the demigod has not been there in some time. Lady Lydia's Tonetti Palace is also clear. Lord Salvor will now start to sweep through the houses inside the town itself.' She paused for a moment. 'I have my doubts that he will be able to find them before they strike again. I spoke to Lord Salvor during our break, and asked him to warn Lady Yvona in Icehaven that she might be a target. She agreed to take reasonable precautions.'

'That brings us on to our next move,' said the King. 'Unfortunately, the Queen and I have been unable to reach a consensus on this matter. Therefore, we will not be sending the Banner forces to raid Tara.' He took a breath, and Kelsey guessed from his features that he had been the one pushing for the soldiers to go in. 'However,' he went on, 'a show of strength remains advisable. Kelsey Holdfast, we would like you and Frostback to fly over Tara. Harm no one, and burn nothing, but make sure as many civilians as possible see you. Let's give them a little reminder of the forces under our command. At the same time, the Banner will remain here in Pella, in case of an attack from either Gloamer or Roser territory. Major-General Logos, I want your staff to prepare plans for all of the options you discussed earlier, so that we are prepared if it comes to it. That is all. Dismissed.'

'Kelsey,' said the Queen; 'could you please remain behind for a moment?'

The Holdfast woman nodded as the officers got to their feet. They bowed, then left the room. The King also got up, kissed his wife, and left by another door.

'How are you feeling?' said the Queen.

'Sorry about the garden,' Kelsey said. 'I had a funny turn, but I'm alright now.'

Emily nodded. 'Good. Listen, if you have a reason for not wanting to put yourself in danger, then you can talk to me about it. We can work out a way around it.'

Kelsey frowned. 'What are you talking about? I don't exactly enjoy being in danger, but I've never shirked my duty.'

'So,' said Emily, 'you're not pregnant?'

Kelsey laughed. 'No, praise Pyre and his glorious arse. Is that what you thought?'

'Well, I saw the way you acted when I passed you Elspeth, and it crossed my mind.'

'Can you imagine me as a mother? Can you imagine Van's face?'

'I think that you and Van would make good parents.'

'Are you drunk?'

'No, but I'm starting to wish I was. Alright; my apologies, this conversation was misguided from the start. The important thing is that you're fine to fly on Frostback and scare some Rosers.'

'That was your idea, wasn't it?' said Kelsey. 'The King wanted to send the Banner in, and you proposed that as a compromise?'

Emily said nothing.

'You can tell me,' said Kelsey. 'It was obvious from the King's face that he wasn't happy about what he was suggesting. If that's true, then all I can say is thank Pyre you're here. Van doesn't want to do any of the things he was suggesting. I think he was trying to frighten you into stepping back from the edge.'

'Well, it worked,' Emily said. 'I felt sick listening to him and Captain Cardova. Children as hostages? Executing prisoners? The terrible thing is, I realised how easy it would have been to say yes. After all, we wouldn't have to see any of the suffering; we would be here, safe in

Cuidrach. As if we could give the order, and then shove our fingers in our ears so we couldn't hear the screams.'

'Does the King share your compassion?'

'Not at the moment. Daniel is very angry. His grand plans for the City are in ruins. They were good plans, written with noble intent, but in his mind they now represent an existential struggle for the soul of the City. Don't be too harsh on him, Kelsey. I know fine well, that if I had allowed the Banner to enter Roser territory, then Daniel would be stricken with guilt and shame, once he realised what he had done.'

'Have you thought about offering one of the palaces to Amalia?'

Emily narrowed her eyes. 'Why would I do that?'

'Well, for a start, she hasn't made any demands, so we don't actually know what she wants.'

'She is a power-crazed tyrant, with no morals and no conscience. She opened the gates in the Middle Walls, Kelsey, which led to the slaughter of tens of thousands of her people. I will not negotiate with someone who acts like that. She is a wild beast, and needs to be dealt with as such.'

Kelsey shrugged. 'When she was holding me prisoner on Lostwell, she didn't seem particularly interested in power. And, before that, in a place called Shawe Myre, she spent ages trying to persuade Belinda to return with her to the City. Their plan was to kill Yendra, and you and Daniel, and then Amalia said she wanted to hide away in a palace, and let Belinda rule. She said that Belinda could govern the City in any way she chose, as long as Amalia could live a life of luxury, and peace and quiet.'

'I assume that Belinda wasn't persuaded?'

'She might have come round, given more time, but she was adamant that any return here would be carried out without bloodshed. Amalia wasn't fussy about that aspect.'

Emily nodded. 'That doesn't change my opinion of her. She would have said anything to persuade Belinda. At heart, Amalia cannot be trusted.'

'You're probably right,' said Kelsey. She stood. 'I should go up onto the roof. No, wait; I'll need a map of Roser territory first. Do you want us to fly over Tara, or the countryside as well?'

'As much as you can manage, please. Come with me; we'll find you a map.'

The queen rose from her seat, and walked with Kelsey to a side door. They went into a part of the palace that Kelsey had never seen before, and stopped by a door.

'This is my little study,' Emily said. 'There are plenty of maps in here.'

She pushed the door open. Inside, the walls were lined with full bookshelves, while a desk sat by a shuttered window. Kelsey frowned. Van was sitting in an armchair, his eyes wide as he glanced up to see Emily and Kelsey. Next to him, on a little table, were a few small, glass vials.

'What are you doing?' said Kelsey.

'Nothing,' he said, sweeping up the vials with a hand. 'Just... taking a break.'

Kelsey peered at him in the shadows. His eyes seemed funny, almost as if he had been smoking keenweed. That was impossible, she knew. There was no keenweed in the City.

Her frown deepened. 'Have you been taking salve?'

Van stared at her.

'Well?' she said.

'Look,' he said; 'it's purely temporary, just to get me through this. I'm in pain, and I need it for my recovery.'

'But, I thought that more salve would be bad for your heart,' said Kelsey. 'That's what Lucius told me. Is that not true?'

'I'll be fine,' he said, trying to get to his feet.

'When were you going to tell me about this?' she said.

'It's nothing to worry about, honestly.'

'Then, why were you hiding away in here to take it? Does Lucius know?'

He stood, wheezed, then sat again.

Kelsey took a step forward. 'Does Lucius know?'

Van shook his head.

'So, you were keeping it from me, and from him? And you expect me not to worry? It's addictive, isn't it? You told me that you used to be addicted to it. Why would you risk your health over this? It's stupid.'

'Excuse me a moment,' said Emily. 'Sorry; I just need to squeeze past.' She reached over onto the desk, and picked up a few rolled-up maps. 'I'll give you some privacy.'

'No,' said Kelsey; 'I'm coming with you.' She glared at Van. 'This conversation will be continued later, and you'd better have some answers for me. And, I'm telling Lucius.'

'Don't,' he said. 'Please.'

'Tough shit, Van; I'm telling him as soon as I get back from terrorising Tara. You could always tell him yourself before then; that would be the decent thing to do.'

Kelsey turned and strode from the room. Emily lingered for a moment, the rolled-up maps clutched against her chest, but Van wouldn't meet her gaze. She decided against saying anything, and followed Kelsey out of the room, closing the door behind her. The Holdfast woman was waiting outside, a deep frown on her face.

Emily handed her the maps. 'Should I be worried about this?'

'I don't know,' said Kelsey. 'I don't have much experience of salve. But, if he's hiding it, then it makes me think that it can't be good.'

'Normally, this sort of thing would be none of my business, but...'

'Aye; I know. He's the Commander of the Banner.'

'Perhaps we should wait and see. He told us that it was temporary.'

'Aye, but that's exactly what an addict would say.' She glanced at the rolled-up maps. 'I'd better have a look at these and get on my way.'

'I'm here for you; if you need me.'

'Thanks, Queenie.'

Emily watched as Kelsey turned and made her way towards the stairs that led to the roof. A couple of guards peeled off to follow her, while the rest remained in the hallway, waiting for the Queen. Emily realised that she was at a loose end. The meetings with the military officers had been expected to last all day, but her disagreement with Daniel had seen them cut short. She thought about going to see her husband, but he had been in a foul mood, and she didn't want to risk another argument. Instead, she turned, and walked in the opposite direction, towards Silva's room.

A nurse was sitting alone in the demigod's living quarters when Emily arrived.

'How is she?' said the Queen.

The nurse jumped to her feet and bowed. 'Your Majesty. Lady Silva is sleeping at present. She ate some breakfast this morning, and then asked me to leave, so that she could sleep.'

The bedroom door opened, and Silva walked out. She looked exhausted, her face drained of any colour, and she was shuffling across the floor as if she were in pain.

'I'm awake,' she said. She bowed before the Queen. 'I heard you come in, your Majesty.'

'Please, sit,' said the Queen. 'Don't tire yourself out on account of me.'

Silva sat.

'Thank you,' said the Queen, also taking a seat. 'I don't think I need to ask how you are feeling. Oh, Silva, seeing you like this tears at my heart. Is there any sign of your self-healing returning?'

'Not yet, your Majesty. This experience has taught me something. I think I understand a little more how it feels to be mortal. Right now, if someone were to wound me, I would die. Really die. Is this how it feels? How do mortals live their lives feeling so vulnerable all the time?'

'You get used to it, if it's all you've ever known,' said Emily.

'I'm scared, your Majesty; scared that they gave me so much anti-salve that I'll never recover. What if I'm mortal for the rest of my life? How long would I have to live? It sounds so selfish to say that, knowing that you are mortal, your Majesty, but it's all I can think about.'

'I understand. Whatever happens, you will have my support.'

'Even if I've lost my powers permanently? What use would I be?'

'I don't judge my friends by how useful they are, Silva. I judge them by their kindness and loyalty. You have nothing to worry about.'

'Thank you, your Majesty; that means a lot to me. Naxor laughed when he gave me the anti-salve. I knew he was self-centred, but I thought he respected me. Corthie was right all along; we should never have trusted him. When he broke Belinda's heart, I should have killed him myself.'

'I always thought that his behaviour was an act, and that, deep down, he was a decent enough man. It seems we were wrong. Has Amalia led him astray?'

'If anything, your Majesty, she was more reluctant to hurt me than he was. She kept asking me to reconsider; she even asked that I stay neutral, if I couldn't join her. It sounds strange, but if I had to guess, I would say that she's been led astray by Naxor.'

Emily narrowed her eyes. 'I realise that you used to be friends with Amalia, but...'

'We were never close friends, your Majesty. She was Queen Belinda's friend, and so I helped her when she arrived in Lostwell. I did it for Belinda, not for her. I know how selfish she can be, but I also saw how much she needed Belinda to forgive her. When the Ascendants came to Shawe Myre, Amalia fled, and I thought I'd never see her again, but she came back. If Naxor hadn't tried to steal her Quadrant, then I believe that Amalia might have been reconciled with the others. I know how ridiculous that sounds, but I believe it.'

'You have a very forgiving heart,' said Emily; 'I'm not sure I can find it within myself to match you. However Amalia behaved in Lostwell, the fact remains that she is responsible for the deaths of tens of thousands of my people. If she had won, then the death toll might have reached a million – everyone who didn't live in Auldan would have been slaughtered, including Belinda. I cannot forgive that, and I cannot allow her to retake control of the City. If what you say is true, then the same applies. If Naxor is the real driving force behind the insurgency, then Amalia has chosen to go along with it. Either way, they must be stopped.'

Silva nodded. 'Yes, your Majesty.'

'I'll leave you to get some rest. Remember, no matter what happens, I am here for you.'

Emily got to her feet. She smiled at the nurse, then left Silva's rooms, her mind swirling with doubt. First Kelsey had questioned whether or not Amalia was truly evil, and then Silva. Were they both simply being naïve? Neither had been in the City when the God-Queen had ruled, but both knew what she had done. She tried to imagine what Amalia had been like on Lostwell. She would have been desperate and wounded; hunted and frightened. Did it matter? She had brought it on herself. Emily pushed any feelings of pity from her mind. Amalia was ruthless, and so she had to be the same; otherwise defeat was all but certain.

She thought about going to see Salvor. The demigod had been keeping to himself since Amalia had returned him to Cuidrach Palace. Would he think that she was prying if she interrupted his search for the rogue gods? His dose of anti-salve had been far weaker than that administered to Silva, and his powers had recovered quickly. Why? Daniel had suspicions that he had been turned, but what if Naxor and Amalia wanted them to think that? Salvor had been loyal throughout their reign; could it all be an act? Emily didn't want to think about it, so she made her way instead to the offices taken over by the Banner leadership. A squad of guards escorted her as she walked to the eastern wing of the palace, where Banner soldiers were unloading and unpacking crates of supplies and equipment. They stood to attention and saluted as she passed, then she saw Captain Cardova by a doorway, organising the soldiers.

'Your Majesty,' he said, as she approached.

'Captain. Could I have a quick word in private?'

The tall officer smiled down at her. 'Of course, your Majesty. We can go into my new office. It's still in a bit of a mess; I hope you don't mind.'

They walked into the small room, leaving the guards behind at the door. Cardova moved a few boxes from a chair, and gestured to the Queen.

'Thank you,' she said, sitting.

'How can I help you?' he said.

'You know quite a lot about salve, yes?'

He shrugged. 'I know some aspects, your Majesty. I have very little experience of refining it, or anything like that.'

'The Banners used to hand it out to their soldiers, didn't they?'

'Yes; that was common practice. I don't know if that's still the case, especially if supplies on Implacatus are running short. It was fine when there was an abundance of it, but the gods will keep it for themselves if there's little left.'

'How was it given to the soldiers?'

'Generally, your Majesty, the officers would hold onto it, until combat was required. Then, they'd hand it out to the sergeants in small vials, and they would distribute them to the troops. Also, if anyone was injured, then they would get some. The ordinary soldiers weren't trusted with it outside of combat situations.'

'Why not?'

'Salve is known by another name – the scourge of the Banners. I've seen many good soldiers brought low by it. It makes you feel great, like a drug, and some can't get enough of it. However, it's also highly addictive, and dangerous if taken too often. Overdoses are common, and deadly. Heart attacks, convulsions, comas and death; I've seen all of these happen. It surprises me, your Majesty, that, in the City where salve originates, you don't seem to have had these problems.'

'The gods and demigods here never allowed any mortals to access salve; they kept it all for themselves. Many citizens were unaware that such a substance even existed. For a long time, I was angry about this – especially when I saw injured soldiers succumb to their wounds. But, after listening to you now, I wonder if it were perhaps for the best. What would the Banners do if a soldier became addicted?'

'Often, they'd turn a blind eye to it, as long as that soldier was still able to carry out their duties. I mean, it was rife in some regiments, and if they'd tried to discipline everyone who took it recreationally, then they would have lost most of their soldiers. If it became so that the soldier couldn't perform, then they'd be discharged from the Banner.' He glanced at her. 'Is there a particular reason for these questions, your Majesty?'

'I'm curious, Captain. One more question. Forget the rules that applied on Implacatus – what would you do, if someone under your command became addicted to salve?'

Cardova gazed at the Queen for a moment, his eyes tightening a little.

'Hypothetically,' she said.

'I would lock them in a room for a week,' he said, 'until all the salve had gone from their system. They would scream and shout, but I would ignore it. Then, I would put them on a training programme to get them fit again, and place them back into their regiment.'

'You wouldn't punish them?'

'No, ma'am. It's a sickness. However, if they kept doing it, despite warnings and so on, then I would dismiss them from the Banner. Salve-addled soldiers are too dangerous – to their colleagues, civilians; in fact, anyone who gets in their way. Addicts can't be trusted. It's sad, but it's true.'

'Have you ever been addicted?'

'No. I would say that a good half of Banner soldiers stay away from salve. I fit into that category. I've taken it a couple of times, when I was injured on Dragon Eyre, but that's all. I never took it before battle. To be honest, I prefer a cold beer. And a cigarette. Gods, I miss those.'

Emily stood. 'Thank you for your help, Captain.'

'No problem, your Majesty. Do I need to be concerned about this?'

Emily caught his gaze for a moment, but said nothing. 'I'll see you later, Captain.'

She left the small office, and her guards followed her as she made her way up to the royal quarters. She knew that Daniel would be there, but hoped that his temper had calmed a little; if not, then she would have a bath and go back to work. She walked through the main door of their apartment, and saw Daniel sitting on a couch, talking to his mother.

'Good afternoon, your Majesty,' said Lady Aurelian. 'I owe you a rather large thank you, it seems.'

Emily frowned as she walked over to where they were sitting. 'For what?'

'For preventing my son from sending soldiers into Roser territory. He's told me all about it. Silly boy.'

Daniel glared at her.

'I think he forgot about the Aurelian estate in the Sunward Range,' said Lady Aurelian. 'Not to mention our mansion on Princeps Row. The thought of a dragon burning both to the ground has left me feeling a little off-colour.'

'I didn't do it, mother,' said Daniel. 'Emily talked me out of it.'

'And praise the gods for that,' said Lady Aurelian. 'What if I'd still been on the estate, son? And your father is in Tara.' She sighed. 'You are quite reckless at times.'

Emily sat. 'Did you have a nice time on the estate?'

'Oh yes; it was wonderful. It's better in summertime, naturally, but I love the peace and quiet there over winter. A few others from Tara were also holidaying in the Sunward Range, and I managed to catch up with some old friends. Although, we did try to avoid discussing politics. As you can imagine, you and Daniel are not the most popular among the Roser nobility at present.'

'You shouldn't be associating with them,' said Daniel. 'Many are our enemies.'

'Oh, what nonsense, Daniel. I am a Roser aristocrat, as are you. They are our people, son. Well, not all of them – I also happened to visit the estate of a certain Lady Sofia; have you heard of her?'

Emily shook her head.

'She's from Lostwell. Very, very rich. Apparently, she's the only Exile who had the presence of mind to make sure she carried her wealth with her to the City. Unfortunately, she donated a large sum of money to the legal fund that opposed the new constitution.'

'Oh, yes,' said Emily; 'I remember hearing about that, though I had forgotten her name. Did you manage to convince her to support us?'

'She was too ill to greet us,' said Lady Aurelian. 'We were entertained instead by a young man, also from Lostwell. Her betrothed, it seems. He had a very strange accent.'

'Is he an aristocrat too?' said Daniel.

'He claimed to be, but I wasn't fooled. No, I imagine that he's just a boy from the slums of that big city they all seem to hail from. I think he struck it lucky, and this Lady Sofia has taken him in. He was quite handsome, so I suppose she has her reasons.'

'I'm glad they're integrating,' said Emily. 'She might be the only Exile who'll fit into the rest of the Rosers.'

'She lives in a nice mansion in Port Sanders, actually, along with Kagan and her servants.'

Emily frowned. 'Kagan?'

'Yes, dear; that's the name of her betrothed. What's the matter? Your face has gone very pale, Emily.'

'Kagan?'

Lady Aurelian raised an eyebrow. 'Yes. That is what I said.'

Emily shot to her feet and rushed from their apartment, taking her guards by surprise. They shouldered their crossbows and hurried after her as she retraced her steps to the eastern wing. She slowed down as she reached the area where the Banner soldiers were working, not wanting to attract too much attention, but her heart was pounding. She pushed open the door to Cardova's office, and found him inside, laughing with a young woman from the Brigades.

'Your Majesty?' he said.

Emily glanced at the young woman, and Cardova gestured for her to leave.

'Are you alright, your Majesty?' he said, once the woman had left.

'I don't know, Captain. Do you remember when you went to Greylin Palace and spoke to Lady Amber?'

'The first time, or the second time, your Majesty?'

'The second. You told me that Amber spoke about Amalia's visit, when she collected the anti-salve?'

'Yes?'

'Amber said that a young man from Lostwell was with her.'

'That's right, your Majesty.'

'What was his name?'

Cardova puffed out his cheeks. 'Um, was it Kagan? Something like that.'

Emily fell into a chair, her eyes wide and her mouth open.

'What's wrong, your Majesty?'

'We need to recall Kelsey and Frostback, and prepare soldiers to move into Port Sanders.'

'Of course, your Majesty; but why?'

She glanced up at him. 'We've found Amalia.'

CHAPTER 19

LONG LIVE THE GOD-QUEEN

Port Sanders, Medio, The City – 15th Monan 3422

Kagan stared at his reflection in the mirror, as if trying to remember who he was. Just a few doors away, in the dining room, three gods and four demigods were sitting down for a late dinner, despite it being after midnight, and Kagan was expected to join them. How had his life come to this? Prior to arriving in the City, he had never left the slums of Alea Tanton, and now he was dining with divine royalty. He straightened his shirt, and smoothed his hair, then noticed that Gellie was watching him.

'I've lost control of my life,' he said.

The Fordian continued to watch him, but said nothing.

'You too, Gellie,' he went on; 'we're being swept up in something I don't understand.'

'We must put our trust in her ladyship,' Gellie said.

'I trust her; it's the others I'm worried about.'

'None of them will harm you. They are too afraid of Lady Sofia.'

'Are you still calling her that? I do too, sometimes; I can't help it. But, it's not true.' He glanced at her. 'Did you check on Maxwell?'

'Your son is fine, Kagan; stop worrying. He's asleep, and his nurse-maid is resting in his room. Are you going to dinner?'

He nodded.

She gestured to the door. He took a breath and walked from the room, with Gellie leading the way. She led him to the dining room, and opened the door. Inside, sitting around a long table of polished oak, were the seven immortals. Amalia glanced up from the head of the table, and gave Kagan the slightest nod. Gellie gestured toward a chair, and Kagan sat down, to Amalia's left.

Felice frowned. 'Is the mortal joining us for dinner? I assumed he was a servant.'

Montieth laughed from his seat on Amalia's right. 'Watch what you say; my mother gets tetchy if you insult her little mortal.'

'She does indeed,' said Naxor. 'She melted my skin off when I referred to him as a boy.'

'His name is Kagan,' said Amalia; 'not "boy" or "mortal."'

Montieth giggled. 'She's in love with him.'

'Don't say that,' said Naxor; 'I want to retain my appetite.'

Amalia raised a fork and pointed it at Naxor. 'Do I need to remind you whose house this is, grandson?'

Naxor's smirk faded. 'No, grandmother.'

'Then, keep your hilarious little quips to yourself.' She turned to the housekeeper. 'Gellie, serve dinner, if you please.'

The Fordian bowed. 'Yes, ma'am.'

'I'm not hungry,' said Vana.

'You are not obliged to eat, granddaughter,' said Amalia, 'but your presence here is not up for debate.' She glanced around the table. 'We are here to plan the next steps. As you all know, a dragon flew over Tara this afternoon, presumably to frighten the Rosers and to scout out the locations of potential targets. However, as of yet, the Banner forces have made no attempts to invade Roser territory. It seems our assumption may have been mistaken. The King and Queen do not appear to have taken the bait.'

'There's still time for that, surely?' said Ikara. 'They might try to invade at dawn.'

'They might, but we need to retain the initiative. We cannot sit and wait. The obvious time to invade would have been today, when the Banner had arrived, but, instead, they seem to be settling into Cuidrach Palace. Felice has thoroughly reconnoitred the environs of the palace, and has seen defences being built. If they were going to invade, why would they waste time doing that?'

'We should act, mother,' said Montieth. 'I have a simple plan.' He looked at the faces of the others. 'We split into two groups, each containing someone with vision, and someone with death powers. We use the Quadrant to position the groups – one in Dalrig, and the other in Tara. Then we move towards Pella. The Holdfast girl can only be in one place at a time with her blasted dragon, and if we attack from both directions at once, they won't be able to kill us all.'

'But,' said Vana, her eyes wide, 'the group that Kelsey chose to attack would be annihilated.'

'She's right,' said Naxor. 'Sorry, uncle, but your plan would almost guarantee that half of us sitting here will be dead in a day. Listen, the greatest advantage we have over our enemies is the Quadrant. With that device, we could sow terror throughout the City with a succession of precise raids; that way, the King and Queen will have no idea where we're going to strike next. On our tenth raid, we go to Cuidrach Palace in numbers and kill whoever remains.' He smiled. 'Except little Elspeth, our future Queen.'

'Where would you suggest we raid?' said Amalia.

Naxor pulled a note from his pocket. 'I made a list.'

'You shouldn't be writing this sort of thing down, grandson.'

Naxor shrugged. 'Right. First, how about the leader of the Banner – Van Logos? I knew him pretty well on Lostwell; he's a good officer; well-organised and efficient. And, Felice is dying to get her hands on him.'

'That's true,' said Felice, 'but he's in Cuidrach Palace. The problem is, so is the Holdfast witch. We should have struck earlier, while she was out riding the dragon. We need to rule out any attack on Cuidrach if the Holdfast witch is there.'

'Clearly,' said Montieth. 'What about killing one of the demigods who bow to the mortal King and Queen? Those feeble-minded traitors don't deserve to live.'

'Would you include your own daughter amongst that group, uncle?' said Naxor.

'I have one daughter – Amber,' said Montieth. 'The other is dead to me.'

'Do you mean the one called Jade?' said Felice; 'my old jailor? She sounds like a likely candidate for execution. And, we know where she is – in the Fortress of the Lifegiver.'

'She's not,' said Vana.

The others turned to look at her.

'I've checked,' said Vana; 'I know the locations of every god and demigod in the City, except for any who may now be in Cuidrach, as Kelsey is there. Jade isn't anywhere in the City that I can see.'

'She can't have left the City,' said Ikara. 'So, she's in Cuidrach; or perhaps she's been forced to take some anti-salve?'

'There's none left in Pella,' said Naxor; 'we have it all.'

'Alright; so, she's in Cuidrach,' said Amalia. 'That rules out an attack on her, or on Van Logos. Of course, our main target has to be Kelsey Holdfast. She is the biggest threat.'

'Unfortunately, she's also the hardest to get to,' said Naxor.

'Do we have to kill her?' said Vana. 'She's young, and she hasn't done anything wrong.'

'I was captured because of that little bitch,' yelled Montieth. 'I agree with mother; she must be eliminated.'

'We could always put her onto the Grey Isle,' said Amalia, 'where she can't do any harm.'

Several of the gods and demigods stared at her.

Amalia sighed. 'Fine. We'll kill her. And her dragon too, I suppose. Are the other dragons in the east a threat?'

'Not if we erect hundreds of ballistae,' said Felice. 'That's what kept them out of Alea Tanton.'

'That is what we shall do,' said Amalia. 'Who else is on your list, Naxor?'

The demigod scanned the paper. 'Adjutant Quill?'

'She is also in Cuidrach,' said Felice.

Naxor frowned. 'Alright; how about Yvona?'

'Why?' said Vana. 'Yvona's done nothing.'

'She sided with my enemies last time,' said Amalia. 'If it comes to war, then I expect her to act in the same manner.'

'I agree,' said Naxor.

Montieth frowned. 'Remind me; who is she?'

'The Governor of Icehaven,' said Amalia. 'Niomi's daughter.'

'Oh, her?' said Montieth. 'Yes; kill her. She's been nothing but trouble, messing around in the Cold Sea as if she owns it.'

'Killing her would achieve nothing,' said Vana. 'The government of Icehaven is solidly behind her. Assassinating Yvona would only drive the Icewarders into the arms of the Crown.'

'Perhaps it's time for another approach,' said Amalia, 'since it's clear we can't agree who to kill first. I propose that we move, as a group, to Maeladh Palace, and announce the formation of an alternative government. The Rosers would rally to us, followed by the Sanders, once Lydia was let into the inner group; and I imagine that Amber would have the Gloamers declare for us. The Bulwark would remain neutral, the Circuit is in chaos and would be unable to respond, and who cares about Icehaven? The Crown would be utterly isolated. Then, we await their response.'

'And lose the initiative?' said Naxor.

'The Aurelians will be hard to dislodge from Pella,' said Amalia; 'they have the Banner, Kelsey, and a dragon. We should do the same – entrench ourselves into Tara and Dalrig, and surround them.'

'There must be a way to weaken them,' said Naxor. 'I mean, you're right, as you usually are – they might be isolated in Pella, but they're also strong and their forces are concentrated.' He snapped his fingers. 'I really am a genius. I have an idea. We do exactly as my dear grandmother suggests, but with a twist. We use the Quadrant to take a small group of us to Outer Pella, and empty a few vials of death-salve into the water supply. Then, we move to Maeladh and announce ourselves. The chaos that will erupt in Outer Pella will be more than enough to keep our enemies busy. We use that time to consolidate our grip on the City.'

'What's death-salve?' said Kagan.

'Never mind that, boy,' said Naxor, then he blinked. 'Oops. Sorry, grandmother; honestly, I forgot.'

Amalia glared at him, then glanced away. 'The idea has some merits.'

'It has many merits,' said Naxor; 'it is many-merited.'

'It could work,' said Montieth, 'and I've always wanted to see the effects of that stuff on a large population. Amber would never allow me to try it out on the Gloamers.'

'I'm with Kagan on this,' said Felice. 'What is death-salve?'

'It kills mortals, then brings them back.'

Felice frowned. 'What's the point of that?'

Montieth grinned. 'When I said it "brings them back," it doesn't bring them back exactly as they were before. A mob of them, unguided by any god, will revert to their basest instincts, and roam the streets, attacking anyone in their path. A few vials would be enough to transform hundreds, maybe thousands of Reapers into mindless savages.' He rubbed his hands together. 'I cannot wait to see it in action.'

Kagan turned to Amalia. 'You can't be serious about this?'

'It seems to be the least of several evils, Kagan, compared to all-out war, or massacres, or dragons razing towns to the ground. If the price of this civil war is a few hundred, or even a few thousand deaths, then that will be fewer than the alternatives.'

Naxor smirked and shook his head. 'He really is your conscience, isn't he, grandmother? I mean, since when did you care about the number of fatalities?'

Amalia frowned. 'I've just said that I'm in favour of pouring death-salve into the water-supply of Outer Pella. What part of that makes you think I've gone soft?'

'Very well,' said Naxor. 'If we go now, we can visit the central cistern under Outer Pella, and be back here in ten minutes. Let's say, me, grandmother, and...' He glanced round the table. 'Ikara. That should do it.'

Ikara smiled. 'You want me to come?'

'You're always trying to prove yourself, aren't you? And, this way, Uncle Montieth and Felice will still be here, so; just as he suggested, each group will have vision and death powers available if needed.'

The door to the dining room opened, and Gellie strode in, leading a young servant who was pushing a trolley.

'Dinner is prepared, ma'am,' Gellie said.

'Thank you, Gellie. Have it set out for us, if you please.'

Kagan watched as the housekeeper and the servant served the gods and demigods at the table, filling their plates with hot food, and their glasses with red wine. He kept his expression level, but his anger and despair were growing. Alone, Amalia had shown she could be kind and loving, but with her family around her at the dinner table, she seemed to have descended into the depths of cruelty; nodding along with any suggestion, no matter how murderous. Perhaps poisoning the water supply of Pella would result in fewer deaths, but murder was murder, and the people of Pella were innocent civilians.

None of the immortals spoke while their dinner was being served, though Montieth leered at the young servant like a predator. Gellie gave Kagan a slight nod as his dinner was placed in front of him, but he couldn't meet her eyes, feeling shame that he had kept quiet during the discussion.

Naxor raised his wine glass as soon as the housekeeper and the servant had left, and took a sip.

'Shall we go?' he said.

'Yes,' said Amalia. 'Naxor, Ikara; come with me.'

Kagan noticed that she didn't look at him while she spoke, nor had she suggested that Kagan go along on the trip to Pella. She got to her feet, and her two grandchildren followed her out of the room.

Montieth rubbed his hands together. 'Felice,' he said; 'I want you to give me a running commentary, once the death-salve has had a chance to reach the homes of the Reapers.'

'When will that be?' she said.

'Dawn will suffice. Most will be sound asleep in their beds at the moment. The fun will commence at breakfast time.'

'I'll take a look,' Felice said. She glanced at Collo. 'Does he ever speak?'

'He's been smoking opium again,' said Vana. 'My brother seems to have been addled with it for some time.'

Felice nodded, then squinted at Vana. 'Have I seen you before? I've not had a chance to speak to you since I was rescued yesterday, but I'm sure I recognise you from somewhere.'

'I was in Lostwell,' Vana said. 'When I was locked up in the Governor's Residence in Old Alea, you visited me for a few minutes.'

Felice smiled. 'That's right. You were the bait to entrap Belinda.'

Vana narrowed her eyes. 'Did it work?'

'Yes. Leksandr and I put her in a restrainer mask. Then Edmond, the Second Ascendant, nearly had me killed for it. Bastion tortured me for hours. You know, the more I think about it, the more I see that I could be happy here, with no Implacatus breathing down my neck all the time, and no more bloody Blue Thumbs games to have to sit through. Vana, whatever happened in Lostwell is in the past. I hope we can be friends?'

'I hope so too,' said Vana.

Kagan stood. 'Excuse me for a moment; I need to use the bathroom.'

He turned his face away from the gods and demigods at the table, and strode for the door. The moment he was out of the dining room, he picked up his speed. He ran up the stairs to the second floor, and hurried into the quarters he shared with Amalia. He slowed, trying to remain quiet, and stole across the hall to the small nursery, where Maxwell was sleeping.

He had five minutes. Five minutes to get his infant son out of the mansion and as far away as possible. As soon as they realised he had gone, he would have two immortals with vision powers looking for him; but he was good at hiding; good at lying low. He knew he would have a far better chance of escaping if he went alone, but the notion of abandoning his son to a band of crazed gods and demigods never crossed his mind.

Pausing to check that no sounds were coming from the room, he pushed the door open and peered inside. Sitting in a comfortable armchair was one of the nursemaids, a young Sander woman. Her eyes were closed, and she had a blanket over her legs. Kagan waited a moment, to see if she would awaken, then crept across the carpet, avoiding the floorboards that squeaked. He gazed down into the cot. Maxwell was wrapped up in a white blanket, his sleeping features peaceful.

Kagan hesitated. This was insanity. He had never once changed the child's nappy, and had only fed him on very rare occasions. How was he supposed to know how to care for a baby on his own? A realisation dawned on him. If he was going to flee, then his only chance of success would be to hand himself in to the authorities in Pella. Surrender himself and Maxwell to the Crown, and pray that they were merciful. Was that really better than staying?

Torn with indecision, Kagan stared at the baby as the minutes passed, then, on an impulse, he reached down and took the child into his arms. Doing the right thing would probably cost him his life, but at least he knew what the right thing was. With Maxwell held tight, Kagan turned for the door. On the floor by the wall was the leather bag that the nursemaids carried around with them. Kagan leaned over and picked it up, slinging the strap over his right shoulder.

He slipped out of the room, and gently shut the door behind him. Maxwell stirred in his arms, but made no sound, and Kagan hurried down the two flights of stairs to the ground floor. He went through the large atrium. The front doors of the mansion would be locked, so he turned for the kitchen. With any luck, Saul would be in the cellar. He padded across the floor and eased the kitchen door open. Inside, the Torduan cook was working by the line of stoves, cleaning up after making the late dinner. Kagan tried to turn back, but Saul glanced up and saw him in the doorway. His eyes narrowed as he caught sight of the baby.

'What are you doing?' said Saul. 'Where are you going with the boy?'

Kagan said nothing, his mind freezing. Why hadn't he thought up a suitable excuse?

'I see,' said Saul. He put down the cloth he had been using and picked up a broad meat cleaver. 'How about you answer me? I know you're her ladyship's favourite, but that doesn't mean I won't slice you up if you're trying to run out on us.'

'I'm not going anywhere.'

'No? You just happened to be creeping about with Maxwell and a packed bag?' He took a step forward, the cleaver clutched in his hand. 'You filthy Shinstran rat. I've never trusted you. Wait until her ladyship hears about this. I wonder if she'll let me torture you before I cut your head off and dump your body in a canal?'

'You've got it all wrong, Saul.'

'Do I? Why don't we let one of the new gods read your mind? Then, we can be sure.'

The cook took another step forward, and Kagan got ready to run. He tried to work out if he could unlock the front doors before Saul caught him, but before he could move, the side door that led to the alleyway burst open, and three armoured soldiers charged into the kitchen. Saul turned, his face twisted with fury, and raised the cleaver. Two soldiers loosed their crossbows, and both bolts struck Saul in the chest. The third soldier aimed at Kagan, then paused, his eyes widening at the sight of the baby held against him. It was all Kagan needed. He turned and ran, not waiting to see Saul's body fall to the kitchen floor.

Kagan sprinted back into the atrium. He made for the front doors, then skidded to a halt as they were smashed in, the tall doors swinging off their hinges as more soldiers entered the mansion. Kagan swerved for the stairs and ran up them as quickly as he could, ignoring the cries from the soldiers to halt. A crossbow bolt flashed by his head, embedding itself into a thick wooden banister post. He reached the first floor landing. Felice had opened the door of the dining room, and was glancing out to see what was causing the noise.

'Soldiers!' Kagan shouted to her.

Montieth pushed Felice out of his way and strode to the top of the stairs. Down in the atrium, over a dozen soldiers had gathered, and more were entering through the broken front doors.

'Fools,' muttered Montieth, raising his right hand. 'Die.'

Nothing happened. The soldiers stared up at the god, then loosed their crossbows. Kagan threw himself back against the rear wall of the landing as bolts flew up at them. Montieth took three to his torso, and staggered back, as the soldiers began to charge up the stairs. Kagan ran for the next flight, hearing Felice sprint up after him. They reached the second floor landing and ran into Amalia's private quarters. Felice bolted the door, then turned to Kagan.

'My powers have gone,' she said, her eyes wide. 'That Holdfast bitch must be here. Can you fight?'

The nursemaid emerged from the nursery, her eyes sleepy. She glanced at the child in Kagan's arms, and frowned.

'What's happening?' she said.

'Soldiers are attacking the mansion,' said Felice; 'we've been discovered.'

'If they come in here,' said Kagan, 'we're surrendering. I'm not risking Maxwell.'

Felice glared at him. 'I'm not going back to prison. Can we get out through the roof?'

He shook his head. 'We're trapped.'

'I don't understand,' said the nursemaid. 'We haven't done anything wrong; why would soldiers be here?'

Felice shook her head at her. 'You poor, ignorant mortal. If you want to live through this, go back into the nursery and hide. The soldiers aren't interested in worthless beings like yourself.'

The sound of someone screaming echoed up through the mansion.

'Give me the baby,' said Felice. 'My self-healing is still working, and I could survive a jump from a window.'

'No,' said Kagan. 'I'm not giving my son to you.'

'He's Amalia's son too, or had you forgotten? And, what were you doing with him, anyway? You told us that you were going to the bathroom.'

She reached out to grab Maxwell, but Kagan took a step back. She glared at him. Without any powers, Kagan was stronger than her, and he could tell from her eyes that she knew it.

The air shimmered, and Amalia appeared in the room next to them, alone. She glanced at Kagan, and gasped in relief when she saw Maxwell in his arms. Without a word, she slid her fingers over the Quadrant, and the room dissolved around them. Their surroundings changed, and they appeared in a large chamber, with faded and worn tapestries covering the walls.

'Stay here,' Amalia said, then she vanished.

Kagan glanced around. Naxor and Ikara were already in the room, sitting on a low couch by a blazing hearth. They looked up at Kagan, Felice, and the nursemaid.

'We have been betrayed,' said Felice.

'Looks like it,' said Naxor.

'Where are we?'

'In Greylin Palace,' said Naxor.

'Where did Amalia go?' said Kagan.

'Where do you think, boy? She's gone to try to rescue the others. We returned to the mansion a few minutes ago, and saw the Banner soldiers break in. She brought us here, then went to fetch you and the baby.'

The only door in the room opened, and Lady Amber walked in.

Her mouth fell open. 'What in Malik's name is going on? Naxor?' She blinked. 'Ikara? You can't be here – Salvor scans the palace every day. You have to leave.'

'We're going nowhere, cousin,' said Naxor.

The air shimmered again, and Amalia appeared, with Vana, Montieth and Gellie.

Amber gasped, and put her hands to her mouth.

Montieth was in a rage. He ripped the crossbow bolts from his chest and stomach and threw them to the ground.

'Bastards!' he screamed.

'Father?' said Amber.

'Get me a drink, girl,' Montieth growled.

'That's a fine idea,' said Naxor. 'Let's drink before the Banner get here.'

Amalia walked over to where Kagan was standing and embraced him.

'Thank you,' she said. 'I almost panicked, but you had Maxwell. Thank you, Kagan.' She kissed him, then turned to the others. 'I had to leave Collo behind. And Saul's dead. Kelsey Holdfast was there, on the roof of the mansion with her damned dragon; there was nothing we could do.'

'How did they find us?' said Vana. 'I thought we were supposed to be safe there?'

'I thought so too,' said Amalia. 'Maybe Salvor got lucky. What's important is that, with the exception of Collo and a few servants, we all made it out alive. Amber, alert the Dalrigian militia, and make sure that you have ballistae on the palace roof, and everywhere else. They won't be able to attack Greylin.'

'Are you joking, grandmother?' said Amber. 'The Banner have already been in Greylin, twice. Are they coming a third time?'

'Yes; as soon as they realise where we've gone. You have no choice, Amber – you must declare for us.'

'It doesn't matter what Amber thinks,' said Montieth. 'Greylin and Dalrig are mine. It's good to be home. Where's my drink?'

Felice walked over and took a seat by the fire. 'Has the water supply of Outer Pella been poisoned?'

'Yes,' said Naxor. 'We emptied four vials of death-salve directly into the cistern.'

Amber's face went pale. 'You did what?'

Felice nodded. 'That means we're probably safe for a day or so. The Banner will be needed to quell the disturbances in Pella come dawn.'

'You're right,' said Naxor; 'it buys us some time. Though, and we need to be clear on this – we deny everything. Claiming responsibility for what we've just done would unite the rest of the City against us. At least we have an alibi; for how could we have done anything while we were under attack? We should issue a statement at dawn, blaming the carnage on the King and Queen, and saying that it proves that they are unfit to lead.'

'Draft something to that effect,' said Amalia.

'You poisoned the water supply of Pella with death-salve?' said Amber. 'What's wrong with you? Have you lost your minds?'

'Be quiet,' said Montieth. 'And fetch us drinks; I will not ask again.'

'I will not be quiet, father,' said Amber; 'you have put us all at risk.' She turned to Amalia, and pointed a finger in her face. 'As for you, grandmother; so much for you wanting to stay hidden. I knew that was a lie. All you've ever wanted is power over the rest of us...'

Amber's skin began to turn green, and she choked, blood appearing on her lips.

Montieth laughed, his finger raised. 'Calm yourself, daughter, or I will bring you more pain; I will turn your guts inside out and upside down.'

Amber fell to her knees, her hands on her throat, as her skin began to peel off.

'That's enough, son,' said Amalia. 'Amber was merely letting off steam.'

Montieth lowered his finger, and Amber fell to the floor, convulsing. Amalia pointed at her, and the demigod healed. From the other side of the room, the nursemaid let out a whimper, and Gellie put an arm over her shoulder.

'We have suffered a setback,' said Amalia, her eyes going over everyone in the room, 'but we are not defeated. Together, we can make Greylin impregnable. Ballistae on the roof, and on the town walls, will keep the dragons away, and we have enough militia soldiers here to keep the Banner out. We will issue a statement in the morning, calling upon the citizens of the City to support us. As Naxor suggested, we will blame the deaths in Outer Pella on the Aurelians' incompetence.' She took a breath. 'As of this moment, I am once again the God-Queen. You will refer to me as your Majesty, and give me all the honours that the title is owed. Now, if you please.'

One by one, the gods and demigods in the large room got to their knees before Amalia, their heads bowed. Montieth frowned, but joined the others, while Amber was unable to keep the fear and anger from her features as she knelt by the hearth.

'Mortals too,' said Amalia.

Gellie went to her knees, pushing the nursemaid down to the carpet at the same time. Kagan said nothing, his arms still clutching onto Maxwell. Amalia gave him a pointed look, and he lowered himself to his knees, cursing his cowardice. His plan to flee had failed, and he was aware that either of the two immortals with vision powers would be able to read his true intentions out of his mind, if they chose to. He bowed his head, ashamed of what he had become.

'Good,' said Amalia. 'This is my City. You will obey me, and you will love me. Long live the God-Queen.'

No one met her eyes.

Felice shuffled on the carpet. 'Long live the God-Queen,' she said, her head bowed.

'I'm waiting,' said Amalia.

The others kept their heads down. 'Long live the God-Queen.'

CHAPTER 20

HIGH EXPECTATIONS

The Eastern Mountains – 15th Monan 3422

Jade opened her eyes, stretched, and smiled. The dawn's first rays were filtering through the front of the tent she shared with Rosie, and, though the air was cold, Jade felt warm wrapped in her blankets. She sat up, pulling the blankets over her shoulders. The tent was low, and her hair was almost touching the condensation that had gathered on the hanging fabric. She heard Rosie breathing, and glanced down at the sleeping figure. The Jackdaw girl had a habit of staying up late each night, and sleeping in each morning, but Jade didn't mind. She eased past her and opened the front of the tent.

Outside, Flavus and Inmara were sitting by the ashes of the campfire. The Banner officer was writing in a notebook, while the militia sergeant had filled the steel kettle, and was sifting through a pile of chopped wood.

'Good morning,' Jade said, as she squeezed herself out of the tent. She closed it behind her, stood, and stretched again.

Flavus glanced at her. 'Sleep well, ma'am?'

'Very well,' said Jade. She pulled the blankets round her and sat on the grass. She looked up. The sky was lightening towards sunward, though it would be a while before any sunlight reached the bottom of the valley. A light breeze was rustling the bare branches of the trees next to the pool, while the tall, dark green pines swayed gently.

'Good morning, ma'am,' said Inmara. 'Sergeant Darvi has gone to fetch more firewood. There will be some hot water in twenty minutes or so, if you want to use it to wash?'

'I'd rather have something warm to drink,' Jade said. 'I can wash in the pool later. Maybe we could get Halfclaw to heat the water up for us.'

Flavus laughed. 'Perhaps, ma'am. If you have a moment just now, I'd like to speak to you about the next stage of our survey.'

Jade nodded. 'There's a next stage?'

'This is our fourth dawn in the valley, ma'am, and I have completed the initial mapping of the area, and of the salve mine. There are two tasks remaining, as far as I can see. Firstly, we need to refine a few ounces of the raw material, which is the most I'll be able to do with the limited amount of alcohol at our disposal. I would have brought more, of course, had I known the purpose of this trip in advance. And, secondly, we need to ascertain if this valley is the sole source of salve, or if the mountains are full of the stuff. Does that sound right, ma'am?'

'I think so,' said Jade, trying to hide her worry. The mapping and survey of the mine had been completed already? That sounded like terrible news to her, as it held the promise of a rapid return to the City, when she had been hoping that their stay would be extended.

'I have finished constructing the necessary equipment,' Flavus went on; 'we can try the refining process later today, ma'am, and then, naturally, we shall need a volunteer to test it upon. With all due respect, ma'am, you would be the most suitable candidate.'

'Me? No. I've had enough salve, thank you.'

'But, ma'am, there is a small risk that whatever I create might well be toxic, and you are the only one with self-healing powers.'

'I'll supervise the process; it won't be toxic.'

'All the same, ma'am, we would be running an unnecessary risk. You would only have to take the tiniest amount for the purposes of checking that it's pure and effective.'

Jade frowned. 'I said no. How old would you say I looked?'

Flavus glanced at her. 'Maybe nineteen or twenty, ma'am?'

'Exactly. If I have any more salve, I'll end up looking like a sixteen-year-old, and I really don't want that. I know the fate of the God-King, and that will not be happening to me. If one of the mortals takes the salve, then I will be on hand to heal them if there are any ill effects, which there won't be; I'll make sure of it.'

Inmara lit the fire, and placed the kettle onto a metal grid above the flames. 'I will take the salve, ma'am.'

'See?' said Jade. 'Sergeant Inmara has volunteered. Problem solved. What about step two?'

Flavus glanced at the sergeant for a moment, then nodded. 'For step two, we will require Halfclaw. I suggest that he takes us over the mountains to iceward, where we can search for more caves. It is clear to me that these mountains were settled by a primitive culture several millennia ago, and there is a fair chance that, if more salve deposits exist, then at least some of them would have been found by the ancient inhabitants. If we find nothing to iceward, then we can look sunward.'

Jade relaxed. That sounded like it would take many days to complete. 'I agree.'

'Excellent,' said Flavus. 'Halfclaw is due to visit us at some point today; I will speak to him and schedule some trips. We can also send him back to the City with our initial results from this site. He mentioned yesterday that he misses his mate, Frostback, and I'm sure he wouldn't mind going back to see her for a day. He could pick up some more supplies for us at the same time.'

'Are we running low on anything?' said Jade. 'I thought we had enough to last us a month?'

'We are short of two things, ma'am – glass apparatus and containers for the refined salve, and alcohol.'

'Why do we need more alcohol?'

'Well, ma'am, I assume that the City will want us to refine as much salve as possible while we are here? It would be far easier to transport back to the City in a refined state. There will be a weight limit to the amount of raw salve that a dragon can carry.'

Jade nodded. She hadn't told anyone about the King's last minute secret orders; that she was to oversee the destruction of the salve mine if it proved to be the only one in the area. That was the outcome she was hoping for. Salve had been nothing but an evil presence in her life, and, although the cost would be that she would slowly age, it would be worth it to see the mine go up in flames.

'Let's prioritise the search for other deposits,' said Jade.

'Yes, ma'am. Might I say, that you are the first immortal I've met who seems ambivalent about salve? Every other one would have bitten my hand off to be the first to try some. If the gods of Implacatus were here, they would be in a salve frenzy by now.'

'Yes? Well, none of them had to spend nine hundred years shut up in a palace with nothing but salve. I was given it as a baby, even before I'd grown to adulthood, because my father wanted to test the effects on infants. He used to put it in my milk. Is it any wonder that my memories of my first century alive are so hazy? I was intoxicated by salve the entire time.'

Inmara sighed and shook her head.

'Do you have something to say, Sergeant?'

'Apologies, ma'am,' said Inmara, 'but listening to you makes me want to grab your father by the collar and ask him just what he thought he was doing. What a way to treat a child! Animals treat their young better.'

'My father is a monster. I knew it for a long time, but it's only now that I can say it out loud. I hope he rots in jail.'

Flavus and Inmara glanced at each other, and Jade grew embarrassed, not wanting their pity. The tent opened behind her and Rosie crawled out into the daylight, groaning. She rubbed her face and sat down, her eyes heavy.

Flavus raised an eyebrow. 'Too much gin last night, Private?'

Rosie shook her head. 'Darvi had most of it, sir. Is he still sleeping?'

'Sergeant Darvi has been up for an hour, Private' said Inmara. 'He complained, but I find that fresh air and hard work is the best cure for a hangover.'

Rosie looked horrified. 'I'm not sure I completely agree.'

Inmara opened a bag and took out a loaf of bread. She set it down onto a wooden board and began to slice it with a knife.

'We'll have some breakfast,' she said, 'and then we can put the theory into practice, Private.'

Rosie rolled her eyes. 'Some holiday this is.'

An hour later, Jade had eaten, washed in the pool, and had changed into fresh clothes inside the tent. Rosie had done the same, but still seemed groggy and disorientated.

'I might need to throw up,' she whispered, after pulling on a clean outfit.

'Don't do it in the tent,' said Jade. 'We'll never get rid of the smell.'

Rosie groaned. 'I'm never mixing wine with gin again; that was my mistake.'

'Are you really feeling terrible?'

'Yes. Sorry.'

Jade touched the young woman's arm, and sent a burst of healing power into her.

'Woah,' cried Rosie. She glanced around, as if she had just awoken. 'Wow, that felt amazing; my hangover's gone. Thanks.'

'It's better than you vomiting over the blankets.'

'Maybe you could do that for me every morning?' said Rosie.

'If you didn't drink alcohol, then I wouldn't need to do it.'

'Hmm. Yes, I suppose that's true. Or, I could drink and never have a hangover again.'

'That seems like an abuse of my powers. I only did it this time so that you wouldn't be sick on my stuff.'

'No, you did it because, deep down, you're kind.'

Jade snorted. 'You know that's not true, Rosie. I wish it were, but it's not. You are kind; I am a murderer.'

'You *were* a murderer,' said Rosie. 'You've changed.'

'I wouldn't be so sure about that. And besides, you've only known me for a few days.'

Rosie opened the tent. 'I have faith in you.'

Jade watched as the young Jackdaw woman wriggled her way out of the tent. Without a doubt, Rosie was the nicest person Jade had ever known, and she realised that she would do anything to protect her, almost as if she really were a friend. Jade shook her head. She had to resist these feelings. In a short while, just a few decades, Rosie would be dead; it was the way of all mortals, and Jade had to harden her heart, and not allow herself to become bewitched by friendship. She took a breath, and followed the mortal out of the tent.

Flavus was standing by the fire, issuing instructions to Rosie and Darvi, while Inmara was tidying away the remains of breakfast.

The Banner officer nodded to Jade. 'We are going to extract a few pounds of raw salve, and make a start on the refining process, if you would like to assist us, ma'am?'

Jade nodded. Darvi was sent back into the trees to forage for more wood, while Flavus, Rosie and Jade walked up the gentle, grassy slope towards the entrance to the caves. They passed the piled up crates and boxes by the opening to the cavern system, and Flavus picked up an oil lamp and lit it.

'Are you actually coming inside today?' said Rosie.

'Yes,' said Jade. 'I promised Flavus I would help with the refining, so that none of you get poisoned.'

Rosie smiled. 'See? You are kind.'

'No. It's so I don't have to explain to the Queen why one of my team died on this operation.'

'So you say.'

Flavus glanced at them, but said nothing, and Jade wondered what the officer really thought of them. He shone the lamp down into the end of the cave, and set off, the two women following a pace behind. They reached the end of the cave, and went through a narrow opening on their right, and walked along the tunnel for several yards, passing the crude scrawling on the walls that had supposedly been made by ancient peoples.

Jade stopped to glance at the walls. The images depicted stick-like figures hunting some sort of cattle-like creature, along with other, more confusing drawings. In one, lines of stick figures were lying horizontally, while another figure was holding a glowing substance in their hands.

'They are incredible, aren't they?' said Rosie. 'Just imagine, they've been here for thousands of years, in a time before the greenhides arrived. It must have been so peaceful back then.'

'Mortals don't need greenhides to be violent,' said Jade. 'They can manage that on their own.'

'I've taken the liberty of sketching most of the wall paintings,' said Flavus, 'and I'm hoping that the Royal Academy in Ooste will be interested in seeing them. Do you know Chancellor Mona, ma'am?'

'Not really. Of all of Michael's children, she was the quiet one. I saw her at the coronation, but she didn't speak to me. I don't think she likes me.' She pointed at the glowing substance depicted above one of the stick figures. 'Is that salve?'

'Presumably, ma'am.' He shone the lamp down the tunnel. 'Not far to go.'

They set off again, following the bobbing light coming from the lamp as Flavus led them through the narrow tunnel. They reached a larger cavern, and Jade immediately recognised the silvery threads running through the rock walls.

'This is the first salve cave,' said Flavus; 'there are another two, deeper within the caverns. I have searched every inch of this cave system, and now estimate that there are over a hundred and fifty tons of salve left. Of course, there may be more – these seams might stretch back further than I've been able to judge.'

He placed the lamp onto the smooth ground and pulled a heavy set of gloves over his hands. He then took a small axe from his belt, and began chipping away at the closest vein of salve, knocking chunks of silver-grey rock onto the ground. Rosie took a bag from over her shoulder, and put on her own gloves. Then, she knelt by Flavus, and carefully placed each lump of rock into the bag, while Jade watched.

Memories flooded her, and she started to feel claustrophobic. She remembered lying on her stomach, in a cave so narrow that she was terrified of getting trapped, scraping salve with a spoon into a sack, her fingers tingling from the constant contact with the substance. While the other demigods of the City had been living their lives of power and luxury, she had been mining salve for her father, barefoot, cold and alone. She shivered and closed her eyes, but it was no good; she could still smell the salve. She started to feel sick.

'Right; that's enough,' said Flavus. 'Is the bag heavy, Private?'

'Nah; it's alright, sir. I can manage.'

'Ma'am?'

Jade opened her eyes.

'We're ready to return to the outside,' he said. 'Are you alright?'

'Fine.'

She turned before they could say anything, then realised that it was too dark to see her way back through the tunnels. She let Flavus move ahead of her with the lamp, and remained silent as they retraced their steps to the entrance cave. Jade walked straight out into the sunlight, and exhaled. It was several moments before she noticed that Halfclaw was standing in front of her, his head just a few yards away.

'Demigod,' he said.

'Hi, Halfclaw,' said Rosie, emerging from the cave behind Jade. 'How are you today?'

'I'm well, little Jackdaw, but something bad has occurred, and we need your help.'

'What has happened?' said Flavus.

'Is there any salve ready? We need some,' said the green dragon.

'Not yet,' said Flavus; 'it'll be a few hours.'

The dragon's eyes flared with impatience. 'That isn't fast enough; Firestone is dying.'

'Firestone?' said Rosie.

'Yes; Dawnflame's son. I must return to the lair with some salve to save him; Deathfang sent me, and told me to do whatever it takes to get some salve.'

'I'll work as quickly as I can; I swear it,' said Flavus. 'Rosie, help me get the equipment set up. I'll need that bottle of gin, and we'll have to get the fire going at a fair old heat...'

'That'll take too long!' cried the dragon. 'Firestone will be dead by then.'

'What happened to him?' said Jade.

Halfclaw bowed his head. 'He is young, and he was foolish. He flew too low over a swarm of greenhides, and they leapt up and dragged him to the ground. Dawnflame and Darksky were there, and they pulled him free, but he has been badly mauled, and has lost a lot of blood. His wings were ripped to shreds.'

Rosie nudged Jade. 'Now's your chance,' she whispered.

Jade frowned. 'Chance for what? Flavus is right, it will take time to refine the raw salve into medicine; I can't speed the process up.'

Rosie pulled Jade's arm, and took her aside.

'Offer to heal the young dragon,' Rosie said, keeping her voice low; 'you have the power to save him.'

'Why would I want to save a dragon? The last time they were here, they threatened to kill me and Flavus. And, it sounds like it was his own fault.'

'You're right; everything you're saying is correct. That's why you need to do it. Show them, Jade; show them that they're wrong about us; show them that we care.'

Flavus coughed. 'Excuse me, Private? I need your assistance.'

'Yes, sir,' said Rosie. 'Jade wants to say something.'

'Do I?' said Jade.

Rosie glared at her. 'Yes; you do.'

Jade sighed. 'I suppose that I could heal this dragon.'

Halfclaw turned his face to her. 'You could? Are you sure?'

'Of course I'm sure,' said Jade.

'Are you powerful enough, demigod?'

'Don't insult me, Halfclaw. If you want this Firestone to live, then take me to the dragon colony.'

Halfclaw stared at her for a moment, then tilted his head. 'Climb up onto the harness, demigod; I will take you there.'

'Wait,' said Sergeant Inmara, hurrying up the slope. 'You shouldn't go alone, ma'am.'

'She will be safe,' said Halfclaw.

The sergeant narrowed her eyes. 'Will she? You guarantee that? That yellow dragon wanted to bite her head off.'

'Then, bring two others,' said the dragon. 'The harness can fit three; but be quick – Firestone's life is draining away.'

Inmara turned, and gestured to Darvi. 'Get up here.'

'I shall come along also,' said Flavus.

'No,' said Halfclaw. 'You are the one the others hate, because you served in Dragon Eyre. They will not accept your presence in the colony.'

'What about me?' said Rosie.

'You are acceptable, little Jackdaw.'

'I should go,' said Inmara. 'It's not fair to put Rosie into danger. I'm the sergeant; it's my job.'

'I'll take Rosie and Darvi,' said Jade; 'that's my decision. Inmara, you stay here and help Flavus refine the salve, in case it's still required.'

The sergeant frowned. 'Yes, ma'am.'

Darvi, Rosie and Jade scrambled up the side of Halfclaw's flank, and strapped themselves into the harness. The dragon extended his wings across the width of the narrow valley and rose into the air. On the ground below them, Flavus and Inmara gazed up, then Halfclaw banked and soared away to sunward, the breeze whipping over his long body.

'How far is it to the colony?' yelled Rosie.

'Less than an hour,' said the dragon. 'I cannot predict how the others will react when I arrive with three humans on my back instead of salve. They will probably insult you, but I will not allow them to harm you.'

'Sounds just great,' muttered Darvi.

'Don't worry,' said Jade. 'If we are attacked, then I will show them just how powerful I can be.'

'It won't come to that,' said Rosie. 'They will see that we are doing a good thing. And, think of the alternative – if we did nothing and Firestone died, then the dragons would be right to hate us.'

Halfclaw cleared the high mountain ridge and increased his speed, racing sunward over the crests and valleys. They crossed the pass used by the greenhides, and soon left it far behind. Jade gazed down at the view. There were many other small valleys and little plateaus above the range of the greenhides. If salve was common in the region, then any one of those would be suitable for exploration. She hoped it wasn't true. If the mountains were filled with salve, then there would be no end to it, but, if their little valley was the sole source, then one day, there would be no more salve; ever. The thought made her heart race with excitement. Imagine that – no more salve. The gods would age and, eventually, grow too decrepit to lead a normal existence. What would happen after that? Would they die? Was such a thing possible? Jade hoped so.

The temperature began to edge upwards the further they flew, until the breeze felt warm against Jade's face. It was still temperate enough for vegetation to grow in wild abundance, but it felt more like summer.

Halfclaw veered a little to the east, then circled over a high rocky plateau that was criss-crossed by deep ravines. In the centre, where three ravines meet, a river spilled over the edge of a cliff, falling into a wide, round pool. Halfclaw descended, and Jade saw Deathfang sitting by the water's edge, his long neck angled upwards so that he could keep a watch on the skies.

The green dragon pulled his wings in and set down next to the waterfall, which sent spray over the three humans up on his shoulders.

'Did you bring salve, young Halfclaw?' cried Deathfang.

'I brought a healer,' the green dragon said.

Deathfang glanced up, and saw the humans. His eyes burned.

'I sent you to bring salve,' he said, 'not humans.'

'The salve is not ready,' said Halfclaw, as the three humans unbuckled their straps and began to clamber down. 'It will take hours to refine it. The demigod here says that she has the power to save Firestone.'

Deathfang lowered his head to stare at Jade. 'Is that so?'

'Yes,' said Jade, reaching the ground. 'Do you want my help?'

Deathfang continued to stare at her, ignoring the other two humans. 'Let me announce this to the others first.'

He turned his great bulk, and entered a vast cavern on the sunward side of the ravine.

'This place is a bit gloomy,' said Rosie, glancing around.

'It is sheltered from prying eyes,' said Halfclaw.

'Oh? Do you get many prying eyes around here?'

A rage-filled bellowing echoed out from the large cavern, and they all turned to look at the entrance.

'Dawnflame does not like humans,' said Halfclaw.

Jade shrugged. 'If she doesn't want me to save her son, then we can go right back to the valley. It makes no difference to me.'

Three dragons peered out from the cavern to stare at the humans. Two were Deathfang and Burntskull, while the other was a dark blue female.

Darvi swallowed. 'My crossbow feels a little inadequate right now.'

'For Malik's sake,' whispered Rosie; 'keep it on your shoulder.'

'You may enter,' said Deathfang. 'However, be warned – Dawnflame is resistant to allowing any human to touch her son.'

'I don't have to touch him,' said Jade, 'but, I'll need to get close if he is severely wounded.'

The dark blue dragon's jaws sparked and flamed. 'Do you think we would let you anywhere near Firestone, insect, if he wasn't severely injured? I will restrain Dawnflame. You will heal Firestone, and be quick at it.'

The dark blue dragon withdrew into the cavern, along with Burntskull.

'Come,' said Deathfang.

The humans stepped forward, and entered the cavern. It was dim, but shafts of daylight were filtering through jagged cracks in the rock, and Jade could see enough of her surroundings to prevent her from stumbling. They walked along a wide tunnel, then entered a vast, open cavern. Deathfang and Burntskull moved to one side, while the dark blue dragon pushed back another female.

'No,' cried the other dragon. 'Get those filthy insects out of here!'

'Quiet, Dawnflame,' said the dark blue dragon. 'This is your son's only chance. He is dying.'

Dawnflame charged forward, and the dark blue dragon raised her claws and allowed a gust of flames to leave her jaws.

'Quickly,' Deathfang said to the humans.

Jade glanced over the floor of the cavern, then saw the wounded dragon. He was small, though still far larger than she was, and was lying in the middle of the floor, his red scales covered in blood. Rosie ran forward, then pulled up a yard away from the injured dragon.

'That's close enough,' said Deathfang.

Jade walked to stand by Rosie, then lifted her hand. She closed her eyes, using her powers to feel for the life force of the young dragon. It was ebbing away. His heart was weak and fading, and he was barely breathing. She felt deeper, and sensed the great wounds covering his body, from the ripped and torn wings, to the slashes gouged across his flesh by greenhide jaws and talons. She had never sensed the insides of a dragon before, and Jade marvelled at its complexity – so different from humans, but sharing the same organs: heart, lungs, eyes, blood. She heard sounds echo through the cavern next to her, but ignored them, concentrating on the body lying motionless in front of her. When she was confident that she understood what she was doing, she sent an enormous burst of healing power into the dragon, enough to heal dozens of humans. She gasped, and staggered backwards, tripping and falling onto the cold, stone floor.

Jade groaned. Her ears were ringing, and she felt weak and drained. She powered her self-healing, and opened her eyes. Dawnflame's jaws were a foot above her. Sparks and little wisps of flame curled about the dragon's teeth. Jade tried to scramble away, then noticed that Dawnflame had brought a great forelimb down onto Rosie, and was crushing her beneath it.

'Get off her!' Jade cried. She rolled, then sprang to her feet, her hand lifted. 'Get off her or I'll kill you.'

Dawnflame didn't seem to hear her; her attention focussed solely on her son. Jade unleashed a blast of death powers at Dawnflame, and the dragon screamed, then lifted her other forelimb and swatted Jade away as if she were a fly. Jade shot through the air, then hit the cavern wall, breaking several bones. She fell to the ground in a heap, breathless, her head hitting the stone. She tried to glance up, but her body was lanced through with pain, and her vision was blurry. Dawnflame turned to her with rage in her eyes, and opened her jaws. Jade covered her face with her hands, preparing herself for death.

'Stop!' cried Deathfang. 'Dawnflame; stop! Look at your son.'

Jade waited for the flames, but none came. She pulled her hands away to look. Dawnflame had turned away from her, and was sniffing Firestone, who had begun to move. The young red dragon opened his eyes, then lifted his wings. They were healed.

'My son!' cried Dawnflame. She stepped forward, and enveloped Firestone with her wings, pulling him close to her.

Jade felt a hand on her shoulder.

'Ma'am?' said Darvi.

She took his offered hand, then Darvi helped her up. Her self-healing was in full flow, and the fractures in her bones had healed, though she was still in pain. Her eyes turned from the dragons and scanned the floor. Lying alone and ignored, was the body of Rosie. Jade pushed Darvi's hands away and ran. She fell to her knees next to Rosie, her eyes welling as she saw the damage the dragon's forelimb had caused. Without hesitating, she placed her hands onto Rosie's face, and gave her every last ounce of power she still had. Her eyes closed involuntarily as she felt her own life force seep away into the young Jackdaw woman, then she fell sideways, collapsing to the floor, unconscious.

When Jade awoke, she was back in her tent. She stretched, then noticed Rosie sitting next to her in the semi-darkness.

'Is it night?' said Jade.

'Yes. How are you?'

'Fine. A good sleep was all I needed.'

'You saved the dragon, and then you risked yourself for me,' said Rosie. 'I'll never be able to thank you enough.'

'It's nothing,' said Jade; 'don't make a fuss.'

'It's not nothing.'

'I used my powers to heal you; that's all.'

'That's not what I'm talking about. Darvi told me – he said that you fought Dawnflame because of me, and that the dragon was going to kill you. I knew you'd changed, Jade, and this proves it.'

Jade sat up. 'It proves nothing. I'm hungry; is there any food?'

Rosie smiled. 'Go outside and see.'

Jade crawled to the end of the tent, glad to be away from Rosie and her over-powering gratitude. She had acted on impulse in the dragon cavern; it didn't mean that she was suddenly redeemed for all the evil she had done. She opened the tent and emerged into the glow of the campfire. Flavus and the two sergeants got to their feet, and applauded her.

'Bravo, ma'am,' said Flavus. 'Bravo.'

Jade stared at them, embarrassment colouring her cheeks.

'Have a seat, ma'am,' said Darvi. 'We've got dinner all ready; we were waiting for you. Will you eat with us?'

Rosie came out of the tent and laughed. 'Look at her; she doesn't know how to handle being the hero.'

'I'm not a hero,' said Jade.

'Maybe not,' said Rosie, 'but you're my hero.'

CHAPTER 21

THE RAID

P ella, Auldan, The City – 16th Monan 3422

Frostback soared down from the sky, her jaws opening, as Kelsey clung onto the harness rail. Below them lay the tight maze of red sandstone streets and houses of Outer Pella. At the corner of a large building, a dozen or so dead Reapers were staggering along the road towards a barricade guarded by Banner soldiers. The flames from the silver dragon burst forth, and the dozen figures were consumed by fire. Frostback banked and rose, and Kelsey watched as a Banner sergeant picked off a smouldering straggler with a well-aimed crossbow bolt, sending the tottering corpse to the ground.

'I think that's the last of them in this area,' said Kelsey.

'I hope it's the last of them in Pella,' said the dragon. 'The sight and smell of these creatures turns my stomach. They are rotten, inside and out.'

She flew low over the barricade, and the Banner soldiers raised their arms to salute the silver dragon. All over Outer Pella, it was the same. The Banner were out in force, along with the Reaper militia, blocking roads and sweeping through neighbourhoods for the last of the roaming dead. The civilian population had been ordered to remain inside their homes, with their doors and windows locked and barred.

Frostback turned for Cuidrach, and raced through the air, passing the old walls of ancient Pella and soaring over the jumble of sandstone houses. The palace reared up before them, and she ascended, and then landed on the roof.

Sergeant Nagel and the rest of the dragon crew were ready. A trough of fresh water had been set out by the edge of the roof, along with a large cauldron of raw meat. Frostback began to eat, and Kelsey slid down from the harness. She saw Captain Cardova among the Banner officers on the roof, and strode towards him.

'We think we've got them all,' she said to him.

Cardova nodded. 'Thanks. You and Frostback have made this a lot easier.'

'I know. Your gratitude is duly noted, Lucius.'

He beckoned for her to walk with him, and they went to the far end of the roof and sat on a bench. Cardova offered her a canister of water, and she took a drink.

'Listen,' he said; 'I know there's a whole ton of things going on at the moment, but I need to speak to you about Van; in confidence. As friends, not as Banner and dragon-rider.'

'Alright; understood.'

He nodded, then gazed at the ground. 'I have discovered where he got his hands on the salve. We assumed that Naxor stole everything that was removed from Greylin Palace, but I checked the records, and a vial of concentrated salve was logged as missing before Naxor escaped. Van must have taken it, and diluted it down. I know it's not much consolation, but I'm glad that he wasn't getting it from someone else in the Banner.'

'Does that mean he has plenty of it?'

'Yes. Enough to last an addict months, maybe years.'

'But, you've told him to stop?'

'I did, but he's also my commanding officer; I can't exactly order him to stop, and it's part of my duty to pretty much do whatever he asks me. He asked me to shut up about it. So, I have a choice – either I do as he says, or I resign my commission as an officer and return to my old regiment. Or, possibly the Brigades. Now, I've decided what I'm going to do, but I also want to hear your opinion.'

'What are you going to do?'

'Your opinion first, then I'll tell you.'

'If you resign, then I assume that you'll be replaced by someone else?'

'Yes. Most likely another captain, but it's at his discretion.'

Kelsey stared out over the view of Pella. 'Shit. You'll have to stay. I trust you, Lucius, and I don't know if I'll trust your replacement. Van will pick someone that won't question him sneaking off to take salve, and I'll have lost an ally in the Command Post.'

'That's the conclusion I came to. I intend to make one last attempt to get him to see sense, and then I'll keep my mouth shut, if he doesn't relieve me of my position. He needs to know that I don't approve, even if I agree to keep quiet.'

'But, he'll be alright, aye? I mean, the way I've heard it told, it's like half the Banner were on salve back in Implacatus. It obviously doesn't kill everyone who takes it.'

'No, you're right. I've known many officers who were addicted to salve, and most of them managed to function enough to do their jobs, and some were able to quit with a little help. However, the stuff Van's taking is extremely pure, and he has a history of heart problems associated with taking salve.'

Kelsey sighed, and stared at the ground. 'I thought things were going too well. I don't know if I can face the prospect of watching a slow decline; or worrying every time I come home that he's lying dead on the floor from a heart attack. If he was ill, it would be different, but he's choosing to do this to himself.'

'It's not time to despair just yet.' He leaned in close. 'Also, if I ever happen to find his stash, I will destroy it, regardless of the consequences.' He straightened. 'Anyway, back to work. The major-general wants to see us in the briefing room downstairs. We have new orders.'

He got to his feet. Kelsey sat for a moment longer, trying to prepare herself to meet Van. They had been avoiding each other over the past day, which wasn't difficult, as both had been busy. She stood, and they walked along the roof to the stairwell, then descended to the next floor down, where a meeting room had been taken over by the Banner. Cardova knocked, then they entered. Inside, Van was sitting at a table with Salvor, in front of a large map of Dalrig.

Van stood, leaning on his walking stick. 'Thank you for coming. Please sit.'

His eyes lingered on Kelsey as she took her place at the table next to Cardova.

'The City, as you know,' Van said, 'is currently in a state of shock. Most people seem to doubt that the God-Queen has returned, despite her announcement from Greylin Palace. That's the good news – everything else is bad. The chaos in Outer Pella is under control, but the entire regiment is still out on the streets, and in no position to assault Dalrig or storm Greylin Palace. The town is now bristling with ballistae batteries, and we're not going to risk losing Frostback in any kind of aerial assault. Or Halfclaw, for that matter.'

'Halfclaw?' said Kelsey.

'He arrived in Pella this morning. He'll be assisting in the clear up of Outer Pella, and then monitoring the frontier with Gloamer territory. That will free up Frostback for something else. Before you ask what that is, I want you to listen to what Lord Salvor has to say.' He nodded to the demigod.

'Thank you, Captain,' said Salvor. 'What I will now tell you is confidential, of course. Our enemies have two immortals with vision powers, and it was wise to keep some secrets to ourselves. For example, we knew yesterday morning what was causing the chaos in Outer Pella. We knew that the water supply had been poisoned by death-salve. Because of that, we were able to close off the central cistern and drain it before too much damage was done. The death toll was kept to the hundreds, rather than the thousands, because of information we received from someone within Greylin Palace.'

'The water was poisoned?' said Kelsey. 'Who did it?'

'Who do you think?' said Van. 'Who stole the supply of death-salve?'

'That wee bastard,' muttered Kelsey.

'Quite,' said Salvor; 'my brother appears to be one of the ringleaders and instigators of the crisis. However, thanks to our informant, not only did we discover the source of the poison, we have also learned of the attitude and dispositions of the cabal sheltering within Greylin Palace.'

'Who's the contact?' said Kelsey.

Salvor lowered his eyes. 'Amber.'

'You read Amber's mind?'

'I didn't have to. As soon as I made contact, she told me everything. Of course, I had to be sure, but every piece of information I checked turned out to be true. To say that Amber is unhappy with the squatters in her palace would be a gross understatement. She told me about the death-salve immediately. She was outraged, and her emotions, I believe, were genuine. For all the problems and inconveniences that Lady Amber has caused the Crown, she has never been a killer. Unfortunately, she is surrounded by killers, including two with the power to read her mind.' He paused. 'An hour ago, I lost contact with her. We must assume that she has been discovered. I have yet to locate her within the palace, so there is also the possibility that she has been killed.'

Kelsey puffed out her cheeks.

'Before I lost contact,' Salvor said, 'I learned several facts about the make up of our enemies. Amalia has a baby son within the palace.'

'The baby we saw in Port Sanders was hers, my lord?' said Cardova. 'I talked to a few soldiers who saw a man carrying a baby inside the mansion. One almost shot them, but the baby made him hesitate.'

'The man is Kagan,' said Salvor; 'Amalia's betrothed.'

Kelsey laughed. 'What? Amalia's getting married? To a mortal? Pyre's cock, that's hilarious.' The others waited for her to stop laughing. 'Do you think he says "Amalia's arse?"' she went on. 'I hope he doesn't mention Malik's rear end to her.'

'He's from Lostwell,' Cardova said.

'Yes,' said Salvor. 'Kagan is also in Greylin, along with Montieth, Vana, Ikara, Naxor and a god called Felice, also from Lostwell.' He glanced at Van. 'She harbours a particularly bitter grudge against the major-general.'

'Why?' said Kelsey.

'It stems from my time in the Golden Fist, but the details aren't important,' said Van, 'because I'm not going to Greylin – you two are. It pains me to place you into such a position of danger, Kelsey. You aren't a trained soldier, and I won't be able to guarantee your safety. Unfortunately, we can't come up with an alternative. A full frontal assault on Dalrig by the Banner would result in an unacceptable level of casualties; but a small strike force might be able to infiltrate the palace and neutralise our enemies before they can do more damage to the City. Your primary targets are Amalia, Montieth and Naxor; the others are of lesser importance, but kill or capture any that you can, with the exception of Lady Amber and, clearly, the child.'

Kelsey leaned back in her chair. 'Alright.'

Van glanced at her. 'I'm sorry about this.'

'Don't apologise,' she said; 'you have a job to do, and so do I, it seems.'

He nodded, then turned to Cardova. 'Handpick ten Banner soldiers; that's all that Frostback will be able to carry, so you will need to travel light. Halfclaw will provide a distraction on the frontier while you and your team are put into position. You have an hour, then assemble on the roof. Any questions?'

'I have one,' said Kelsey. 'Say that we get in, and it goes wrong; how do we get out again?'

'You will need to use your initiative. We can't risk sending a dragon to collect you. Lord Salvor will be monitoring your progress, but his vision will be limited by your presence. If it wasn't for the current state of my health, I'd be coming with you.'

'The Queen has ordered the major-general to stay here,' said Salvor. 'He tried to persuade her that he should go along, but she forbade it.

Both the King and Queen have asked me to pass on their best wishes for the success of this operation; much depends upon it.'

'What about you, Lucius?' said Van. 'You've been very quiet. Any questions?'

Cardova shook his head. 'No, sir.'

A flicker of frustration passed over Van's eyes, then he nodded. 'Very well. Dismissed.'

'Can I speak to you in private?' said Kelsey.

Van gestured for Salvor and Cardova to leave the room. The captain got to his feet, saluted, then he and the demigod walked out, closing the door behind them.

'I'm worried about you,' she said.

Van raised an eyebrow. 'You're worried about me? You're the one being sent into that nest of snakes. If anything happens to you...'

'You know what I'm talking about, Van.'

He narrowed his eyes. 'I can handle it, Kelsey.'

'Can you? Lucius and I are concerned...'

'Lucius can mind his own business.'

'And me? Should I mind my own business too? I thought we were a team; you and I? This is my business.'

'I told you that I can handle it. It changes nothing between us.'

'I'm not sure I agree.'

'Come on, Kelsey; when I first met you, you were smoking weed like there was no tomorrow. How is this any different?'

'I knew you'd bring that up. Salve is much worse.'

'That's a matter of opinion. Right now, I need it to function; I need it to keep my mind clear so that I can deal with all the shit that's being thrown at us. Once things calm down, I'll be able to ease myself off it, and then you'll wonder what all the fuss was about.'

Kelsey chewed her lip for a moment. 'Alright, but I'm interpreting that as a promise.' She stood. 'I'll see you when we get back.'

'Good luck, Kelsey.'

She nodded, then walked from the room.

An hour later, Frostback extended her silver wings and lifted into the air above Cuidrach Palace. Grasped in her forelimbs was one of the small wooden carriages. It had been stripped to its minimum weight, and had nine Banner soldiers packed inside, while up on the harness, a sergeant sat alongside Kelsey and Cardova.

To iceward, Kelsey could see Halfclaw in the distance, flying over the frontier between Reaper and Gloamer territory. Frostback turned, and sped off towards the west, crossing the harbour of Pella, and then the bay, which was shining in the light of the morning sun. The dragon soared across the water, then passed the town of Ooste on their right. As soon as they had rounded the headland, Frostback banked again, and raced up along the edge of the high cliffs. To their left was the impenetrable fog and wind of the Clashing Seas, and waves were battering off the ragged shoreline. Frostback descended as low as possible, hugging the cliffs as she battled the rising winds from the sea. Beneath her, the carriage swayed and shook, as gusts battered them. Grey banks of thick fog stretched up the western slopes of the Shield Hills, and they lost visibility several times amid the giant rocks and the high waves of sea spray.

After a mile, the turbulence dropped, and the skies to the west cleared to reveal the waters of the Cold Sea, while, on their right, the high cliffs of the Shield Hills continued.

'That was fun,' said Kelsey, her clothes and hair soaked through. 'Still, I'm glad I'm not in the carriage.'

'At least they're dry down there,' Cardova said. 'And it'll be worth getting wet if we've retained the element of surprise. With you up here, they shouldn't be able to see us.'

The dragon ascended to the height of the cliffside. The Shield Hills were mostly barren, with a few patches of gorse and heather, and Frostback kept as low as possible, the carriage barely skimming the ground. She navigated to the location that Salvor had given them, and set the carriage down at the bottom of a dry gully, then landed next to it.

The nine Banner soldiers piled out of the carriage, and were joined by Kelsey, Cardova and the sergeant on the ground.

Frostback lowered her head towards Kelsey. 'Take care, my rider. This is a hard moment for me, leaving you here inside the territory of our enemies. I understand the reasoning, but it sits badly with me. You and I belong together, and I should be there, to protect you.'

'You know that you can't come any further; the ballistae would shoot you down. And, don't worry; I'll be fine.'

'Every soldier here would give their life to save her,' said Cardova.

Frostback turned her gaze to him. 'Do you include yourself in that promise?'

'Of course,' said Cardova.

Frostback tilted her head. 'You are a good man. Take care of my rider.'

The dragon swept her wings out and launched herself off the cliffs, heading away to the west, towards Westrig. Kelsey and the soldiers watched her disappear into the distance, then turned, and began walking down the gully.

It was hard going, as the valleys and ridges of the Shield Hills were pathless and wild, and the winds were relentless and bitterly cold. Frost spread over the rough ground, and large flakes of snow swirled about the high slopes as the group made their way down through a succession of gullies that were thick with brambles and thorns. At the bottom of a valley, Cardova consulted the map he had brought, as the others gathered round him.

'The first Gloamer pickets are over the next ridge,' the captain said; 'but we're not going that way.' He pointed to the map. 'Just iceward of here is an old, abandoned mineshaft that leads down into the salve caverns. These caverns are connected by tunnels to the basement of Greylin Palace. Lord Salvor has scouted the route, and it appears to be lightly defended. Speed and silence are needed here; our objective is to get as close as possible to our targets inside the palace. Let's go.'

Cardova led the way, and they set off again. The entrance to the mineshaft was almost hidden by undergrowth, and when it had been cleared, they realised that the ladders descending into the dark depths had long since rotted away. They fixed ropes to the top of the shaft, prepared their oil lamps, and climbed down into the darkness. Cardova stayed close to Kelsey during the descent, making sure that her ropes were correctly secured, and Kelsey's arms and legs were sore and tired when they reached the bottom. Cold, ankle-deep water was sloshing about at the base of the shaft. A soldier shone his lamp down a tunnel, and then the squad set off in single file, their crossbows ready. After twenty minutes of splashing through the dark, narrow tunnel, they reached a stout door blocking their way.

Cardova raised a hand. 'The salve mine should be on the other side of this door,' he whispered, 'along with a few Gloamer militia. Kill them all.'

The soldiers nodded. Cardova signalled in the direction of the door, and two soldiers squeezed forwards, and unpacked the tools they had brought with them. They positioned a series of steel crowbars along the side of the door, then, at a nod from Cardova, they heaved, and the door rose up off its hinges, then crashed forward into the tunnel.

Six crossbows thrummed, and the two Gloamer soldiers on the far side of the door fell to the ground. The Banner squad rushed through the entrance, their bows levelled, but there were no more militia guarding the tunnel. The squad extinguished their lamps, as the interior of the mine was well-lit, and dumped them and their tools, retaining nothing except what they needed to fight. They set off at speed, racing through the tunnels in the direction of the palace, with Kelsey bundled into their midst. She had been given a thick leather cuirass to wear, but was unarmed. Her nerves were stretched taut, but she tried to keep her fear from being noticed by the others. If it all went wrong, she knew her arms lacked the strength to climb all the way back up the mineshaft, but she pushed such thoughts from her head and tried instead to focus on what they were doing.

The squad turned a corner, and found themselves gazing into a basement chamber of the palace. They paused, then stepped out from the tunnel into the empty room.

'From now on,' said Cardova; 'kill everyone we meet, except for Lady Amber and the baby. The last known location of Amalia and Montieth was in a large room on the ground floor; that's our next target.'

They crept through the chamber, then Cardova peered through a doorway. He gestured to the rest of the squad, indicating that two more militia guards were in the passageway. Four soldiers nodded, got into position, then burst out of the room, two down on one knee, the others standing behind them. Together, they loosed, and Kelsey heard the sound of two bodies hitting the floor. The squad ran out into the corridor, then raced along it, heading for the stairs. Kelsey glanced around, trying to get her bearings. She remembered both of her previous trips to Greylin, and noticed the room where the King and Queen had been caged. The cages were still there, piled up along the walls, and Kelsey shuddered at the sight. They reached the servants' stairwell, and started to ascend, keeping as quiet as possible. None of the soldiers were wearing steel armour, and they moved silently, their bows ready. At the top of the stairs, another pair of Gloamer militia was standing on duty, but they had their backs to the steps, and didn't hear the Banner soldiers coming. Cardova took one, and a sergeant the other, reaching up silently with knives from behind, and slitting the throats of the two men. They pulled the bodies down the stairs, then Cardova pointed at a doorway. The squad gathered at the top of the steps, then charged the door. The sergeant kicked it open, and the Banner soldiers rushed inside.

Kelsey ran with them into the room. From a collection of low couches, several faces turned at once, then Kelsey was pushed down by Cardova as the shooting began. The squad formed up into two lines, and unleashed bolt after bolt into the sitting gods and demigods. Amalia was struck in the face, and fell to the floor, while Montieth was riddled with four bolts and toppled off the couch. Kelsey watched, transfixed, as Ikara went down screaming, then Vana and Naxor were hit.

Cardova drew his sword, and half of the squad followed him in a charge, the others continuing to loose. Two soldiers reached Ikara, who was lying on the carpet with a bolt in her back. One plunged his sword into the demigod's stomach, and the other swung at her neck, cleaving her head from its body. Cardova reached Montieth, who was raising a hand, vainly trying to use his powers. The Banner captain lifted his sword.

The air shimmered, and several immortals vanished, including Montieth.

'Shit!' cried Cardova. 'Fan out, they could return at any moment.'

Kelsey was bundled into the centre of the room by a Banner soldier, and pushed onto an empty couch as the others in the squad formed a protective cordon around her. Aside from Ikara's corpse, two others remained in the room – Vana, whose arms and legs were quickly bound with ropes, and a green-skinned Fordian woman, who was dying from three bolts in her chest.

'Did you see who got away?' said Kelsey, trying to ignore the cries of pain from the mortal woman.

One of the Banner leaned over the Fordian, and loosed his bow into her heart, ending the cries. Kelsey stared, her mouth opening.

'Amalia, Montieth,' Cardova said, 'Naxor, Felice, and the mortal man. I saw them all in here.' He snapped his fingers. 'The baby; Amalia will return for the baby, just as she did in Port Sanders. Come on.'

The squad moved off, keeping Kelsey in their centre as they left the room. Gloamer militia were charging down the stairs in the main hallway, and the squad formed up into lines and cut them down with a hail of crossbow bolts, their bodies falling down the steps and leaving bloody trails on the faded carpets. More Gloamers loosed their own bows from the top of the stairs, and two Banner soldiers went down with bolts in their guts. Cardova led the others in a charge up the stairs. Another Banner soldier was hit, in the face, and flew backwards to the ground. The others reached the landing, and drove into the Gloamers, their swords bloody as they cut them down without mercy.

Cardova led them on, and they reached the rooms where Salvor had indicated that Amalia's son was being cared for. They burst through the door, and a lone woman raised her hands above her head.

'Don't shoot! I'm only a nursemaid!'

Cardova raised a hand to prevent his squad from loosing, and they entered the room. The nursemaid had her hands tied behind her back and was placed in the corner of the room with a guard, while Kelsey and Cardova walked over to a cot by a huge, faded tapestry.

Kelsey looked down at the baby's face. The infant boy was awake, and he smiled up at her.

'Take up positions,' said Cardova. 'If Amalia returns, this is where she will come.' He gestured to the sergeant. 'Get up onto the roof and release the orange smoke, then get Lady Vana and our wounded up here into this room.'

'Yes, sir,' said the sergeant. He selected another two soldiers to accompany him, and they raced out of the nursery.

Kelsey continued to gaze down at the baby. 'Are we using a child as bait?'

'Yes,' said Cardova. 'Does that offend your principles?'

'I don't know.'

'No harm will come to him; I'm under strict orders to ensure that the baby is treated well.'

'What if you'd been ordered to kill him? What would you do then?'

Cardova met her glance. 'I don't have to answer that. We're Banner; you know what we'd do.'

'I would stop you.'

'Then thank the gods it won't come to that.' He turned to his squad. 'Stay alert; Amalia could return at any second. If and when she does, bring her down.'

CHAPTER 22
DOUBLE-EDGED

Dalrig, Auldan, The City – 16th Monan 3422

Emily strode across the roof of Greylin Palace, a thick winter coat keeping out the cold night air. Banner soldiers were manning the large ballistae at the corners of the roof, just as they were occupying the rest of the palace. Emily stopped at the roof's edge, and gazed down into the lamplit streets of Dalrig.

'I don't think she's coming back, your Majesty,' said a voice behind her.

Emily turned to see Lady Amber standing close by. The demigod had been found, gagged, hooded and bound in a basement cellar. She had also been poisoned by anti-salve, and the bruises on her face bore testament to the fact that her self-healing powers had yet to recover.

'It's been twelve hours since they vanished,' Amber went on. 'They've abandoned the baby.'

'You should be resting,' said Emily.

Amber snorted. 'How can I rest? My own father put these bruises on my face, after that rat Naxor told him I'd been speaking to Salvor. My own father.'

'We owe you a debt of gratitude, Amber. Your courage enabled us to be standing here.'

'But the raid failed, your Majesty. My grandmother and father are still on the loose, along with Naxor and Felice.'

'And the mortal too, I heard?'

'Yes. Kagan.'

'We have people out searching the City for them,' said Emily. 'We'll find them, and when we do, we'll attack again and again until we get them. For now, the surrender of the Gloamer militia will suffice as a triumph. For that, we also owe our thanks to you.'

The demigod shrugged. 'I wasn't sure that they'd obey me, not after the God-Queen announced that she was back in charge.'

'We'll have to leave a garrison here in Greylin; I hope you understand?'

Amber said nothing, her gaze on the town and the dark harbour basin.

'The rest of us will be gone before dawn,' the Queen went on, 'and we'll be taking Vana and the child with us. A hundred Banner soldiers will suffice as a garrison.'

'Are you leaving Kelsey Holdfast too?'

'No, she will be returning with us to Pella. I need her available to go anywhere within the City at a moment's notice.'

'Have you searched Maeladh? I heard Amalia talk about going there.'

'It was the first place we looked. Listen; when this is all over, what can I do to thank you? You have proved to be loyal; there is a place for you in the government if you wish it?'

'I just want to be left alone, here, in Dalrig. I may have helped you, but it doesn't mean I like you, your Majesty. And, I will never agree to those foolish new constitutional laws, and you can tell the King I said that. Scrap the elections, and go back to the way things were.'

'I appreciate your honesty, Amber. If we defeat Amalia and Montieth, then we shall need to try a new approach.'

'Does your husband agree?'

'He will.'

Amber smiled. 'I'm amazed your monarchy has survived for as long as it has. What are you going to do with Ikara's body?'

'Burn it,' said Emily, 'then inter the ashes in the crypts under the Royal Palace in Ooste with the remains of the rest of the former Royal Family.'

'The Banner have turned out to be a fearsome weapon.'

'I wish I had more of them.'

'I've thought of one thing you can do for me, your Majesty,' Amber said. 'Hand the Grey Isle back into my possession.'

Emily narrowed her eyes. 'I'll consider it. I might want to place Vana there, if I decide not to execute her.'

Amber laughed. 'She wouldn't last a month locked up in the old dungeons. What if you give me the island, but keep the fortress?'

'Alright, but it's conditional on Monteith never being in charge of Dalrig again. To be sure of that, we need to kill him whenever we capture him. No mercy this time.'

Amber nodded.

A Banner officer approached the two women and bowed. 'Your Majesty, Lady Vana is pleading to speak with you.'

'Is she, indeed?' said Emily.

'Yes, your Majesty. She is refusing to eat or drink.'

The Queen glanced at Amber. 'If you'll excuse me, I'd better talk to our prisoner.'

Amber gave a slight bow, then turned back to gaze out over the town. Emily followed the officer past the overgrown and neglected gardens on the roof, and they descended into the lamp-lit corridors of the palace. They went to a set of rooms on the top floor, and passed through a thick line of Banner soldiers, who all saluted. The officer removed a key from a pocket in his uniform, and unlocked a door. Inside, Vana was sitting on a low bed, with her knees drawn up by her chin.

Emily entered the small, windowless chamber, along with the officer, and a soldier who kept his crossbow trained on the prisoner. There was only one seat in the room, and Emily took it.

'Good evening, Lady Vana,' she said.

Vana stared at her with red, tear-filled eyes. 'This is all a terrible mistake.'

'I see. You joined a rebellion by accident?'

'I didn't know what they were going to do. Naxor tricked me.'

Emily sighed. 'How gullible do you think I am? Your mistake was getting caught, Vana; you knew what you were doing.'

Vana burst into tears. 'They chopped Ikara's head off; then they shot the Fordian mortal, even though she was already wounded. I thought they were going to kill me.'

'So did I. Frankly, I was a little surprised to hear that you had been taken alive, especially as my orders stated that you were all to die.'

'Are you going to execute me?'

'That depends, Vana. If you would prefer to keep your head on your shoulders, then I'm going to need more than a few tears of contrition.'

'What do you want from me?'

'Let's start with the most basic question – where has Amalia gone?'

'I don't know – I swear it. Maeladh? She talked about going to Maeladh Palace, but that was before you raided the mansion in Port Sanders.'

'She's not in Maeladh, Vana, nor is she back in her old mansion. I'm not asking you to guess – use your powers.'

'I have! I can't see her anywhere, just as I can't see the others who fled. They must have taken more anti-salve.'

'But, Vana, we found most of the anti-salve; they didn't have time to gather up their possessions before Amalia whisked them away with the Quadrant.'

'Then, I don't know. Maybe Naxor had some anti-salve in a pocket. Or, they might have moved out of my range. Tarstation?'

Emily frowned. 'Lord Salvor will read every last secret out of your mind when we arrive in Pella. I'm asking you these questions now, as a courtesy. If I discover that you are lying to me, then nothing will save you.'

'I'm not lying! I don't know where they are. Ask yourself – why did they leave me behind?'

'Incompetence? It was a panicked situation, or so I heard. Abandoning you proves nothing; I'm more interested in why they seem to have abandoned the child. Maxwell, yes? Amalia and Kagan's son. Why hasn't she tried to rescue him?'

Vana looked confused. 'You have Maxwell?'

'Yes. Amalia left him when she vanished, but that was predictable. She did the same in Port Sanders; only, there, she came back for him a few minutes later.'

'I don't understand; truly. I know my grandmother can be cold, but I really believed that she loved that baby boy. She hasn't come back for him? I wonder if...'

'Yes?'

Vana frowned. 'I wonder if Naxor or Montieth have taken the Quadrant from her. That's the only thing that would prevent her from coming back.'

Emily raised an eyebrow. 'I doubt that. Amalia is a monster – she poured death-salve into the water supply of Outer Pella. She has it within her to abandon her own child.'

'I can see how you'd think that, but I disagree. She's changed. The baby has changed her. And the mortal too – Kagan. While Naxor was advocating the mass murder of half of the City, it was Amalia who restrained him.'

'I don't believe that. And, even if it is true, then it's just for show. Trying to kill thousands of Reapers is not showing restraint, Vana.'

'I know.' She lowered her eyes. 'I'm sorry for my part in the rebellion, your Majesty.'

'No, you're not. You're scared that you're going to be executed, and that's not the same thing. If Amalia had won the day, you would be standing by her side.'

Emily stood and turned to the Banner officer. 'Transport Lady Vana back to Pella and place her in the dungeons next to Lord Collo. Lord

Salvor can read her mind first thing in the morning, and then she is to be executed along with her brother.'

The officer bowed. 'Yes, your Majesty.'

'No; please!' cried Vana, getting off the bed and falling to her knees in front of Emily. 'I'm begging you; don't kill me. I don't deserve to die.'

'You are a traitor,' said Emily. 'Death is exactly what you deserve.'

She walked from the room before Vana could say another word, then took a moment in the hallway to breathe. A few minutes later, the officer and soldier escorted Vana out. Her hands had been bound, and she had a hood over her head, and Emily watched as the soldiers led her down the stairs to a waiting wagon. She thought that she would feel pity for the demigod, but she felt nothing. She turned, and went down another two flights of stairs to the nursery, which had been transformed into an armed camp. The corridors leading to the room had been barricaded, and dozens of well-armoured Banner soldiers were surrounding it. Emily squeezed past a blockade and entered the room. Kelsey Holdfast was sitting by the cot in the corner of the room, while soldiers lined the walls, their crossbows at the ready.

'Wrong Queen, guys,' said Kelsey; 'don't shoot.'

'It's a strange time to have a sense of humour,' said Emily, as she walked up to the cot.

'Aye? Well, it's either that or I go crazy; I've been sitting here for hours. She's not coming.'

Emily glanced down into the cot, and watched as the baby slept.

'That's typical,' said Kelsey. 'The damn baby's been crying for ages, and he goes to sleep just before you come in.'

'Has he been fed?'

Kelsey nodded. 'Twice, and his nappy's been changed. I hadn't realised that babysitting for Amalia was in my job description.'

'You know why you're here, Kelsey.'

'Aye, for the same reason that anyone's ever been interested in having me around – to block powers.'

Emily sat down on a chair next to Kelsey. 'I just sentenced Vana to death.'

'Vana? Oh.'

'Do you disagree with my decision?'

'You're the Queen.'

'That doesn't answer my question.'

'I've never got on with Vana. But, execution? I don't know. Back in Lostwell, I remember arguing with her brother about the same thing. Irno wanted to execute a few Banner prisoners, because they had infiltrated his castle. I appealed to his better nature, and he backed down. One of those prisoners turned out to be Van.'

'Are you going to try to appeal to my better nature?'

'Do you want me to? You sound like you want me to.'

Emily sighed. 'I confess to having had some fairly murderous notions concerning the gods and demigods recently. Part of me thinks it might be better to kill every one that has shown disloyalty. Lady Ikara, for instance? I won't mourn her. She was a terrible Governor of the Circuit, and the City is better off without her, just as it'll be better off without Amalia and Montieth. And Naxor, as it turns out. He might be the worst of them all, in some ways, because at least the other two have never hidden their intentions.' She paused. 'The other part of me worries that, if I carry on down this road, I will become just like them.'

Kelsey glanced at the cot. 'Say you could get rid of Amalia and the others permanently, by killing Maxwell – one solitary child, to potentially save hundreds, or maybe thousands; would you do it?'

'Of course not, Kelsey.'

'Then, you're not as bad as them. Imagine what they would do to Elspeth, if the circumstances were reversed, and they captured her?'

Emily bowed her head, feeling sick.

'Do what you need to do,' said Kelsey. 'You're stronger than I am. It was me who stopped Van from throttling Montieth, remember? Several of your problems would be solved if I hadn't intervened. I'm not sorry that I did it; I'm not saying that, but I don't think I'm capable of killing. Yesterday over Outer Pella was bad enough, and those poor bastards were already dead. I don't envy you having to make these decisions, Queenie. I used to watch my mother rule the Holdings, and I've experience of watching the Empress on my homeworld, and if it's taught me anything, it's that I never want to be a leader.'

Emily gestured for a lieutenant to approach.

'Your Majesty?' he said.

'Please fetch Captain Cardova for me.'

The officer bowed and left the room. Emily turned back to Kelsey. 'Thank you for listening, and thank you for your advice. I know that I've asked you to do all manner of unpleasant and dangerous things, as well as frustrating things, like sitting all day and night in this room waiting for the God-Queen to turn up. The funny thing is, you've done all this without ever signing a contract, like the Banner, or swearing loyalty to me, like everyone else in the City who works for the Crown.'

'I consider myself an Exile; an honorary member of the Brigades, and you pay me.'

'I know what you get paid; you receive the same pittance as the rest of the Brigade Exiles, and you live in a tiny brick house with no heating or running water.'

'That's not true; I have a hot-water pipe that works twice a day.'

Emily smiled. 'Very well, I'll concede that. My point is, that you could be so much more. Lady Kelsey of Jezra, for instance. I'm sure I remember Corthie and you telling me that your family was aristocratic. When all this is over, I'm going to make sure that you are suitably rewarded.'

Kelsey gave her a wry smile.

'And, of course,' Emily said, 'Major-General Logos might well end up as Lord Van of Jezra.'

'I wouldn't count on that.'

'Why? I thought the two of you were getting along well?'

'We were, but... never mind. We'll either get through it, or we won't.'

'I assume this is related to the salve? I won't pry any further, though I'm tempted. All I will say is that I hope you stay together. I like you as a couple – my best soldier and my dragon rider, who rescued me and my husband from this very palace.'

'Excuse me for interrupting, your Majesty,' said Cardova, as he walked across the room, 'but, as I recall, they had some help.' He smiled, bowed, then his face grew serious. 'Before we say anything else, please allow me to apologise for the failure of the operation. I take full responsibility for the escape of Amalia and the others. We were quick, but not quick enough, and the Quadrant was activated before we could reach the main group.'

'That was a funny choice of words, Captain,' said Emily.

Cardova blinked. 'Which part, your Majesty?'

'You said "the Quadrant was activated," instead of something like "Amalia activated the Quadrant."'

'Yes, your Majesty. Amalia took a crossbow bolt to her face and fell to the floor. I didn't see her move again, and my eyes were on her the whole time. I don't know who activated the Quadrant.'

Emily glanced at Kelsey. 'Did you see?'

'No. I was being held down by a burly soldier.'

'Damn it,' said Emily, shaking her head. 'Vana might have been right. Captain, prepare to leave Greylin. Amalia's not coming back. I don't think she's in possession of the Quadrant. Let's return to Pella.'

———

The sun had yet to rise when the convoy of wagons drew through the gates of Cuidrach Palace. The Queen had travelled back to Pella in a plain carriage, with Cardova, Kelsey and baby Maxwell, while Banner soldiers had flanked them. In the last wagon of the convoy lay the bodies of Lady Ikara and the Fordian mortal, along with the corpse of the one Banner soldier who had died in the raid, from a crossbow bolt to his throat. The bodies of the thirteen Gloamer militia that had been killed were being returned to their families in Dalrig, and the Queen had offered compensation for each life lost.

Cardova caught Emily's eye as the carriage slowed down in the palace courtyard.

'Your Majesty,' he said, 'without wishing to be a nuisance, you haven't yet commented on the failure of the operation, nor have you accepted or rejected my apology. I will be speaking to the Major-General when we arrive, and I would like to pass on your response.'

'I'm disappointed, Captain,' she said. 'In truth, I would have preferred it if we were transporting the bodies of Amalia and Montieth back to Pella, but I don't consider the Banner to be at fault. Learn from it, and move on.'

Cardova bowed his head. 'Thank you, your Majesty.'

'A couple of other details regarding the raid have come to my attention,' Emily said. 'Vana claimed that one of the soldiers killed the Fordian when she was already wounded. Is that correct?'

'Yes, your Majesty. Without salve or a healer, the Fordian woman would have died a long, lingering death, and it was felt that a quick end would be more merciful. Should I change the guidance given to the soldiers regarding these situations?'

Emily frowned. 'No. If you put it like that, then I suppose you did the right thing.'

'They would have killed the baby, if you'd ordered them to,' said Kelsey. 'Did you know that?'

'No,' said Emily, 'but I suspected it might be the case.'

'The Banner obey orders,' said Cardova, 'and I'm not going to apologise for that. I am, however, relieved on a personal level that we didn't receive those orders. On Dragon Eyre, and on Lostwell, the gods commanded us to do far worse than kill a single child. We wiped out the entire population of Yoneath because the two Ascendants ordered us to; and we slaughtered every trainee within Gadena's compound. The Banner of the Lostwell Exiles consists of the same men who carried out those atrocities. So far, your Majesty, you have never ordered us to do anything like that. It's a relief to work for someone who shows compassion and mercy, if I'm being honest. It makes a nice change.'

The carriage stopped, and the captain opened the door. He climbed out, then extended his hand to help Emily descend to the ground. Kelsey emerged last, the child in her arms.

'Get some rest, Captain,' said Emily. 'Kelsey and I will take Maxwell inside.'

Cardova saluted, then went to join the other Banner soldiers gathered in the courtyard.

'I like Lucius,' said Kelsey, as she and Emily walked towards the palace, a squad of Royal Guards flanking them, 'but he scares me a little at the same time. He seems like a good man, but we know what he and the others in the Banner are capable of. I was in Yoneath; I saw what they did there. It was terrible. Women, children, old folk – they killed them all. The streets were running with blood.'

'I will never order them to do that, Kelsey.'

'Your husband wanted to send them into Tara.'

'Yes, and I stopped him. The Banner are a weapon, an extremely sharp one, and they need to be handled with care. On top of that, I trust Van, and he rebelled against some of the more ruthless orders he received from the gods. They're in good hands.'

They entered the palace and walked through the quiet hallways. They reached the royal quarters, and went into the living room, where Emily lit a few lamps, while Kelsey took a seat, balancing the sleeping baby on her knee. Emily smiled at the sight, then knocked on the nursery door. She opened it and stole inside. Elspeth was fast asleep in her cot, and Emily gazed down at her for a few minutes, before turning to wake her mother, who was resting on a bed by the other wall.

'Mother,' she whispered, shaking her shoulder.

Lady Omertia opened her eyes. 'What is it, dear?'

'Can you get up, please? I need to ask you something.'

Her mother yawned, and sat up. 'What time is it?'

'Nearly dawn,' Emily said. 'I've just got back from Dalrig.'

Her mother pulled the covers back and slipped her arms into a long dressing gown. They tiptoed out of the nursery, and entered the living room.

Emily pointed towards the child. 'This is Maxwell; Amalia's son.'

Lady Omertia stared at the baby.

'Hi,' said Kelsey.

'Amalia has fled,' Emily went on, 'and she left the baby behind. Mother, I want you to look after Maxwell for me. You can bring in a couple of extra people to help, but I want the child cared for as if he were my own.'

Lady Omertia walked to the couch and sat next to Kelsey. 'How old is he?'

'The same age as Elspeth,' Emily said.

'May I hold him?'

'Sure,' said Kelsey, passing her the bundle. 'Is that me done? No more baby duties?'

'Get some sleep, Kelsey,' said Emily; 'and thank you for everything.'

Kelsey stood. 'He's alright, for a baby, but I still don't want one of my own.'

'You might change your mind,' said Emily. 'I hope you do.'

Kelsey smirked. 'Right. See you later, Queenie.'

Emily sat as Kelsey left the royal quarters. 'Thank you, mother.'

Lady Omertia held the child close to her chest. 'It's fine, dear. Are you going to get some sleep too? You look tired.'

'Is Daniel in bed?'

'No, dear; he's been up for hours. I think he's with Lord Salvor.'

Emily stood again. 'I'd better speak to them.'

'Don't work yourself too hard, dear. Even queens need to rest now and again.'

Emily's gaze lingered on her mother and the child for a moment, then she left the apartment. Kelsey had already gone, and the Queen walked with her guards down the stairs to Salvor's grand office. She entered it, and saw the two men deep in conversation by the flickering shadows of a low fire. They fell silent as she approached, and turned to her.

'I assume you know roughly what happened?' said Emily, as she approached.

'Yes,' said Daniel. 'Salvor's been keeping me updated. He couldn't see everything of course, due to Kelsey's presence, but I think we've pieced it all together.'

Emily noticed that the expressions on both of the men's faces were grim.

'It didn't quite go according to plan,' she said, sitting on a chair next to them.

'I have contacted Chancellor Mona,' said Salvor; 'the search for Amalia, Naxor and Montieth has begun afresh. Hopefully, Lady Silva will be recovered enough soon to assist.'

'I thought that Mona was scanning the forests to the west of Jezra?'

'She was, your Majesty. Should I have kept her doing that? I thought that, in the circumstances, we would need every available god and demigod with powers helping with the search.'

Emily frowned. 'Vana told me that she couldn't detect any of the missing immortals within the City. Could they have gone elsewhere?'

Daniel and Salvor exchanged a glance.

'Possibly,' said Daniel. 'Tarstation, perhaps?'

'I was thinking of somewhere more exotic. My greatest fear is that they have gone to Implacatus.'

'Then, your Majesty, we should conduct our search as quickly as possible,' said Salvor, 'so that, hopefully, we can rule out such a possibility.'

Emily nodded. 'Maybe we should talk to Vana again. She might still have her uses. I assume that she and Collo arrived back at the palace?'

Daniel narrowed his eyes. 'They got here a couple of hours ago.'

'Good. Let's visit them and see if they are willing to help in return for their lives.'

'What?' said Daniel. 'They're both dead. The Banner executed them not long after they arrived. We were told it was on your orders.'

Emily blinked. 'Vana and Collo are dead?'

'They were beheaded, your Majesty,' said Salvor. 'A Banner officer asked me if I had finished reading their minds, and I replied that I had. Ten minutes later, the same officer returned to inform us that both had been executed, as per your specific orders.'

Emily stared at them.

'You did order it, didn't you?' said Daniel.

'I... I may have done. Dear gods, I thought that I would still have a chance to change my mind. What have I done?'

'Three demigods killed within a day,' said Daniel. 'Salvor's sister, and two of his cousins. Are you trying to compete with the God-Queen in ruthlessness?'

'They were traitors,' she said, her voice low.

'They were, your Majesty,' said Salvor, not meeting her eyes.

'We'll announce it in the morning,' said Daniel, 'and see how the City reacts to the news.' He glanced at his wife. 'I understand why you did it, but I wish you had consulted with us first.'

Emily said nothing, her gaze turning to the low flames in the hearth as she went over the words she had said to the Banner officer in Vana's room. She had ordered the demigods' executions, but it felt unreal, as if it had been vague and conditional, but the officer had taken her words and acted upon them. How had she not realised what would happen?

Three immortals in one day. Emily felt numb as she stared at the flames.

Three down; four to go.

CHAPTER 23

AMID THE SANDS

Yocasta – 17th Essinch 5254

Kagan tumbled through the air, his eyes almost blinded by the fierce sunlight. As he fell, he caught a glimpse of a desert, then he landed on a sand dune, the impact winding him. He rolled down the steep slope, coming to a halt on the roasting hot sand at the bottom of the dune.

He lifted his head. Amalia was lying a few yards away, her hands on a crossbow bolt embedded into her left cheek. She ripped it from her face, spraying blood over the sand. Close by, Montieth was groaning in pain, his torso riddled with bolts. Naxor staggered to his feet, his bloody hands holding a bolt that he had removed from his side. He dropped it, and raced across the sand towards Felice, who was lying motionless. He scooped up something from the ground, then glanced at Amalia.

'Give that back to me; now, Naxor,' Amalia cried.

'No, grandmother; I think not,' Naxor said, backing away.

Amalia stood, her face wound healing. She raised a hand towards Naxor. 'Give me the Quadrant, Naxor; I won't ask again.'

'Wait,' said Montieth, standing. 'Where are we?'

'Never mind that,' said Amalia. 'I need to go back and rescue Maxwell.'

'That's exactly why I won't hand it over, grandmother,' said Naxor. 'Do you think I'm a complete idiot? If I give you the Quadrant, you'll vanish, and the rest of us will be marooned here; wherever here is.'

'No,' said Amalia. 'I'll be back in two minutes; I swear it.'

'The Banner soldiers will be waiting for you,' said Naxor. 'Kelsey was there; your powers will be useless. They will cut you down, and we'll be stranded.'

Felice sat up on the sand, and rubbed her head. 'Where are we?'

Naxor smirked. 'I was hoping you could tell us that; it was you who activated the Quadrant and brought us here.'

Felice glanced around. 'I thought I was taking us to Implacatus. This isn't Implacatus.'

The others stared at her.

'Why would you want to take us to Implacatus?' said Amalia. 'Are you insane?'

'I panicked. Those Banner soldiers were tearing us to shreds. I must have made a mistake.'

Amalia turned back to Naxor, and extended her open palms. 'Give me the Quadrant; I can fix this.'

Naxor shook his head.

'I agree with the little runt,' said Montieth. 'If he gives you the Quadrant, you will leave us here, and you will most likely be killed by the soldiers.'

'But those bastards have Maxwell,' Amalia cried.

'So?' said Montieth. 'Your mortal's still alive. Have another brat.'

Amalia raised her hand towards her son.

Montieth laughed. 'My death powers are more than a match for yours, mother. If you attack me, or try to take the Quadrant from the little fellow; I will strike you down.'

Kagan struggled to his feet, his eyes on the immortals. A searing pain rose up from his left ankle, and he fell back down to the burning sands. Amalia glanced at him, then edged towards where he was lying, her hand still raised at her son.

She crouched down next to Kagan. 'Are you hurt?'

'I might have broken my ankle in the fall.'

Amalia placed a hand onto the side of his face, and he felt a powerful surge ripple through him. He shuddered, then realised that all pain had ceased.

'Listen to me,' she whispered. 'We must get the Quadrant. Our enemies have Maxwell.'

'I can hear what you're saying, mother dear,' said Naxor; 'so you can forget trying to play any tricks on us. I'll give the Quadrant to Montieth if it makes you feel better, but I don't think it's a good idea to let you have it; not until you've calmed yourself down.'

Amalia glared at him, rage burning in her eyes. 'You'll pay for this, you rat. If anything happens to Maxwell, I'll build my own restrainer mask, just for you.'

Naxor laughed.

'Don't give me the Quadrant,' said Montieth; 'I have no idea how to use it. We might end up in the middle of a mountain, or perhaps at the bottom of the sea.'

'I can look after it,' said Felice.

'Why; so you can take us to Implacatus?' said Naxor. 'No; I don't think so. I'll hold onto it for now. Incidentally, Felice, can you show me exactly what you did? We might be able to work out where we are.'

'I don't actually want to go to Implacatus,' said Felice, as she walked over the sand towards Naxor. 'It's just that I'm unfamiliar with the geography of the City, and, apart from Lostwell, Implacatus is the only other world I know how to get to.'

Naxor held the Quadrant up, and Felice leaned in close, showing Naxor the finger movements that she had used.

'That's strange,' said Naxor. 'Some of the workings of Quadrants are a mystery to me, but if I had to guess, then the Quadrant has taken us somewhere it has been before.'

They turned to Amalia.

'Why are you staring at me?' she said, as she and Kagan stood.

'This Quadrant has been in your possession for millennia; correct?' said Naxor.

'Yes.'

'Then, where are we, mother? We are not in the world of the City, and, clearly, we are not on Lostwell. Where else have you been?'

'Who cares?' she cried. 'While you're standing there chatting, my son might be... I don't want to think about it. You bastards.'

Montieth raised a hand. 'Don't make any funny moves, mother; I'm watching you.'

'Why don't we give her the Quadrant,' said Felice, 'and we'll all go back?'

'We'd be slaughtered in seconds,' said Naxor. 'I guarantee it. The Banner will be in Maxwell's nursery right now, with crossbows and Kelsey Holdfast. It would be a bloodbath. In my opinion, the child will be safe, for that very reason – they will want to tempt us into returning, and they'll ambush us if we do.'

'Don't pretend that you care about my son, Naxor.'

'I'm not pretending; I don't care. What I do care about is remaining alive. Now, think, grandmother – where are we?'

Amalia bowed her head, her fists clenched. 'I have only ever been to three worlds: the City, Lostwell, and Yocasta. This must be Yocasta; my homeworld.'

Montieth frowned. 'Never heard of it.'

'Why would you? I've never mentioned it to anyone in the City. Only Malik knew anything about my homeworld. I met him on Lostwell, after I'd fled this place. That was over five thousand years ago. I've never been back since. The entire world is a wasteland, devastated by the god wars.'

Kagan glanced around at the desert surrounding them. 'This is where you come from?'

'Yes. It used to be green and beautiful. I fought for centuries to save it, but the gods were relentless and, in the end, there was nothing left to save. I fled to the rebels in Lostwell, where I met Belinda and Nathaniel, as well as Malik.'

'What about your family?'

'They were wiped out. Only I survived, out of all of my brothers and sisters, and their children. My parents were also killed.'

'I'm sorry.'

'It was five thousand years ago, Kagan; but thank you.'

'Perhaps I should take a look around?' said Felice. 'If I can find somewhere to shelter from the sun, somewhere with water, then we could put our heads together and work out what to do next.'

'Do so, girl,' said Montieth. 'I dislike this heat.'

Felice narrowed her eyes at him, but said nothing. She sat onto the sand, and her eyes glazed over.

'Gellie's dead,' Kagan said to Amalia. 'I saw her get shot before we left. Ikara too. The soldiers beheaded her.'

'Damn them,' said Amalia. 'Damn the Banner and damn all those who gave the orders.'

'If Felice hadn't brought us here,' said Naxor, 'we'd all be dead.'

'I know that.'

'I say we give it a day before we return. That way, they won't be expecting us.'

'Shut up, Naxor.'

'Your son will be safe.'

'You don't know that. The Banner were loosing bolts at us without checking who was in the room. They could have easily killed my son by now.' She broke down, and began to weep.

'We'll get him back,' said Kagan; 'whatever it takes.'

Felice's eyes snapped open. 'We need to move,' she said, getting to her feet. 'There are greenhides all around us.'

'What?' said Naxor.

'A few greenhides are no problem,' said Montieth. 'Let them come.'

'You don't understand,' said Felice. 'There are thousands of them, and they are moving in coordinated patterns, as if someone is guiding them.'

Montieth snorted. 'Impossible, girl. No one can control greenhides. Your imagination is running away with itself.'

'You're wrong,' said Felice.

'How dare you? I have killed others for less.'

'Let me check,' said Naxor. 'I'll soon clear it up.'

He tucked the Quadrant into his clothes, while Felice glared at both him and Montieth. The demigod's eyes glazed over for a second, then he coughed.

'Malik's ass; she's right,' he said. 'Formations of greenhides are approaching, and... and, they're in ranks; ordered ranks. How is this possible?'

Felice folded her arms across her chest. 'Perhaps you should listen to me.'

'Well?' said Montieth. 'Get on with it, girl.'

'Don't call me girl, Montieth; I am far older than you, and, it seems, a little more experienced in the ways of the worlds. If you hadn't been hiding in the City for so long, then you might know that greenhides can be controlled.'

'By whom?' said Naxor.

Felice took a breath. 'By an Ascendant. Greenhides were designed that way.'

Naxor's eyes went wide. 'We need to get out of here.'

'That's what I was just saying!'

Do not run, little creatures. I see you.

Kagan fell to his knees with his hands over his ears, grimacing in pain from the voice that had ripped through his mind. From the cries of the others, he knew he wasn't the only one to have heard the voice.

My warriors will escort you to me; do not resist them.

The voice faded away, and Kagan opened his eyes. Clouds of sand were rising into the air around the dunes, and a low rumbling sound was growing. A greenhide appeared at the top of the nearest dune, then hundreds more, all around them, until they were surrounded. The greenhides halted as one, forming a thick ring around the five humans, who clustered together in the centre.

'If you and I unleash our full powers, mother,' said Montieth, 'we can destroy them.'

If you try, I shall destroy you first.

Montieth yelled out in pain.

'Do nothing,' snapped Naxor. 'Whoever you are, if you're listening; we surrender.'

A path opened up amid the dense ranks of the greenhides.

Follow the path; follow my warriors.

'Alright,' cried Naxor; 'we'll do it.'

'Coward,' muttered Montieth.

The group set off, walking between the lines of watching greenhides. Kagan glanced to either side at the rows of sharp fangs, and long, deadly talons. He had seen greenhides in the arenas of Alea Tanton, but the sight of hundreds of the beasts so close made his heart race. Next to him, Amalia was keeping her eyes on the ground. His thoughts went to Maxwell. He knew what the Banner was capable of, having seen them in action in the Shinstran slums, but he had hope that Naxor had been right. They would use the child as bait to lure Amalia back to the City, and they would keep him alive for that purpose. All the same, a dread was growing in the pit of his stomach. They needed to return to the City soon; otherwise the authorities might come to believe that they were never coming back, and then they might decide to dispose of the child. Ahead of them, Naxor was walking with Felice, while Montieth remained at the rear, no doubt keeping an eye on Amalia, in case she tried to seize the Quadrant.

The sun blazed down on them from the bright, blue sky as they trudged over the hot sands. The greenhides kept on the move, funnelling forwards in ranks to show the way, and always staying to either side of the group. They walked until thirst and exhaustion were starting to wear Kagan down, and he envied the others for their self-healing powers.

Naxor pointed. 'Look. A city. Well, what used to be a city.'

They glanced up, and Kagan saw the ruins of a large settlement, half-covered in high drifts of golden sand.

'Do you recognise anything, grandmother?'

'From a few heaps of bricks and stone? No. This could be any one of a dozen cities on Yocasta that I used to know.'

The greenhides guided them down a wide boulevard, towards the centre of the settlement, and they passed ancient streets and the stumps of old buildings, their stone weather-beaten and eroded.

'I'm so thirsty,' Kagan mumbled.

'There will be water here,' said Felice. 'All these greenhides must be drinking something.'

They reached a large, circular opening in the ground, with a ramp that descended at a steady angle into the dark depths. The greenhides flanked the entrance, blocking off every other route.

'This looks suspiciously like a greenhide nest,' said Felice. 'Are we sure about this?'

You have no choice. Descend, so that I can judge you.

'No one's judging me,' barked Montieth.

I could strike you down from here, little creature. Descend.

'Stay close to me, Kagan,' Amalia said. 'If it's a trap, then I'll make it quick for you.'

Kagan said nothing, and they entered the large cavern, walking down the ramp into the darkness. The greenhides kept pace with them, leading them onwards into the gloom. High shafts pierced the roof of the cavern, sending beams of bright light down into the shadows. After a hundred yards, the tunnel levelled off, and they walked onwards, seeing dozens of openings to their left and right, where soldier and worker greenhides were gathered, watching them as they passed.

They walked into a vast cavern, large enough to fit Greylin Palace into. It was crowded with swarms of greenhides, including several towering monstrosities as tall as a tree, who were clustered around a high pedestal. The group were led towards it, and Kagan realised that a throne was perched upon the top of the pedestal. He squinted into the gloom. A figure was sitting on the throne. A man; an extremely old man. His skin was withered and wrinkled, and he was hunched over, his long, white hair hanging in wiry tangles about his shoulders. His face was pale and drawn, but his eyes flashed with life.

Welcome to my palace, his voice boomed into their heads. *I am Simon, the Tenth Ascendant. Kneel.*

Naxor and Felice fell to their knees immediately, while Amalia and Montieth both frowned before they joined them on the ground. Kagan hesitated, then did the same.

What do we have here? A god from Implacatus; a god from Yocasta, and a god and a demigod from a place unknown to me. You are the first guests I have entertained in four thousand years; for that is how long I have been stranded here. Naxor; give me the Quadrant that you are hiding within your clothes.

Naxor swallowed. 'Um, why? We need it, I'm afraid.'

My need is greater. Approach.

Naxor stood, glanced at the massed ranks of greenhides, then shrugged and walked up to the pedestal. He reached its base, and climbed the rough steps to the top. He pulled the Quadrant out and held it in front of the old man. Simon didn't move, and so Naxor laid it down onto his lap, and placed one of the withered old hands onto it.

Thank you. I can sense the Quadrant through my skin, and all of its many owners.

'I am its owner,' said Amalia.

Yes, Amalia of Yocasta, but you have only been in possession of this device for five thousand years; it was fashioned long before that. I know; I was there. Now, Naxor, you have something else in your pocket; a substance that I am unfamiliar with. Salve. Give it to me. If it does what you believe it does, then you will have my eternal thanks.

Naxor put his hand into a pocket, and withdrew a vial of concentrated salve.

Pour some into my mouth.

'It's extremely potent,' said Naxor. 'A few drops should do.'

'Is this wise?' muttered Montieth. 'He's powerful enough even in that decrepit state. Malik knows how strong he'll be if rejuvenated.'

Malik would indeed know. Malik was a young friend of mine on Implacatus. Amalia; I sense your thoughts – you were his wife, and you killed him because salve had addled his mind and body. That is enough warning for me. Naxor, just a small amount, as you advised.

Naxor held the vial away from him, and pulled out the stopper. He moved his hand to Simon's face.

I see you are tempted to throw the salve into my face, Naxor, because you fear me. If you do so, you will be dead in an instant. On the other hand, if you help me now, I will repay you a thousand fold.

Naxor frowned, then tilted the vial above the ancient man's mouth until a drop spilled from the edge. It landed on Simon's lips, which started to burn and smoke.

Let me inhale the vapours; quickly!

Naxor moved the vial under Simon's nose, and the Ascendant screamed – not in their heads, but out loud, the noise echoing off the cavern walls. His body began to convulse, and he toppled off the throne, landing onto Naxor, who fell backwards down the steps. The greenhides began to glance around, as if a spell had been broken, and a few called out, their shrieks tearing through the air. Naxor scrambled back from Simon's shaking body, and a greenhide tried to slash at him. Montieth raised a finger, and the greenhide's head melted, the flesh dripping off to reveal the bare skull. More greenhides shrieked, and two of the enormous queens started to fight each other.

Amalia pushed Kagan behind her, and stood back to back with her son, their arms raised. Felice dragged Naxor over to them, and they crouched by the feet of the two gods with death powers, as the greenhides encircled them.

A cry tore through the cavern, and Simon stood. At once, the greenhides became submissive again. The two queens pulled back from each other, and the workers and soldiers quietened, and lowered their talons. Kagan turned. Simon was standing upright, almost seven foot tall, his old clothes hanging off his muscled form in tattered rags. Long black hair flowed down his back, and his face seemed to glow with its own radiance. His sharp blue eyes turned to the group.

'Gaze at me,' he said, extending his arms to either side; 'look upon my majesty, and worship me.'

Felice got to her knees without another word, and bowed her head. She glanced at the others.

'Get on your knees!' she hissed.

Naxor was the next to kneel, followed by Amalia and Kagan, and finally a scowling Montieth.

'Thank you, my friends,' said Simon. 'For four long millennia, I have been stranded upon this desolate, poisoned world; and today you appear, with a Quadrant, and with salve. My prayers are answered, and my heart leaps with joy. My body is whole again, and young, and I feel...' He paused, and stared at Amalia, then at Felice. He pointed at the Lostwell god. 'You. I wish to mate with you. It has been four thousand years since I touched a woman. Everything else can wait.'

'Uh, excuse me?' said Felice.

'Or, perhaps food?' Simon said. 'I haven't eaten in centuries, and I hunger for that, also.' He picked up the Quadrant from where it was lying by his feet, and a moment later, the group appeared in a different cavern, filled with decayed and broken furniture. Simon frowned, then vanished.

Kagan and the others glanced at each other.

'This is insane,' Kagan said. 'The Tenth Ascendant? I haven't even heard of the Tenth Ascendant.'

'He disappeared four thousand years ago,' said Felice. 'The story goes that he was about to activate a Quadrant, when he was attacked, and the device was knocked from his hand as he was swiping it. He vanished, but the Quadrant stayed behind. He hasn't been seen since; people thought he'd gone for good.'

Montieth eyed her. 'And now he wants to mate with you.'

Felice shrugged. 'If he comes back.'

'He'd better! Otherwise, we're stuck here with a million damn greenhides.'

Naxor rubbed his face. 'And now he knows every single thing about us. Including salve, and the location of the City. If he's gone to Implacatus, we're...'

Simon reappeared in a shimmer of air, along with a huge table filled with food and drink. The Ascendant was dressed in a complete set of shining steel armour, and had a massive sword strapped to his back.

He beamed. 'Let us feast.'

Simon had also transported two long benches into the room, and they and the table had crushed the original furniture under their weight. Simon sat, and the others did the same. Felice and Naxor sat on the same side as the Ascendant, while Amalia, Kagan and Montieth sat opposite.

For a few minutes, Simon ate, his attention focussed solely on the food in front of him. The others also ate, and Kagan drank several pints of water. Simon eventually pushed his plate back and sighed. He glanced at Felice, and smiled.

'You are a beautiful young goddess. Would you care to mate with me later? I hunger for you as I hungered for the food.'

'That proposition was slightly more romantic that the last one,' said Felice.

'Answer me, beautiful one.'

Felice smiled. 'Maybe.'

'Good enough, for now.' He glanced at Amalia. 'Don't be jealous. You too are a stunning young goddess, but I perceived your love for the mortal. And do not fear – we will find your child when I return to the City with you.'

'You're coming to the City?' said Montieth.

'Your world is hidden from the other Ascendants, most of whom are my enemies.' His face darkened. 'Especially that vile serpent known as Edmond. I will kill him one day for what he did to Theodora.' He glanced at Kagan. 'I feel your raw terror, mortal man, but you do not need to be scared of me. All of you sitting here are now under my protection. You rescued me, and I do not forget such things. I will crush your enemies in the City, and you shall all have palaces, and slaves, and harems; whatever you desire. And then, I shall grow my strength, before taking the fight back to Implacatus and the worthless Second Ascendant.'

'You would help us retake power in the City,' said Amalia, 'and then you would leave?'

Simon smiled, and leaned on the table. 'You are a tricky one, Amalia of Yocasta. I will have to watch you. You would feel better if you stopped hating yourself; accept that you are a monster and be done with it.' He turned to Montieth. 'You, on the other hand, already know that you are a monster, but you don't care; that is why you are happier than your mother.' He shifted to his left to face Naxor.

'Please don't start on me,' said the demigod. 'Everyone already knows what I'm like.'

'You're worse,' said Simon; 'effortlessly worse. I seem to have been rescued by a band of scoundrels. None of you are innocent, but, neither am I.' He stared at Felice. 'Come; I wish to bed you now.'

'What if I say no?'

He shrugged his enormous shoulders. 'Then I would ask you again tomorrow.'

Felice stood, her eyes on Simon. 'Alright.'

The air shimmered, and the pair of them vanished.

'Thank Malik for that,' said Montieth. 'I thought they were going to do it on the table.'

'I have no idea what's going on,' said Kagan.

'You're coping well,' said Naxor; 'most mortals would be cowering in the corner right now. What do you all make of him? And, remember, he'll read whatever we say and think out of our heads the moment he returns. His vision skills are on a different plane altogether from mine. Let me tell you what I think first. It's simple; we have no choice. He has every power imaginable, and could kill us all in a heartbeat. We have to follow him. We have to do whatever he says. If he wants to rule the City for a while, and then go to Implacatus, then great. He said he's going to save Maxwell and crush our enemies; that sounds pretty good to me.'

'What if he likes the City too much, grows fat and lazy, and doesn't leave?' said Montieth.

'That depends on how accommodating he is,' said Naxor. 'You want Dalrig, mother wants Tara, and I'd settle for Port Sanders, or Pella; I'm not fussy. If he rules from the Royal Palace in Ooste, then so be it. We either look upon this as a complete disaster, and despair, or we try to make the best of it.'

Amalia sighed. 'I was God-Queen again for two days; but I'd gladly give up all of that to have Maxwell back. You are correct in what you say, grandson. We have no choice but to accede to his wishes and demands, but if he sticks to his word, then it might turn out fine for us.'

'What about the people of the City?' said Kagan.

'If we can't stand up to him,' said Amalia, 'then the mortals of the City will have no chance. They will need to submit, and quickly.'

'About what he said,' Kagan went on. 'He's trying to make you doubt yourself. I know the real you, and you are not a monster.'

The air shimmered, and Simon appeared in the room, naked, with the Quadrant in his left hand.

He smiled. 'I thought I'd come back to let you know that I'll be in bed with Felice for at least a day, maybe longer. There should be enough food and drink for you all, but don't leave the room. I'll be too busy to keep control of the greenhides, and they'll be roaming free. Make yourselves comfortable; there's a bathroom at the back, although it hasn't been used in centuries.' He laughed. 'Gods, it's good to be back.'

He grinned, and vanished.

CHAPTER 24

A PLACE FOR ANGER

Dalrig, Auldan, The City – 18th Monan 3422

A thin column of grey smoke was rising from the valley. Down on the grass by the entrance to the cave, Rosie was feeding the flames with wood that had been cut and foraged by Darvi, while Flavus watched carefully, a sack of raw salve lying next to his feet. Over by the circle of tents, the two sergeants were also busy, cleaning and repairing their gear.

Jade smiled from her vantage point halfway up the cliffside. She was sitting on a narrow ledge of rock, facing sunward, the valley spread out below her. It was only their seventh day there, but she viewed it as a better home than anywhere else she had lived. The previous night, she had dreamt that the City had been destroyed, and that they were stranded in the valley forever. It had been a good dream. Rosie had asked her why she was smiling when she had awoken, but Jade hadn't told her. She knew that the others had family or, in the case of Flavus, colleagues, waiting for them back in the City that they would miss if everyone died in a fiery cataclysm. Jade understood their feelings, but didn't share them. Her cats would be the only thing that she would save from the City; they would love it in the valley, and she pictured them lazing on the grass in the sunshine, or scampering about the under-growth, hunting for birds and mice.

A dark speck in the sky caught her attention, and she watched as Halfclaw approached from sunward. The green dragon seemed to spend most of his time in the mountains with Deathfang and the others in the colony, only passing the valley to check up on the small group now and again.

Jade got to her feet, and brushed the dirt and fallen leaves from her dress. The track down to the valley bottom was steep, but she had made the journey several times, and reached the grass by the banks of the stream in a few minutes, as Halfclaw was beginning his descent. She strode along by the rushing water towards the pool. The others had stopped what they were doing to watch Halfclaw as he landed close to the tents. He pulled in his blue-streaked wings and lowered his great head. He gazed around, until he saw Jade.

'Demigod, greetings.'

'Good morning, Halfclaw,' she said.

'How's Firestone?' said Rosie, wandering over from the fire.

'He is well, little Jackdaw,' said the dragon, 'though I have been so busy that I have barely seen him over the last day.'

'You're busy, eh? What are you doing?'

'I have begun transporting carriages filled with workers and tools to the colony. A mere half an hour ago, I delivered the second batch – there are now twelve humans inside the caves, all working away with pickaxes and hammers. They are living in the cavern that Frostback and I used to share.'

Jade frowned. 'How has Dawnflame reacted to this?'

'She is keeping quiet. She has decided to ignore their presence, rather than allow herself to be provoked. Darksky was going to adopt the same approach, but I saw her speaking to some of the workers earlier today; she was telling them exactly how she would like her cavern to be extended, and where she wants a new tunnel to be dug out.'

'I'd like to see that,' said Rosie, 'and I'd like to meet the workers. Is that why you're here? Are you offering to take us to visit the workers?'

'Not quite, little Jackdaw,' said the dragon. 'I came here to speak to the demigod.'

'What about?' said Jade.

He turned back to face her. 'I have been collecting the workers from the Fortress of the Lifegiver – they are all Blades, from the artificer and engineering battalions. Quill is organising it. She spoke to me this morning.'

'Yes? What did she say?'

'Your father has escaped from prison.'

Jade's face fell. 'How?'

'The God-Queen, Amalia, was responsible. She released your father and another god from the dungeons, and the King and Queen have been hunting them down. Frostback and Kelsey have been helping.'

'Do you know where my father is?'

'No one knows. They were hiding in the palace in Dalrig, but Banner soldiers stormed it two days ago, and the fugitive gods vanished. I hear that your sister acted honourably.'

'Amber? I doubt that.'

'That's what Quill told me. Your sister was secretly helping the King and Queen, and was punished for it by your father, and poisoned with anti-salve. Her powers still haven't returned, or so I was told. The King and Queen have officially thanked her.'

Jade's temper bubbled over. 'They thanked her? They thanked that stupid, ugly bitch? I'm the one they should be thanking, not her. I've been loyal for years, while she's been nothing but a back-stabbing traitor. The King and Queen are weak; they should have executed her.'

The dragon tilted his head. 'Weak, you say? The King and Queen have already executed three demigods for their part in the rebellion. That doesn't sound weak to me.'

'They did what?' said Rosie. 'Which ones?'

'Let me try to remember,' said the dragon. 'Ikara, Collo, and, I think the other one was named Vana. Yes. Those three. They have lost their heads, by the orders of the Queen.'

Rosie puffed out her cheeks. 'Wow. I didn't think she was that ruthless.'

'But, they let Amber live?' said Jade. 'She was worse than those three. Far worse. What happened to the others?'

'They escaped,' said the dragon. 'Amalia has a Quadrant.'

'Is Amber in jail?'

'No, demigod. I told you; she has been thanked, not punished. She is still in Greylin Palace.'

'Take me there,' said Jade. 'I want to speak to her.'

'I thought you might. I am due to return to the Fortress of the Life-giver today, to collect the third consignment of workers. I shall deliver them to the colony, and return to the fortress tomorrow at dawn. If I take you to Dalrig, then I can bring you back, if you are waiting for me in the Bulwark at sunrise.'

'You're leaving us?' said Rosie.

'Just for a day,' said Jade. 'I'll be back tomorrow. Flavus, you're in charge.'

The Banner officer bowed. 'Yes, ma'am. Could I possibly give you a little list of items to bring back with you? They should be relatively easy to obtain.'

Jade nodded. 'Alright, but be quick about it.'

Flavus smiled, then ran off to his tent.

Rosie frowned. 'Is this a good idea?'

'I want to see if it's true,' said Jade. 'I need to know if my sister is genuine, or if she's tricked the King and Queen. I can't believe it. My sister has always been loyal to my father. People like that don't change.'

'She might have changed,' said Rosie, 'or, maybe she just became sick of what your father was doing?'

'You don't know her. She used to laugh when father was beating me; do you understand? She used to stand there, and laugh at me.' Her eyes welled up, but she refused to succumb to tears, her anger flaring. 'If she has changed, which I don't believe, then I want to hear her say it. And I want an apology. A big apology. On her knees, preferably.'

Rosie nodded. 'Do you want me to come along?'

'No. You dilute my anger, and I'll need it.'

'You don't need it. No matter what has occurred in the past, she is still your sister. Do you think you can forgive her?'

Jade snorted. 'No.'

'Then, you shouldn't go.'

Jade walked away. 'Stay out of it, Rosie.'

Flavus emerged from his tent, and handed Jade a scrap of paper torn from his notebook.

'The alcohol is the single most important thing on the list, ma'am,' he said. 'If you can only get one thing, then please make it that. Without it, we cannot refine any more salve. The other items are luxuries in comparison.'

Jade scanned the list. 'I'll see what I can do.'

'Thank you, ma'am; it would be much appreciated. When will you return?'

Jade glanced at the dragon.

'If the demigod is at the Fortress of the Lifegiver at dawn tomorrow, then she will be back here for noon.'

'I'll be there,' said Jade.

'Then, climb up,' said Halfclaw, 'and we will leave now.'

Jade glanced at the others. The two sergeants were standing together in silence, while Flavus's attention was already drifting back to the sack of salve by the fire. Rosie was also silent, but her eyes revealed exactly how she felt about Jade's imminent departure. Jade looked away, unable to meet her gaze. Not everything was sunshine and flowers, that was what the Jackdaw girl didn't understand. Not everything could be cured by being nice all the time. Some people were rotten, and that was that.

Jade climbed up onto the harness. 'Take me to the City, dragon.'

Jade tried to rest during the four hour journey across the greenhide-infested plain between the mountains and the City, but her mind wouldn't let her. Twisted memories and thoughts trampled over each other, as she replayed countless encounters with her sister. They had lived in the same building for nine centuries, and there was no shortage of events that inspired feelings of bitterness and rage within her. That time Amber had destroyed her rose garden; or when she had held Jade down while their father had forced a new blend of concentrated salve into her mouth to test its effects; or when she had mocked Jade's stupidity in front of a roomful of merchants from Dalrig – round and round they went, an unending succession of humiliations and degradations.

And that bitch was being thanked?

She barely noticed when the dragon crossed the Great Walls of the City. He soared over the Bulwark, and then over Medio, drifting to iceward as they passed the Union Walls. He approached Dalrig from the direction of Pella, and Jade saw the town walls of her old home. They were bristling with ballistae, but none of them were pointed upwards. Her heart sank further as she saw the high, dark bulk of Greylin, squatting by the harbour. More ballistae batteries were positioned on the roof of the palace, and Jade noticed that the soldiers standing by them were wearing the uniform of the Banner of the Lostwell Exiles.

Halfclaw circled, then descended onto the roof.

'Remember,' said the dragon. 'Dawn tomorrow at the Fortress of the Lifegiver. Quill knows where I land to collect the workers.'

'Alright,' she said, unbuckling the harness straps.

'Unless you wish me to take you back now, demigod? Little Jackdaw seemed to consider this a poor idea.'

'Never mind what she thinks; this is something I have to do.'

'Very well.'

Jade climbed down the side of the dragon, then stood back as he extended his wings and soared away into the sky.

A Banner officer approached. 'Lady Jade? We weren't expecting you.'

'Where is my sister?'

'I'm unsure of her exact location within the palace at present, ma'am. Shall I send someone to find her, and to let her know that you have arrived?'

'No. I'll find her myself.'

She tried to walk round him, but he moved to block her way.

'I have to ask, ma'am,' he said; 'are your intentions hostile?'

'That's none of your business.'

'I'm afraid it is, ma'am. The Banner are under orders to protect this palace, and Lady Amber. I cannot allow you to proceed if you intend to carry out any aggressive act towards your sister.'

'Yes? And how would you stop me?'

'The same way we stopped Lady Ikara, ma'am.' He gestured towards the ballistae, and Jade noticed that all four of the machines were pointing at her. 'If you were to assure me that you will behave peaceably, then I can allow you to enter the palace. Otherwise, ma'am, we'll have to escort you off the premises.'

Jade glanced at the ballistae. 'Fine. All I want to do is talk. Happy now?'

'Yes, ma'am.' He signalled to the crews, and they turned the weapons away.

Jade brushed past the officer, and strode towards the stairs, angrier than ever. Greylin Palace had been her home, and she had already been humiliated by Banner soldiers. Who did they think they were? She was a demigod, a mighty being, an immortal; and yet that officer had spoken to her as if she were nothing. She hurried down the steps, then paused at the bottom of the stairwell, her nostrils catching the unmistakeable odour of Greylin. She hesitated, feeling nauseous; a hundred bad memories fighting for attention in her mind.

She set off again, passing rooms that had been familiar to her since childhood. She made her way to her sister's private quarters, an area of the palace she had been too scared to enter while she had lived there.

The décor and furnishings were much nicer, she noticed, as she walked into Amber's apartment. She strode through the living area, and walked into Amber's study without knocking.

Her sister glanced up from her desk. 'You?' She narrowed her eyes. 'What do you want?'

Jade stared at her. 'An apology.'

Amber laughed. 'Then you've come a long way for nothing, because I have absolutely nothing to apologise to you for.'

Jade took a step forward, her fists clenched. 'Yes, you do. You treated me like shit my entire life.'

'My, your memories are a little one-sided, because all I remember is you being a spoilt brat, always causing trouble, and making my life a misery. I should be asking for an apology from you, but I won't waste my breath on that. Scurry back to wherever you've been lurking, and let the grown ups get on with the real work.'

'I hate you.'

'Oh, boo hoo, Jade. You should try growing up a bit; it's like you've been stuck as a miserable teenager your whole life. Yes, like an angry fourteen-year-old girl with a chip on her shoulder, who blames everyone else for her problems. You're even still wearing the same stupid dress you always wore; you haven't changed a bit.'

'Neither have you. You were disloyal then, and you're disloyal now.'

'Disloyal to whom? The only person in this room who has broken their promises is you. You're a disgrace. You abandoned us when you ran off with that idiot Aila, or have you forgotten? And then, what did you do? Oh yes, I remember – you slaughtered hundreds of Evader mortals. Aila was so disgusted with you that she ran away. She preferred to marry Marcus than remain in your company. I don't blame her; I think I'd have done the same. How does it feel to be a mass murderer?'

'I... I turned out that way because of you and father.'

Amber sighed and shook her head. 'Is that what you tell yourself? That the innocent people you murdered were really killed by me and father? How pathetic you sound, Jade.'

'But you have disowned father too.'

'Yes, I have. He went too far. He deserved to be in prison for killing Yendra, and now, he deserves to be executed for poisoning the water supply of Outer Pella. It's a sad fact, but father has lost his mind. Part of the reason, I suspect, is because of your betrayal of him. It broke his heart when you ran away. Perhaps if you'd stayed, then he wouldn't have done those things. Yes, the more I think about it, the more I see that this is your fault, Jade. All of it. You should have killed yourself years ago, and done us all a favour.' She smiled. 'There's still time.'

Jade started to cry.

'Oh, stop snivelling,' said Amber. 'I had to put up with your endless tears when you lived here. "Father, Amber is being mean to me again."'

'Stop it.'

'Or what?'

Jade pointed at Amber's face. 'Are those bruises?'

Amber fell silent.

'You were poisoned with anti-salve, weren't you? And look, you're powers haven't returned. What a shame.'

'Get out of my rooms, Jade, before I call for the Banner.'

'I could kill you, right now. I could flail your skin off, piece by piece, and make you suffer, just as you and father made me suffer.'

Amber edged back, her eyes wide.

'Are you scared, sister? For the first time in our lives, I have the upper hand. Apologise.'

'No. If you're going to kill me, then do it. Father almost killed me two days ago, because I was giving information to Salvor. If I didn't back down to him, I'm certainly not going to back down to you.'

'Apologise, Amber. Say you're sorry, and I'll let you live.'

Amber closed her eyes. 'No.'

Jade focussed her powers, feeling them tingle at the end of her outstretched fingertips. She pictured Amber's head melting, her screams, the blood. With a single burst of power, her sister's life would be over. She frowned. Why was she hesitating? She hated her sister so much it hurt.

Amber remained still, even serene. 'Father will be very proud of you if you kill me,' she said. 'Is that what you want? Do you want to be like him?'

Jade stared at her hand, curled it into a fist, and punched Amber in the face.

'Ow!' Amber cried, opening her eyes and raising a hand to her bloody nose. 'You little bitch!'

'I hope it hurts, Amber. Goodbye.'

She turned, and strode from the study. Several Banner soldiers were standing outside the room, their crossbows in their hands.

'Were you out here listening?' she cried.

'We were ensuring that events didn't get of hand, ma'am,' said the officer.

'Get out of my way, you stupid mortals!'

She pushed past them and fled Amber's private apartment, then ran all the way down the stairs to the ground floor. She looked around, but there were no servants, only more Banner soldiers. She blinked. What was she going to do? She had no money, and no carriage. She cursed her lack of preparation, then she cursed Amber and the stupid Banner soldiers. She hurried to the front doors of the palace, flung them open, and ran down the street.

———

'You walked here from Dalrig?' said the Queen, as they strolled through the gardens of Cuidrach Palace. Behind them, the Queen-Mother was pushing a double pram, and they were surrounded by soldiers from the Royal Guard.

'Yes, your Majesty,' said Jade.

'How long did it take?'

'I don't know; a couple of hours? Why have you forgiven my sister? It's not fair. Her soul is rotten, while I've been trying my best to be good.'

'I know you have, Jade, and I'm very pleased with your work.'

'Are you? It doesn't feel like it. You killed Ikara, Vana and Collo, yes?'

The Queen glanced down at the gravel path. 'Yes.'

'Their crimes were less than my sister's. Collo was probably too numbed by opium to even know what he was doing, and Vana was just following Naxor, as she always does. Always did, I mean. Yet, they lost their heads while Amber gets to lord it in Greylin? It's not fair.'

'Your sister's information saved the lives of hundreds of Reapers, Jade. Was I to ignore that?'

'Yes. Amber is not a kind person.'

'I don't execute people for being unkind, Jade. The demigods were executed because they joined a rebellion.'

'Amber will stab you in the back when you least expect it, your Majesty. I know her better than you.'

'I'm sure you do. However, again, I don't execute people for things that they might do in the future.'

'She's done plenty of bad things in the past.'

'Her recent conduct has allowed the Crown to forgive her previous lapses of judgement.'

'You're an idiot.'

The Queen took a slow breath. 'Ah, here we are; your little cottage. You'll find that your cats have been well looked after. Now, if you'll excuse me, I have important matters to attend to.'

The Queen gestured to her mother and the soldiers, and they began walking back towards Cuidrach Palace. Jade glared at the Queen's back, then turned and walked up the path to the front door of the cottage where she had lived after leaving the Bulwark. She tried to clear her thoughts, so that her anger with her sister wouldn't ruin the experience of seeing her cats again. She pushed the door open, and walked into the front room. Inside, a young woman in militia uniform was sitting on Jade's old couch, with Poppy on her knee.

The woman glanced up, her eyes widening.

The demigod looked down at her. 'I'm Jade.'

'Hello,' said the woman. 'Are you back for good? No one told me you were coming.'

'Just visiting. How are my cats?'

'Great. I mean, this is the best job I've ever had. All I have to do is live here, and look after your pets. Before this, I was on guard duty on the Gloamer frontier. My name is...'

'I don't care. Get out, so that I can have some peace with my babies.'

'Oh. Alright.'

The woman lifted Poppy from her knee, and placed her onto the couch. She stood.

'I'll wait outside, I guess.'

'Go for a long walk. I'll close the shutters when I leave; that way you'll know.'

'Yes, ma'am.'

Jade waited until the woman had left the cottage, then she sat on the couch, and picked up Poppy.

'I missed you,' she said, kissing the cat's head and rubbing her nose into her soft black fur. She heard a meow from the floor, and saw Ginger and Fluffy sitting by her feet, while Tab-Tab came wandering in from the bedroom. 'All my babies together,' she said. 'Come to momma.'

The cottage was dark when she awoke. She had fallen asleep on the couch with three cats sitting on her, lulled by their warm bodies and soft purring. She sat up and scratched her head, then removed Tab-Tab from her lap. She got to her feet and looked out of the window. The sky was purple, though there was a faint light to sunward. She said her goodbyes to the cats, kissing each of them, then walked out the front door, where she nearly tripped over the young militia soldier.

'What are you doing out here?' Jade said.

The young woman was shivering from the cold. 'Waiting for you to leave, ma'am.'

'You've been sitting here all afternoon?'

The woman frowned. 'It's nearly dawn, ma'am.'

Jade's mouth fell open, then she took off down the path, sprinting for the palace. She ran through the empty gardens, then turned at a corner, and entered a large courtyard, where a few guards were standing.

'I need a carriage!' she yelled.

The officer on duty narrowed his eyes. 'Lady Jade; is that you?'

'Yes. Listen; I need a carriage to take me to the Fortress of the Lifegiver, or I'll miss my dragon.'

The officer pointed at a soldier. 'See to it at once, Sergeant.'

'Yes, sir.'

'I was informed that you were here, my lady,' said the officer, 'but we thought you'd departed hours ago.'

'I fell asleep. Damn it.'

'Not to worry, my lady. The sergeant won't be long. I have to advise you, however, that the carriage will be going via Sander territory, as the main routes through the Circuit are currently too dangerous. Several wagons and carriages have been attacked in the last few days. It will add an hour or so onto your journey.'

Jade groaned.

The sergeant emerged from the shadows at the far side of the courtyard, leading a set of ponies. They were hitched to the front of a carriage, and a couple of guards and a driver were rustled up from the palace. Jade stared at them, willing them to work faster, but the sun was starting to rise before the carriage was ready to leave. Jade piled into the back, and they set off, just as the first rays of dawn appeared over the horizon.

'Halfclaw waited for you, ma'am,' said Quill, 'but he had to leave. He has a schedule to keep.'

Jade frowned as she stared over the battlements on the roof of the Duke's Tower. It was mid-morning, and the plains in front of the Great Walls were filled with roaming greenhides.

'He'll be back tomorrow,' Quill went on; 'probably around noon; if you want to stay here?'

'Where else am I going to stay?' said Jade.

'I, uh, live in your old rooms now,' said Quill, 'but you can sleep in the spare room under my quarters tonight.' She smiled. 'It will be like the old days.'

'Don't depress me further, Quinn. I hated the old days.'

'Halfclaw's been telling me about your little valley in the mountains. It sounds idyllic.'

'I wish I could live there forever. I shouldn't have said that out loud.' She bowed her head. 'I hate it here; the City, everything. Rosie was right; I shouldn't have come back.'

'How is the young Jackdaw girl? I used to know Maddie quite well.'

'She's... better.'

'Better than what?'

'Better than me. I don't deserve her.'

Quill raised an eyebrow. 'I'm not sure I understand, ma'am.'

'That's funny, Quinn, because neither do I.'

CHAPTER 25

ON PATROL

Jezra, The Western Bank – 19th Monan 3422

Kelsey awoke in the bathtub. The hot water had cooled, and her back was sore, not only from lying in the same position for so long, but from the countless hours she had spent flying on Frostback over the previous few days. She wondered what had woken her up, then heard a banging on the front door of her little red brick house.

She got up and stepped out of the bath, dripping cold water all over the stone floor, and reached for a towel that she had draped over the hot water pipe. She wrapped it round herself, and went through to her main room.

'Hold on,' she said, as she approached the door.

She opened it a crack, peered out and saw Sergeant Nagel and Vadhi from the dragon crew.

'Hi, guys. What do you want?'

'We're supposed to be having a meeting this morning, ma'am,' said Nagel.

Kelsey frowned. 'Are we? What day is today?'

'The nineteenth, ma'am.'

'Is it? Bollocks.' She opened the door wider. 'You can come in while

I get dressed.' She stood to the side to allow them to squeeze past. 'Take a seat. There's nothing to eat or drink; sorry.'

'We actually went to the Command Post first to look for you, ma'am,' said Vadhi, as she and the sergeant sat. 'We didn't think you'd be here.'

Kelsey nodded, then walked into her tiny bedroom. She pushed the door, but left it slightly ajar, so that she could continue the conversation.

'Where are the rest of the crew?' she said, as she dried herself.

'Up on the palace foundations, ma'am,' said Nagel. 'Frostback is there too.'

Kelsey pulled on her underwear and sat on the bed, yawning. 'How late am I?'

'Just an hour, ma'am.'

Kelsey shook her head, feeling exhaustion seep its way into her. 'I think I'm supposed to return to Pella today. Or is it tomorrow? Sergeant, what am I doing today?'

'Well, ma'am, in the morning, you are patrolling over the City, and then, in the afternoon, you're back in Jezra to defend the Brigades while some urgent repairs are carried out to a stretch of palisade wall.'

'And Pella?'

'That's tomorrow, ma'am; you have a briefing with Salvor an hour after dawn.'

'I may as well stay in Cuidrach tonight,' she said, as she finished dressing. 'That way, there's less chance of me sleeping in again.'

'I'll get the little carriage organised, ma'am,' said Nagel, 'and we'll all stay over.'

'Great,' said Vadhi; 'I like Pella.'

'You're not supposed to say things like that when we're in the middle of a major crisis, Vadhi,' said Kelsey.

'Sorry, ma'am.'

'Pyre's arse; I'm starting to sound like my mother.'

'No comment, ma'am.'

Kelsey opened the door. 'You've never met my mother. She'd knock this City into shape.'

Vadhi glanced at her. 'Is your mother as ruthless as Queen Emily?'

'My mother would have massacred every immortal on her first day in power.' She sat down on the couch and pulled on her boots. 'If you ever do happen to meet her, don't tell her I said that. So, you think Emily is ruthless, eh? Is that what you wee scamps are gossiping about?'

'Most folk are talking about it, ma'am. Three demigods in one day. Was it revenge for Yendra?'

'It wasn't revenge; it was punishment for rebelling.'

'Some folk are saying that the Queen plans to kill the rest of them, you know, when she catches them.'

'If by "the rest of them" you mean Amalia, Montieth, Naxor and Felice, then aye. Well, that's my guess, anyway. But, the facts are that they've been gone now for three days. I'm starting to wonder if they are coming back.'

'I worry that they have gone to Implacatus, ma'am,' said Nagel. 'Right now, the Ascendants could be mustering their Banners to invade. The first we'll know of it is when they open a giant portal and send thousands of soldiers through.'

'What a cheery thought,' said Kelsey, standing. 'Come on; let's go.'

'Your hair's still wet, ma'am,' said Vadhi, 'and it's freezing outside.'

Kelsey pulled her hair back and tied a black ribbon to keep it in place. 'The cold air might wake me up. Back on my homeworld, I would have had three cups of coffee and four cigarettes by this time of the morning. That's what Amalia should have done with her Quadrant. Never mind trying to take over, she should have used it to fetch some coffee plants.'

She pulled her heavy winter coat over her shoulders and opened the front door. A bitterly cold wind was gusting through the narrow streets of Jezra, and they kept their heads down as they hurried towards the foundations of the ancient palace. They climbed the steps, and saw the rest of the dragon crew standing around, sheltering from the wind next to Frostback.

'You are late,' said the silver dragon, as she lowered her head towards Kelsey. 'And you look tired.'

'I am tired,' she said. 'I fell asleep in the bath. I think we should cancel the meeting and leave now. Are you ready?'

'I have eaten and am refreshed. However, the colonel was here. Have you spoken to him yet?'

Kelsey frowned. 'No.'

'When was he here, Frostback?' said Nagel.

'While you were waking my rider,' said the dragon. 'He told us that the major-general wants to speak to you in the Command Post, which was strange, as we all thought you were sleeping there.'

'I was in my own house last night.'

'That explains it, rider. Perhaps in the future, you should tell us where you are intending to sleep. That way, I won't have to stand out here in the cold wind waiting for you for hours.'

'Sorry,' Kelsey muttered. She glanced at the shivering members of the dragon crew. 'I'll have to go back to the Command Post.'

They groaned.

'Go to the common room for a bit,' she said, 'and warm up by the fire; I'll be as quick as I can.'

She hurried back down the steps, not waiting for the crew's response, and set off for the Command Post. With an entire regiment of Banner soldiers stationed in Pella, the streets of Jezra were quieter than usual, but the market was busy, with Brigade workers out buying supplies to supplement their daily rations. She reached the harbour front. The wind was coming off the sea, sending cold spray across the quayside, where dozens of boats were tied up.

The Command Post was well-insulated against the weather, and she stopped shivering as she passed through its entrance, the soldiers on duty saluting her. She made her way upstairs to Van's quarters, and knocked on the door of his office.

'Enter,' came a voice from within.

She opened the door and walked in.

Van glanced up from his desk. 'It's unlike you to knock; you usually just barge in.'

She sat. 'Excuse me for being polite.'

'Where were you last night?'

'Why?'

'You're supposed to be on call, at any time of the day or night, in case the rogue gods are spotted.'

'Have they been spotted?'

'No.'

She shrugged. 'Then, what's the problem?'

He frowned. 'You need to tell us where you are. I can't have soldiers running about Jezra looking for you. What if there's an emergency?'

'Are you just annoyed that I wasn't in bed with you last night?'

'This has nothing to do with my personal feelings, Kelsey. Right now, I'm speaking as your commanding officer, not as your... whatever we are.'

'Does it matter? You're perfectly capable of being a numpty either way.'

'This is serious. What if Amalia had appeared in Pella this morning, and we had no idea where you were?'

'Pyre's arse, Van; I was in my house. You're making it sound as if I had run away and hidden among the ruins, or wandered off into the forest. I wanted a night of peace; I wanted to be on my own.'

'That's fine, Kelsey, but next time – tell me.'

Kelsey yawned. 'So, what did you want to see me about?'

'We've just discussed it.'

'Really? You dragged me all the way over here just to tell me off? That was a fine use of everyone's time. You know, I can tell when you've taken salve. It makes you more annoying than usual. Where's Lucius?'

Van glared at her for a moment, then glanced down at the documents on his desk. 'In Pella.'

'Why? He's your personal aide. Shouldn't he be here, by your side?'

'I need an officer to stay in Cuidrach Palace.'

'Aye; but why him? You have other officers.'

'It's none of your business.'

'Is it because he disapproves of you taking salve?'

Van kept his eyes on the documents. 'You are dismissed, Kelsey. Go back to work.'

She got to her feet. 'You're being a right bawbag, you know that? Oh, and I'll be in Pella tonight, so you won't need to send out scouts to search for me. I'll pass on your regards to Lucius.'

She strode from the room, anger rippling through her. The soldiers on duty moved aside for her, then a door further down the corridor opened and Mona appeared.

The white-robed demigod raised a hand. 'Kelsey; do you have a minute?'

'Not really.'

'I know that you're very interested in the finds we've discovered in the ancient library, and I was wondering if you would like…'

'Not now, Mona.'

The Chancellor gave a weak smile. 'Is everything alright?'

'No. Van's being an arsehole. And, how come you've got time to be reading dusty old scrolls? I thought you were meant to be looking for your delightful old grandmother?'

'I don't use my vision powers every moment of the day. I need to rest sometimes, and when I do, I like to keep up with my work; my real work.' She paused. 'Is there anything I can do to help?'

'About Van? No.'

Mona looked relieved.

'I'll tell you what,' said Kelsey; 'next free day I get, we can sit down and you can show me what you've learned from the scrolls and stuff, and we can avoid all talk about Van.'

'That would be wonderful. None of the Banner or Brigade Exiles seem particularly fascinated by the history of the City; whereas you make a very attentive student.'

Kelsey turned for the stairs. 'That's not what my university lecturers in Plateau City used to say, but thanks, I guess. See you later, Mona.'

Half an hour afterwards, Frostback rose up from the brick houses and streets of Jezra, with Kelsey strapped to the harness. The silver dragon ascended to the height of the cliff tops, then soared towards the east, crossing the Straits in minutes. They reached the Taran headland, then flew along the range of hills, passing Maeladh Palace, where a small Banner garrison had been stationed. The Roser militia and leadership had objected, but hadn't yet used force to try to eject them, partly due to the fact that Frostback patrolled the area daily. They circled over the town of Tara for a few minutes, and Kelsey watched the small fishing vessels in the harbour, and the Rosers strolling through the markets near the water front. Several faces turned upwards to glance at the sight of the dragon, and Kelsey wondered if their presence inspired fear, contempt or respect. Their patrol of Tara complete, Frostback headed east again, and they crossed the fertile fields and farms of Roser territory. Once they had passed the Union Walls, they repeated the patrol over Port Sanders, reminding the locals of the reach of the Crown. Kelsey looked out for the mansion where Amalia had lived, and saw a squad of Banner soldiers on the roof. An officer waved up to them as they circled overhead, but didn't raise the red flag they had been given in case they needed to request the dragon to land.

'That's the nice bits done,' said Kelsey. 'The Circuit's next.'

'Ah,' said Frostback, 'so you do remember how to speak, rider. You have been quieter than usual this morning.'

'Hmm.'

'I'm going to guess that your silence has something to do with your meeting with Van.'

'He's a numpty.'

'Maybe. However, he is the same man that you were seemingly devoted to just a short time ago. What has happened? I know that he is the one who has been pursuing you over the last two years; has his ardour cooled? Is he no longer worshipping the air you breathe?'

Kelsey frowned. She hadn't told the dragon about Van taking salve, but maybe she had a point. Prior to Van's new addiction, he had been relentless in his love for her, but his passion had cooled considerably since rediscovering the joys of salve. It struck her that, given the choice between her and salve, he had chosen salve; and he would rather lose her than stop taking the narcotic. Her shoulders slumped, and she felt the knot of tension in her guts flare.

'Van and I are finished,' she said, realising the words were true as soon as she had spoken them.

'Have you severed your relationship with him?'

'Not yet, well, not to his face. I will, the next time I see him.'

'Are you sad?'

'Angry. I might cry later, when it's sunk in, but all I feel right now is anger. He chased me for years, and when I finally decided to give it a try, he... changed. I don't actually think he'll care if I break it off. He might even be relieved.'

'Remember, my rider – my loyalty to you outweighs any other ties. If you wish, I will incinerate him, for you.'

'We might get into a bit of trouble for that.'

'Love does not ponder the consequences – love acts.'

'Thanks, Frostback. Even though I don't want him dead, I appreciate the offer.'

They crossed the fields of Sander territory, heading iceward, and began to fly over the vast, grey, concrete labyrinth of the Circuit. Kelsey counted four columns of smoke rising from the slums. The other tribes were containing the Circuit with a ring of walls and militia, allowing no Evaders to leave the territory, in case, like an infection, the rioting spread. Kelsey had tried to make sense of the various factions engaged in a fight to the death within the narrow, winding alleyways of the Circuit, but it had been a fruitless task, as the revolutionary and anarchist groups seemed to splinter, merge and re-splinter with bewildering frequency. A street battle was underway to the west of the Great Racecourse, and several bodies were floating in the polluted canals that ran close by. Up on the roof of the enormous Racecourse, a band of Evaders loosed their crossbows at Frostback. None of the bolts came near the underside of the dragon, and Frostback didn't react. Getting shot at from the Circuit had become a regular event, but the rebels had no ballistae, and the dragon was under strict instructions not to retaliate.

The dragon banked towards the east when the hills of the Iceward Range loomed near, and they soared over the Middle Walls, entering the Bulwark. Blade children were playing among the overgrown and derelict housing sectors that lay sandwiched between the inhabited areas. Frostback turned sunward, and they went over the Scythe Wall. A single camp containing Exiles still existed, huddled against the walls close to Arrowhead Fort. It had a high fence surrounding it, and looked more like a prison camp. Held within were all those deemed unsuitable for any kind of civic work –murderers, criminals and thieves, and the remnants of the Banner soldiers who had refused to sign up with Van's new regiments. During the previous summer, they had been conscripted to work in the fields of Scythe territory, and had required an armed presence of Blades to ensure that they didn't escape.

Frostback banked again and flew east towards the Fortress of the Lifegiver – the final stop of their patrol. Kelsey scanned the battlements, then searched the sky.

'No sign of Halfclaw today,' she said.

'We always seem to miss him,' said the dragon. 'However, I see Quill on the roof of the Duke's Tower, along with a demigod.'

Kelsey groaned as she recognised the figure of a woman in a dark green dress. 'Jade. That's all we need. Let's make this visit a quick one.'

Frostback circled over the fortress, giving Kelsey an excellent view of the thousands of greenhides out on the plains beyond the Great Walls, then she alighted onto the wide roof of the Duke's Tower.

'Greetings,' said Quill, smiling up at them.

'Adjutant,' said Frostback. 'Have we missed Halfclaw?'

'He was here at dawn,' said Quill. 'He was meant to take Lady Jade back with him, but she was late.'

'I slept in,' said the demigod.

'Aye? Me too,' said Kelsey, as she unbuckled the straps keeping her to the harness. She slipped down to the flat roof and stretched her arms and legs.

'When I saw the dragon,' said Jade, 'I had hoped it was Halfclaw.'

'Aye? Well, sorry to disappoint you, Jade.'

'Can Frostback take me to the Eastern Mountains?'

'No. We're needed back in Jezra this afternoon to help repair part of the town's defences.'

Jade nodded.

Kelsey waited, expecting her to make some sort of arrogant, demigod comment, but instead, Jade turned and stared out over the plains.

'How's the City today?' said Quill.

Kelsey shrugged. 'Same as always. The Circuit's up in flames again. No sign of the wicked god-grandmother. Hopefully, she, and the rest of them, are lying dead in a ditch somewhere.'

She glanced at Jade, remembering that the demigod's father was among the fugitives, but she didn't respond. Somehow, Kelsey was almost disappointed.

'Of course,' Kelsey went on; 'I'd rather they did return, so we can string the bastards up.'

Jade turned. 'Do you agree with the executions of Vana and the others? If you do, then why did you stop Van Logos from killing my father?'

Kelsey blinked. 'Em, I don't know. Should I have let him do it?'

'Yes. My father is evil, and you allowed him to live.'

'Oh. I thought...'

'You thought I was sympathetic to him because he's my father? He was my jailor for nine hundred years, Holdfast witch. As far as he is concerned, I no longer exist. You look at me and make your assumptions, but you're wrong.'

'Alright; steady on. No need to get angry.'

'I have every right to be angry. My father hates me, and my sister is being rewarded, when she should have suffered the same fate as Vana and the others. You know nothing about me; you're mean and spiteful, just like everyone else.'

Frostback lowered her head to face the demigod. 'Do not insult my rider, demigod.'

'It's alright, Frostback,' said Kelsey; 'I can handle Jade.'

'I don't need to be handled,' said Jade, her voice rising, and her fists clenched.

'No?' said Kelsey. 'Tell me; what do you need?'

Jade stared at Kelsey. 'To be left alone. I'm sick of this City, and I'm sick of everyone in it, including you. I am treated like a child, but I hear all the nasty little comments that people make about me. I know that you all hate me, and I don't care any more. I'm tired of being bullied and hurt.'

The demigod turned, and ran across the roof. She reached the stairs and disappeared from sight.

Kelsey glanced at Quill. 'Woah. She's changed.'

'I know,' said Quill. 'Something's happening to her, something to do with living out in the mountains. I'm actually a little concerned about her, and I didn't think I'd ever say that. She seems so fragile.'

'Tell her that I'm sorry,' said Kelsey. 'I'm having a rough day myself, and I should have been friendlier.'

'I will.'

'Thanks.' Kelsey shook her head. 'I didn't think demigods were capable of changing.'

'I doubt many are,' said Quill; 'but, then again, I doubt many spend the first nine centuries of their lives trapped in a palace with no windows, while being tormented by their father and sister.'

'Good point. Right, we'd better be off.'

'Halfclaw's due here about noon tomorrow, if you want to see him.'

'Thank you,' said Frostback.

Quill stood back and watched as Kelsey climbed back up onto the dragon's shoulders.

'See you tomorrow,' Kelsey said, then the dragon lifted into the air, swept round in a wide arc, then sped off to the west, for Jezra.

It was dark by the time Kelsey and Frostback finished assisting the Brigade Exiles in their work repairing the palisade walls. The green-hides had been persistent in their attacks, and the dragon had needed to clear a whole stretch of forest in order for the workers to safely set the new posts in place. Rumours about the young greenhide queens had made the workers jumpier than usual, and there were several false alarms before the stretch of wall was finished. Once everyone was back behind the defences, Frostback soared down the face of the cliffs and landed onto the foundations of the ancient palace, where her crew was waiting.

Kelsey dropped to the ground, and took an offered waterskin.

'Get packed up and ready to leave for Pella,' Kelsey said. 'I have something I need to do first.'

'We've already loaded the carriage, ma'am,' said Nagel.

'Aye? Well, eh, just hang around until I get back.'

Kelsey hurried down the steps before any of the crew could ask her where she was going. She pulled her winter coat round her, feeling the chill wind gusting through the streets. She tried not to think about what she was doing; her decision had been made, and she didn't want weakness to make her falter. She walked towards the harbour, passing the little street where the town's bars were located, and entered the tall Command Post. Soldiers saluted her as she ascended the stairs to the major-general's quarters. She walked into Van's rooms, and saw him sitting on a couch, his eyes closed.

'Are you sleeping?' she said.

His eyes opened. 'No.'

She peered at him, wondering if he had just been taking salve.

'I wasn't expecting you back here today,' he said. 'I thought you were travelling to Pella.'

'I am; as soon as I've spoken to you.'

'I'm glad you're back. I wanted to say sorry for being in a foul mood this morning. I hate having to be your commanding officer.'

'Apology accepted.'

'Good. I was worried that it would come between us.'

'One little argument hasn't got between us – something else has, Van, and that's why I'm here.'

He frowned. 'Take a seat.'

'No; I'll stand for this. Van, our relationship is going nowhere, and you know the reason why. I had plans to demand you choose between me and salve, but I already know what you'd say, and I don't particularly feel like being humiliated.'

Van's mouth fell open. 'What do you mean?'

'I think you know, Van. It's over. I can't trust you any more, not when you're prepared to lie to me about something like this. I'm glad that I was here for you when you were ill, and I'm glad we gave it a try, but it'll never work if you love salve more than you love me.'

'But...'

'No, Van; this time you listen. I care about you, and so does Lucius. But, I am not prepared to sit and watch you kill yourself.'

'I see.'

'Is that it?'

'It appears so.'

Kelsey glared at him. She had gone over the scene many times on the journey back from the Fortress of the Lifegiver, and had imagined him begging and pleading for her to stay. If he had done so, then her resolution might have cracked, and in a way she was relieved that he had made it easy for her.

'Goodbye, Van.'

He glanced away. 'Goodbye, Kelsey.'

She turned and strode from the room, her thoughts spinning and her emotions numb. She was halfway down the stairs before the tears came, and she quickened her pace, not wanting any of the Banner soldiers to see her. It was too late. A couple of sergeants glanced at her, their eyes narrowing as they saw the tears rolling down her cheeks. No doubt the entire town would soon know what had happened, and she and Van would once again be everyone's favourite topic of gossip.

She brushed past the sergeants and walked back out into the dark, cold street. She would be in Pella within half an hour, and she realised that her ordeal wasn't over. She would have to tell Frostback, Lucius, and probably the Queen.

And then, she would get drunk.

CHAPTER 26

UNDERHANDED

P ella, Auldan, The City – 19th Monan 3422

Emily glanced at the window clock, and smothered a sigh of relief. The Tribal Council session was due to end at sunset, and there wasn't long to go. A delegate from the Hammers was on her feet, speaking about the need to train more apprentices in iron-working – a worthy topic in peacetime, but with Amalia and Montieth on the loose, Emily's patience was at its limits. Next to her, Daniel was giving every appearance of paying attention to the delegate's words, and she wondered if he was pretending.

The Hammer sat back down, and a council clerk got to his feet.

'The Tribal Council thanks the delegate for her words,' he said. 'We now come to the last part of the session – does anyone have other business to raise?'

Emily scanned the benches where the delegates were sitting. Out of the nine tribes, three were absent. The Rosers hadn't attended since withdrawing from the governance of the City, while the Gloamers had rarely been seen in the previous two years. The other missing delegates were from the Circuit. So divided were the Evaders, that they had been unable to send anyone who commanded the respect of a majority of their tribe. Without the three most troublesome tribes, the council meetings had become dull and uneventful.

The clerk waited a few moments, but no one raised their hands.

'Very well,' he said; 'in that case...'

His voice tailed away as the doors to the large chamber opened. There was a low gasp as five men strode in.

Daniel frowned. 'I see the Gloamers have seen fit to turn up for once,' he said. 'It's a little late – we are about to end the session.'

The five delegates bowed before the twin thrones.

'Greetings, your Majesties,' said their leader; 'Lady Amber has sent us here to raise one specific issue with the council, and, as the session has not yet ended, we are entitled to lodge it.'

'Get on with it,' muttered the King.

The delegates took their seats on the Gloamer benches, though their leader remained standing.

He nodded to the clerk. 'We have a proposal that can be put to a quick vote.'

The clerk bowed his head. 'I recognise the Gloamer delegation's right to speak.'

'Thank you,' the Gloamer said, as the clerk sat. 'Your Majesties, fellow delegates of the City; Lady Amber would like to introduce a piece of emergency legislation, one that can be enacted by this council here today. The City is in the midst of a terrible crisis; I don't think anyone would deny that simple fact, and, it is imperative that the stability of the tribes and the City are placed at the forefront of our decisions. To prevent further disorder, we therefore propose that the elections scheduled for the end of Darian be cancelled. We demand a vote on this issue.'

'Out of the question,' said the King. 'This issue was settled many months ago, and the elections have taken a considerable amount of planning. It is too late to postpone them.'

The chief Sander delegate stood. 'We second the proposal of the Gloamers. With all due respect, your Majesty; it is never too late to correct a faulty course. Lady Lydia of Port Sanders is in agreement.'

'Of course she is!' thundered the King. 'It is well known that some of the former Royal Family are opposed to losing even a tiny portion of their power over the mortals. The elections will forever shift the balance of power in the City, and they are well aware of that fact.'

The chief Gloamer returned to his feet. 'This goes beyond the personal wishes of a few demigods, your Majesty. The Gloamers will boycott the elections, as will the Rosers and Sanders, while it is clear to everyone in this chamber that the Evaders are in no fit state to run even a simple ballot. We move for a vote; we demand a vote.'

The clerk stood.

'Wait,' said the King. 'There is no mandate for this piece of business. If the Gloamers want to vote on cancelling the elections, they need to go through the correct channels.'

The clerk bowed. 'Unless we first vote on whether a vote can take place, your Majesty.'

'This is a nonsense,' muttered the King.

'You wrote the rules, your Majesty,' shouted the chief Gloamer.

'A show of hands is all that is required,' said the clerk. 'Would those in favour of holding a vote on the proposal from the Gloamers please raise their hands?'

Arms shot up across the chamber.

'Very well,' said the clerk; 'I count the Gloamers, Sanders, Icewarders and Blades as voting in favour. The formal vote on the Gloamer proposal shall proceed.'

Daniel glanced at Emily, his face growing pale. 'What is happening?' he whispered.

Emily said nothing. The clerk picked up the voting urn, and began to walk by the benches of each tribe. When he passed them, the chief delegate from each tribe dropped in one of the three voting tokens available. When he reached the last tribe, he accepted their token, then returned to his desk, where he upended the urn.

The chamber stilled.

'Your Majesties,' the clerk said, 'delegates of the Tribal Council; the votes are as follows – for the Gloamer proposal, three votes; against, two votes; and two abstentions. The elections scheduled for the end of Darian are hereby cancelled.'

Half of the chamber erupted in joy. The Sander and Gloamer delegates started hugging each other, grins plastered to their faces.

'This session has now ended,' said the clerk. 'Good day to you all.'

The King stood, his face red with anger. 'This outrage will not be forgotten,' he called out over the noise. 'We have tried consensus; we have tried careful negotiation, and we have tried to appease and compromise at every stage. No more. You will soon feel the true power of the Crown, and you shall have no one to blame but yourselves.'

The King stepped down from the low platform, and strode from the chamber. A few of the celebrating delegates glanced in the King's direction, but to Emily's mind, none seemed overly concerned by his words. She got up from her throne and thanked the clerk. The Hammer and Reaper delegates approached her.

'This is madness, your Majesty,' said the chief Hammer; 'we have been preparing for the elections for well over a year. Our people will be angered by the vote held here today.'

'I understand,' said the Queen.

'The Gloamers ambushed us, your Majesty,' cried a Reaper. 'They must have planned this little conspiracy with the Sanders.'

'But who gave the third vote in favour?' said the Hammer.

'I imagine it was the Blades,' said Emily. 'The Scythes always abstain in these matters, and I cannot believe that Lady Yvona of Icehaven voted with the Gloamers. Do not lose heart – this is a painful setback, but we shall overcome all such obstacles in the end; the will of the people shall prevail. Please excuse me, as I must now discuss these events with the King.'

The delegates of the two tribes bowed low before her, and she walked from the chamber, picking up a squad of Royal Guards at the doors. They escorted her to the royal quarters, and Emily let herself in. She opened the door to their living room, to see Daniel on his feet, a look of ferocious anger on his face. Standing a yard from him was his mother, whose face was equally lit up.

Emily glanced at both of them. 'Have I interrupted something?'

'It's quite alright, your Majesty,' said the King-Mother.

'No, it's not,' snarled Daniel. 'My own mother is pleased about today's vote – can you believe that? That bitch Amber has betrayed us, after all we did for her.'

'Lady Amber was clear about where she stood,' said Emily, 'and she has stuck to her principles. I can think of a few words to describe her behaviour, but "betrayal" is not one of them.'

The King-Mother smiled. 'Well said, your Majesty. Today's vote has given us all a little space in which to breathe. Perhaps now, the Rosers will reconsider their position and re-enter the negotiations in good faith.'

'Who cares about the stupid Rosers!' Daniel shouted. 'I should have sent the Banner soldiers in. A few hundred deaths would have concentrated minds, and then the other tribes would never have voted to cancel the elections. They see us as weak, and with good reason. Yes, yes; I know we executed three demigods for treachery, but they were the most useless, and harmless, demigods in the City. Where's Frostback? Dalrig and Port Sanders should be punished for what they have done.'

'Really?' said Emily. 'What would you suggest? Burning Tonetti Palace to the ground? Or perhaps some housing estates? A school, maybe? Or a hospital?'

Daniel turned his rage-filled gaze to his wife. 'Do you want to be the Queen of the City? Answer me.'

'I am the Queen, so the question is irrelevant.'

'If we fall from power, what do you think will happen to us? To Elspeth? We'll be beheaded, and our heads will decorate the gates of Cuidrach Palace.'

'The Banner will protect us.'

'You're a fool. The Banner doesn't serve us out of loyalty; they signed a damned contract – a piece of paper. They serve whoever pays them the most. If we lose our positions, then their contracts become void; it'll be Banner soldiers wielding the swords that take our heads.'

'Van would never...'

'Van's head will be on display next to ours!' Daniel cried.

Emily sat down, debating whether or not to make an issue of the fact that her husband had just called her a fool. Her own temper was simmering away, but someone needed to keep their head.

'Let's consider every peaceful solution before we do anything rash,' she said.

'We've tried,' he said. 'You thought up the plan of the dragon patrols; has it made any difference? No. Tomorrow, we should unleash Frostback upon Tara and Port Sanders; burn their ships, and raze their marketplaces to the ground. Hit them economically.'

'The Reapers and Evaders also depend upon the food those ships bring in, Danny.'

'It'll be worth it, if by doing so, we are able to introduce... what was the word that Kelsey taught us – democracy?'

'You just witnessed democracy in action, Danny; and we were out-voted three to two.'

The King picked up a vase of flowers from the table and flung it across the room. His mother ducked, and the vase exploded against the rear wall, sending water, flowers, and shards of broken pottery flying through the air.

'That is quite enough, Daniel,' said his mother. 'Did I raise you to act like a savage?'

'Shut up, mother. You're dismissed. Go on, get out. Confine yourself to your quarters. If I catch you anywhere else in the palace, I'll evict you from Cuidrach.'

Lady Aurelian's features went cold. She raised her chin, gave a brief nod to Emily, then strode from the room, slamming the door behind her. Daniel stared at the door for a moment, then sat down, putting his head in his hands. Emily watched him, wondering where the man she had married had gone.

'I'm sorry,' he said, not looking at her. 'I went too far. I feel as though I've been betrayed, that everything I've worked for has been reduced to ashes. It was my mother's smirk that set me off. When I walked in, she was gloating about the vote, and I lost my temper.'

'You lost it in the council chamber,' Emily said. 'You threatened the delegates.'

'Did I? I'm so angry that I can't even remember what I said. I thought that becoming King would allow us to improve the lives of everyone in the City, but instead, it's turned me into an asshole.'

'Perhaps we misjudged how long these things take. Perhaps we tried too much, too soon. The lesson here is not to give up, Danny, but to plan for a longer future. We should learn how to treat failure with the same serenity as success.'

'Easy to say that. I need a break.'

'Take the evening off, Danny. Rest.'

'I meant a longer break than that. I need to recover whatever I've lost, before I do something that can't be undone. I've failed, Emily.'

She kept her gaze on him, saying nothing. She knew that he was waiting for her to tell him that he wasn't a failure, or an asshole, and that everything would be alright, but she couldn't summon the will to do so. Was it her job to pander to his ego and his temper? She was his wife, not his damn mother.

She stood.

Daniel looked up at her. 'Where are you going?'

'I have work to do, Danny. I need to draft a statement so that the City understands the implications of today's vote, and to let the people know that we are still firmly in charge. The worst thing would be to allow panic and uncertainty at this time. Stay here and rest, or get drunk; I don't care.'

She walked away, leaving him staring at her. She left the apartment, and a squad escorted her through the palace. The shutters had been closed, and oil lamps were illuminating the quiet corridors of Cuidrach. She went into the area containing Salvor's grand office, but stopped at an open door. Inside a small ante-room, Captain Cardova and Kelsey were sitting by a fireplace, talking.

Emily knocked, and entered. 'Good evening.'

Cardova got to his feet and bowed. 'Your Majesty. Commiserations on this evening's vote.'

'You heard?'

The tall officer nodded. 'I think the entire City has heard by now, your Majesty.' He gave her a funny look. 'Do the Banner have any new orders?'

'No.'

Kelsey puffed out her cheeks. 'Thank Pyre for that. We thought you might be planning some kind of violent retribution.'

'We were merely going over the options, your Majesty,' said Lucius.

Emily eased the door shut and walked over to them. 'Do you mind if I sit?'

'Please,' said Lucius, gesturing to a seat.

'It's your damn palace,' said Kelsey. 'Sit where you like.'

Emily sat, and Lucius returned to his chair.

'I have something to say to both of you,' the Queen said, 'and it must not be repeated outside of this room under any circumstances.'

'This sounds interesting,' said Kelsey.

Emily noticed that the Holdfast woman had a glass of brandy in her hand, but chose not to mention it.

'If,' she said, 'you are approached by *any* other person, from the lowest station to the very highest, who orders you to undertake what I would consider to be an aggressive policy, then that order must not be carried out without my express permission.' She paused. 'Do I make myself clear?'

Kelsey and Lucius glanced at each other.

'Perfectly, your Majesty,' said Lucius. 'All operational orders must be confirmed by you.'

'By me, in person.'

'That might be tricky,' said Kelsey. 'I mean, I assume we're talking about the King, aye?'

Emily sighed. 'I was trying to be subtle about it.'

'Nothing beats the naked truth, Queenie. Alright, what if the King and a dozen soldiers come up to me and Frostback, and he tells us to go and burn something, or someone, immediately; am I supposed to say "no; I'll have to run it by your wife first?"'

'That is precisely what I am asking of you both.'

Lucius wrinkled his nose. 'That could be difficult, contractually speaking. The Banner is tied to both of you, your Majesty – the King and the Queen. That's not what I would call an unambiguous chain of command. If the King orders me to do something, and I don't have time to consult with you, or if you happen to be somewhere else, then I would be breaking my contract if I were to disobey him.'

'And let me guess – the Banner never break their contracts?'

Lucius gave a gentle shrug. 'Exactly, your Majesty.' He frowned for a moment. 'However, I can delay, and I'll certainly take whatever measures are practical to have the orders confirmed by you before any action is taken. Also, if the King asks me directly about this, I will be duty-bound to tell him, just as I would be bound to tell you if the King had issued a similar request.'

'Has he?'

'No, your Majesty.'

'Tell me if he does.'

'I will, your Majesty.'

'Pyre's sake,' muttered Kelsey; 'the Banner and their weird rules.'

'It's what keeps us right,' said Lucius. 'Being apolitical is what keeps the Banner from splitting.'

Emily leaned forward. 'If the King and I were deposed, would the contract become void?'

'These situations can get very complicated, your Majesty. Every soldier in the Banner would be analysing their contract word-by-word, looking for guidance. "Was the deposition legal?"; "Does the contract state your names, or does if refer vaguely to the Crown?"; "Is the new government legitimate or illegitimate?" The list goes on. Ultimately, after some debate, the Banner should obey the advice of its commander, but, if a majority disagrees, or thinks that the commander's personal feelings are leading them to act illegally, then the Banner can vote to remove them from authority and appoint new leadership. In other words, Van and I, and a few other senior officers, would be arrested and replaced. It rarely happens, though, because the commanders usually go along with what the bulk of the Banner want. I guess that was a long way to say that it depends.'

Kelsey squinted at him. 'Arrested?'

'Yes. Then put on trial by the Banner, to see if we broke the law, or tried to force the Banner to break the law. If found guilty, the Banner would then execute us. That's another reason why commanders rarely go against the wishes of the majority if the contractual situation becomes unclear.'

Emily nodded. 'Then, it's just as well that I had my name, and that of my husband, inserted into the contract. If such an event were to occur, then I would simply claim to still be the Queen. I think I could argue my case in front of the Banner.'

'That might well swing it in your favour, your Majesty. Is this scenario likely?'

Emily sat back in her chair. 'I don't think so. If Amalia returns, then it'll be a fight to the death.'

Kelsey drained her glass and refilled it with brandy.

Emily glanced at her. 'I hope you can ride a dragon while drunk.'

'What? Do I have to fly tonight? I thought I...'

'No, no. It's just in case, you know. Is there a particular reason you're gulping down brandy?'

Kelsey scowled. 'I broke up with Van.'

'Oh no. When?'

'Earlier this evening.'

'Why?'

Lucius looked uncomfortable, and lowered his gaze. Emily eyed him, wondering if the break-up had anything to do with Kelsey and her catching Van taking salve. 'I assume that you know, Captain?'

'He does,' said Kelsey, 'but I'm not going to tell you, Queenie. Sorry, but it's personal.'

'No, that's fine,' she said. 'It's none of my business, as long as it doesn't affect his performance as Commander of the Banner. It doesn't, does it?'

'No,' said Lucius.

That's good to hear, though it's still a pity,' Emily said. She narrowed her eyes. 'Wait a moment – you two aren't...?'

Kelsey laughed. 'No. Pyre's arse; imagine that.'

'No, thanks,' said Lucius; 'if it's all the same to you.'

'You're too tall for me anyway, Lucius,' Kelsey said. 'I get a sore neck looking up at you.'

'All the same,' said Emily, smiling; 'whatever caused you to break it off, can it not be fixed? You seem to have given up on it fairly quickly.'

Lucius gave a wry smile. 'That's exactly what I've been telling her, your Majesty. One might even accuse Kelsey of being a tad flighty.'

'Flighty?' said Kelsey, raising an eyebrow. 'I'm the opposite of flighty. I'm decisive. I weigh up all the advantages and disadvantages in my head, and make a decision. There's no point living in a world of wishful thinking.'

'Seems a little cold,' said Emily.

'Oh, I'm hurting,' said Kelsey. 'I might not look it, but I already miss him, the stupid numpty. That's why I've decided to get drunk tonight.'

'Pour me one of those brandies,' said Emily.

Lucius picked up the bottle, and half-filled a glass.

'Thanks, Captain.'

'You're welcome, your Majesty.'

'I met Jade today,' said Kelsey; 'and she is pissed off.'

'I know,' said Emily. 'I talked to her yesterday after she had visited her sister.'

'She was also less... I don't know; arrogant? Less full of herself. She was sad, but at the same time, better company than usual. I felt sorry for her.'

'Then, you did better than I,' said Emily. 'She was driving me crazy; no. Apologies, I shouldn't have said that. She was trying my patience. She thinks her sister should have been executed.'

'Maybe she should have been,' said Kelsey, 'especially after she screwed you over with today's vote.'

'Yes, well, I can't go around executing everyone who disagrees with me. What Amber did in the Tribal Council was underhanded, but perfectly legal. She played Daniel's system to perfection. On the other hand, I can see why Jade is so annoyed; she's been loyal for years, and I believe her when she says that Amber was a nasty bully. But, that's hardly a valid reason to take her head. When it came to a crisis, it was she who warned us about the death-salve in the water supply. She saved the lives of hundreds of Reapers – an act for which she was severely beaten by her father.' She sighed. 'It's impossible to please both sisters.'

She took a large sip of brandy.

'Are you also getting drunk, your Majesty?' said Lucius.

'Why?'

'I didn't think you got drunk,' he said; 'you always seem to be in control, your Majesty. Plus, there's the prospect of spending my evening with two drunken young women. I might need to mentally prepare myself.'

Emily considered for a moment. She knew that she shouldn't drink too much, in case an emergency arose, but after the evening she had endured, she decided that one night wouldn't hurt. Also, Daniel had probably already started on the gin, and if he could do it, then why couldn't she?

'I might get a little tipsy,' she said, taking another sip. 'From this point on, anything I say stays in this room; understood?'

Kelsey smirked. 'Everything you've said is already confidential.'

'You can trust us, your Majesty,' said Lucius. 'I will remain sober.'

'You can keep our glasses topped up,' said Kelsey, 'and I'll be wanting some snacks soon.'

Lucius bowed to her. 'Yes, Lady Holdfast of Jezra.'

'That's more like it, Lucius. That's how you should address me from now on.'

'Yeah, right. I'm not your bloody servant.'

Emily smiled as she watched them. Kelsey continued to look at Lucius, her mouth opening to say something, then she froze, her eyes widening. She dropped her glass of brandy, but, lightning quick, Lucius's hand shot out and caught it before it could fall to the ground.

'Nice reactions, Captain,' said Emily, then noticed that Kelsey was still staring at the officer, as if she were in a trance. She frowned. 'Are you alright, Miss Holdfast?'

Kelsey blinked. 'Eh, what?'

'Are you alright? You seemed to blank out for a moment there.'

'Oh. Uh, sorry.'

Lucius handed her back the glass of brandy, and she drank the contents in one. Emily and Lucius shared a glance.

'How's Silva doing?' said Lucius. 'Is she still sick in bed?'

'No,' said Emily. 'She's up and about, but is keeping to her rooms. Her powers haven't returned, though she told me that she could feel them a tiny bit, so hopefully it won't be much longer before she's fully recovered.'

Lucius nodded. 'Good, because we could really do with her powers at the moment, your Majesty.'

The Holdfast woman leaned forward and lowered her voice. 'Lucius, eh? Who'd have thought?'

Emily frowned. 'You're not making any sense, Kelsey.'

'She seldom does,' said Lucius.

'Shut up, smartarse,' said Kelsey. 'Bollocks. I really don't want to tell you this, and I'm only doing it because I'm half-drunk, but... No. I've changed my mind. Ignore what I just said.'

'That's an impossibility now,' said Emily. 'Do you know something about the captain? If so, then I think we should also know.'

Kelsey smiled and refilled her glass. 'All in good time, Queenie; all in good time. Now, get that brandy down you; we've a long night ahead of us.'

Emily frowned, then drained her glass.

CHAPTER 27
GIVER OF GIFTS

Yocasta – 19th Essinch 5254

'For the sake of my sanity,' yelled Montieth, 'tell that little runt to stop pacing the floor.'

Amalia sighed. 'Tell him yourself.'

'I'm pacing,' said Naxor, 'because it helps me think better. My head is spinning with a hundred plans and schemes, and, as I am the most intelligent among us, I advise you to let me continue.'

Montieth reached over the table of half-eaten food, picked up a chunk of meat, and hurled it at Naxor. The demigod dodged it, moving faster than Kagan had thought possible, and the meat splattered over the wall.

Naxor glanced at the mess. 'I could have eaten that. Who knows when Simon will return to give us more food? How long would you say that we have been stuck in this room? Two days? Three?'

'How should I know?' cried Montieth from his chair. 'Long enough to want to throttle you, you filthy miscreant.'

'Stop bickering,' said Kagan; 'you're like a pair of children.'

Montieth and Naxor turned to stare at him.

'No mortal has ever addressed me thus,' spat Montieth, his face reddening with rage. He raised a finger. 'Time to suffer.'

'No,' said Amalia. 'Kagan's right. I would be most obliged if you two held your tongues for a while. Even ten minutes would do. If I had to guess, I would say that we have been in this chamber for a little over two days, but without any windows or clocks, there's no way to tell.'

'This room has been designed with that in mind,' said Naxor. 'The seals on the doorframe are perfect – no gaps, and there's no keyhole, so there's no way for my vision to leave the room. Do you think we'll eventually run out of air?'

Montieth picked up a jug from the table. 'At least he left us a load of booze.' He grinned. 'I wonder how Felice is getting on?'

'I'm trying not to think about that,' said Amalia.

'Jealous, are you, mother?'

'Not in the slightest.'

'You're just saying that because your pet mortal is here.'

'No, I'm not. Let's change the subject. I...'

The air in the corner of the room shimmered, and Simon appeared in his full battle armour, Felice by his side.

The Ascendant beamed at them. 'I am sated. Felice has reminded me how good life can be. However, that doesn't mean that I favour her over the rest of you. You are all my rescuers.'

Felice frowned at him.

'When we get to your City,' Simon went on, oblivious to Felice's expression, 'I shall take for myself a harem of truly godlike proportions. Are the women there beautiful?'

'They are the same as everywhere else,' said Naxor. 'The Royal Palace in Ooste was where the God-King had his harem. I think you'll find the facilities there to your liking.'

'That sounds promising, young Naxor,' said Simon. He plucked the Quadrant from behind his breastplate, and glided his fingers over the surface. The room around them vanished, and was replaced by the open air. Kagan glanced around. They were on the top of a high tower, overlooking the ruins of the city they had walked through two days before. Swarms of greenhides were circling the tower, raising great clouds of dust and sand.

'I know everything about the City now,' Simon said, 'and I have a plan.'

'You do?' said Amalia.

'Yes. My plan is so gorgeous I could kiss it. I have identified the main threat – one Kelsey Holdfast, and have devised a simple strategy, taken from a thought that Montieth had, combined with some of Naxor's more devious schemes. By this time tomorrow, we will be in control of the City. I now wish to grant each of you a boon, in thanks for your help in delivering me from this hideous world. Amalia, as you are the eldest, you shall go first.'

'That's easy,' she said. 'I want my son Maxwell back, and I wish to live in Maeladh Palace.'

'Granted,' said Simon. He turned to Felice. 'And you, my young beauty...'

'I'm five thousand years old, Simon.'

'I know. As I said, you are young in my eyes; you all are.'

'Yes, but Montieth and Naxor are only in their second millennium. Amalia and I are many generations older than them.'

'Oh, you're an ambitious one, Felice. I can see that you hoped to become my consort, as if spending a few days in bed with me were enough to warrant that. Let me disabuse you of such a naïve notion – there was only one woman fit to be my bride, and she has been dead for almost as long as you have been alive.'

Felice narrowed her eyes. 'Who?'

'The glorious, unequalled First Ascendant – Theodora. Ah, how I loved her; her beauty and wisdom shone like the stars. She taught me how to use the Sextant, and we created the most beautiful worlds together. Next to her, all other women are crude imitations.' He shook his head as he gazed out over the desert wastes, and a tear rolled down his cheek. 'I believed that bastard Edmond when he denied murdering her. I believed him for a long, long time.'

'Do you know what happened?' said Felice. 'It's always been shrouded in secrecy.'

He turned to her. 'I know everything. It was Belinda's fault, or so I used to believe. Against my wishes, Theodora married Edmond instead of me. It destroyed me for a while, and I used to watch them from afar, pondering on how such a woman could possibly be attracted to that vile creature. Then Belinda returned to Implacatus after a long time away, and Edmond turned his eyes towards her.' He spat on the dusty roof of the tower. 'Bitch. She seduced him, and enticed him away from Theodora. Edmond's head was so full of Belinda that he planned to leave Theodora, but she discovered his infidelity first. That is when he killed her. All my dreams died that day. Except, Edmond denied it. I went after Belinda, for she had run off to be with Nathaniel. I intended to kill her, to avenge Theodora, but she told me the truth, that it had been Edmond who had murdered the First Ascendant. In a rage, I went back to Implacatus to confront Edmond, but he had set a trap for me, and I was taken unawares. I tried to escape, but the Quadrant slipped from my fingers, and I ended up here instead. And, in my absence, Belinda and Nathaniel lost the god wars. I had been intending to join their rebellion, and should never have returned to Implacatus.'

He fell into silence for a while, his features heavy.

'During my long exile here,' he said, 'I was consoled by the thought that Edmond and the other Ascendants would be as old and decrepit as I had become. Yet, for many centuries, they had been reinvigorated by salve, and were enjoying a second youth. I will smash them; I will grind them all under my heel.'

'Even Belinda?' said Amalia.

Simon glanced at her. 'I might allow Belinda to enter my harem. I have not forgiven her for seducing Edmond, but I also owe her a debt for revealing the truth to me.' He turned to Felice. 'You may also enter my harem – that honour I will grant you.'

'No, thanks.'

'Then, name your boon.'

Felice shrugged. 'A palace, I guess; along with some authority. A place in the government, and there's a mortal man, ex-Banner, whom I want to personally kill.'

'That will be easy to fulfil. Montieth? I can already see that you wish to reclaim Greylin Palace in Dalrig. Is that so?'

'Yes.'

'So be it. Naxor?'

'Port Sanders and a government post, please.'

'Certainly. Mortal? What do you desire?'

Kagan narrowed his eyes. He didn't want to be part of whatever Simon was planning, and knew that by asking for something, he would be as complicit as the others.

Simon shook his head. 'Those sorts of thoughts will get you killed, mortal man. I am offering you a gift, in gratitude. Do not twist my intentions.'

'Alright,' he said. 'Like Amalia, I want my son back, but I also want the mortals in the City to be treated with the same rights as the gods and demigods.'

Simon started to laugh, then Felice and Montieth joined in.

'My answer is no,' said Simon. 'I will, however, treat *you* with the same rights and respect as the other immortals. For such a lowly creature as yourself, that is the greatest honour I could possibly bestow.' He glanced at the gods and demigods. 'I think we are ready to leave. With only one Quadrant, I will not be able to open a portal, therefore the size of our army will necessarily be somewhat limited.'

'Army?' said Naxor.

'Yes,' said Simon, gesturing with a hand at the greenhides swarming in the ruins below them. 'Behold; my warriors.'

'No,' said Amalia; 'you can't be thinking of taking greenhides into the City.'

Simon gave her a piercing stare. 'Why not? They are under my control, and are more obedient and reliable than human soldiers. They are better than the best Banner; ideal warriors. Why would I not take some?'

'The citizens would panic,' she said. 'For thousands of years, their greatest fear has been that greenhides get into the City.'

Naxor smirked. 'You would know about that, grandmother – you brought the damn greenhides to our world.'

'Yes, but Malik and I miscalculated, and they escaped our control. Nevertheless, the people of the City will not accept a ruler who brings greenhides in to patrol the streets.'

Simon laughed. 'I can read from your mind that you opened the gates in your defensive walls to let the greenhides in; are you going to deny me the same privilege? And, my greenhides won't wantonly slaughter the mortals, as yours did.'

Amalia lowered her eyes. 'I realise that I sound like a hypocrite, but I implore you not to do this.'

'You're over-reacting,' said Felice. 'There's bound to be some opposition from the mortals in the City, and that opposition will have to be overcome. Does it matter how we do it?'

'Of course it matters,' said Kagan.

'Don't question me,' Felice said. 'I helped rule Lostwell for centuries. I was among the first wave of gods sent from Implacatus to subdue that sad, horrible little world. All you've ever known, until very recently, is how to survive in a slum.'

'Did you ever care about the Blue Thumbs, or the mortals of Alea Tanton?'

'Don't be ridiculous; of course not. You should consider yourself very fortunate, Kagan. Due to your ties to Amalia, you are now under the protection of the Tenth Ascendant. If I were you, I'd keep my mouth shut and be thankful for what I have.'

Simon laughed. 'It's settled. With a single Quadrant, I can transport about a hundred greenhides with us to the City. Not enough to cause a mass panic, but sufficient to act as a bodyguard and to instil a certain amount of healthy terror among the mortals. Are we all ready?'

'Where are we going first?' said Naxor.

'Dalrig,' said Simon. 'From the moment we arrive, you will all address me as "your Grace," is that clear? Failure to do so will result in your immediate death. I owe you all for my rescue, but one must remember the proper protocol. I am, after all, far more radiant and glorious than any of you. Next to me, in fact, you might be considered mere insects.'

His fingers slid over the Quadrant, and the air crackled all around them. Kagan closed his eyes, and when he re-opened them, he was standing on a cold street, with stone buildings on either side. Simon and the other immortals were next to him, along with a mass of green-hides. Screams rose up into the red sky of dawn, as the terrified citizens of Dalrig fled in panic. Men and women barged past each other as they raced away in both directions, despite the fact that the greenhides remained motionless.

'So, this is Dalrig?' said Simon, gazing around. 'It's not exactly Serene, is it?'

'None of the City compares to Implacatus, your Grace,' said Felice. 'It's all very "small-town."'

'Well, I won't be here for too long,' Simon said. 'A century at the most.'

A group of armed Gloamer militia began approaching from around the street corner, then halted when they caught sight of the greenhides. A few immediately turned and ran, while others stood, staring in disbelief.

'I'm guessing those soldiers work for your elder daughter, Monti-eth?' said Simon.

'Yes, your Grace,' Montieth replied, his tone showing his displeasure at having to use the Ascendant's correct address.

'Then, we shall allow them to live. Such is my magnanimity. Now, let us progress through the streets towards Greylin Palace. I want the mortals to see us.'

Simon led the way, with the others close by, while the greenhides formed up into ranks and marched behind them, their long talons sparking off the cobblestones. On either side of the street, the locals were frantically barring their doors and closing their shutters, but Kagan could see many faces watching them from the upper floor of the tenements. The party walked towards the harbour front, where Simon stopped for a moment to look at the many ships tied up by the piers and quayside. The market was deserted, the locals having fled at the first sight of the greenhides, and Simon browsed through a counter of silver jewellery, selecting several items for himself. While he amused himself in this way, Kagan watched the sailors and merchants standing up on the decks of their vessels, their eyes wide with terror.

'Halt!' cried a voice.

Kagan and the immortals turned. At the end of the road, next to the corner of the huge, imposing bulk of Greylin Palace, two squads of Banner soldiers were assembling, their shields held out to the front in a wall.

'Ah,' smiled Simon. 'The Banner of the Lostwell Exiles, I presume?'

'State your name and your purpose,' cried a Banner officer, as the soldiers levelled their crossbows.

Simon placed his hand on his hips. 'I am the Tenth Ascendant,' he said, his voice booming out over the harbour. 'I have come to liberate this City. Bow before me.'

The Banner officer raised his hand, and his soldiers loosed their crossbows as one. Amalia pushed Kagan behind her as the bolts whistled through the air. Felice took one to her leg, while Naxor staggered backwards as he was hit in the chest. A bolt ricocheted off Simon's wide breastplate, and he laughed, then clicked his fingers. At once, the head of every Banner soldier on the street exploded in a flash of brains and fragments of bone. The headless figures remained upright for a second, then they collapsed to the blood-streaked cobblestones.

Simon smiled. 'Let's hope as many citizens as possible saw that. Word will spread quickly that we have arrived in Dalrig, which is precisely what I want.'

Felice pulled the bolt from her leg, then pointed upwards. 'Amber saw it, your Grace. She's watching from the roof of the palace.'

'So she is,' said Simon. 'Come; let us pay Amber a little visit.'

'Are you going to kill her, your Grace?' said Monteith.

'That depends upon her attitude,' said Simon, setting off again.

They followed the road to the palace, stepping over the ruined bodies of the two dozen Banner soldiers scattered across the cobblestones. Kagan tried not to look at the corpses, and tried to keep all negative thoughts about Simon from his mind. A weight of base fear settled onto his shoulders. One wrong thought, or idea, or look, or gesture, and it would be his head that next exploded.

Amalia took his hand as they walked.

'Think about something happy,' she whispered.

'I'm trying to.'

'Stay in the background, where he won't notice you.'

Simon turned. 'I can hear you; just so you know. My battle-vision powers give me unparalleled hearing. I know that your mortal is terrified, Amalia, but that's quite alright. I would be more concerned if he showed no fear of me.'

They turned the corner and strode up the road that ran along the front of the palace, the greenhides keeping pace behind them. When they reached the mighty front doors, they were closed. Simon stepped forwards, crossing the short bridge over the dry moat, and thumped on the doors with his fist.

'Amber!' cried Montieth, also walking forwards. 'It's your father. Open the doors.'

'There are more Banner soldiers inside the building,' said Simon. 'Your daughter seems to have allied herself to your enemies, Montieth.'

'Utter nonsense, your Grace. My Amber is more cunning than that.'

'She betrayed you before you left for Yocasta, did she not? I can see the beating you gave her through your own eyes, and the way that you poisoned her with anti-salve. Her powers have yet to return. Will she not hold you responsible, Montieth?'

'She will help us, your Grace; I know her.'

They walked back across the moat bridge, then Simon turned to face the doors again. He lifted his left palm, and sparks flew between his fingers, like little arcs of lightning. He then brought his other hand up, and pushed the sparks outward. They spread, sizzling, and formed a ball of tight, white fire. Simon flexed his fingers, and the fireball grew in size, until a roiling cloud of flames as large as a wagon was suspended in the air in front of the Ascendant. He shot his hand out, and the fireball responded to his will. It shot across the gap and smashed into the double doors of Greylin Palace, blowing them off their iron hinges in an explosion of fiery fragments. As the smoke and flames plumed upwards, Simon clicked his fingers, and the greenhides set off at a run, funnelling past Kagan and the immortals, and piling through the ragged entranceway. They surged into the palace, until every one of them was inside.

'Don't look so upset, Montieth,' said Simon. 'I have ordered our little army not to damage any property, and to leave your daughter alive. This is simply the most efficient way to rid ourselves of the hundred or so Banner soldiers inside.' He turned to the others. 'Let's chat while we wait. Young Naxor, I want you to stay in Greylin with Montieth and his daughter, while I take the others to our second destination. Your task here in Dalrig will be to keep the Crown's attention on you. Use your powers to send a message to our enemies – tell them to come and get you, but do it subtly, otherwise they might realise that it's merely a diversion. I will signal you later with your next steps.'

Naxor bowed his head. 'Yes, your Grace.'

Simon smiled. 'I'm growing to like you, young Naxor. You remind me of a less powerful, shorter, younger version of myself. And not as handsome, obviously.'

Screams and cries were coming from the interior of the building. A Banner soldier ran out of the front entrance, fleeing from a greenhide. Simon pointed at him, and his head evaporated into a cloud of red mist. Moments later, more greenhides emerged. Two were dragging Amber by the heels, while she struggled and screamed. The greenhides deposited her onto the ground in front of Simon.

'Good morning,' said the Ascendant, looking down at her. 'Your father thinks I should spare your life. What do you say, Amber? Hmm? Are you willing to beg for your life and swear fealty to me, to save yourself from being torn to pieces?'

Amber glanced around, her eyes wide. She noticed Amalia and Monteith, then her eyes climbed up to see Simon towering over her.

She calmed her expression, got to her feet, and brushed the dirt from the front of her dress.

'To whom am I speaking?' she said, her voice even.

Simon laughed. 'You have nerves of iron, young Amber. But you already knew that, didn't you? How else could you have betrayed your father by giving secrets to his enemies?'

Amber held his gaze, then turned to Montieth. 'Who is this gentleman, father?'

Felice stepped forward before Montieth could speak. 'He is Simon, the most sacred and honourable Tenth Ascendant, and you should be on your knees in front of him, traitor.'

'I have already been dragged into his presence,' said Amber, 'and I don't wish my dress to get dirty again.' She frowned at Simon. 'An Ascendant? I've heard of those, though your present company leaves a little to be desired. What do you want?'

'You don't care that my greenhides slaughtered your soldiers?'

'They weren't my soldiers, Ascendant. They were placed here by the Queen.'

'A Queen that you have pledged loyalty to.'

'I am loyal to one thing – the Gloamer tribe who live in Dalrig under my protection.' She lifted a finger as Montieth began to speak. 'No, father. You lost the right to rule the Gloamers when you poisoned and beat me. Dalrig is mine. If you and the others don't accept that, then kill me now and be done with it.'

'Oh, I like you,' said Simon, grinning. 'Pledge yourself to me, and you can keep Dalrig as your personal fiefdom; you've already shown me more courage than your father has.'

Amber raised an eyebrow. 'I wouldn't have thought that Dalrig was your gift to give, Ascendant. Are you in control of the City? Have you overthrown the Aurelians and defeated their allies? Dalrig is mine, with or without your permission. I will say this, however – I will not hinder or obstruct your plans, nor will I go running to the Aurelian Crown. Yesterday, I destroyed their attempts to hand all power in the City to the mortals, and I doubt very much that they consider me a friend. In fact, I half expect the palace to be attacked by dragons.'

'It will be, Amber, this very day, if my plan comes to fruition. Take Montieth and Naxor within your walls, and allow the young vision demigod to contact the enemy in order to sow his webs of deceit. Then, prepare the town defences of Dalrig for attack. I would recommend multiple batteries of anti-dragon ballistae, but I can see that you have already thought of that.' He leaned his head down, until his face was an inch from hers. 'Will you do this for me, Amber? You shall be rewarded. I will not interfere in your little Gloamer realm – that is all you truly want; I can read your deepest desires. A simple nod will suffice; you do not need to kneel.'

Amber held his piercing gaze for several seconds, then blinked and looked away. She nodded.

Simon turned to the others. 'Greylin and Dalrig belong to Amber. Montieth, you shall stay here as her guest, along with Naxor. Do either of you object?'

Naxor shrugged. 'That's fine by me, your Grace.'

Montieth said nothing. His eyes were bulging, and he was shaking with rage.

'I hear no objections,' said Simon. 'Good. Go into the palace, and await my instructions. Defend Greylin to the best of your ability.'

He snapped his fingers, and the rest of the greenhides emerged from the palace. Many were streaked in blood, and some had strands of flesh or hair hanging from their talons.

Simon grinned at Amber. 'Sorry about the mess, Mistress of Dalrig.' His hands slid over the Quadrant, and the air sizzled. The landscape around them changed, and they appeared, minus Montieth and Naxor, but with the greenhides, on a rocky ridge overlooking a bay. To their right, the low sun was shining in the purple and pink sky, and its reflection was dazzling on the still waters. Far below them lay a town, with wide avenues of villas and red-roofed houses, with trees lining the routes to the harbour.

'This is much nicer,' said Simon, his eyes lit with delight.

'I'm glad you think so, your Grace,' said Amalia. 'Tara has always been my favourite location. The view of Pella and Ooste across the bay lifts my heart every time I see it.'

They turned, and Kagan saw a huge building that dominated the terraced slopes of the ridge. The area where Simon had brought them was high among the barren rocks, and there was no sign of any other buildings close by.

Amalia sighed. 'There it is, your Grace. My home for centuries – Maeladh Palace. Have you brought us here for the same reason that you took Montieth and Naxor to Dalrig?'

'I have. Maeladh is yours, Amalia. You will, however, have to share it with the greenhides, at least for a little while.'

He raised a hand, and the greenhides began trotting up the path towards the rear gates of the palace. They increased their speed as they approached, and Kagan saw Banner soldiers come out of a guard post by the gates. A cry rang out into the morning sky, but was quickly stilled, as the greenhides broke down the gates and surged into a court-yard. They ripped their way through the soldiers, destroying a dozen in a few seconds. A few soldiers loosed their crossbows, but the green-hides ignored any that struck them, and carried on towards the palace. They tore down a door and entered, filing into the building in patient queues.

Simon laughed. 'It'll be fine, Amalia. The palace is almost derelict anyway, and I'll confine the greenhides to the iceward wing on the western side. You'll be safe if you keep out of that part of the palace. And best of all, it'll only be for a day. Wait here and, when you are required, I will send my instructions. Felice will be coming with me.'

Amalia turned from watching the last of the greenhides enter Maeladh Palace. 'Where are you going?'

'To speak to the largest military contingent of mortals in the City.'

'The Banner?'

'Of course not. The Blades, Amalia. Their active forces outnumber the Banner ten-to-one. The Aurelians can keep the Banner; it's the Blades I'm after. Yes; I think I might put on a bit of a show for them.'

He activated the Quadrant and vanished, along with Felice.

Kagan turned to Amalia. 'We should run for it. We could steal a boat and be in Pella in a couple of hours. If Maxwell's alive, that's where he'll be.'

Amalia rubbed her forehead. 'We can't. If we disobey Simon, he'll kill us. Our only chance of getting Maxwell back is if we do exactly as he orders. No hesitation, no arguing; simple obedience. I need to know if you can do that, Kagan; I need to know that you are able to smother your more... compassionate feelings. Many mortals will lose their lives over this day and the next; that is inevitable, and there is no point in us dying over something we cannot change. Only by living can we get Maxwell back. Kagan, are you listening to me?'

'Yes.' He closed his eyes. 'Shit. How did this happen? We're in the entourage of a madman with unlimited power. We're either the luckiest people in the City, or the unluckiest.'

Amalia smiled. 'Let's hope for the former of those.'

He took her hands. 'I'll behave,' he said. 'I'll do whatever it takes to get our son back – you and Maxwell are all I care about.'

They kissed, then turned, as screams began to rise from within the palace.

'Come on,' she said, 'let's go and see what remains of my old belongings. I might even have a few bottles of Taran brandy hidden away somewhere.'

Hand in hand, they walked through the twisted remnants of the iron gate, and entered Maeladh Palace.

CHAPTER 28

LIBERATION

Fortress of the Lifegiver, The Bulwark, The City – 20th Monan 3422

Jade shuffled through from the bedroom and opened the shutters, letting the morning light spill into the small apartment. Quill had taken the good rooms on the floor above, where Princess Yendra, and then Jade, had stayed when they had ruled the Bulwark.

She sat down, wishing she could go back to bed. She had hardly slept the night before, unable to get comfortable in the unfamiliar surroundings, and, when she finally had managed to fall asleep, she had experienced a horrible nightmare about her cats being chased by monsters. Upon awakening, she had been tempted to rush back to Pella to check that they were alright, but knew that she couldn't afford to miss Halfclaw again. Her ideal solution would have been to bring the cats with her to the Eastern Mountains, but she worried about them running away, or becoming lost in the valleys and ridges; at least in the Pellan cottage they were safe.

'Lady Jade,' sounded a voice through the door; 'are you awake?'

'Come in, Quinn,' Jade said, then watched as the door was opened and the officer entered.

Quill bowed her head. 'Sorry to barge in like this, but I have news – your father has been seen in Dalrig, along with Amalia and... others.'

'What's this got to do with me?' said Jade. 'I'm going back to the mountains today.'

'Lord Salvor has put the City militia garrisons on alert, and has asked that the Blades be prepared.'

'Prepared for what? If my father's in Dalrig, then that is where he will probably stay. What "others" did you mean? Naxor, I assume?'

'Yes; Naxor was also seen, but the "others" I was referring to were greenhides.'

Jade stared at her, trying to tell if the officer was joking.

'That's what Lord Salvor told me,' Quill said. 'From his tone, he seemed sure about it; he saw them enter Greylin Palace with his own eyes, he said. He thinks that Amalia might have brought them back with her, from wherever she has been hiding these last few days.'

'That sounds like something my grandmother would do,' said Jade. 'Am I needed to go and kill them? I can do that. Maybe Halfclaw can take me when he arrives. Is my sister dead yet?'

Quill sat opposite Jade. 'She might be. Lord Salvor saw her being dragged out of the palace by greenhides. I'm awaiting more news from him, but I'm sure he's got his hands full at the moment. I'm sorry, Jade, but it doesn't look good for Lady Amber.' She shook her head. 'Green-hides, inside the City; it's like a nightmare. Thankfully, there's only a hundred or so, but even a hundred could do terrible things. They've already annihilated the Banner garrison assigned to Greylin; tore through them in minutes, apparently. There was also someone else with them – another god, but Lord Salvor was unable to identify him.'

'Another god? From where?'

'We don't know. The same place as the greenhides, presumably. Anyway, your plans haven't changed for now; I just wanted to let you know about your father. Frostback is being assigned the task of investigating, along with Kelsey Holdfast.'

Jade frowned. 'Her? I hope she falls off her dragon and gets eaten by a greenhide.'

'Kelsey was sorry for what she said to you yesterday. I know she can be a little curt at times, but she's not a bad person.'

'She should have apologised to my face.'

'She had to leave; she was needed back in Jezra.'

'They all hate me.'

'Kelsey doesn't hate you, Jade. Listen; I need to go back to work; I have orders to muster the garrisons of the wall fortresses, just in case they're required.'

'What am I supposed to do?'

'Rest. You still have a couple of hours before Halfclaw is due to arrive.'

'I might kill some greenhides from the battlements.'

'Sure; you can do that.' Quill stood. 'I'll see you before you leave.'

Jade nodded, then Quill bowed her head and left the room. Jade got up, and walked over to the window. It faced west, and overlooked the vast internal courtyard in the centre of the fortress. On the left were the tall tenement-like barracks that housed the main garrison, and Blades were issuing from the doors and forming up into their battalions in the middle of the courtyard. What a waste of time, she thought. There was no chance the Blades would be sent to Dalrig.

She went into the small bathroom, took off her nightdress and washed, taking her time and savouring the hot water. If she could do one thing to improve the living conditions in the mountains, it would be to have hot water coming out of a pipe every morning. She dried herself and pulled on the same dress she had been wearing for two days. She had checked the closets, but Quill was several inches taller than she was, and her taste in clothes was appalling, which was probably why she wore her uniform most of the time. She walked through to the bedroom, and spent twenty minutes on her hair and make up, so that she would look good when she arrived back in the mountains. She had just finished when she remembered that the wind from the journey on the back of the dragon would wreck her hairstyle anyway. She put down the brush and admired her reflection. She was much prettier than Amber, she decided. The only woman in the City that could be compared to her was Queen Emily, but that was because she got to wear fancy dresses and a crown all the time. Perhaps Amalia also qualified, she thought, now that the former God-Queen had taken the plunge and used salve to make herself seem as young as the demigods.

She glanced down, her heart growing despondent. She was nine hundred years old – why was she concerned about who was the most beautiful woman in the City? It was ridiculous. She glanced at the window clock, longing for the dragon to come and take her away. This time, Jade was sure that she wouldn't return to the City. She would live in the little valley, in peace and quiet, and go for walks every day to look at the trees and flowers. Maybe once she had rested there for a few decades, she might be able to face coming back.

She remembered the list that Flavus had given her, and searched the apartment for it, but gave up after a few minutes and sat down again. Alcohol, she thought; that's what he had requested above all else. If she could procure some, then she could make up a story about being too busy to get the other things. She got to her feet and walked out of the apartment. Two Blades were standing on duty in the stairwell, and they saluted her while she was closing the door.

'Can you get me some booze?' she asked.

One of the Blades blinked. 'Yes, ma'am. What kind?'

'Any; I'm not fussy. But make sure it's very strong; I need lots of alcohol. A crate will do. Get it now for me, and leave it on the roof.'

'Yes, ma'am,' said the Blade, then hurried off down the stairs.

Jade followed him, but at a more leisurely pace. She reached the ground floor of the tower, then strode out into the winter sunshine. The shadows in the courtyard were still long, and a chill wind was swirling dust around as the garrison continued to assemble. Jade turned towards the high Inner Walls that lined the eastern edge of the fortress, and climbed the steps to the battlements, which were busy with Blades watching the swarms of greenhides on the plains below. A ballista battery sat next to a large catapult, and the Blades operating them were training young apprentices in their use. They saluted Jade when she arrived on the parapet at the top of the wall, and she watched them for a minute while they loosed their iron ballista bolts and large stones upon the Eternal Enemy.

More futility, she thought. The Blades were doing what they had been doing for centuries, and it made as little difference now as it had then. She turned to face the greenhides, and raised her hand, sending a wave of death powers into a large group clustered by the moat. A few dozen shrieked in agony and collapsed. One toppled forward, and broke through the thin ice covering the moat, its body sinking into the dark depths.

'Impressive,' said a voice to her left.

She frowned. A large man in full battle armour had appeared next to her on the battlements. There was something odd about his skin, she realised; it seemed to glow of its own accord.

'May I have a try?' he said.

Jade was about to respond, when she noticed a woman standing to the man's left, almost hidden by his wide and powerful frame.

'Felice?' Jade cried.

The woman smiled at her. 'Good morning, Lady Jade.'

The huge man turned to face the Blades on the battlements.

He raised his arms. 'Blades! Listen to me,' he called out, his loud voice echoing off the walls of the fortress. All around them, the soldiers up on the battlements stopped what they were doing to pay attention, the voice irresistible.

'Your day of liberation is at hand,' the man said. 'The City has a new ruler, one far more powerful than any of the petty godlings and worthless mortals that you have suffered under for so long. You are truly honoured to be among the first to hear this good news. As a small token of my might, witness what I now do.'

He turned back to face the greenhides, then swept a powerful arm from left to right. There was a roar of noise from down on the plain, and Jade stared in disbelief as thousands of greenhides lost their heads in a cacophony of exploding skulls. The air filled with a cloud of green blood and tattered ribbons of flesh, then the bodies fell, carpeting the blood-soaked ground for a distance of a hundred yards in every direction.

Silence fell over the battlements as the Blades watched, their mouths falling open, then someone roared in celebration, and a dam of emotions burst as the Blades raised their hands in the air to cheer.

The man smiled at Jade. 'Did I win our little contest? I think I might have. Your feeble powers are like a child's next to mine, young Jade. Shall I spare you, or shall I kill you?'

'Kill her, your Grace,' said Felice. 'She is a tool of the Aurelians.'

'Well,' said the man; 'that's one opinion. But, I saved her sister. Perhaps young Jade possesses as much courage as Amber?'

Jade took a step back, her ears filled with the sound of the Blades cheering. More mortals were running up the steps of the Inner Walls to see what was causing the commotion, and each stared in amazement at the sea of dead greenhides out on the plain.

The man reached behind his breastplate and took out a Quadrant. He winked at Jade, then glided his fingers over the copper-coloured metal. In an instant, he, Felice and Jade had been transported to the roof of the Duke's Tower, from where the entire fortress could be seen.

'Time for a little speech,' the man said; 'don't worry, my young Jade; I'll keep it short.'

'Who are you?' she said, her hands shaking.

'Listen and learn.' He turned to face the assembled garrison. 'Greetings,' he called out, his voice filling the fortress. 'I am Simon, the Tenth Ascendant. I am here to liberate the City from the hands of the unworthy, and to set it back onto its correct course. All those who stand by my side will be protected and rewarded; those who oppose me will be destroyed.'

Down in the courtyard, the thousands of Blades were all gazing up, as if spellbound by the god's words.

'The regime of the sad little Aurelians is at an end,' cried Simon, his arms raised. 'I have taken control of the City. Already, I have returned Montieth to his rightful home, and installed Amalia in her Taran palace, but it is to the Blades that I have come, for the Blades are the only military force in the City that commands my respect. The foreign Banner soldiers will be hunted down and destroyed in their entirety; their reign of terror is over. You may rejoice; you may worship me...'

'You are under arrest,' cried a voice.

Simon turned, and Jade saw Quill appear at the top of the stairs, a squad of armed Blades by her side.

The Ascendant smiled. 'Here I am, Adjutant Quill. Come and get me.'

Quill gestured to the soldiers, who rushed forwards, their crossbows levelled at the god. Simon clicked his fingers, and the soldiers fell down dead, their faces contorted with pain.

'I felt heart attacks would be more appropriate for Blades,' said Simon, as Quill staggered backwards in horror. 'More dignified that way; and considerably less messy. Get on your knees, Quill, and surrender the Great Walls to me.'

Quill stared at him, then she noticed Jade.

'I'm not with this madman,' Jade cried.

'Tut tut, young Jade,' said Simon. 'For those unkind words, I now also require you to kneel before me and beg for your life. If you do so, then I may let you live; perhaps in my harem, or perhaps as a kitchen slave.'

In a flash of anger, Jade raised her hand and unleashed her death powers at Simon. He flinched, as if someone had slapped him across the face, but otherwise seemed unaffected.

'So, you do have some courage,' he said.

He raised a finger, and Jade felt her heart give out in a burst of excruciating pain. She fell to the ground, her eyes open, but unable to breathe.

'Did you kill her, your Grace?' said Felice.

'No. I merely stopped her heart. Her self-healing will bring her back.'

'You are too merciful, your Grace.'

He shrugged his huge shoulders. 'If I kill everyone, then who will I rule?'

Jade started to convulse as she lay on the cold surface of the roof. She saw Quill forced to her knees by a click of Simon's fingers, then the Ascendant turned once again to the watching garrison.

'Adjutant Quill has surrendered her authority to me,' he called out. 'The Blades are now under my command, along with the rest of the City. Do any here choose to defy me?'

Among the massed ranks of Blades were were a small detachment of seconded Banner officers, and Jade watched as they stepped forwards.

Simon shook his head. 'They're like innocent creatures in a slaughterhouse,' he said, his voice low. He raised his finger, and every one of the Banner officers fell to the stone slabs of the courtyard, where they writhed and screamed in torment in front of the watching Blades. Blood gushed from their noses, their ears and then their eyes, before they quietened and lay still.

Simon turned to Quill who was still kneeling, her face wearing an expression of terror and defiance.

'Carry Jade downstairs,' he said to her. 'I intend to speak to the Blade officers of the garrison, in order to hear them recite their oaths of loyalty to me. Once the transfer of power along the Great Walls is complete, then I will think of a suitable punishment for you both – something public, I'd imagine. The Blades will need to see your bodies displayed, so all can marvel at my power.'

He set off for the stairwell, Felice by his side. Quill rose to her feet, then staggered towards Jade. The officer glanced down at the crowds of Blades, and Jade thought that she was going to throw herself from the top of the tower. Instead, she turned, and crouched down next to the demigod.

'Can you hear me?' she whispered.

Jade nodded. She was still unable to speak, but her heart had restarted. She tried to move her legs, but they wouldn't respond, and she lay as if paralysed.

'If only Yendra were here,' Quill said, sobbing; 'or Corthie. I'd rather die than submit to that beast.'

She reached out with her hands and lifted Jade clear of the roof, then stood. She carried her over to the stairs, stepping over the bodies of the dead Blades, and began to descend. They passed the commander's quarters, and then the rooms where Jade had spent the night. Simon was waiting for them at the bottom of the stairs. He pointed towards the empty guardroom near the front entrance of the tower.

'In there,' he said; 'your new home for a while. When I return, you will have one final opportunity to pledge yourselves to me. If you refuse, I will have you tortured and executed in front of every Blade in the Bulwark. If you accept, then you will stand proudly by my side, and the Blades will see how I reward loyalty.'

Quill carried Jade into the room, then Simon closed and barred the door.

With only a silent Quill and her own pain for company, Jade lay on a wooden bench inside the guardroom, feeling her strength slowly return. Through a narrow slit window, she listened to the endless queue of Blade officers read out their pledges of loyalty to the Ascendant.

'Cowards,' she gasped.

Quill glanced at her. 'What choice do they have?'

'You said you'd rather die than serve him.'

'I would, and, when he returns, I shall. But I'm the commander; it's my job. Most of the Blades out there are married, and have children to think about. No one sane is going to refuse, not if the alternative is instant death.'

Jade pushed herself up into a sitting position, grunting with the effort. 'I'm not giving up,' she rasped, her chest burning with pain.

'Good for you,' said Quill.

'At least I tried.'

'And look where it got you.'

Footsteps sounded from outside the guardroom. Quill turned to the door, her face paling.

'My powers have returned a little bit,' said Jade. 'I'm going down fighting, Quill.'

The officer gave a wry smile. 'You called me by my proper name.'

Jade tried to stand, but toppled back onto the bench, just as the door opened. Four Blade soldiers entered the room.

'Quickly,' a sergeant hissed.

'What's the hurry?' said Quill. 'Is your new master so desperate to see us dead?'

'We're still loyal, ma'am, but we haven't got much time; entire battalions are switching sides to work for that bastard Simon.'

Jade stared at them. 'You're on our side?'

'Yes, ma'am. Not all of us are traitors. Can you walk?'

Jade shook her head.

Two of the soldiers ran into the room. They approached Jade and hauled her to her feet. Quill sat, watching but not moving.

'Ma'am?' one said to her.

Quill shook her head. 'Let me die; I have failed you all.'

'Please, ma'am. Simon told us that he's going to string you up in the courtyard. If that happens, then every Blade will lose heart and join him. But, if they hear that you have escaped, then it will give them all hope.'

'Get up,' said Jade. 'Get up, or I'm staying too.'

Quill glared at her, then got to her feet. The soldiers escorted them out into the stairwell of the tower, two of them supporting Jade.

'This is the difficult part,' said the sergeant. 'We need to smuggle you out past the Blades in the courtyard. We brought some spare uniforms with us, to pass you off as apprentice artificers; that way, we should be able to sneak past.'

Quill sighed. 'While your courage is to be applauded, your escape plan will get us all killed.' She shook her head. 'Come with me.'

She strode off, entering another chamber on the ground floor. The others followed her in, then Quill lifted a rug from the floor, revealing a hatch.

'Duke Marcus built secret tunnels under the tower,' Quill said. 'One of them leads to a turret in the Outer Walls.'

The sergeant stared at the hatch. 'This changes everything. Lads, we might actually survive this.'

'You assumed you would die?' said Jade.

'Yes, ma'am.'

'But, you came for us anyway?'

'It was the right thing to do, ma'am.'

'What next, Sergeant?' said one of the other soldiers. 'Do we drop them into the tunnel and go back to our battalion?'

'You can't,' said Jade. 'Simon will read your minds and discover the truth. If you wish to live, you will have to come with us.'

'Her ladyship's right,' said the sergeant. 'If that big bastard reads our heads, then he'll know where they've gone, and then this will have been for nothing.'

Quill opened the hatch. Below was a dark shaft, with a ladder attached to the side. The sergeant ordered the two soldiers carrying Jade to go down first, and the demigod was lowered down into the darkness. Her strength was returning with every moment, and she was able to stand unaided at the bottom, except for a hand leaning against the wall of the tunnel. Quill came down next, with a lit oil lamp, followed by the sergeant and the last soldier, who closed the hatch.

Quill led the way down the cold, damp tunnel, her lamp sending flickers of light into the darkness. Jade stumbled along behind her, a soldier by her elbow to offer support whenever she tripped or staggered. At the far end of the tunnel was another ladder going up, and Jade was strong enough to pull herself up on her own, though her arms were sore, and she was out of breath by the top. She emerged through another hatch into a small, empty chamber, and sat by a wall while the others climbed up.

'We're on the Outer Walls,' said Quill, glancing out of a slit window. 'And, it's almost noon.'

'Where now, ma'am?' said the sergeant.

She turned to face them. 'Over the moat.'

The four soldiers looked horrified.

'Over the moat, ma'am? You mean, out of the City?'

'That's exactly what I mean. In a few minutes, Halfclaw will be arriving. If he lands on the Duke's Tower, Simon will kill him.'

Jade pulled herself to her feet. 'My powers have returned. I will slay any greenhide that gets too close.'

Quill went to the chamber's only door and peered outside. 'It's deserted.'

'Every Blade in the fortress has been summoned to bow before Simon,' said the sergeant.

'We'll never get another opportunity,' said Quill. 'Follow me.'

They hurried out of the chamber, and descended a set of steps cut into the inner side of the Outer Walls. They ran along the channel that lay between the Inner and Outer Walls until they came to one of the frequent postern doors. The sergeant and another soldier lifted the heavy bar, and flung the stout door open.

'One of us will have to remain here,' he said. 'This is how the breach happened a couple of years ago – it only takes one gate to be left open, and the Bulwark falls.'

'I can do it,' said Jade. 'I can bar the gate, then I can run up onto the parapet and jump down the other side. I can survive breaking a few bones.'

'No disrespect, ma'am,' said the sergeant, 'but are you strong enough to lift the bar?'

Jade leaned over and tried to pick up the wooden beam, but it was too heavy.

'I'll do it,' said the sergeant. 'If I jump from the parapet, ma'am, will you heal me?'

She nodded. Quill led them through the gate, leaving the sergeant in the channel. He closed the door, then they heard the heavy wooden bar drop back into place. They stepped away from the wall and stared up at the parapet. Moments later, the sergeant's head appeared above the battlements. He waved, then scrambled up and over the crenulations. He paused for a moment at the top, his eyes widening at the view, then jumped. He landed onto the frost-covered ground, and rolled over, clutching his left ankle, his face grimacing in silent pain. Jade rushed to his side, and sent a blast of healing into him. He shuddered violently, then gasped.

'Thank you, ma'am. I would kiss you for that, if it weren't disrespectful.' He got to his feet. 'I have good news,' he said. 'I looked out over the plain – there's nothing but headless greenhide corpses everywhere.'

'How do we get across the moat?' said Jade.

'This way, ma'am,' said the sergeant.

They followed him to the five-foot high moat wall, where he bent down and picked up a coil of rope. He secured one end to an iron hook embedded into the wall, and tied the other round his waist.

'I'll swim for it,' he said, 'then tie the other end to the stonework on the far side. I've watched the Rats do this a hundred times; never thought I'd be down here myself.'

He scrambled up onto the moat wall and dived into the dark depths, breaking through the thin crust of ice on the surface. While the others watched his progress, Jade scanned the skies.

'There!' she cried, pointing up at a dark speck that was approaching from the east.

Quill and the three soldiers began waving and jumping up and down, trying to attract the dragon's attention, as the sergeant reached the far side of the moat and hauled himself clear of the freezing waters. He ripped the rope from his waist and secured it to an iron hoop rising from the stonework.

'Come on,' he cried. 'Crawl along the rope – one at a time.'

'Jade, you first,' said Quill.

Jade glanced up at the dragon. So far, he hadn't noticed them, and was making straight for the Duke's Tower. Quill pushed her in the back, and she set off. She scaled the moat wall, then grabbed the rope. She pulled herself along, wrapping her ankles around the rope, so that she was hanging two feet above the level of the icy water. At the other side, the sergeant helped her, and she scrambled up onto the far bank.

'Stay here,' she said to the sergeant; 'I'm going to get the dragon's attention.'

She ran off, then slowed as she took in the quantity of dead green-hides littering the plain. They were lying in heaps, piled up where they had fallen, and the stench from the vast carnage was almost unbearable. She climbed up onto the tallest heap of headless corpses, covering her hands and dress in thick green blood, and started yelling up at the dragon, her arms in the air.

Halfclaw soared overhead, passing the moat and the Outer Wall, and Jade lowered her arms, cursing. An awful scream rose up from behind the walls of the fortress, and Halfclaw reappeared, spiralling away from the battlements, his head down. His wings folded, and he plunged through the air, crashing into the ground, and ploughing his way through the heaps of greenhide bodies. Jade jumped down from the mound and ran towards him.

She dodged round the bodies and reached the dragon. His head was lying still, his eyes closed, while blood was trickling from his nostrils. Without hesitating, Jade placed her hands on his head. He was dead, his life force gone. She knew what she had to do. It might kill her, but hadn't those soldiers been prepared to lose their lives to try to save her? What kind of person would she be if she couldn't match the selfless courage of mere mortals? She had revived dead animals before, but only rodent-sized ones – never a fully grown dragon. She closed her eyes, and summoned her power.

It was evening when she awoke. She was lying out on the grass by a blazing fire, wrapped in blankets, and surrounded by her rescuers, along with Quill, and the salve mountain team. To her right, she saw the little circle of tents, and the pool by the entrance to the mine.

'Where's Halfclaw?' she croaked.

'Welcome back, ma'am,' said Quill. 'He's gone to tell the dragon colony what's happening in the City.'

'This time,' said Rosie, taking her hand, 'don't you dare say that you're not a hero.'

'Hear, hear,' said Flavus. 'Though, it does seem that we are in a bit of a pickle. The Tenth Ascendant, found after so long? I thought he was a mere myth. We should think about what we should do next, for Simon will come here, once he learns that the mountains have salve. Should we evacuate, ma'am?'

'You're asking me?' Jade said.

'You are the leader of the operation, ma'am. We are yours to command.'

Jade tried to get up, and Rosie helped her into a sitting position.

'How do you feel?' said the young Jackdaw woman.

'Like a greenhide's been squashing me. Flavus is right. Simon's not going to let us live in peace out here.'

'Let him have the salve,' said Rosie; 'we should hide in the dragon colony.'

'Would they allow it?'

'You saved Firestone, and now Halfclaw,' said Rosie; 'of course they'll let us stay.'

Jade glanced around at the expectant faces watching her. They were waiting for her to speak, to make a decision, but she was too tired to think. Images of Amber, and Simon's cruel smile, swirled around her mind, then she remembered the secret orders that the King had given her. Perhaps that was the answer. If they destroyed the mine, then would Simon be interested in the valley, or who dwelt there?

'I don't know what to do,' she said. 'My mind is too jumbled to think. Have we got food?'

'With the increased numbers,' Flavus said, 'we have enough rations to last us a dozen days – more if we go out hunting. The workers in the colony have plenty of supplies, but no weapons.'

'Weapons are useless against Simon,' said Quill. 'I've never seen power like it.'

'I meant,' said Jade, 'have we got food right now? I'm starving. All I want to do is eat, then sleep. I'll come up with a plan tomorrow.'

Quill frowned. 'What if Simon attacks tonight, ma'am?'

'He won't,' she said, casting her gaze at the flames of the campfire; 'he'll be too busy conquering the rest of the City.'

'But what if he does?' Quill went on.

'Then,' said Jade, 'we shall die fighting him.'

CHAPTER 29

PLAYED

Pella, Auldan, The City – 20th Monan 3422

Kelsey's attention drifted as she sat in the small waiting room down the hall from Salvor's grand office. Her head was pounding, and she felt as though she could throw up at any moment. A small group of senior Banner officers strode past her towards the office, but Kelsey hardly noticed. She had been due to meet with Lord Salvor for a briefing an hour after dawn, but had been kept waiting, while others had come and gone.

She wondered if Queen Emily was suffering from the same hangover. The Queen had been more restrained in her drinking, but Kelsey suspected that Emily's tolerance for alcohol was far lower than hers. Her thoughts turned to Van. She had talked far too much about him the previous evening, and she worried that she might have embarrassed herself. She had even drunkenly declared her love for him to the Queen, an act that she was now regretting. For the entire evening, Lucius had sat there sober, listening while the two women had become steadily more inebriated. Emily had been amusing company, but had somehow retained the ability to stop herself from saying anything too personal, and had kept her secrets hidden. Kelsey had been nowhere near as discreet, though she was sure that she hadn't told them about her ability to see visions from the future. She had told them about pretty much everything else, but at least she had possessed the sense not to blab about that.

She lowered her head, groaning, then heard the sound of a man quietly laughing.

She glanced up. 'Do you find my suffering funny, Lucius?'

'Do you want an honest answer to that?' said the tall captain, standing close by. 'Dear gods, you were drunk last night, Kelsey. Do you remember anything?'

'I think so.'

'You would have matched any Banner sergeant in the bars of Serene with that performance.' He took a breath. 'Certain events have taken place in the City this morning.'

'I guessed as much. My meeting was supposed to start an hour ago, and I've seen loads of folk passing to and fro.'

'Lord Salvor needed to use his powers, so you were stuck in here – it's just a little more than a hundred yards from his office. I had a squad measure it out this morning while you were still sleeping.'

'Aye? Bollocks. I was hoping that you had all forgotten about me, and that I would be allowed to go back to bed.'

The captain took a seat next to her. 'That won't be happening, I'm afraid. I've been sent to fetch you, and to brief you. You and Frostback are going to be in action this morning – proper, god-fighting action. Montieth and Naxor have been seen, in Dalrig. They've entered Greylin, and the Gloamer militia have gone on full alert.'

'Against them?'

'No. The Gloamers have moved into defensive positions around the palace.'

'Does that mean Amber's switched sides? Is she helping her father now?'

'We think that she has no choice. She is still unable to use her powers to defend herself, and the gods brought greenhides with them – the Banner garrison has been slaughtered.'

Kelsey's mouth fell open.

Cardova eyed her. 'That was most people's response. The good news is that there appears to be only around a hundred of the beasts, which is probably as many as a single Quadrant can transport at once. The bad news is that we don't know the current location of those said beasts. They seem to have left Greylin after killing the Banner soldiers, but we have no idea where they went after that. Chancellor Mona is currently searching the City for them, while Lord Salvor has alerted the other tribes, including the Blades, who are mustering.'

'What about Amalia?'

'She was also in Dalrig, along with Felice, and the mortal man the God-Queen has taking a liking to. And, one other, as yet unidentified god. According to Salvor, they seem to have gone, leaving only Montieth, Naxor and Amber in the palace.'

'Is that where I'm going? To Dalrig, again? Can Frostback and I burn down the palace this time? I'm sick of going there.'

'If that's what it takes to kill Montieth and Naxor, then yes.'

Kelsey blinked. 'Seriously?'

'Yes. There's no one else in the palace, and the Crown want a rapid response.'

'Fine. I can go now.'

'Wait. There's something else. It concerns this other god that Salvor thinks he saw.'

'Aye?'

'According to Gloamer witnesses that Salvor has read this morning, the greenhides were organised and disciplined. They marched through the streets in ranks, following the gods to Greylin, and they didn't touch a single civilian. If that's true, Kelsey; then it can mean only one thing.'

'Well? Don't leave me in suspense.'

'Only one type of god can control greenhides – an Ascendant.'

Kelsey groaned. 'Shit. Amalia must have betrayed us to Implacatus.'

'We don't think so. If that were the case, then the Ascendants would surely have opened a portal and flooded the City with greenhides and fresh Banner forces. However, the evidence seems to point to only one Quadrant being used. Regardless, the god no longer appears to be in

Dalrig. They have split their forces, and the Crown wants the Greylin faction eliminated. This morning, if possible. Come on; I'll take you to Salvor's office.'

He stood and offered Kelsey a hand. Normally, she would have refused it, but she was worried that her legs would wobble, so she gripped his hand and pulled herself up. Her head went spinning, and she staggered.

'Are you going to be sick?'

She puffed her cheeks and breathed. 'Why did you let me drink last night, Lucius?'

'That's right; it's my fault entirely. I held you down and poured that brandy into your mouth.'

'Do you want me to punch you in the face, Lucius?'

'I'd like to see you try. Do you think you could even reach my head with those little fists of yours?'

'How's the Queen?'

'She's fine. I'd say that she drank about a third of what you put away.'

'You were counting, were you?'

'I needed something to do while you sobbed about Van.'

Kelsey's cheeks burned hot. 'How embarrassing was I?'

'It's fine, Kelsey; you're a friend. These things happen.'

'Have you told him?'

'Of course not. You should know that he's acting as if he doesn't care that you broke up, but I can tell he's putting on a brave face. The current crisis needs him to behave that way. Don't take it personally.'

He led her along a quiet, marble-floored corridor, until they reached the doors to Lord Salvor's office. The guards moved aside, and they entered. In the middle of the room, every seat was taken at the long table, and a mixture of Banner and militia officers, as well as Salvor, Silva and the King and Queen turned to watch as Cardova and Kelsey walked in. Van was also there, she noticed, sitting to the left of the King. A courtier hurried over with two extra chairs, and those sitting moved up to create some space.

'Take a seat, Kelsey,' said the King; 'and thank you for your patience. I assume that Captain Cardova told you the reason for you having to wait in a different room?'

Kelsey nodded, then fell into her chair.

'Miss Holdfast has a severe headache, I'm afraid, your Majesty,' said Cardova. 'It will not prevent her from carrying out her duties, but she may find it difficult to speak this morning.'

A few of the officers exchanged glances.

'That's perfectly alright,' said the King. 'This won't take too long. Kelsey Holdfast, we require your particular skills today, along with those of your dragon. Greylin Palace is the location, and Montieth and Naxor are the targets. Use whatever methods are necessary to eliminate the enemies of the City. Understood?'

Kelsey nodded again.

'Excellent. To avoid any further delay, I propose that Kelsey and Frostback depart immediately.'

'May I interject, your Majesty?' said Van. 'While I can see the advantages of a quick response, we should be aware of the risks of what we are proposing. As soon as Frostback leaves Cuidrach with Kelsey on her shoulders, she will become invisible to Lord Salvor and Chancellor Mona's vision powers. As such, we will be unable to communicate with them until they return. There is a chance that we are walking into a trap. Might we consider the possibility that our enemies want Frostback and Kelsey to attack Greylin?'

'This risk is understood,' said the King, 'but we have no alternative.'

'In that case, your Majesty,' said Van, 'might I suggest that the operation be time-restricted? Say, a maximum of two hours altogether? That way, if the situation changes, we will be able to react.'

'That seems sensible, Major-General,' said the Queen, who looked, to Kelsey's eyes, to be refreshed and alert, though there were worry lines around her eyes.

'We can allow a little leeway here, I think,' said the King. 'If Kelsey feels that the destruction of the targets is imminent, then she should stay to finish the job, even if that means she goes over the time limit a little. We can be flexible here, yes? Miss Holdfast, the decision will be yours. Return directly to Cuidrach once the operation is over. Dismissed.'

Kelsey's eyes went to Van, and their glances met.

'Good luck,' he said.

She nodded, performed a rudimentary bow, then walked from the chamber, hoping that she didn't stumble. Cardova followed her out, and they took the stairs to the roof.

She glanced at him. 'A headache?'

He shrugged. 'It was better than telling them that you were hungover. And, it saved you from having to open you mouth. Your breath reeks of booze, madam.'

She shook her head. 'You've covered for drunken officers before, aye?'

'I don't know what you're talking about. What a preposterous suggestion.'

'I didn't like the bit about me having to make the decision on when to end the operation.'

'Your blocking powers make it difficult to do it any other way. I suggest using extreme levels of violence when you get to Greylin.'

They emerged from the stairwell onto the roof. Frostback was sitting there, surrounded by her dragon crew.

'Rider,' said the dragon. 'Am I to be briefed?'

'I'll tell you on the way,' she said.

The dragon lowered her head. 'You look terrible. I have seen healthier looking corpses, and your odour is that of a dead rat.'

Kelsey frowned. 'That's a little brutal.'

'Yes? Well, I am somewhat chagrined this morning. Vital meetings, important decisions, matters of great urgency – all of these things take place and are discussed in my absence, yet I am expected to mutely agree to whatever has been decided. It would be nice if, for once, I were included in such deliberations.'

'You make a fair point,' said Cardova. 'I'll pass on your words to the King and Queen.'

Kelsey pulled herself up the harness straps. 'I didn't think these things bothered you.'

'No? How would you feel if you were left out of these meetings?'

'I was, Frostback. I was made to sit in a room on my own for an hour, so Salvor could do his vision thing.'

'I see. Well, that makes me feel a little better. Perhaps I should attend these meetings, and then I can brief you afterwards.'

Kelsey buckled herself into the saddle. 'That would be fine by me. We're going to Dalrig.'

'Again?'

'Aye,' she said, as the dragon extended her long wings; 'only, this time, you can burn Greylin to the ground if you want.'

Frostback ascended into the air, banked once, then sped off to iceward.

'Why the change in strategy?' said the dragon.

'Montieth and Naxor are in the palace. The Crown want them eliminated.'

'You mean killed?'

'Aye, I suppose so.'

'Are you fine with this, my rider?'

'I'm too hungover to have a debate about the morality of it. Let's just get it done, and then I can dwell on it morbidly afterwards.'

They soared over the red sandstone streets of Outer Pella, then crossed the fields of Gloamer territory. Kelsey knew every detail of the short journey, and closed her eyes, feeling the cold air whip her hair into tangles. Van's face popped into her head, and she felt a well of regret in the pit of her stomach.

'Have I made a mistake?'

'Indubitably, my rider. All sentient creatures make them. Were you thinking of anything in particular?'

'Van. I might have been too quick to jump to a conclusion. He doesn't seem to be acting weirdly because of the salve; maybe he can handle it.'

'You never seem to doubt your decisions, rider. If you are worried about this one, then perhaps you would do well to reconsider.'

'Do you like him?'

'To be honest, I prefer the captain.'

'Lucius? Well, that's never going to happen. Lucius is more like a big brother. What's wrong with Van?'

'I didn't say anything was wrong with him. But, now that you mention it, I think Van is a little arrogant, a little too sure of himself; but he also has a self-destructive streak. A dangerous combination.'

Kelsey shrugged. 'But he's very handsome.'

'Is he? I am unable to discern that. Enough of Van; Dalrig approaches.'

Kelsey peered ahead, and saw the town walls loom in front of them. Frostback started to ascend and, moments later, the first ballista bolt whistled through the air towards them, followed by a heavy barrage. Frostback soared upwards, twisting as she went, and the long, steel bolts fell away below her. Kelsey's stomach heaved as the dragon banked and climbed.

'I think they might be expecting us, rider,' Frostback said, once she had ascended out of range of the batteries on the town walls.

Kelsey looked down. They had flown over the walls, and she could see Greylin Palace in the distance, it dark bulk rising above the streets next to the harbour. As they approached, she caught movement on the roof of the palace.

'The Banner soldiers inside Greylin were slaughtered,' said Kelsey. 'Those soldiers on the roof will be Gloamer militia.'

'Are they to be treated as enemies?'

'Aye.'

Frostback circled over the palace.

'Pyre's arse,' Kelsey muttered. 'The roof of the palace has at least six ballistae on it.'

'And they are all pointing at us, rider.'

'Is it safe to attack?'

'No. However, I am supremely fast and agile. I dodged the many bolts loosed at me over Yoneath without injury. I am prepared to risk it.'

Kelsey swallowed. 'Alright.'

Frostback pulled her wings in, and surged downwards in a blur of speed towards the palace. She opened her jaws in readiness, and then the first bolts were loosed at her. Out of the corner of her eye, Kelsey noticed further ballista batteries on the roofs of the buildings close to the palace, and the air filled with two-yard-long steel bolts. Frostback twisted and turned, and a bolt sped past Kelsey's head, missing her by a few feet. The barrage intensified, and a bolt glanced off the thick scales of the dragon's flank, with only the angle of approach saving her from being skewered. Kelsey cried out in terror, as a blizzard of steel surrounded them.

Frostback pulled up, banking and diving, then sped away towards the Cold Sea, leaving the palace and its ballista batteries behind them. She ascended to a safe altitude, then circled the harbour.

'I am sorry, rider; my nerve failed me.'

'Don't apologise for not dying; any lower, and we'd both have bolts sticking out of us. Shit; what do we do now?'

'We tried an assault from above; let's try one from below.'

The silver dragon sped out to sea, then banked and soared down, until her forelimbs were barely clearing the waves. She turned back towards Dalrig, and put on another burst of speed, keeping low as the harbour approached. Again, she opened her jaws, but the Gloamers had installed more ballistae along the waterfront, and some were positioned on the stern platforms of the larger merchant vessels tied up by the quayside, and the barrage resumed. The bolts flew out towards them, loosed horizontally at the low-flying dragon. Frostback tried to evade them, but a bolt tore a long wound across her left flank, and she turned aside, soaring back out over the Cold Sea.

Kelsey leaned over to look at the dragon's injury. She had been lucky – the bolt had opened a wound a yard long, but hadn't embedded itself into her flesh.

'That looks sore,' said Kelsey.

'It is, rider, but I can bear the pain. For a third attempt, perhaps we should attack from...'

'No. I'm ending this now. The defences are too strong.'

'The notion of failure sits ill with me.'

'Aye? Well, the notion of death doesn't sound much better. Come on; we'd better report back to Cuidrach.'

'Naxor will be laughing at us.'

'His day will come, Frostback; have no doubt about that.'

The dragon ascended, and turned towards sunward.

Someone must have noticed the dragon's approach, as both Van and Cardova were on the roof of Cuidrach Palace when Frostback and Kelsey returned.

'Our assault failed,' said the dragon, once she had alighted onto the roof.

'We know,' said Van, whom Kelsey noticed was walking without his stick. 'Lord Salvor was able to piece together what happened.' He signalled to the dragon crew. 'See to Frostback's wound. There is salve available if she requires it.'

'Aye?' said Kelsey, as she clambered down onto the roof. 'From your personal stash? Very generous of you.'

'We have some bad news,' said Cardova.

Kelsey frowned. 'What?'

'The new god has travelled to the Bulwark,' said Van. 'Chancellor Mona witnessed him at the Fortress of the Lifegiver. He killed Halfclaw. I'm sorry.'

Frostback turned her head, her red eyes burning. 'Tell me everything.'

'It seems that this new god was speaking to the Blades when Halfclaw returned to pick up another batch of workers for the dragon colony. He didn't even make it to the Duke's Tower before he was attacked. The god used his powers, and Halfclaw fell onto the plains, beyond the Great Walls.'

'Rider,' said the dragon, her voice quavering. 'Climb back up onto my shoulders; we are going directly to the Bulwark, where I will take vengeance upon this god; terrible, bloody vengeance.'

'Be careful,' said Cardova. 'The Fortress of the Lifegiver has more ballistae than Dalrig.'

'So?' said Kelsey. 'One god can't operate them all.'

Van lowered his gaze. 'The Blades have turned. The god killed several of them, then threatened the rest into submitting. He's an Ascendant, Kelsey; they had no choice. If he commands them to loose upon Frostback, we think that they'll obey.'

'Is it Edmond?'

'No. He's called Simon, the missing Tenth Ascendant.'

'Missing?'

'Not any more, clearly. He's been lost somewhere for thousands of years; Amalia must have found him. Listen, the Crown wants you both to go to the Bulwark, but you must take great care. If you see the Ascendant, and have an opportunity, then strike with everything you've got. He's planned all this, and, at the moment, he's playing us like a fiddle. I would be surprised if he isn't expecting you.'

'I care not for any of that,' said Frostback. 'If this vile creature has slain my betrothed, then I will face him without fear.'

Van took a step closer to Kelsey. 'I know you hate me right now, but my world would fall apart if something happens to you. You mean more to me than anything else in my life.'

'If that's true, then give up salve.'

Van frowned, but said nothing.

'Hurry, rider,' said Frostback.

Kelsey pulled her gaze from Van and clambered back up onto the harness. Frostback immediately extended her wings and ascended into the pale red sky. She circled once, then shot off towards the east.

'I'm sorry about Halfclaw,' Kelsey said.

'I will not believe it until I see him with my own eyes, rider. He may be hurt and require our assistance. But, if it is true, then I fear my anger and despair will push me beyond the bounds of restraint.'

They crossed the Union Walls, then flew over the Circuit, between the drifting columns of smoke rising from the never-ending riots that had consumed the territory. Frostback surged ahead, and they passed the Middle Walls in a burst of speed. Rather than angling towards the Fortress of the Lifegiver, the silver dragon held her course to the west, and they crossed the Great Walls between the fortresses of Stormshield and Arrowhead. Frostback flew over the plain, then began to bank to sunward. She descended, until she was only a few yards above the sea of greenhides roaming the plains, then turned in a long slow arc. Kelsey looked up. The Fortress of the Lifegiver was directly in front of them, and she could see the high platform on the roof of the Duke's Tower. Then, she noticed the greenhides. Before the walls of the fortress lay a carpet of the dead, spread in a vast semi-circle. A few living greenhides were rooting around the mounds and heaps of corpses, but most were staying clear of the area.

'The land is saturated with the blood of the fallen beasts,' said the dragon. 'Did the Ascendant do this? Look, every greenhide is missing their head.'

'Van said that Halfclaw had fallen down here somewhere; do you see him?'

The dragon twisted her neck to look beneath them. 'No. However, I see evidence that a dragon was here.'

She pulled up, and hovered over a stretch of ground that looked as though it had been ploughed up. Frost and blood-covered mud lay folded into the heaps of dead greenhides.

'This is where Halfclaw fell,' said the dragon. 'But he is no longer here.'

'What does that mean?'

'I'm not sure. My hope is that he was only lightly injured, and has made his escape, but I doubt that an Ascendant would have acted so carelessly. Do you detect Simon's presence within the fortress?'

Kelsey calmed herself and closed her eyes. 'No; nothing. That doesn't mean he's not here; he might not be using any of his powers.' She gazed up at the tall battlements on the Inner Walls. 'Shit. They're preparing the ballistae up there. The damn Blades are going to loose upon us.'

Frostback powered her wings, and began to rise back into the air as the first bolts were released. The dragon surged upwards, dodging the steel missiles as they whistled past. She ascended to a safe height, then gazed down.

'They have made a grave error,' said the dragon; 'and they will pay for their folly.'

'What error?'

'Those ballistae are fixed to aim towards the plains. They have never imagined that an attack could come from the other direction.'

She soared down again, without waiting for Kelsey to respond. The dragon crossed the fortress, and then descended over the Bulwark in a tight curve.

'Are the Blades our enemies now?' said Frostback, as she began to approach the fortress from the eastern side.

'I think so,' said Kelsey, her heart pounding, as she realised what Frostback was about to do.

'Then, they shall pay for their treachery.'

The dragon hurtled over the eastern edge of the fortress and opened her jaws. Flames surged out, enveloping the high artillery platform next to the Duke's Tower. The catapults and ballistae erupted in flames. Frostback slowed, then hovered over the fortress's vast internal courtyard. She aimed at the massed batteries of ballistae along the Inner Walls. Kelsey saw that she had been right. Each catapult and ballista was fixed in position, facing the plains. Blades were loosing their crossbows at the dragon, but to no effect. Frostback opened her jaws again, sending a great stream of fire along the crowded battlements, incinerating every Blade and ballista that had been positioned there in an inferno of red flames. Blades screamed as they were consumed, some falling from the parapet, their bodies burning as they plunged downwards. Frostback turned to the Duke's Tower.

'Rider, do you sense the Ascendant?'

'No,' Kelsey gasped, her voice sounding strange as she stared at the destruction along the walls.

The dragon turned to the Duke's Tower, and released another thick surge of fire. The building began to smoke as the flames penetrated the interior, and the roof platform exploded into flames. Frostback then glanced at the barracks, and opened her jaws again. Down in the courtyard, Blades were screaming, and running in every direction.

'Enough, Frostback,' said Kelsey. 'Maybe this is what the Ascendant wants us to do. Maybe he's trying to divide us; turn us against each other. Like Van said, he's playing us a tune, and we're dancing along to it.'

'They attacked us first, rider.'

'You've killed every ballista operator; you have your vengeance. The Ascendant isn't here – he's already moved on to his next target.'

'Which is?'

'I have no idea, Frostback.'

The dragon gazed down into the courtyard, then swooped, her wings pulled in. The Blades scattered, fleeing in panic, and Frostback reached out with a forelimb and plucked one from the ground. She extended her wings again and soared away. The man screamed in her grasp, his eyes wide with terror, as the silver dragon surged away to the west. She found a deserted patch within Scythe territory, and landed, dropping the Blade when they were a few feet above the ground. The man cowered on the frozen mud, curling himself into a tight ball.

'Where is the Ascendant, Blade?' said the dragon, pushing at him with a long claw.

'Please don't kill me,' he yelled, his hands over his face.

'Answer me, and you will live. Where is the Ascendant?'

'I don't know; I swear it.'

'Did you pledge loyalty to him?'

'I had to! We all had to! I have a wife and three children, and he was killing anyone who disagreed with him; we had no choice!'

'You pathetic little traitor.'

'If it saved my family, then I would do it again.'

'When did the Ascendant depart the fortress?'

'I'm not sure; I didn't see him leave. He locked Lady Jade and Adjutant Quill inside the Duke's Tower, and told us all that he was here to overthrow the Aurelians. He ordered us to defend the fortress from attack, then I never saw him again.'

'Wait,' said Kelsey. 'Jade and Quill were in the Duke's Tower?'

'Yes.'

'Oh, shit; what have we done?'

'Perhaps something unforgivable,' said the dragon. 'My temper went too far.'

Kelsey glanced over at the smoke belching up from the Fortress of the Lifegiver. Flames were still rising from the battlements, and from the Duke's Tower in the interior of the fortress.

'Blade,' said Frostback; 'you may return to your home.'

The man glanced around, then pulled himself up and bolted across the field in the direction of the fortress.

'You were right, rider,' said Frostback; 'we have been played for fools. Every Blade will now fear and hate the dragons, and those who sent me here. We have done the work of the Ascendant for him.'

'Let's go back to Cuidrach; there's nothing else we can do here.'

Frostback turned her head to gaze at Kelsey, their eyes meeting, then, without a word, the dragon rose back into the air and turned for Pella, leaving the burning ruins of the Fortress of the Lifegiver behind them, the thick, dark smoke filling the red sky.

CHAPTER 30

OUT-MANOEUVRED

Pella, Auldan, The City – 20th Monan 3422

Emily stood by the tall bay window, gazing up into the red sky as Frostback faded into the distance, bearing Kelsey to the Fortress of the Lifegiver. She had misgivings about ordering the dragon to the Bulwark, but when Daniel had suggested it, she hadn't been able to come up with an alternative plan.

The King was still sitting at the huge table behind her in the grand office, chatting to Salvor, while Silva was on his left, listening in silence.

Emily turned. 'They've gone. Frostback and Kelsey are on their way.'

'Excellent,' said the King. 'If Simon is in the Bulwark, then let's hope they find him.'

Next to him, Salvor shuddered, closed his eyes and lowered his head.

The King frowned. 'Something wrong?'

'Naxor was in my head again, your Majesty; I don't know how long he's been listening. I've pushed him out, but he's stronger than I am, and he's learned how to remain quiet and undetected.'

'Damn him,' cried the King. 'Is there no way that you can shut him out completely?'

'He might have been inside your head, your Majesty,' said Silva; 'or the Queen's. Most likely, you would have had no inkling that he was there.'

'You mean, he could be in my head right now?'

Emily strode to the table, trying to keep her temper. 'Naxor is irrelevant. He's not the one in charge of this invasion; he's just trying to distract us with his games. It's the Ascendant we need to be focussed on.'

Daniel nodded. 'You're right. Lord Salvor, can you scan the Fortress of the Lifegiver again? If Adjutant Quill is still there, we can warn her that Frostback is on her way.'

'Jade was there too,' said Emily. 'She was due to be collected by Halfclaw today.'

Salvor nodded. 'I'll look now, your Majesties. Hold on; Chancellor Mona wishes to speak to me from Jezra. If you could please wait a moment?'

Emily caught Daniel's glance, then they both looked away. For the entire morning, the militia and Banner officers, and the palace demigods, had seen the King and Queen work well together, as a team. She wondered how many of them had guessed it was a façade. When they had been awoken that dawn, they had each been tormented by savage hangovers, and they had rowed bitterly over Amalia, the election, the Banner, and anything else that had come up in conversation. The Queen had even found herself in the bizarre position of defending Lady Aurelian against the accusations of the King, while Emily had uttered a few things of her own that didn't exactly fill her with pride.

The news about the greenhides had stopped the arguments, the abrupt shock silencing both Emily and Daniel. The news had been followed by a careful explanation from Captain Cardova, stating that the City was now facing an Ascendant with a Quadrant. From that moment on, and without anything being said, Emily and Daniel had come together to present a united front.

Salvor coughed. 'Chancellor Mona has located the greenhides, your Majesties.'

'Where?' said Daniel.

'In Maeladh Palace, your Majesty.'

The King frowned. 'What are they doing there?'

'Nothing, your Majesty. Mona reported that they are motionless. They're taking up a few chambers in a derelict wing of the palace. Amalia is also in the palace, but at the other end from the greenhides.'

'The creatures might be awaiting orders from Simon,' said the Queen.

The King shook his head. 'I know that Van and the captain told us all about it, but it still seems incredible to imagine that any god can control those beasts.'

'I saw it happen many times on Lostwell, your Majesty,' said Silva. 'King Nathaniel and Queen Belinda often controlled entire armies of greenhides. Khatanax was the only continent that was kept clear of them. If the greenhides in Maeladh Palace are being controlled, then the being that arrived with Amalia has to be an Ascendant.'

'Do you know this Simon?' said the Queen.

'No, your Majesty, though I have heard of him. Queen Belinda occasionally mentioned his name to me.'

'Shall I resume my scan of the Fortress of the Lifegiver, your Majesties?' said Salvor.

'Yes,' said the King.

'I need to get some air,' said the Queen, once Salvor's eyes glazed over. 'Lady Silva, would you care to join me?'

'Certainly, your Majesty,' said the demigod, rising to her feet.

'Don't be too long,' said Daniel.

'Ten minutes,' said Emily. 'Just a quick walk to the gardens and back.'

He nodded, then glanced away. Silva bowed to him, then she and Emily walked to the main door of the office. Outside, a squad of Royal Guards was waiting to escort them, and they followed a few paces behind the Queen and the demigod.

'We have lost control of the City,' said Emily, her voice low.

'Not yet, your Majesty,' said Silva, 'but its fate is in the balance. Have you made any plans to evacuate Pella?'

'No. Should we?'

'It would seem prudent, your Majesty. May I offer a few other suggestions?'

'Of course.'

'Keep Kelsey Holdfast by your side, your Majesty, as soon as she returns from the Bulwark. Dalrig was a distraction, and so, I fear, is the Fortress of the Lifegiver. Simon is trying to draw Kelsey away from you, and he has so far succeeded. Secondly, send Frostback to the Eastern Mountains, for it is only a matter of time before Simon discovers the existence of the salve deposits there, and the dragons should be warned. They should also be informed about the death of Halfclaw. They might be open to an alliance. Deathfang remembers his victory over the Ascendants in Alea Tanton, and there is a chance he may be stirred into action.'

They stepped out into the chill winter sunshine, and Emily led the way to the gardens.

'A few dragons would certainly help,' said Emily. She smiled as she noticed her mother sitting on a bench next to a line of rosebushes. Next to her was the double pram, and at least twenty Banner soldiers, who were forming a ring of steel around the bench.

'Mother,' said Emily, as she and Silva squeezed between the soldiers.

Her mother bowed her head. 'Your Majesty.'

Emily stopped by the pram and gazed down at Elspeth, who was wrapped up in a thick blanket, with a hat to keep her head warm. Lying next to her was Maxwell, also wrapped up against the cold weather.

'Simon will have informed Amalia that her son is here, your Majesty,' said Silva.

'Will he?' said the Queen. 'He might be keeping it from her, so that she stays where she is and does what she's told. If he'd informed her, then she would be here.'

'Perhaps, your Majesty. However, I have known of gods who

abandon their children. After a few millennia, some come to lack the kind of maternal instincts possessed by most mortal mothers.'

'Vana said the baby had changed her.'

'It's possible, your Majesty.'

'He's certainly no trouble to look after,' said Lady Omertia; 'he's a very quiet child, especially compared to Elspeth when she gets going.'

Emily smiled. 'They look sweet together.'

'I can see Amalia in the boy's face, your Majesty,' said Silva.

'Can you sense his self-healing powers?'

Silva closed her eyes, and placed her hands over the infant. 'Very faintly, your Majesty. My own powers are slowly starting to return.'

She and the Queen sat on the bench next to Lady Omertia, and Emily felt her headache finally clear. She recalled the previous evening. Poor Kelsey; she had been weepy-drunk for a while, and had talked for long periods about her complicated relationship with Van. She had mentioned salve a few times, and Emily had kept a close eye on Van during the meetings that morning. He had seemed calm and organised, and she hadn't noticed any oddness about his behaviour. Maybe taking salve now and again was on a par with drinking; if so, she could hardly judge him harshly, as she had consumed far too much brandy the night before; though less than the Holdfast dragon rider had.

Silva and Lady Omertia chatted about the weather for a while, and Emily was content to let them, her eyes drifting over the empty flower beds, working out plans on how to fill them in the coming summer.

'Emily?'

The three women glanced up to see the King standing next to them.

'I thought I'd come out and find you,' he said. 'Salvor has news. He's scanned the Fortress of the Lifegiver – the Ascendant's gone, but we have no way to recall Kelsey.'

Emily nodded. 'I'll just be another minute, Danny.'

The King glanced down into the double pram. 'There's more. We should move back into the palace. It might not be safe out here.'

'Would we be any safer inside?' said Emily. 'There are nearly two dozen Banner soldiers surrounding us, and hundreds more are close by.'

'The Gloamer militia are on the move,' he said. 'We've had reports of a few border posts being attacked, and Gloamer soldiers have been seen crossing into Reaper territory. If they come at us, the gardens will become a battleground.' He reached down into the pram and took Elspeth into his arms. 'I'll take her indoors.'

'Have the Gloamers invaded in force? Did Salvor confirm it?'

'He's checking it now, but I don't think we should take any chances.'

'Alright. We'll move inside.'

The King gave her a long glance. He seemed scared, and his eyes reflected her own feelings of helplessness. He crouched down next to the bench, Elspeth cradled in his arms.

'I'm sorry,' he whispered.

'I know.'

'I've been behaving like an idiot. Please don't give up on me, Emily. I've been so obsessed with the constitution that I've lost sight of what's important – you and Elspeth. Everything that's happened today has forced me to put it all into perspective, and if we get through this, I promise I'll be a better husband and father. I love you.'

'I love you too, Danny.'

He got to his feet, tore his eyes away from Emily, then strode off towards the palace with Elspeth in his arms, two full squads of Royal Guards flanking him.

Emily's mouth went dry. Next to her, Lady Silva and Lady Omertia remained silent.

Silva shifted on the bench. 'I'm looking forward to some rain, and no more frost.'

'Really?' said Emily's mother. 'I'll bet you change your mind after a few days of Freshmist storms. Last year…'

Her voice tailed off as Emily began to cry.

'Stop that at once, Emily,' said her mother. 'You are the Queen; you must be strong.' She took her daughter's hand. 'If you need to weep, then I beg you, do it alone.'

Emily forced herself to stop crying, driving down the feelings of despair that threatened to overwhelm her.

'Listen to your mother, your Majesty,' said Silva. 'You are in control of your actions; smother your emotions; don't let them rule you.'

Emily wiped her face, and tried to smile. 'Do you never cry, Lady Silva?'

Silva returned her smile. 'I wept like a baby when Queen Belinda sent me away. But the advice we have given to you, is the same as I always gave to my beloved Queen, my great-grandmother – keep your feelings private. Your subjects need you to be firm and unyielding in a crisis such as this. If you give way, then so will they.'

'Let's go back inside,' said Emily, standing.

She glanced around the gardens as the other two women got to their feet. If the Gloamers attacked with their full militia force, then more than her beautiful gardens would be destroyed. Her thoughts went to her husband. She was still angry with him, and disappointed, but the strains of ruling the City during a series of never-ending crises had changed her too, and not in ways that she liked. She would give him another chance.

They began to walk towards the palace, Lady Omertia pushing the pram, and the squads flanking them.

A terrible scream tore through the air, and every soldier in the gardens turned in the direction of the palace. The officer leading their escort raised his hand for Emily to halt on the path.

'We should check what caused that, your Majesty,' he said. 'I'll send a soldier ahead to make sure everything is as it should be.'

Emily frowned. The officer turned to the squads, and began speaking to them. Before he could finish, another rending scream came from the palace, followed by more shouts and cries. The side door of the palace burst open, and two greenhides bounded out into the gardens, their talons raised. They ripped through the soldiers closest to the entrance, then turned and charged straight for the Queen.

The gardens erupted into chaos. Several of the Royal Guard broke and fled in panic, but not a single Banner soldier retreated a step.

Without waiting for orders, they formed up into close lines between the two greenhides and the Queen, and began loosing their crossbows into the beasts from close range. The greenhides barrelled into the Banner ranks, their bloody talons slashing through flesh and leather armour. Crossbow bolts thudded into their bodies. One fell, a bolt hitting its left eye, but the second ploughed through the soldiers surrounding the Queen. It opened its jaws to reveal rows of sharp teeth, and lunged at Emily, and the Banner officer shot it in the face. The greenhide staggered, then collapsed onto the path a yard from the pram.

Emily stared at the carnage. A dozen Banner soldiers had died to defend her, and not one had flinched in the face of the greenhides.

The officer glanced at her. 'We need to move, your Majesty.'

Another officer ran into their midst.

'I'll take it from here, Lieutenant,' said Cardova. 'Good job.'

'Lucius,' said Emily. 'We have to get to Danny and Elspeth.'

'The Major-General is leading that operation, your Majesty; you are my responsibility. Cuidrach Palace is swarming with greenhides; it looks like Simon has transported every one of them here. It's time to evacuate Pella.'

'What? We didn't plan for any evacuation.'

'I took the liberty of planning it as soon as the regiment arrived, your Majesty. The ships in the harbour have been alerted, and are awaiting us. We must hurry.'

'Ships?'

'Yes, your Majesty; to take us to Jezra.'

'And then what? What if Simon and the greenhides follow us there?'

A horrendous chorus of screams echoed out from the palace.

'One step at a time, your Majesty,' said Cardova. He turned to the waiting Banner squads. 'To the harbour. Protect the Queen and her entourage.'

The soldiers began to move, and Emily found herself being bundled along with them. Her eyes went up to the floor of the palace where the royal quarters were located. Somewhere inside were Daniel and Elspeth. She started to turn, so that she could run towards the palace, but the soldiers were in a tight formation, and refused to let her pass their ranks.

'Elspeth!' she cried.

'Major-General Logos has two companies with him, your Majesty,' said Cardova; 'please allow him to do his job, and I will do mine. Lady Omertia, leave the pram here and carry Maxwell, if you would.'

'All my belongings are inside the palace,' said Lady Omertia, lifting the baby out of the pram, 'and all the things the infants need.'

'It's too late, ma'am,' said Cardova; 'Cuidrach has fallen.'

Flames exploded from a window on the second floor of the building, sending a shower of glass down into the gardens. Smoke belched out from the shattered window frame, thick and grey. Captain Cardova led the group onwards, picking up more Banner soldiers as they went. He commanded them to retreat in good order to the harbour, and they obeyed without question.

They reached the front corner of the palace, and the Banner soldiers forced open a gate that led to the main road that lay between the palace and the waterfront. The road was crowded with soldiers and fleeing civilians, and a steady stream of people were emerging from the main gates of the palace fifty yards away. Cardova gestured towards the line of transport vessels tied up along the quayside, and the soldiers herded Emily, Silva, Lady Omertia and Maxwell towards the closest ship.

Greetings, citizens of Pella! a voice boomed out.

Emily clasped her hands to the sides of her head, while even the Banner soldiers hesitated.

'What a sight to behold!' the voice went on, but not inside their heads.

Emily and the others glanced up, to see a huge figure in full battle-armour standing upon the roof of the palace gatehouse, facing the harbour. The steel plates covering his body were shining in the sunlight, and his skin seemed to match their radiance.

'Keep moving!' cried Cardova.

The figure on the roof laughed, his voice echoing across the harbour.

'The battle is over,' the Ascendant said; 'I am victorious. Dalrig is mine, Tara is mine, the Blades on the Great Walls have submitted, and now Pella has fallen.' He reached down, and dragged up a man by the hair. 'And, I have your pathetic King.'

Emily opened her mouth to cry out, but Cardova covered her face with a hand and pulled her back into the crowd of soldiers. She struggled in his grip, but he held onto her firmly, and the soldiers round her kept moving towards the ships.

'Shall I execute his Majesty in front of you?' Simon called out. 'No. I am merciful. I understand the petty needs of mortals, and will not elevate this feeble creature to the status of a martyr. He will live, and he will crawl at my feet.' He let go of Daniel's hair, and the King slumped back down to the roof of the palace. Simon reached down again, and picked up a small bundle. 'Behold,' he cried out; 'the infant princess.'

Emily bit Cardova's fingers and tried with all her strength to free herself, but the captain was resolute, and she was hauled ever closer to the line of ships. The Banner soldiers were boarding the vessels as quickly as they could amid the panic and screams on the quayside. More flames rose up from the wings of the palace, and a fire reached up behind where Simon was standing, silhouetting him in a fiery glow.

'I will hold onto Princess Aurelian, I think,' said the Ascendant. He grinned. 'Is her mother in the crowd?'

Cardova reached the gangway by the closest ship, and dragged Emily on board, then the soldiers shoved Silva and Lady Omertia down onto the crowded deck.

'Go!' Lucius screamed at the helmsman. 'Now!'

Banner soldiers sliced through the ropes connecting the ship to the quayside. The sails had already been unfurled, and they filled with the winter breeze, as the vessel began to move. Other ships had already cast off, and the small fleet was moving out into the bay.

'Leaving so soon?' cried Simon, his voice continuing to reach them. He raised his left hand, his right still clutching Elspeth, and a pillar of flames arose from the fires behind him. It soared up into the red sky, then a huge ball of flames separated from the pillar, and shot downwards. It struck one of the fleeing ships, the fires consuming the sails, and incinerating the soldiers on the deck. Another fireball loosed itself from the pillar, and a second ship was enveloped in flames, the explosion hammering through Emily's ears as she stared. Banner soldiers were jumping from the sinking vessels, their hair and uniforms on fire, and their screams tore at Emily's heart.

One by one, the retreating vessels were targeted by the Ascendant as they tried to cross the bay, until the calm waters were filled with burning and sinking vessels. Hundreds of dead Banner soldiers were floating on the surface, their bodies bobbing amid the wreckage. A fireball struck the forward mast of Emily's ship, and it split in two, the top half toppling over into the bay. A fire broke out near the bow, and the soldiers battled to put it out as the ship slowed.

Lady Omertia fell to her knees, weeping, Maxwell held close to her chest. On the roof of the palace gatehouse, the figure of the Ascendant was still visible, his arm aloft as he directed the firestorm. Emily stared at him, for a moment oblivious to the death and chaos surrounding her. A mere five ships were still sailing, out of more than a dozen that had departed the harbour. In a few moments, she thought, none would be left.

Behind the Ascendant, the pillar of fire wavered. It seemed to lose strength, then toppled away to nothing. Something flashed through the air, coming out of a cloud of smoke above the palace – a dragon at full speed, hurtling down towards the gatehouse, its jaws opening. Simon looked up, clutching the child to his breastplate.

'No!' cried Emily, her hands going to her mouth.

At the last second, the dragon pulled up, hovering over the Ascendant. Simon hesitated, then disappeared from the roof.

'Frostback and Kelsey have saved us,' said Silva.

'Saved us?' said Emily. 'Simon has Elspeth and Daniel, and more than half of the regiment is dead.'

'But,' said Cardova, 'you are alive, your Majesty.'

'Where's Van?'

The captain didn't respond.

'I am the Queen of nothing,' said Emily. 'Simon has destroyed us.'

'He has made it clear by his actions that he plans to annihilate the Banner,' said Cardova. 'Our fate is now tied to yours, your Majesty. You mustn't give up.'

Emily pushed him out of her way, and ran to the side of the boat. She bowed her head, fighting back the tears, as her hands gripped the side rail. Their ship was still moving, though slowly, and they passed the gigantic statue of Prince Michael by the Taran headland. Beyond, the rougher waters of the Straits beckoned, but Emily turned to the east, her eyes staring at the smoke rising from Cuidrach Palace, her home.

She sensed Cardova by her elbow. 'We're sinking, your Majesty. The ship won't make it to Jezra.'

Emily said nothing.

'Sir,' shouted a soldier; 'look.'

They turned, and saw another fleet approaching them, from the west. At least a dozen ships were sailing from Jezra, the flag of the Banner flying from their masts. The five surviving vessels from Pella were swallowed up by the larger group; and Frostback joined them, circling overhead as the crews and passengers from Emily's sinking ship were transferred to the new fleet. Emily was handed a blanket and a mug of warmed wine when she arrived onto the deck of her new ship. Wounded soldiers were being laid out beneath the sails, many suffering from burns. She glanced at her old vessel, which was slipping beneath the waves, then the rescue fleet turned, and sailed into the west.

Van was waiting for her on the crowded docks of Jezra, his head bowed. His armour was battered and ragged, and he had a blood-stained bandage on his left arm.

Emily walked down the gangplank and stared at him.

'I'm sorry, your Majesty. I failed to rescue the King or the Princess. We fought hard, but the greenhides and the Ascendant were too strong for us. I offer you my resignation...'

'Shut up, Van,' she said. 'Where are the two companies of soldiers who were with you?'

'There were six survivors, ma'am.'

'You sacrificed two hundred soldiers to try to rescue my husband and my daughter? I don't accept your resignation, Major-General. I'll need you to negotiate our surrender to Simon.'

'Surrender, your Majesty?'

'What else can we do? It's over. If he crosses the Straits and attacks us, the Banner regiments, and every worker in the Brigades, will die.'

'And we'll die if you surrender, your Majesty,' said Cardova, standing by her side as the Banner forces limped down from the vessels. 'The Ascendant will show no mercy to the Banner.'

'The captain is right, your Majesty,' said Van. 'If we don't surrender; if we defy Simon, then we can hold Jezra.'

'But, he has Elspeth and Daniel.'

'And we have Maxwell, your Majesty,' said Silva. 'Don't give up.'

A shadow flickered overhead, then Frostback landed onto the high roof of the Command Post.

'We also have those two, your Majesty,' said Van, pointing upwards at the dragon and Kelsey. 'The Ascendant's powers will be useless in Jezra, as long as Kelsey is with us.'

'Simon will attack us.'

'And the Banner will fight, to the end.'

Emily glanced around at the faces looking at her. For a moment she felt angry with them; how dare they have hope, when all was clearly lost? Kelsey ran into their midst. Her eyes caught sight of the state of Van's armour, and his injuries, and her mouth opened.

'I've screwed everything up,' the Holdfast woman said. 'I wasn't in Pella when I should have been, and then we nearly burned Elspeth and Daniel on the roof. Also, we... we might have accidentally killed Jade and Quill.' She lowered her head, her face tormented with guilt.

'It's not your fault, Kelsey,' said Emily; 'the Ascendant has made fools of us all.'

'Are you still the Queen, Emily?' Kelsey said. 'Please tell me that you're still the Queen.'

Emily recalled the advice given to her by Silva and her mother, and smothered her own feelings. Later, when she was alone, she would weep and mourn, but now, standing on the harbour of Jezra, she needed to be strong. A huge crowd had gathered around them – Brigade workers trying to find out news about their friends and loved ones in the Banner, and wounded and dazed soldiers.

'I am the Queen,' said Emily, her voice clear and even; 'and we will not be surrendering to Simon.'

City of Salve - The Royal Family

The Gods	Title	Powers
Malik (deceased)	God-King of the City - Ooste	Vision
Amalia	Former God-Queen - Exiled	Death

The Children of the Gods

	Title	Powers
Michael (deceased)	ex-Prince of Tara, 1600-3096	Death, Battle
Montieth	Prince of Dalrig, b. 1932	Death
Isra (deceased)	ex-Prince of Pella, 2001-3078	Battle
Khora (deceased)	ex-Princess of Pella 2014-3419	Vision
Niomi (deceased)	ex-Princess of Icehaven, 2014-3089	Healer
Yendra	Cmdr of the Bulwark, b. 2133	Vision

Children of Prince Michael

	Title	Powers
Marcus (deceased)	Duke, Bulwark, 1944-3420	Battle
Mona	Chancellor, Ooste, b. 2014	Vision
Dania (deceased)	Lady of Tara, 2099-3096	Battle
Yordi (deceased)	Lady of Tara, 2153-3096	Death

Children of Prince Montieth

	Title	Powers
Amber	Lady of Dalrig, b. 2035	Death
Jade	Adjutant of the Circuit, b. 2511	Death

Children of Prince Isra

	Title	Powers
Irno (deceased)	Eldest son of Isra, 2017-3420	Battle
Berno (deceased)	'The Mortal', 2018-2097	None
Garno (deceased)	Warrior, 2241-3078	Battle
Lerno (deceased)	Warrior, 2247-3078	Battle

Vana	Lostwell Returnee, b. 2319	Location
Marno (deceased)	Warrior, 2321-3063	Battle
Collo	Courtier in Pella, b. 2328	None
Bonna (deceased)	Warrior, 2598-3078	Shape-Shifter
Aila	Has left the City, b. 2652	Shape-Shifter
Kano (deceased)	Adj. of the Bulwark, 2788-3420	Battle
Teno (deceased)	Warrior, 2870-3078	Battle

**Children of
Princess Khora**

Salvor	Royal Advisor, b. 2201	Vision
Balian (deceased)	Warrior, 2299-3096	Battle
Lydia	Gov. of Port Sanders, b. 2304	Healer
Naxor	Lostwell Returnee, b. 2401	Vision
Ikara	Courtier in Pella, b. 2499	Battle
Doria	Royal Courtier, b. 2600	None

**Children of
Princess Niomi**

Rand (deceased)	Warrior, 2123-3089	Battle
Yvona	Governor of Icehaven, b. 2175	Healer
Samara (deceased)	Lady of Icehaven, 2239-3089	Battle
Daran (deceased)	Lord of Icehaven, 2261-3063	Battle

**Children of
Princess Yendra**

Kahlia (deceased)	Warrior, 2599-3096	Vision
Neara (deceased)	Warrior, 2601-3089	Battle
Yearna (deceased)	Lady of the Circuit, 2604-3096	Healer

THE NINE TRIBES OF THE CITY

The Nine Tribes of the City (in 3422, when *Red City* takes place)

There are nine distinct tribes inhabiting the City. Three were in the area from the beginning, and the other six were created in two waves of expansion.

The Original Three Tribes – Auldan (pop. 300 000) Auldan is the oldest part of the City. United by the Union Walls (completed in 1040), it combined the three original tribes and their towns, along with the shared town of **Ooste**, which houses the Royal Palace.

1. **The Rosers** – (their town is **Tara**, est. Yr. 1.) The first tribe to reach the peninsula where the City is located. Began farming there in the sunward regions, until attacks from the Reapers forced them into building the first walled town. **Prince Michael** ruled until his death in 3096. **Queen Amalia** ruled until her expulsion in 3420.

2. **The Gloamers** – (their town is **Dalrig**, est. Yr. 40.) Arrived shortly after the Rosers, farming the iceward side of the peninsula. Like them, they fought with the Reapers, and built a walled town to stop their attacks. **Lady Amber** rules from Greylin Palace in Dalrig.

3. **The Reapers** – (their town is **Pella**, est. Yr. 70.) Hunter/Gatherer tribe that arrived after the more sedentary Rosers and Gloamers. Settled in the plains between the other two tribes. More numerous than either the Rosers or the Gloamers, but are looked down on as more rustic. **Prince Isra** ruled until 3078. **King Daniel and Queen Emily** rule the City from Cuidrach Palace, with **Lord Salvor** as their senior advisor.

The Next Three Tribes – Medio (pop. 220 000) Originally called 'New Town', this part of the City was its first major expansion; and was settled from the completion of the Middle Walls (finished in 1697 and originally known as the Royal Walls). This portion of the City was devastated by the Greenhide incursion in 3420. The name 'Medio' derives from the old Evader word for 'Middle'.

1. **The Icewarders** – (their town is **Icehaven**, est. 1657.) Settlers from Dalrig originally founded a new colony at Icehaven to assist in the building of the Middle Walls, as the location was too cold and dark for the greenhides. After the wall's completion, many settlers stayed, and a new tribe was founded. Separated from Icehaven by mountains, a large number of Icewarders also inhabit the central lowlands bordering the Circuit. **Princess Niomi** ruled until her death in 3089. Her daughter, **Lady Yvona**, now governs from Alkirk Palace in Icehaven.

2. **The Sanders** – (their town is **Port Sanders**, est. 1702.) When the Middle Walls were completed, a surplus population of Rosers and Reapers moved into the new area, and the tribe of the Sanders was founded, based around the port town on the Warm Sea. Related closely to the Rosers in terms of allegiance and culture. **Lady Lydia** governs from Tonetti Palace in Port Sanders.

3. **The Evaders** – (their town is the **Circuit**, est. 2133.) The only tribe ethnically unrelated to the others, the Evaders started out as refugees fleeing the greenhides, and they began arriving at the City c.1500. They were taken in, and then used to help build the Middle Walls. The other tribes of Auldan and Medio look down on them as illiterate savages. Former rulers include **Princess Yendra** and **Lady Ikara**.

The Final Three Tribes – The Bulwark (pop. 280 000) The Bulwark is the defensive buffer that protects the City from greenhide attack. Work commenced on the Great Walls after the decisive Battle of the Children of the Gods in 2247, when the greenhides were pushed back hundreds of miles. They were completed c.2300, and the new area of the City was settled. The Bulwark faced the worst destruction in the greenhide incursion of 3420.

1. **The Blades** – (est. 2300.) The military tribe of the City. The role of the Blades is to defend the Great Walls from the unceasing attacks by the Greenhides. Officials from the Blades also police and govern the other two tribes of the Bulwark. Their headquarters is the **Fortress of the Lifegiver**, the largest bastion on the Great Walls, where **Lady Jade** is the commander.
2. **The Hammers** – (est. 2300.) The industrial proletariat of the Bulwark. Prior to the establishment of the Aurelian monarchy, the Hammers were effectively slaves, forbidden to leave their tribal area, which produces much of the finished goods for the rest of the City.
3. **The Scythes** – (est. 2300.) The agricultural workers of the Bulwark, who produce all that the region requires. Prior to the establishment of the Aurelian monarchy, they were slaves in all but name. Eighty percent of Scythes were killed in the greenhide incursion.

NOTE ON THE CALENDAR

In this world there are two moons, a larger and a smaller (fragments of the same moon). The larger orbits in a way similar to Earth's moon, and the year is divided into seasons and months.

Due to the tidally-locked orbit around the sun, there are no solstices or equinoxes, but summer and winter exist due to the orbit being highly elliptical. There are two summers and two winters in the course of each solar revolution, so one 'year' (365 days) equates to half the time it takes for the planet to go round the sun (730 days). No Leap Days required.

New Year starts at with the arrival of the Spring (Freshmist) storms, on Thanalion Day

New Year's Day – **Thanalion Day** (approx. 1st March)
   -- **Freshmist** (snow storms, freezing fog, ice blizzards, high winds from iceward)
   - Malikon (March)
   - Amalan (April)
   -- **Summer** (hot, dry)
   - Mikalis (May)
   - Montalis (June)
   - Izran (July)
   - Koralis (August)
   -- **Sweetmist** (humid, stormy, high winds from sunward, very wet)
   - Namen (September)
   - Balian (October)
   -- **Winter** (cold, dry)
   - Marcalis (November)
   - Monan (December)

- Darian (January)
- Yordian (February)

Note – the old month of Yendran was renamed in honour of Princess Khora's slain son Lord Balian, following the execution of the traitor Princess Yendra.

AUTHOR'S NOTES
SEPTEMBER 2021

Thank you for reading *Red City* – Book Eight in the Eternal Siege series. I think we are now at the stage that anyone picking up this book would be utterly lost if they hadn't read what has come before (or did we pass that point a while ago?). Back in the Blade trilogy, I wanted to focus on the external threats to the city, so I concentrated on the Great Wall and the greenhides – for the City trilogy, I decide to look instead at the enemy within.

I also intended to take two characters with less than favourable histories – Amalia and Jade, and examine their possible paths to redemption. To Jade, I gave Rosie; while Amalia got Naxor. How it turns out, for both of them, will be revealed in *City Ascendant* – the final book of the City trilogy. After that, it'll be time for Dragon Eyre...

RECEIVE A FREE MAGELANDS ETERNAL SIEGE BOOK

Building a relationship with my readers is very important to me.

Join my newsletter for information on new books and deals and you will also receive a Magelands Eternal Siege prequel novella that is currently EXCLUSIVE to my Reader's Group for FREE.

www.ChristopherMitchellBooks.com/join

ABOUT THE AUTHOR

Christopher Mitchell is the author of the Magelands epic fantasy series.

For more information:
www.christophermitchellbooks.com
info@christophermitchellbooks.com

Printed in Great Britain
by Amazon

26171917R00260